Alyssa

P.D. Shaw

PublishAmerica
Baltimore

© 2006 by P.D. Shaw.
All rights reserved. No part of this book may be reproduced, stored in a retrieval system or transmitted in any form or by any means without the prior written permission of the publishers, except by a reviewer who may quote brief passages in a review to be printed in a newspaper, magazine or journal.

First printing

All characters appearing in this work are fictitious. Any resemblance to real persons, living or dead, is purely coincidental.

ISBN: 1-4241-3264-9
PUBLISHED BY PUBLISHAMERICA, LLLP
www.publishamerica.com
Baltimore

Printed in the United States of America

This book is dedicated to my parents, Elizabeth and Derek, for their passion and drive in encouraging me to read at an early age, and be creative when I wanted to write my own stories.

I would also like to thank my wife Barbara for allowing me to lock myself away during every free moment I had to write this book. It was a rough year, my love, but it was worth it.

Chapter 1

Alyssa left "Government House" on the planet Natoth in a huff, fuming in frustration for the umpteenth time at the never changing, ever inflexible, bureaucratic mind. Her one-piece coverall changed from black to red as it reflected the rise in body temperature as she stormed across the room. Stamping and cursing under her breath she flung open the large ornate wooden doors slamming them behind her. But even that small satisfaction was denied her as the compressors eased the doors shut with a soft whoosh. Faithfully, the coverall activated all of the nanobots woven into the fibres to keep pace with her mood till it was as red and angry as her hair, making her appear more like the devil rather than a professional engineer.

"Idiots. Fools. Morons," she growled as she kicked the large inoffensive door and stamped across the concrete walkway.

Humanity may never be able to harness the awesome and limitless powers of the cosmic universe, but Alyssa's temper would suffice until then. An esteemed engineer and still in her early twenties, spoke much of her attitude and personality. But it was her temper that controlled her. While she stood only a breath above five and a half feet, passers-by gave her distance as she stormed down the stairs, her long red hair streaming behind her as if she bore a tail of fire. The grey overcast sky was a perfect compliment to her mood.

Unfortunately not all the occupants of the steps were as observant and she slammed directly into a young man ascending the stairs. His long coat tails were flapping madly in the breeze he created as he hurried up the steps. His head and face were down as he scrutinized and studied the notes on his reader when the redheaded whirlwind knocked the unit from his hand and spilled his data crystals. As he desperately tried to catch the wayward crystals, he lost his footing and tumbled down the steps landing flat on his back while the crystals made tinkling sounds as they bounced and careened off the cold grey steps.

"Sorry," she growled between clenched teeth. He coverall dimmed slightly as she realized what she had done.

"No problem," replied the man casually. She bent over and helped him collect the scattered data crystals. Handing him her pile, she looked at the man for the first time. He stood just over 6 feet tall and had that air of authority that seemed to emanate from every pore. Strong rugged features, and a fit physique, showed his well-defined but not bulky muscular form. His eyes though, were what held her attention; Deep green, with swirling flakes of gold that had an almost hypnotic effect on her. Glancing down at her coverall she noted the deep blue shade that began appearing.

Damn these stupid clothes, she thought. *Can't even have a private thought without everyone knowing all about it.* As her anger at the ever-changing clothes rose, the colour began changing back to red.

"Thanks," said the man, gently taking the crystals from her hand. His voice—soft and mellow—encouraged Alyssa to lean in closer to hear him speak. She could hear the controlled power of a man used to being in charge behind that soft token of gratitude. He had a calming influence on her and the coverall returned to its normal black colour.

"What's the rush?" he asked, gently staring into her wide, moisture-laden eyes.

Alyssa snapped out of her daze and her anger returned. "Oh, the fools in Government House! Tell me? Why would Planetary Government send for a Drive Engineer from the Council of the Star League, and then refuse to provide her with the tools and equipment necessary to do her job. Politicians, HA! Shakespeare was wrong. We don't need to kill the lawyers. It's the politicians that need wiping out."

"Indeed," said the man, amused, looking at her once again red outfit. "I assume that you're this engineer that's having difficulties?"

"Sorry," she said, holding out her hand. "Alyssa Krychech. Engineer on loan from the Council to assist the Government of Natoth in rebuilding its fleet."

"Glad to meet you, Miss Krychech," he said, taking her hand and pumping it gently. "My name is Trenor, Trenor Adwell. I am here as Ambassador Plenipotentiary for the Council to the Government of Natoth."

Alyssa's face fell and took on a ghostly shade of white as the blood drained from her features. "I am so sorry, Mr. Ambassador. Please accept my apologies."

"No need to apologize, and please call me Trenor. I happen to agree with your sentiments. Most of the time, politicians have their own agendas and have little regard for the disturbance they cause. Now please, tell me what's wrong. Perhaps I can help."

Reluctantly at first, but under Trenor's seemingly eagerness to help, Alyssa explained how the Government had been blocking her operations. How her repeated requests for material and personnel, kept going unanswered. And every time she visited—to get a straight answer—they delayed her by pushing her off on some junior clerk who had no idea of the problem.

"In short, Trenor," she said, as her anger returned, "they're giving me a lot of double talk and the run around. I've filed a complaint with the Council, but I still haven't received any word."

Trenor's face hardened into a mask of determination. "Come with me, Miss Krychech. I believe I can assist you with this problem." He whirled around and bounded up the steps of Government House two at a time. His coat tails streamed out behind him as he flew up the stairs. Alyssa had no choice but to follow him quickly or be left behind.

They paused at the desk of the receptionist leading to the Council chambers. The receptionist looked up—A hawk-faced man who had his nose in the air. When he saw Alyssa his sneer of contempt was obvious. "I told you, Miss Krychech, that the ruling Council will not hear your petty complaints today. Now, please leave before I have security escort you from the premises. As for you, sir, if you are in the company of this woman, I must assume that you are here to cause trouble as well. Therefore I must ask that both of you leave immediately!"

Trenor reached across the desk, grasped the man by his well tailored, brightly coloured, coat of office, and pulled him forward so that their faces were only inches apart. "You will learn some manners, my good man, or I will teach you how to behave. Now, you will announce me to the Council, or I will enter myself."

The man brushed Trenor's hand away violently, adjusted his ruffled tunic, and smoothed his hair. "I think not," he said haughtily. "Just what gives you the right to come in here and demand to see the Council?"

"This gives me the right," said Trenor, reaching into his coat and withdrawing his identification naming him the Ambassador to Natoth from the Star League Council. "This gives me full jurisdiction and the power to veto your planet's acceptance into the Star league. Now do I get to enter? Or do I have you removed from this post!"

"Certainly, Ambassador," said the man sweetly. "I will announce you immediately. As for you, Miss Krychech…Be-gone! You have wasted enough of the Council's time."

"Miss Krychech, is here at my request," said Trenor menacingly, "and if I ever hear you talk to her like that again, I will have you removed and replaced with a trained Zargot. Understand me?"

"Yes, sir," he replied but glared at Alyssa. He stood and moved to the intricately carved door to the Council chambers. Flinging open both sides he motioned for Trenor to wait and moved across the room to the head table. Bending down he whispered in the ear of the ruling President—a squat little man with a large double chin—then straightened and marched stiffly out the door at the rear of the Council bench.

"Mr. Ambassador," said the President, rising, his face beaming with a toothy grin. "Please come in. We are honoured to meet you, sir. I must admit to being taken by surprise, we were not expecting to meet with you until later this evening. How may we be of service?"

"There seems to be a problem," said Trenor calmly—now in full diplomatic mode—as he shook the hand of the President. "This young woman has been sent here at your request. Now I find that an employee of the Star League Council is being denied access to the people and materials she requires. Ladies and gentlemen, let's not start our discussions on an unfavourable topic. Miss Krychech is only trying to do her job. As you know, the League takes great pride in the skills and abilities of its people. We don't take kindly to having them dismissed. I suggest you grant her the boon. Then we can continue to discuss your acceptance into the Star League."

His tone was clear to everyone. Unless the Council quit playing games, Trenor would refuse to discuss their petition to join the Star League. The President shuffled his feet nervously for a few seconds, then his political savvy reasserted itself. "Of course, of course," said the President. "Miss Krychech. I do apologize for any inconvenience that may have been caused. If I had known about your plight, I would have rectified the matter immediately." He held his hand out to Alyssa. "My name is Ken, and I hope that I can make amends for any discomfort I have inadvertently caused you. In future, please don't hesitate to contact me directly, if you have any difficulties."

"Trenor," whispered Alyssa, "that's the bastard who threw me out. He didn't even want to listen to my reports. Instead he followed the advice of the weasel over there." She pointed to hawk faced receptionist peering through the door.

"Don't worry," he whispered and gave a conspiratorial wink. "I didn't get this job on my good looks alone. Let me handle it. Now go home and prepare you requirement list. If you have any problems, come and see me."

"How can I thank you?"

"You can't," said Trenor. "You see, I work for the Council, but, you can do me a favour though?" She looked into his hypnotic eyes, willing to grant almost anything. "Have dinner with me tonight?"

"I'm honoured, Mr. Ambassador," she said, lowering her eyes. She felt like a school child again with her first crush.

"Trenor! I'll pick you up at eight. Till then, Miss Krychech."

"Alyssa," she said and smiled at him. "Mr. President," she said acknowledging Ken and bowed slightly. She turned slowly around and as her self-assurance returned, walked sedately out the door, fighting the impulse to whirl around and stick her tongue out at the Council.

Precisely at eight o'clock that evening, Alyssa's automated butler announced Trenor's presence at the door. Not knowing what to expect she had dressed in a simple yet elegant sarong type outfit currently favoured on Natoth. It was a logical choice. When complete, it could do for almost any formal occasion. With the removal of the outer wrap, she would be comfortable in a more relaxed atmosphere.

"Right on time," she said, as she greeted him at the door. He still wore the suit of a diplomat, but it seemed appropriate for him.

"Wow," he exclaimed when Alyssa opened the door.

"You'll have to do better than that," said Alyssa with a smile.

He stammered and flustered a moment, "I meant no disrespect. That is I meant to say you look wonderful!"

"Thank you," said Alyssa, "and you, sir, are not too bad yourself."

"Shall we go," he said extending his arm. Natoth still held to old world customs and Alyssa found she enjoyed it immensely. With a touch of glee, she took his arm and they left the confines of her small apartment.

"Where are we going? Do I have to change?"

"Not for me," he said. "I think you look perfect as you are. As for where we're going, I thought I'd leave that up to you. I'm new here, and don't have clue what's around."

"It depends," said Alyssa thoughtfully. He helped her step into the carriage floating gently on the roadway. The door slid shut and soft lights turned brighter inside the cabin.

"If it helps," he said with a smile, "the whole evening's on me. Wherever you want to go, is fine by me."

Alyssa laughed gently. "Careful," she said, "that type of attention could get you in trouble. Suppose I said I wanted to go to the Angel Room, the most expensive restaurant on the planet, then what would you do?"

"I'd take you there," he said firmly.

"Don't even joke about that," said Alyssa with a sigh. "You have to have a reservation booked months in advance. Plus I wasn't kidding about the price. A meal there would be worth almost two months salary."

"Well, we can't just sit here," said Trenor. He reached over to the control pad on his left and entered instructions. "I've told it to cruise around until we've made up our minds." The windows darkened completely and tiny carriage lifted higher and moved away from the building.

"I really don't know where to go," said Alyssa. "I admit I'm a little uncomfortable about choosing a place. Especially when I don't really know you."

"No hurry," he said calmly and leaned back in his seat. "We can cruise around for a while if you want. Get to know each other better."

"I'd like that," she said, "but if we don't find a place soon, we won't get in. Restaurants in this town fill up quickly with all the politicians. I'm afraid even your status wouldn't rate us a seat in a drop house in another hour. Tell the carriage to find us a nice place. You can enter the price range on the keypad if you want. I promise I won't look."

Trenor laughed heartily. His eyes twinkled and the swirling flecks danced merrily with his smile. "I like you, Alyssa," he said. "You're a woman after my own heart." He turned and entered instructions on the pad. Alyssa couldn't see what he entered, but didn't worry about it. She was having a wonderful time.

The tiny carriage banked sharply and headed off in a new direction. Trenor leaned back in his seat. "So tell me about this place, what did you call it? Angel something or other?"

"The Angel Room," said Alyssa, "but if you really want to go there one evening, I suggest you have your office book it now. I kid you not when I say it would take nearly two months before they could fit you in. I understand it's quite exclusive. But, let's not worry about that. Tell me a little about yourself."

He told her about his career in the Diplomatic Corps of the Star League and how it eventually led him to this position of importance on Natoth. Then he questioned her about her background. Alyssa rarely talked about herself, but soon found herself warming to his easy-going relaxed manner.

"As long as I can remember," she said, "I've wanted to be an engineer on a Starship. I took all the advanced courses in school, and then joined the Academy. I found I was good. Really good! I worked a couple of years on the interplanetary milk runs then moved up to the smaller system freighters. Eventually I worked myself into the big star jobs.

After my last tour, I was asked to come here and help Natoth rebuild its fleet."

"Yes," he said nodding. "I understand that they lost most of their ships when poorly constructed plasma injectors sent half the fleet into their sun."

Alyssa nodded sadly. "Many good people lost their lives from shoddy workmanship. I've gotten to know a lot of people here, and aside from the problems with the Government; they are a very likable race. When they applied to the League for help, I jumped at the chance to go along." Her eyes sparkled. "Just think I've been given a chance to design and construct the Star Drive engines for a whole new fleet of ships. An engineer dreams of these chances."

"You really like your work, don't you?"

"It's my life," she admitted.

"But what about other things," he prodded gently. "Anyone special in your life?"

"Not really," she said, her face blushing slightly. "A few moments here and there, but nothing permanent."

"I find it hard to believe that a woman as beautiful and as intelligent as you, doesn't have men camping outside her door."

"It's my own fault really," she said. "I've just never truly been interested. I've worked my whole life with engines. I know and trust them."

"But you don't trust people?"

"On the whole, yes. But individually…" She shrugged her shoulders.

The autopilot beeped for attention. Trenor turned to the panel and entered some more information. "It seems that this little life boat of ours has found a suitable place. I've ordered it to book us in, and park. According to the readout, we should have a table in ten minutes."

"Where are we?"

"I didn't ask," said Trenor. "Are there places we should stay out of? Should I make an inquiry first?"

"No," said Alyssa. "The restaurants around Government House are all reputable. Besides, I kind of like the mystery." They chatted about everyday things until the autopilot indicated their table was ready.

The lights dimmed slightly in the carriage and the door slid open. A hand reached in to gently grasp Alyssa's and a soft voice said, "If you will come this way, Sir, Madame, your table is ready."

Alyssa took the hand and bowing her head in the doorway, exited the tiny carriage. When she stood up to look around, her eyes opened in astonishment and her mouth dropped open. Crystal spires that shimmered and sparkled in the light cast flickering shadows over the richly decorated tapestries on the walls. A fountain shot water almost thirty feet into the air to be caught in a shimmering, gold-encrusted basin. All around were the obvious signs of opulence and wealth.

Trenor stepped out of the carriage and looked around. "Very nice," he said.

"Trenor," whispered Alyssa, "there must be a mistake. This looks like the Angel Room."

Just then, the man who had met them stepped forward He stood tall and straight His jacket twinkling with jewels. "Ambassador, Miss Krychech, your table is ready. Please follow me."

Realization dawned on Alyssa. She whirled around and glared at Trenor. "You set me up," she exclaimed. "You had this all planned. Just one question! How did you get reservations so quickly?"

"I had heard about this place before," said Trenor, "so when I received my assignment for Natoth, I booked myself in. When you consented to have dinner with me, I changed the reservation to two. Are you mad?"

"I should be," she said, then her face beamed, "but how can I be. It is a wonderful surprise. Thank you, Trenor."

"Ahhh, but the evening has just begun," he said mysteriously. The concierge escorted them to their private table and departed as quietly as he had first appeared.

As much as she detested the cheap romance fiction that so many of her friends enjoyed, she had to admit she revelled in the attention Trenor showed. He spared nothing in impressing her; he even had the orchestra play her favourite tunes. When pressed, he admitted using his influence to get a background check on her likes and dislikes. Only later did Alyssa found out how powerful his charms could be.

The evening stretched late into the night and Alyssa finally called a halt to the merriment. "Really, Trenor," she said hugging him tightly. "I must call it a night. I have to report for work in less than two hours."

"Of course," he said. "Now that your equipment is ordered, I assume you're eager to get to work."

"I am," admitted Alyssa.

"Then you must go out with me again. Say, next week?"

Alyssa looked into those hypnotic swirling eyes. This man was special. He wined and dined, but didn't try to force himself on her. Not that she worried about that, but it was refreshing to meet a man who cared more for her than for himself. Before she realized it, she agreed to a second date.

"Goodnight, Trenor," she said kissing him softly on his smooth cheek. She stood in the doorway to her small apartment and watched him leave. A smile escaped her lips as she found herself looking forward to their next meeting.

The second date became a third, then a fourth and fifth in rapid succession. Alyssa, finally free to do the work she enjoyed, relaxed and accepted his companionship. She even forgave Ken and he frequently joined the two for a night on the town. He apologized so often that Alyssa threw a temper tantrum and promised to kill him if he apologized once more. Red faced and embarrassed he just stammered until Alyssa kissed him gently to show they were still friends.

Several months after their first date, Alyssa lay nestled in the crook of Trenor's arm, while he reclined casually on the sofa. They had taken to retiring to Trenor's quarters, as Alyssa's were too small.

"You know," she said softly, "I can't remember when I've been this happy."

"Neither can I," admitted Trenor.

"All I've ever cared about is my engines," she said, "but lately..."

"Lately?" He prompted.

"Never mind," she said abruptly. He pulled her tighter and she snuggled closer, breathing deeply his scent. That's what she liked about their relationship. He never pushed, when she didn't want to talk about a subject. He accepted her for what she was and she liked that immensely.

Their mild infatuation for each other grew into a loving relationship in a short time. More and more, Alyssa found herself looking at Trenor and wondering about the future. It worried her a little, but she realized that something new had replaced her engines. Love!

She had built a close friendship with Ken and told him about her feelings for Trenor. "So why don't you marry him?" Asked Ken.

"Don't be absurd," she replied. They were sitting in Ken's spacious office and Alyssa gazed wistfully out the window into the courtyard below. "We're from two different worlds," she said. "We go where the League needs us. I can't give up my career and I certainly won't ask him to give up his."

"Alyssa," said Ken softly, "there is always a way to work around things. Just don't be afraid to take a chance. When the opportunity comes, grab on with both hands and hang on tight."

Alyssa laughed gently and turned from the window. "You're a sweet lovable man," she said moving nearer to hug the portly president, "but in the real world, there are no jobs that require both an Ambassador and an Engineer."

"Really," said Ken, "then explain why you and Trenor are here?"

"But..." She stopped when she saw the smile on his face. She hugged him tighter and kissed his cheek loudly.

Nearly a full year had passed on the planet Natoth when Alyssa received word from the Council that she had been recalled. The fleet of ships she had been working on had finally reached a point where the local populace could maintain them.

"Oh, Trenor," she said that night while cuddling in his arms. "I wish I didn't have to go. For the first time in my life, I'm truly happy."

"Then don't," said Trenor.

"Be serious," she said. "You know the rules here. Once my tenure is over I have no legal claim to remain."

"You can if you were, oh say, married—to someone who lived here?" Raising his left eyebrow in question.

"Why, Mr. Ambassador. That sounds suspiciously like a proposal?"

"Stay with me, Alyssa," he said gently. "You can remain here as my wife."

"But what am I to do? I'm an engineer and a damn good one. Without a job I'll just whither away."

"I've got that covered as well. I plan to present a proposal to the Council to retain you permanently. They can't afford to let someone with your expertise go. They need you full time."

"I don't know," she said slowly, then recalled Ken's advice. "Why not," she said and melted into his embrace and smothering kisses.

Trenor and Alyssa were married three days later in what had to be the biggest event in the planet's recent history. Ken—resplendent in full diplomatic dress—proudly gave the beautiful young bride away.

Chapter 2

For the next year, Alyssa lived the type of life others could only dream about. She married the only man she had ever loved and he worshipped the ground she walked on. Her career took a tremendous boost when she was appointed to the post of Chief Engineer for Research and Development for the planet Natoth

Alyssa hunched over her latest batch of test fuel in her lab. Ken had persuaded the government to provide a fully equipped lab, able to meet all the demands and requirements Alyssa may have. Two walls were filled with monitors. Some displayed ever-changing graphs; others monitored different test procedures in progress. The consoles and computers jutted out from the wall and continually displayed by blinking multi-coloured lights, the results of the hundreds of different programs they were running. As the research developed, Alyssa and her assistants needed more and more equipment. Now the tiny lab was cluttered with machines that whirred and whizzed continually.

In the far corner of the room was another enclosed room with an airlock. Large window-like sections made of transparent Arenak, Natoth's hardest known substance, allowed unlimited vision into the room. This was the test-firing chamber, designed to withstand the tremendous explosive forces of a drive engine. The walls—while clear—were several inches thick. Inside, a smaller, test version of a Starship Drive motor, lay securely bolted to the floor. Thick dark metal straps held it snugly in place.

Alyssa stood up and stretched to take the cramp out of her muscles. Not for the first time she looked around her lab with pride. With her handpicked team, they had designed and built the lab to their dream specifications. Lately though, with all the testing that was going on, it was becoming increasingly crowded. Again, she thought about requesting a larger space. She and her team could hardly move now for all the equipment in the tiny lab.

She returned her attention to the tabletop chamber in front of her. Waldoes moved with precision control as she deftly mixed a beaker of brownish-green liquid that bubbled and seethed. It had been several months since her appointment and she was hard at work. With her team, she was trying to create a new more powerful, stable, and cost effective fuel to power the Star Drive engines in the ships. They believed this last batch could very well be the one. Carefully she extracted a small amount of the liquid and transferred it to a sealed canister.

She took the canister over to the test engine in the booth and dropped it into the special designed slot. "I hope that's not dinner. If it is I think I'll eat out tonight," said a voice behind her as she carefully sealed the room behind her.

"It will be if you ever come sneaking in here again," she said. Removing her syntha-skin gloves she whirled around quickly and planted a big kiss on Trenor's lips. "What are you doing here? I thought you had a sub-space conference with the Star League."

Trenor's face clouded over. "I just finished. Sweetheart. I have some news. I've been recalled to the Star League—only for a month or so. Then I'll be back in your arms."

Seeing the depressed look on his face, Alyssa said cheerfully, "Hey, that's all right. It's only for a month. Besides if this batch works out, I'll be so busy refining it, I probably won't have time for you anyway."

"I love you," he said and hugged her tightly. A few seconds later, conscious of the amused stares of Alyssa's staff, they broke apart. "When will you know whether this batch is the one or not?"

"Right now," she said pulling away gently from his embrace. "Garret," she said addressing her assistant. "Let's give it a test run."

Garret was her right hand man and in Alyssa's opinion, Natoth's leading engineer. A studious looking man in his late fifties, he had a reputation for spontaneous genius. When he was offered the opportunity to work with the famous Engineer from the Star League he jumped at the chance. His slightly greying hair belied his youthful boyish exuberance that delighted Alyssa no end. It didn't hurt that Garret had a cherub face and kept a constant smile on his face. She saw a lot of herself in Garrett and encouraged him to ask as many questions as he wanted.

He double-checked the chamber. No one took the word of another when firing, then followed Alyssa and Trenor to the control panel on the other side of the lab. He touched a switch and a horn sounded. The other assistants scrambled out of the way and retreated to safety at the back of the lab.

"Ready," he said. When Alyssa nodded, he adjusted the settings on a couple of dials and plunged a switch.

Inside the chamber, the blast from the engine exhaust sounded loud enough to rattle the panes of Arenak in the protective booth. Garret and Alyssa furiously adjusted different dials and switches, measuring and controlling the blast output from the engine. Twenty seconds later, silence descended over the room as the motor cut out.

Garret whooped with delight. "I think that did it, Alyssa. I'll have the exact readings for you by tomorrow, but I'm sure it has at least twice the energy potential of our best fuel. Congratulations!"

"To both of you," said Trenor. "Now I must leave. Alyssa, can you get away early today. My ship leaves tomorrow morning, and I…"

"She can leave now," said Garret. "Go on. There's nothing more to do here today except clean up. Take off, have fun." Alyssa gave him a quick peck on the cheek in thanks and scooped up her coat.

"It seems my services are no longer required here. Perhaps you have some duties for me, Mr. Ambassador," she whispered in Trenor's ear and gave him a nibble that promised more.

The next morning Alyssa watched the ship lift off, through tired, sleepy eyes. "You can sleep on the trip," she said to him before he boarded, "but I have to go to work."

"You didn't have to stay up all night," he said.

"As long as you stayed up, so would I," she said. A big huge grin crossed her face.

She returned to lab and found Garret already hard at work. "Morning," she said trying to sound wide-awake.

Garret looked at her and chuckled. "Hard night, eh?" Then ducked as Alyssa playfully through an electronic tablet at him for the pun.

"Back to work, you bum," she said affectionately. "What did the results show?"

"Better than we dreamed," he said reading the results from another tablet. "Output nearly three times more energy than anything else out there. You've really done it, Alyssa."

"We've both done it," she said hugging the man. "Now we have a lot of work to do. We've got to refine this into something a little more usable." The two scientists plunged into their work. Alyssa, glad to have something to take her mind off missing Trenor, devoted herself to the project.

Unfortunately like all great discoveries, it's 95% perspiration that makes it work. The fuel they had invented was too unstable and needed to be refined. Optimism ran high at first then dwindled as the months passed, as they still couldn't turn out a usable fuel that would provide cheap power without blowing up the ship as well.

Several months after their first triumphant discovery of the fuel, Alyssa, looking haggard and worn, entered the lab. "You look like hell," said Garret. Then noticing her expression he asked gently, "Still no word from Trenor?"

"Oh, I received an official communiqué from him this morning. It says the same thing that all the others do. *Taking longer than I thought. Be home as soon as possible. Love Trenor.* Garret, this is the fourth message he sent in three months. I'm beginning to have my doubts."

"Don't worry," said Garret. "He'll be home soon. By the way, the President stopped by early this morning, he wants to know if you'll meet him for lunch?"

"Okay," she said. She really didn't feel like it, but Ken had been so helpful during the months that Trenor was gone, she felt obligated.

Alyssa went to the President's office just before noon. His secretary smiled knowingly and admitted her. She entered the opulent office and bowed slightly. "Good afternoon, Mr. President," she said formally.

"Good afternoon," he said and waved for his secretary to be dismissed. "Never mind waiting around, Mrs. Williams. Go have your lunch, we'll get something here." The secretary nodded and left, closing the door behind her. Alyssa smiled at the elderly woman. Thankful that the hawk-faced man she had dealt with before had transferred to another department. When the door shut, the President opened his arms wide and said, "Alyssa my dear, you look like hell. Come here and give me a hug."

"You're the second person to say that to me today, Ken," but she moved into his embrace, happy to feel the warmth and comfort. "Have you received any word from Trenor? When's he coming home?"

A dark cloud passed over his jovial face. "Sit down, Alyssa," he said gently.

"What is it? Has something happened to him?" Her heart raced as her panic that Trenor had been injured surfaced.

"Now don't get all worked up. Trenor's fine." Said Ken calmly.

"Then what's wrong? Ken? Is there something you're trying to tell me?"

"This arrived this morning," he said holding a small black box in his hands. "It's addressed to you, but it arrived by diplomatic courier. I was going to bring it down, but…"

"But what?"

"There was a message for me encoded on the surface. It's from Trenor and he asked me to present this to you in private."

Alyssa took the box and pressed her thumbprint on the scanner. Immediately the tiny scanning mechanism read the myriad of lines and wrinkles in her thumb and compared it to the one assigned to its memory chip. Finding the two compatible, it unlocked the box and the lid popped open.

Inside, Alyssa found a data crystal and a small pouch. She took the pouch and upended it into her hand. A small ring fell glittering into her palm. She picked it up and examined it closely. Then trembling she placed it slowly on Ken's desk.

"Its Trenor's wedding ring," she mumbled.

"Damn," said Ken smacking his a fist into his palm. "I'm so sorry, Alyssa. If there's anything, anything I can do?"

"Let me borrow your reader for a minute," she said. Her lips were pursed tightly, as if afraid to open.

"Of course, of course," said Ken and handed her the portable reader on his desk. "I'll leave you alone."

"No," she almost shouted, "don't go. Just...Give me a minute." She slipped the crystal into its slot and activated the reader. The unit hummed slightly and her face was bathed in a cool soft green glow from the screen.

"It's a standard divorce form," she said. "He didn't even have the nerve to hire a lawyer. He just sent a generic form."

"Anything else on the crystal?" Ken asked softly.

"No," she said quietly, "just the form. At least he had the decency to fill it out. All it needs is my signature."

"May I look at it," Ken held his hand out carefully. "I was a lawyer before I got into politics."

"Afraid I'll try to challenge it and hurt your friend," spat Alyssa angrily.

"On the contrary," he said and placed an affectionate hand on her shoulder. "I want to make sure he hasn't stripped you of what's yours."

"I'm sorry, Ken,' she said softly. " I didn't mean to spout off at you. Please, go ahead."

He took the reader and thumbed the repeat switch. After reading the information for several minutes he handed the unit back to her. "It's perfectly split," he said. "Neither of you gains or loses. Also, he's filed it as automatic. If you don't respond in thirty days, then your divorce will be automatically granted."

"What happened?" she asked as her eyes filled with tears. "Was it something I said or did, or maybe something I didn't say or do. I...I never expected this. Can you talk to him? Let me call him. Why didn't he call me and talk to me. What...Why...?" She broke down, as her control was lost in a wave of pure grief.

Ken crouched beside her and gently placed a comforting arm around her. "I don't know why this happened, but I think he's making the biggest mistake of his life," he said gently. "If you want to, I can arrange a sub-space link so that you two can talk."

Alyssa shook her head, her red mane flying violently about. "Not right now, I'm too upset and angry. I know we should be talking, but I guess I'm too stubborn." Slowly she relaxed but the tears continued to flow freely. When she spoke again it was with a quiet controlled anger that worried Ken. "If he wants a divorce, who am I to stand in his way. After all I'm just his wife, nobody important obviously."

Ken tried to reassure her and berated her for her negative outlook. "Any man would be thrilled to have you as a companion. You are a warm, loving, beautiful woman who loves unconditionally. Do you know how rare that is these days?"

"Thanks," she said sniffing back the tears. "You're a true friend and I love you deeply, but obviously this is not true or otherwise I would still be married to Trenor. No…it's me. I…I knew…Somewhere deep in my heart, that it wasn't going to work."

"That's your anger and guilt feelings talking. I know it isn't true and so do you." Said Ken forcefully. "Look, why don't you take a few days to think and relax, then we'll place the call to Trenor together. Maybe it is all a misunderstanding. I know that before my wife died, we had many arguments, and sometimes I wished we were free of each other, but we managed to talk about things and resolve those issues. I love her as much now, even though she's gone as I did the day I married her…Perhaps it's the long distance and time away from each other that's caused these feelings. It happens!" He said hopefully.

"He could have called! I would have made the trip to the League, but he didn't. In fact he gave no indication at all. I should have suspected something when he stopped writing and started sending official communiqués instead. No…He means this. It's over." She picked up the reader again and slowly read the document that destroyed her life.

"Well, I've never been one to sit around waiting," she said firmly. She hesitated a moment then picked up the attached stylus and signed her name the screen. The unit checked her signature and found it acceptable. Then it shut itself off. Silence filled the large office of the President of Natoth.

Ken took the reader from Alyssa's hand and removed the crystal. "I'll send this back with the courier if you like?"

"Thanks," she said softly.

"Alyssa?"

"No, I'm fine. Really! Do you mind if we have lunch another day? I don't feel up to it today."

"Of course," said Ken warmly, "anytime you want." Alyssa stood and plodded slowly to the door. Her shoulders drooped with each step as if a great weight lay on her back and was getting heavier with each step.

"Alyssa," said Ken softly, "don't blame yourself."

"But I do," said Alyssa pausing in front of the door. "I'm going back to my engines. At least I understand and trust them. Good-bye, Ken."

"Alyssa," he called, but it was too late. She had already closed the door behind her as she left.

Over the next month, Ken saw little of Alyssa. She had buried herself in her work. Arriving early at the lab every morning and staying late into the night. With the help of Garrett and the others he maintained a close watch on her. She seemed to be coping quite well and after a few weeks his concern for her well being relaxed.

After nearly 6 weeks of trying he was finally able to persuade her to join him for dinner. They had a wonderful evening of dining and dancing. Ken kept the conversation light or about work. He carefully avoided mentioning Trenor or any subject that could be linked to him.

Alyssa had lost some of her enthusiasm for her work, but kept diligently trying to perfect the new fuel. She felt hollow and empty and was just going through the motions. A fact that did not go unnoticed by her coworkers and Ken.

Over the next several weeks, Ken repeatedly offered to take her away on vacation for a few days, but each time she declined politely. "We're almost there," she would say, or, "just another few days and I'll have that fuel. I can't leave now."

Since he received daily reports about the work progress, he knew she was making excuses, but could do nothing about it. Still she did seem happier lately and he felt much better.

"Strange as it may seem," she confided one day, "I still love him."

*

Ken sat in his office, his head in his hands. He'd been wrestling with his feelings all morning. Finally he decided that as a friend he had only one course of action and called Alyssa to his office. "I received this in the morning courier pouch," he said gently. "I don't think it really was intended for me, somebody slipped up. Here, you'd better read it."

"To the right honourable President Ken Tomath of the planet Natoth. The Council of the Star League is pleased to issue this invitation to you to join in the festivities of our newly commissioned Chief of Protocol, His Honour Trenor Adwell. As an added bonus we will be celebrating the marriage of Chief Trenor to Miss Karen Southerside of the Protocol Office."

"The second half of the message is the official notification that Natoth had been accepted into the Star League," he said softly. "Some mix-up must have happened and I was included on the guest list."

"Congratulations, Ken," stammered Alyssa. "I know Natoth will be a wonderful addition to the League."

"Alyssa...I'm so sorry. I don't know what to say..."

"Don't! Don't say anything. If you will excuse me, Mr. President, may I return to my work?"

"Alyssa, why don't you take a few days off? You've been working round the clock. I hear the leaves are falling in Campau province and it's a sight to see."

"Not right now. The fuel is not ready. There's a ton of work to be done..." Ken came over and put his arms around Alyssa. She stiffened up and held firm in his embrace. "If you'll excuse me," she said and left before he could say another word.

Alyssa returned to the lab and plunged herself even more into her work. She drove herself at a fantastic pace, pausing to sleep only when she could no longer keep her eyes open. The days stretched into weeks. Garret and Ken became concerned for her health. She had started drinking in the evening and more than once had shown up for work in the morning still drunk.

Her friends tried to get her to take a break, but she had become sullen and resentful, lashing out at anybody who tried to help. More often than not, she began to make mistakes in the lab, small ones at first, then in increasing levels of danger. Garret watched for and repaired these mishaps. His friendship for Alyssa demanded no less.

Garret contacted Ken, voicing his worry about Alyssa. Ken immediately ran to the lab to talk with the distraught young engineer.

"Alyssa, you've got to get yourself under control. You're killing yourself and I can't stand idly by and watch. Snap out of it!" He said angrily and shook her roughly by the shoulders. Alyssa broke down sobbing and Ken gently ushered her away and back to her apartment. He stayed with her all night she as she slept in a restless, haunted state, tossing and turning all night.

The next morning after she assured him she would be alright and thanked him for his concern, he left still filled with doubt. He returned to his office and wearily began perusing the morning mail. Most of the pile was the usual stuff and he signed off and placed it into the action pile for his secretary, but one piece suddenly caught his attention.

Carefully he read the contents of the communiqué. *Damn*, he thought. *This all we need.* He knew there was no getting around it. He had to tell Alyssa that the Star League had assigned Trenor permanently to Natoth and he would arrive in 2 days. Unfortunately he couldn't bring himself to delivering the bad news to his friend. He would wait until the day Trenor would arrive…

That morning, Alyssa came in, obviously she had been up all night drinking again. "Ready for the test?" She barked at Garret.

"Are you sure you feel up to it," he asked concerned. "We can do it another time if you wish."

"Stop playing around," she lashed. "You think I'm incompetent. Come on tell the truth. That's what you think. Trenor left me because he knew I was no good—now you feel that."

"No, Alyssa. That's not true."

"Well, to hell with you. I'll show you. I'll show everybody. I'm an Engineer, first and foremost, and a damn good one. Now are you going to help me or do I have to do it by myself?"

"I'll help, Alyssa," said Garret softly. Together they prepared the test engine for firing with the newly refined fuel. Garret rolled it into the chamber and reattached the straps and bolts. Then he joined Alyssa in the control booth.

Silently, they worked setting the controls. Twice he had to readjust her settings—slyly because of her temper. Unfortunately he missed one of her mistakes. They fired the engine and watched the readouts. Suddenly, alarms bells clanged loudly through the lab. The engine thrust climbed higher and higher.

"It's a run-away," cried Garret furiously punching the futile controls. The alarm cleared the fuzziness in Alyssa's head and she realized what had happened.

"Shut it down," she ordered.

"Can't. It's locked open."

"Dump the fuel core. It'll cause a hell of a mess, but it's better than blowing up."

"It's not responding," said Garret. "I'll have to do it by hand."

"Are you kidding," she cried. "The radiation in that room will kill you in minutes. No. It's my mistake. I'll do it." But it was too late; Garret had already started across the room.

He swung open the airlock into the blast chamber; entered and secured the door. Alyssa pounded on the door screaming for him to get out. He opened the inner door and secured that as well. Reaching over he flipped on the internal speakers.

"Alyssa," he said. "The core has reached critical mass. Get out while you can. I can't stop it now. Alyssa...I just want to say...I'm sorry about Trenor, but if it's any consolation...I love you. I have since we first met. Now go...this thing's going to blow any minute. I'm dead already from the radiation, nothing can save me, but you still have a chance. Go. Please."

Alyssa refused to leave. She continued to pound on the door of the blast chamber. Just then Ken ran into the room. He'd been on his way over to see Alyssa when the alarms sounded.

"Ken," shouted Garret. "It's going to blow and I can't stop it. Get her out of here. Get to the blast shelter. Hurry man. Hurry!"

Ken's eyes quickly noted that Garret was beyond help and grabbed Alyssa around the waist. She fought like a wildcat, clawing, kicking, and screaming to get Garret out. With precious seconds ticking away, Ken did the one thing he'd never done before. He hit a woman.

The strain combined with the alcohol in her bloodstream gave her no resistance to the punch. She blacked out and sagged in Ken's arms. Slinging her over his shoulders in a fireman's carry he darted for the door—pausing only long enough to wave a sorrowful "wish-I-could-save-you-as-well" good-bye to Garret.

Slamming the door behind him, he dashed down the stairs to the shelter. Inside, he sealed the door and activated the emergency systems. Air from sealed containers pumped into the room and dim emergency lighting from a generator provided him with enough light to set her down safely. No sooner had he deposited her unconscious form on the floor when the building rocked with a tremendous explosion. Ken flew through the air landing heavily on his right arm. The sound of a snapping twig told him that his arm had just broken. Waves of nausea washed over him then mercifully he blacked out beside Alyssa's crumpled body.

He awoke a few hours later. "Easy Ken. That's it. I've set your arm. It will ache but I think I got it right." Alyssa adjusted his sling, then leaned over, and kissed his bruised face. "Thanks!"

Ken looked at her, her hair all dishevelled and sporting a shiny black eye. "Sorry," he said, "guess I don't know my own strength."

Chapter 3

Nearly three days had already passed while Alyssa and Ken lay entombed in the shelter, cut off from the outside world. By the end of the first day, denied her crutch of alcohol, Alyssa grew embittered then a raging anger possessed her. She stormed around the tiny shelter beating her fists in futility at the cold unyielding metal door. When at last her strength failed her, she collapsed in a heap and shook uncontrollably. Ken lay beside her and held her tightly in his good arm. Slowly, over a couple of days, the shakes eased and she was able to think clearly. Ken encouraged her to face her fears and vulnerability. Released from the tension and frustration she had been harbouring, Alyssa sobbed loudly on Ken's shoulder.

"You're a survivor, Alyssa," said Ken soothingly. "I see greatness about you."

"Thanks," she sniffled. "I know you're just trying to make me feel better, but it helps anyway."

"No," he protested gently. "There is something about you. It's hard to describe, but once in a lifetime someone crosses your path that is destined for more than the average person." He leaned over and kissed her matted hair gently. "I feel privileged to have met you."

"You're sweet," she said and kissed him, "but once we get out of here, I'm afraid the only thing I'm destined for is jail."

On the sixth day, the door to their tomb swung open and several people bearing stretchers and emergency equipment entered. One of the medical officers knelt beside Alyssa, while another serviced Ken. As she leaned in close to Alyssa, her nose wrinkled in disgust, but that was the only outward sign she gave of the stench from Alyssa's unwashed body.

Ken and Alyssa survived in the tiny shelter, but lacking sufficient water for cleaning, produced an odour approaching a pigpen. The medical officer looked closely at Alyssa. Her trained eyes and senses showed that the young woman had had a rough time. Without a word she surmised that Alyssa had been through DT's. She reached in her med-pack and withdrew a vial of light brown liquid. This she inserted in a hypo-spray and pressed it against Alyssa's neck. Immediately Alyssa slumped unconscious and the medical officer waved a stretcher over.

"She'll be all right," she said. "Her system has had a severe shock. It needs time to recuperate. Tell me, Mr. President. Was she a drinker?"

Ken said nothing, unwilling to embarrass Alyssa further, but his eyes fell earthward. "No need to say anymore, sir," said the medic. "Don't worry, I won't embarrass her or you." She signalled the others to pull out. As the last one left she looked around the cramped room and wrinkled her nose again.

"Incredible," she whispered. "Going through the DT's, trapped in this god-forsaken hole." She shook her head and left the bunker.

The results of the blast had devastated the building housing Alyssa's lab. The shock hit her hard. Of the 200 people working in the research labs, twenty-five had not escaped in time. Another hundred or so suffered minor breaks and cuts. So bad was the disaster that the people of Natoth cried for her head. In one act of drunken foolishness, she had become the most hated person on the planet.

The hardest part for her to face was the resulting explosion had not only destroyed the labs and her friends, but had blown debris across the whole complex. Innocent men, women, and children, visiting the capital had been injured or killed.

She looked over the names of the dead feeling a strong sense of remorse and guilt when one name caught her attention. Trenor Adwell! It couldn't be!!!

Ken came into the hospital room and she showed him the list and pointed out Trenor's name. Ken sank heavily into a chair beside the bed. "It's true," he said softly. "I was on my way to tell you that he was coming when everything went to hell. I didn't want to tell you when we were trapped because I feared for your sanity and your life…I'm so sorry, Alyssa!"

"So not only did I cause our divorce, I killed him as well," she said in a quiet whisper. The strain of living suddenly became too much for her abused system and she lapsed into unconsciousness. Ken quickly summoned the doctor and left when they reassured him that she would be alright. She just needed rest and time.

After recovering in the hospital, Alyssa was formally charged with wilful manslaughter and ordered to appear before the Supreme Court. The Supreme Court of Natoth found her guilty and ordered her confined for the rest of her life. Ken, as President and counsel, stepped in pleading for leniency.

He argued her achievements and advancements in helping Natoth secure its future in the Star League. The court reviewed the appeal and gave her the choice of staying and serving her sentence or being banished from the planet Natoth—never to return.

Ken, acting as her guardian because of her severe mental depression, accepted the banishment for Alyssa. He gained permission for her to be treated by a psychiatrist before she was to be exiled. Since their rescue, Alyssa had withdrawn in a deep cloud of guilt and self-doubt. She blamed herself for Trenor leaving, and dying in the explosion, and felt the guilt of the killing nearly 40 people, researchers, visitors, and children, who perished in the blast. The court sympathized and released her into the custody of the hospital.

Six months later, she boarded a ship for the Star League University world. The Mind-Techs had returned her to usefulness, but said she must work through her guilt and remorse. They could do no more, so the court evicted her.

"I've obtained a special release," said Ken before she boarded. "Because of all the good work you've done and certain mitigating circumstances, they will not publish your conviction. As far as anyone outside Natoth knows, you have completed your tour of duty and are free to pursue other opportunities."

"Thank you, Ken," said Alyssa softly. "You're a true friend. I just want to say…"

"Never mind," he said gently. "Alyssa, I don't want you to go, but I think this is better than living in prison for the rest of your life. I'll sleep better knowing that you are alive and well somewhere out there. I'm only sorry I couldn't do anything about finding you another post."

"You've done so much for me already," she said hugging the man. "I don't think I could ever repay your kindness. And since I'm banished from Natoth, the chances of me seeing you again are…" The effort proved too much and Alyssa hid her face in her hands as the tears flowed freely down her face.

"Be well, Alyssa," said Ken and gently ushered her into the waiting hands of the Purser.

The Purser didn't know the details, but could see she was under stress. Besides it was none of his business. His job was to see to the safety and well being of the passengers. Gently he guided her into the ship, allowing her to rest on his tall lanky frame.

She kept to herself on the trip to University and only reluctantly allowed herself to emerge from her self-imposed exile while on University. She made few friends, but never got close to anyone. She even refused dating offers, which were numerous, and angrily lashed out at friends who tried to set up blind dates for her.

Alyssa stayed on University for a few months, trying to regain a semblance of normal life. Vowing never to work on another engine again. Three times she changed her major, but she found the lure of the engines on the ships that visited too strong. She yearned to work on the drive coils and challenge herself with the intricacies of FTL flight. She spent more and more of her free time at the spaceport watching with longing the ships that docked there.

One morning, Alyssa was in the observation tower as had been her habit for the last few weeks. She enjoyed watching and feeling the immense power of the giant star ships as they came and went. A ship awaiting take-off clearance activated its motors in preparation for departure. Alyssa, in the observation tower suddenly bolted from the window. She dashed down the carpeted corridor, knocking several people down in her haste.

Muttering apologies she burst through the door into the communications room of the spaceport. "Stop that ship," she cried. "Don't let it lift off!"

The control officer reacted instantly. He didn't know who Alyssa was, nor did he care. When someone came in, in an obvious state of worry, he acted first and would sort out the details later. "Contact that ship," he ordered to the Comm-Tech. "Tell it to stand down."

Thirty minutes later, an inspection showed a flaw in the shielding of the ship's reactor. Alyssa, so in tune with the vibrations of a ship's engines, had heard a note resonate from the ship that shouldn't have been there. Only a handful of people in the Star League could have expertly diagnosed the condition from outside.

The Captain of the freighter—a large woman with a voice loud enough to rattle the rafters—was impressed and thankful to Alyssa for saving her ship, cargo, and the lives of herself and her crew. She offered Alyssa a post as Assistant Engineer on board her ship. At first Alyssa declined, but several days later, after repairs had been made, she changed her mind.

*

"We're going to really miss you around here," said the Captain of the giant freighter Hellion. Alyssa stood at-ease, wrapped in a one-piece light blue jumpsuit, with the ship's crest over her right breast. Her red hair, normally tied up in a bun because of the machinery, hung loose and wavy, framing her face and softly falling to rest on her shoulders.

"You're a good officer and a damn good engineer. The Carriolion doesn't know what she's getting. You take care of yourself. Hear? Come and see me before you depart."

The Captain whirled around and thumped sedately off the upper grid work in the engineering bay. His massive frame shaking the grid works with each step. Alyssa could tell from his formal posture and quick departure that the Captain had left before he created an emotional scene. Rarely in the last two years had she seen him so ruffled and upset!

A feeling of sadness and loss almost overwhelmed her, but old painful memories surfaced, reminding her of why she had chosen to leave her friends on the Hellion, and she buried her emotions. She whirled her powerful lithe frame around and clumped noisily back to her one and only true love—the ships' engines, tying up her hair as she walked.

Hammering loudly on a stuck valve, she failed to hear the Chief Engineer come up behind her. He watched her struggle with the annoying valve for a few moments. He admired the way she could handle the sometimes-troublesome motors. She could wield a space wrench as easily as the delicate tools needed for the plasma drive. This time though, the energy exerted from her tiny but powerful frame seemed to have a more definite purpose other than relieving a stuck valve.

"Alyssa," he said in between the ringing blows of the hammer. The hammer came up and paused in mid-air. She looked over her shoulder, annoyance on her face.

"Yes, sir," she said, the lines on her face smoothing. She stood up and carefully laid the gleaming silver tool on the deck.

"I just wanted to say my good-byes now," he said gently. "I will be off-ship by the time you leave."

"Oh, that's right," she said smiling at the elderly engineer. "Your daughter lives on this planet with her husband and. three children? It must be wonderful to have a family…who loves you!" The latter she almost whispered regretfully.

"Yes, it is" he said avoiding the unspoken question. "I get to visit so infrequently, that I jump ship as soon as we ground. Now I suppose I'll have lots of time. . Alyssa…I just wanted to say how much…"

"I know, Chief," she said. "I feel the same way."

"I don't know what the problem is—you've been pretty quiet about your past—but I hope you find the answer you're looking for."

"I don't know if there is an answer. I just know I have to keep moving, and the reasons are, as you said—my own."

The Chief Engineer quickly pulled Alyssa into a hug and kissed her in a fatherly way on the cheek. "If you need anything—anything at all—you call me. Okay?"

"I will, and thanks." The two friends separated and the Chief left to prepare. Downside would be in 10 minutes. Alyssa turned back to the stuck valve. Suddenly she didn't seem to have the strength anymore. The little fatherly talk with the Chief had drained her of the pent up anger and frustration. She picked up the hammer and swung a few feeble blows at the valve. Her mind drifted to a similar place and time two years ago.

*

"Why don't you stay, Alyssa? We need a new Chief Engineer and your one of the best I've seen."

"I'm sorry, ma'am," she said, "but I can't. I've been offered a post on board the Hellion, and I hear she's making the run into the Markus sector."

"Sounds to me like you're running—away or to, I don't know. I gave you a chance when you saved my ship and I've never regretted that decision. I had hoped you would stay, but... Well good luck."

*

A loud clang brought Alyssa back from her memories and the valve suddenly swung freely. She quickly dropped the hammer and spun the wheel to close the valve. After ensuring the integrity of the seal, she picked up her tools and put them away. She took one last look around the place she had called home for two years then went to her cabin.

Inside she closed the door and leaned weakly against it. "Damn," she said to no one in particular. She opened her eyes and stared at the sparse furnishings of her cabin. Wiping a single tear away absentmindedly, she began packing.

The alarm gong sounded indicating planet-fall in two minutes. Hastily she finished stuffing her few belongings in the haversack. Throwing it into the net hanging on the wall, she dropped into her chair and cinched the straps tight. The need to buckle in during take-off and landing had long passed, but experience teaches—better safe than sorry. Accidents can happen and those who were standing free usually ended up dead.

The Hellion grounded with a slight bump and Alyssa grabbed her things. Making her way forward, the liberty gong echoed through the ship. All crewmembers not engaged in duties could now leave the ship for some much needed rest and relaxation. Alyssa sped up. She had to still meet with the Captain.

Standing outside his cabin waiting for permission to enter, she quickly smoothed the ruffles in her tunic and ran her fingers through her hair, regretting she still hadn't combed it. A gruff "Enter," sounded from within the cabin. She opened the door and stepped in.

"Come in, Alyssa," he said. "Please sit down. I won't keep you long. The Carriolion grounded ten minutes ago and I don't expect her Captain will want your services right away." He closed his journal and pointed to a seat in front of the desk. Captain Renforth was a giant of a man, with a heart to match.

Over the last two years, Alyssa had seen him happy, sad, angry, and downright mean. Once, when she had gotten into trouble in a bar—on a small backwater world in the Markus sector—it was Captain Renforth who had come in, fists waving. In seconds he had cleared the room. Scooped her up and carried her back to the ship. Then he proceeded to give her the sternest lecture she had ever had concerning drunken sailors and bars. Afterward, he took her into the ship's small gymnasium and taught her how to fight and defend herself. A career Captain, he had no children of his own, but he considered his crew his children. Alyssa admitted that never having a father of her own, Captain Renforth would be the type of man she would wish for.

Now she saw a look on his face she rarely saw before, one of anguish and indecision. Getting up he moved around front and sat on the edge facing Alyssa. "I don't usually get involved with my crew's private lives, but as of the moment we grounded, you no longer worked for me," he laughed, then seriously he said. "Alyssa, are you sure you're doing the right thing? As you know, this is the last trip for the Chief. He's put in a request for retirement. You must know that he expected you to replace him, and I concur with his recommendation."

"I know, sir," she said softly.

"Then why are you doing this? I admit the Hellion isn't as big, or as prestigious as the Carriolion, but we are one of the best ships in the fleet. We are like family here, and we look out for each other. You know you could have a very lucrative and happy career here."

"I know that, sir," she said, "but I can't stay. I have my reasons." She stood up and thrust out her hand. "I want to thank you though. You made me feel welcome and gave me a home. I won't forget any of you."

"Well…if you're sure!" He got up and took the proffered hand and pulled her gently. She came into his bear hug embrace and clutched him tightly. Wiping a betraying tear she quickly left the office. Scooping up her bundle she made a mad dash for the gangway, determined to put the warm, comfortable, but also painful memories behind her.

Once ashore, she checked in with the Dock officer concerning her transfer orders to the Carriolion. There she found out that the Captain had left instructions that all new crewmembers and replacements were to report at 17:00 hours later that day—she still had 4 hours to kill. The Dock Officer made a few lurid suggestions on how she could waste a few hours. Alyssa smiled meekly. She had come across this before. These smaller spaceports seemed to be worse than the rest.

Smiling politely she asked where the Commissary could be found. The Officer gave her directions and true to his nature watched her closely as she walked away. Alyssa could feel the hungry officer's eyes burning in her back. His attention flattered her, but it also gave her cause to wish she were elsewhere.

The Commissary was just as she thought. Small and sparsely furnished. A few small tables and chairs set along the window, overlooking the spaceport. In the entranceway, a series of locker boxes beckoned. Not looking forward to lugging her belongings—meagre as they were—around for 4 hours, she picked an empty one and thrust her bundle inside.

"Credit chip or retinal deposit," said the automated teller. Alyssa dug into her pockets and retrieved a small handful of credit chips. Carefully she counted the chips nearly twenty credits—enough to last all day if she was careful, but not enough to cover the locker and expenses.

"Retinal deposit," she replied and placed her right eye over the soft padded view screen. A small beam of light quickly scanned the myriad of blood vessels in her eye and made an electronic note to deduct the amount of the locker from her account at the Galactic Bank. Since her pay usually went straight into her bank account, and she rarely took landfall, Alyssa never found the need to carry large sums of credits.

The locker box beeped for attention and Alyssa placed a thumb on the scanner board. Now it would only open to her thumbprint. Beside the locker boxes, an automated vending machine dispensed hot and cold drinks, sandwiches, and full meals if you so desired. Being an early model it only accepted credit chips. Alyssa studied the menu and quickly decided what she wanted.

After placing her order and depositing some of her meagre supply of chips, the machine prepared her order with its usual quick efficiency. A compartment door slid aside and Alyssa removed a steaming cup of Aldeberan coffee and a small plate of assorted finger sandwiches. She took the tiny repast to an empty table and sat down.

From her viewpoint she could see most of the spaceport. About twenty ships were currently docked. Mostly freighters, a few military vessels, the odd personal skiff, and the two ships that meant the most to her—the Hellion and the Carriolion. The Hellion being a freighter stood proudly at one end of the field, towering over the other ships beside it. The Carriolion stood at the other end, alone.

The Carriolion was the latest in passenger comfort, a cruise ship that carried a crew of 200 and a passenger complement of nearly 500. This would be her new home. These giant ships, once relegated to orbiting worlds, could now land safely thanks to the invention of the gravimetric compensators. It allowed more efficient loading and unloading. It also gave the engineers and mechanics time to go over her systems and hull, without the cumbersome space suits.

"Excuse me? Do you mind if I join you? There doesn't seem to be any free tables." Alyssa looked up into the face of man carrying a tray of food. She nodded and motioned to the empty seat, then resumed staring out of the window.

The man fussed and meticulously rearranged his meal on his tray. Carefully he placed his drink in one corner and his plate in the opposite. Alyssa glanced—trying not to be rude—at this process. When he had placed the last item in its proper position, the man made a gesture of supplication then began eating.

"Awheya," she said quietly.

"Awheya," responded the man. "Are you from Horath as well?"

"No," she said. "I had a roommate on university who performed the same rituals. She taught me the proper greeting."

"Remind me to thank her," he said smiling. "My name is Lexxencrattergg—call me Lex. Most people find our names more than a mouthful, and mine is one of the easier ones to pronounce."

Alyssa laughed. Very few people from Horath ever ventured into space. They preferred to stay on their home world. Those that did usually struck her as stiff and totally devoid of humour. Only her roommate had been different. She would and could laugh at anything.

"Alyssa," she said holding out her hand. Lex took her hand in the custom of his race placed the palm to his forehead.

"If it doesn't infringe on your privacy taboos," he said gently. "What brings you to this desolate outpost?"

"Work," she said. "I've just transferred to a new ship. You?"

"Oh, I already have a job, thanks."

"Not that," she snickered at the poor joke. "What are you doing here?"

"Having a drink and a bite to eat. Would you like some?"

"You're exasperating, Lex. Do you know that?"

"So I've been told." Calmly he took a bite of his sandwich and smiled slightly while eyeing Alyssa. "Please continue eating. I didn't mean to intrude."

Alyssa looked into his deep green eyes, so reminiscent of the ocean. Suddenly shivers ran through her body. She'd seen eyes like that before. Trenor! Memories flooded her mind and her eyes glazed over as she remembered her first love, so many years ago.

"Are you all right?" Lex's voice brought her back to the present. She looked again. Yes, he had the same eyes.

"Sorry," she said. "I'm fine. You just remind me of someone I knew...casually."

"Is that good?"

"Depends on what time of the day you ask me," she said laughing.

"Listen," said Lex, "I don't have to report in for another couple of hours. What do you say we take a look around? That is, if you are free?"

"My price is very high," she said, straight faced. Carefully she looked him over: Handsome, but none of those pretty-boy features that so many men had been going for lately, probably in his early thirties, obviously well educated. She made her decision in a blink of an eye, "but since I don't have to report for several hours myself, I'd love to."

Quickly they finished their meal and departed the Commissary. The facilities at the spaceport were limited. Not being in the main shipping lanes, it still hadn't installed all the different amenities that tourists were accustomed to. They did find a Holo-Theater and sat down to watch a three-dimensional play based upon a Solara fable.

As the story of love and friendship unfolded in front of them, Alyssa and Lex began talking. Their conversation, like their meal, seemed open and friendly. They subconsciously drew closer together, and even though the actors were not real, they started whispering and giggling quietly.

By the time the story had reached the climax of love lost then re-found, the two strangers were sitting close together, hands barely touching. When the theatre brightened after the closing scene, they were holding hands like long time friends.

Lex looked at his watch and muttered, "damn. I've got to go. I didn't realize the play would be so long. If I don't hustle, the Captain will have my head on a platter."

"I'd better get going too," she said nodding. "I still have a little while, but I have to run some errands before I report. Will I see you again?"

Lex smiled and her heart skipped a beat. "Maybe," he said, "space isn't that big. I'm sure we'll meet again."

Hesitantly she pulled him towards her and quickly kissed him. "I've had a wonderful time Lex. I sincerely hope we do meet again."

"As do I," he said and again, repeating his planet's ritual, he placed her hand to his forehead then scurried off down the corridor.

Alyssa watched him go. Thoughts of friendship and possibly even love raced through her head. Not since Trenor—all those years ago—had she thought about another relationship. She just couldn't bring herself to do it again. Now this strange man in a couple of hours had brought those deeply buried feelings back to the surface.

"Not this time," she said softly. "I fell for a pretty face and smooth talker once. Never again!" Resolution set on her face as she returned to the Commissary to retrieve her belongings.

Alyssa picked up her bundle and made her way back to the Dock Officer. "Alyssa Krychech, reporting for duty aboard the Carriolion. May I enter?" The Dock Officer looked over his orders and checked Alyssa's name off the crew manifest for the Carriolion. He directed her to the correct docking bay then returned to his work.

Alyssa swung her pack over her shoulder and marched down the long metal corridor connecting the spaceport to the ship. Pausing at the hatch, she checked her appearance in the bright work. Wouldn't do to show up on a new job looking like a slob. Satisfied with her looks, she entered the hatch and located the deck officer of the Carriolion.

"Alyssa Krychech, reporting for duty," she said and handed him an electronic chit containing her transfer orders. Absentmindedly, the deck officer ran them through his system and after checking her identification welcomed her aboard. His face broke into a wide grin at the sight of Alyssa. His peak cap tilted back on his head revealing the sparse growth underneath.

"The X.O. will meet with you in twenty minutes," he said and signalled for a junior officer standing by. "Please take Engineer Krychech to the X.O's wardroom."

The junior officer took her bag. "If you'll follow me, ma'am," and moved off down the corridor.

Alyssa followed, wondering at the ship's routine. The X.O. or Executive Officer was the second in command. On a ship this big, he wouldn't personally meet new crewmembers. They stopped outside a small door emblazoned with the words 'X.O's Wardroom' and the officer quickly ushered her inside. He placed her duffel on the deck and bid her make herself comfortable, then took his leave.

Alyssa sat on the plush couch in the richly decorated room. This much opulence was more than she was used to. For the last few years she had served aboard freighters'—rooms and quarters that resembled a monk's cell. Weight still meant a lot, so frills were reserved for the Captain only. Everyone else had to do with bare minimum.

She ran her hand gently over the plush material covering the couch, suddenly she noticed that the walls were covered in real wood paneling and not textured plastic. She whistled appreciatively at the whole room. The furnishings alone must have cost more than a year's pay, never mind the paintings and the wood paneling. She got up and started wandering around the room, admiring the statues in the alcoves and the fish tank in the corner.

While trying to attract the attention of a brightly coloured fish swimming in the tank, she heard a commotion outside the door. A muffled voice could be heard from the other side. "I want a full inspection in two hours. Until then I don't want to be disturbed. I will be in conference with our new Engineer."

Alyssa smoothed her tunic and stood in the at-ease position and waited for the X.O. to enter. Again she worried about this assignment. Second Assistant Engineer on the biggest cruise ship in the fleet. For years she had avoided promotion and responsibility, but when this position became available, something in her said, *take it*. At the time she rationalized by saying to herself, *I'm not really in charge. I'm only the second assistant*. Now she had second thoughts.

The door opened slowly and Alyssa prepared to introduce herself to her commanding officer. Instead of speaking clearly and loudly, she gasped and her mouth hung open in shock.

"Told you we would meet again," said Lex with a smile. "Welcome aboard, Alyssa. I'm the Executive Officer of The Carriolion, and your boss."

Chapter 4

"So, I'm going to ask you one more time," said Lex. "Will you marry me?" He shuffled closer to Alyssa who was seated at the other end of the velvety couch. She leaned back into the crook of his arm, and fidgeted herself into a comfortable position.

"I can't," she replied softly. "Lex, I love you more than you realize, but I can't marry you. I can't marry anyone—ever again!"

"Lys, you say you love me, but you won't marry me. I'm sorry, sweetheart, but I need reasons." Alyssa felt the warm glow she always felt when he called her Lys. Most of the other crewmembers called her Alyssa or Lyssa, but only Lex could call her Lys.

"Well," she said mischievously, "you set me up. Then took advantage of the opportunity."

"For heaven's sake that was three years ago. I told you. I didn't set you up. I really was on my own and needed a place to sit. I didn't know who you were. It's just good fortune that I recognized your name. Besides, I would have been a complete fool not to want to spend some time with a beautiful woman like you. Can you truly say you're still mad at me for not telling you who I was?"

"No. I'm not mad, and I really do cherish the love and friendship we have." Since her arrival on board the Carriolion, Alyssa and Lex found themselves being more than an item of occasional gossip. At first the physical attraction was all they had, then gradually, a deep understanding and affection had grown between them.

"Talk to me, Lys. Tell me what's wrong. If I can change it, I will. Is it something about me?"

"No, my love," she said tenderly, as she stroked his cheek softly. "It's not you. I love you with all your faults."

"What faults?"

"Shush, I'm trying to be open and personal with you...Many, many years ago, I married an attractive, intelligent—and ambitious man, named Trenor."

"I know all that, it's in your file. So your marriage failed, life goes on."

"You don't understand. It didn't just fail...Oh you wouldn't understand."

"Try me. I promise I will listen and understand. As a matter—"

"Attention, please. Will Engineer Krychech, and the First Officer, please report to my cabin immediately. That is all." The two lovers looked in frustration at each other after the announcement from the Captain. Alyssa in a way felt both relieved, and depressed.

"Come in, please," came the reply to their inquisitive knock on the Captain's door. They entered the room and stood at ease waiting for the Captain to acknowledge their presence.

Seated behind a large oak desk, neatly arranged with files and papers, sat Captain Beth Bomar a woman in her late fifties, but possessing the drive, and energy, of a woman half her age. The little bit of grey in her hair, accentuated the feeling of power and wisdom one felt around her. Captain Bomar had logged thousands of Star hours, but the strain didn't show. If anything, it seemed to energize her even further.

"Sit down please," she said. "I sent for you two because I have some good news." Alyssa and Lex looked on expectantly. Good news from the Captain came rarely on the Carriolion. Not because she was a miser with it, but because nothing much happened that affected the giant cruise liner.

"I'm sure you've heard of the new class of ship being constructed at Plentara 4." Both nodded. The ship would be the first of the Nebula class of Star Ships As far in advance of the Carriolion as she was to Alyssa's old ship, The Hellion.

"It is almost completed and trials will begin in six months," continued the Captain.

"And you've been offered the Captain's chair," blurted Alyssa excitedly.

"Yes, I have," said Captain Bomar calmly. "But that's not why I called you. I have been Captain of the Carriolion for ten years. She's a good ship and we've seen many wondrous things together. The new ship is called the Argosy and has twice the capacity and power of the Carriolion. It needs a good Captain. It needs a person who can do it justice. I like where I am and what I do. So I turned down the nomination."

"WHAT," cried Lex. "Forgive me for being blunt Captain, but this is an opportunity of a lifetime. Captain of the first new class of ship— reputedly the biggest and most powerful ever built. You've earned her. I suggest you rethink your ideas!"

"That's heavy talk coming from you, Lex," she said and smiled sweetly. "That's why I like having you as my Number 1. You're not afraid to speak your mind when the need arises. All the more reason why I'll miss you."

"Excuse me?"

"I've recommended to the Council that you be given the position of Captain of the Argosy, and I want to make Alyssa, First Officer of the Carriolion. Now don't just sit there gaping like a Verterran Jackfish, say something." Lex closed his open mouth and looked at Alyssa. Her eyes sparkled and shone with and intensity he'd never seen before.

"Captain, I don't know what to say," stammered Lex.

"He accepts," said Alyssa. She turned and faced him and. "Lex, as you say, it's the opportunity of a lifetime. You've worked hard for this chance."

"But-"

"No buts. Captain...When will he have to report?"

"After we complete this run. By the way Lex, the Council unanimously voted you in. You were their next choice; my recommendation just sealed the deal. It's up to you my friend, but I think you would be a fool to turn it down."

Lex sank back in his chair, shock registering on his face. "I...I need time to think, to sort this out. Can I give you my reply later?"

"Of course," she said and looked affectionately at Alyssa. "I appreciate some of the difficulties that you may face in making such a decision. And what about you? Are you going to accept the position of First Officer?"

"Captain, I'm deeply honoured," said Alyssa, "but I'm just an Engineer. I'm not suited for the job."

"Nonsense," said the Captain waving her hands as if dismissing the whole notion. "You've taken the requisite courses and completed all the requirements. You even have experience. When Lex took ill last year, who filled in for him for 4 months? No, don't answer, I will. You did—and a damn good job you did as well."

"But, Captain,"

"No buts from you either. Now both of you get out of my office, I have work to do, and you two have a lot to discuss. My only advice is to go with your guts. Sometimes logic in these cases can mislead you. Now get out. Wait…Lyssa, I need to talk to you."

The Captain rarely called her Lyssa, only when something personal was involved. She gave an involuntary shudder and waited while Lex departed, still in a daze from the news.

"It's time you and I have a heart to heart," said the Captain after the door closed. "Just how do you feel about Lex?"

Alyssa bristled at the flagrant disregard for privacy, but she could understand the Captain's reasons for wanting to know. Alyssa would be a determining factor in deciding whether Lex would take the post or not. "I love him," she replied matter-of-factly.

"Good," said the Captain. She moved around the desk and sat in the chair previously occupied by Lex. "Lyssa, I have to ask this question, so please forgive me. Are you going to marry him?"

"Why? Will it affect his appointment?"

"No," she said shaking her head. "That's a done deal if he wants it. No, the reason I asked is that if you and he intend to get married, I have enough influence to get you assigned to the Argosy as well. I can't promise the job as First Officer, but I can guarantee the Chief Engineer's position."

"First Officer on the Carriolion or Chief Engineer on the Argosy. If you don't mind me saying so, Captain…You're a real bitch!"

Captain Bomar laughed loudly. "Comes from being alone and

miserable all these years. Honey, I'm not trying to pressure you. I just wanted you to know there is another option for you."

"What if I don't want either? Can I stay here as Assistant Engineer?"

Captain Bomar frowned. "We had this conversation before, when I made you Assistant Engineer. I think it's time you told me the real reason you don't want to advance. Oh yes, I can tell. You've refused every opportunity to permanently upgrade and improve yourself through your whole career. You take the courses and will serve in a temporary capacity, but actively shun any permanent posting. Now what you do doesn't affect only you, but Lex as well."

Alyssa stared at her superior. A kind, understanding face peered back. No judgment, just a desire to help. "Maybe you're right," said Alyssa. "I've carried this for many years. Are you sure you want to hear this? It may affect your opinion about me."

"Honey," said the Captain warmly, "whatever you did, or whatever happened to you is in the past. You've already proven you're the best. Your service record is exemplary and your devotion to duty is equalled only by the glowing reports from your previous Commanding Officers. I can't think of anything that could have happened to tarnish that record—short of blowing up the President of the Council."

Alyssa chuckled nervously. "No. I didn't do that—not quite anyway."

"I'm listening!"

"Well, it all started years ago. I was a Drive Engineer working for the Political Branch of the Council. I was sent to Natoth to assist in rebuilding their Star Ships. There I met and fell in love with the man who would become my husband, and the reason for my problems…"

*

"So that's the whole story," said Alyssa softly. "You're the first person I've told it to. Jilted and abandoned, drunk and disorderly, and a convicted murderer to boot. Banished from Natoth and exiled to live with my guilt."

"My god, child," cried the Captain. "What you've been through! I understand now. The reason you hesitate about marrying Lex, and the reason you pass up Command options. You're afraid aren't you?"

Alyssa nodded her head meekly. Shame and guilt washed over her like waves on the shore each wave bringing her deeper and deeper into depression. Captain Bomar grabbed her gently by the shoulders and shook her until Alyssa looked up again.

"We'll get through this. I promise. We'll talk again, and I will help you. Now dry your eyes. There's a man out there who's waiting to hold you. I think you should tell him, but it's up to you."

A klaxon suddenly pierced the air. Captain Bomar slapped a switch on her desk. "Bridge. What's wrong? Why the collision alert?"

"Asteroid field dead ahead, Captain. It just came out of nowhere. I think you should come up here. This thing is huge, and we're too close to avoid it by going around."

"Very well. Call the Exec to the bridge. Out." She turned and faced Alyssa again. "Hope you're feeling better because I need you in that engine room now." Alyssa quickly straightened her tunic and nodded. She was less than half-a-pace behind the Captain as they left the room in a dash. At the end of the corridor, the Captain turned left to head for the bridge and Alyssa turned right.

"We're going to get orders for some wild manoeuvres," she shouted to her staff and the Chief Engineer as she burst into the engine room. "Be alert." Thumbing her mic, she reported in. "Engine room standing by."

Orders from the bridge came rapidly: More power, less power, more power starboard side, more power portside. The giant ship weaved and dodged as the Captain and the bridge crew tried to manoeuvre her through the swarm of asteroids. Occasionally the ship shuddered as one of the pieces of rock slammed into the side.

"A few more of these hits and we'll crack open," said Alyssa to no one in particular. Her eyes were glued to the strain gauges and they were well beyond the safety limits. Suddenly the whole engine compartment shook and the lights dimmed briefly. Alarms sounded all over the ship while Alyssa tried to contact the bridge.

"Captain. Engine room! That last hit weakened the seams. Another hit like that and the strain will tear her apart. Bridge? Bridge?"

Instead of answering, a ship wide announcement came blaring over the speakers. "Abandon ship. All hands, Abandon Ship. Passengers to lifeboat stations! Crewmembers will assist. This is not a drill. Abandon ship." The message repeated itself. It would continue doing so until stopped by the Captain.

Alyssa turned to the Chief Engineer and finally noticed the woman slumped in her chair. She ran over and quickly examined her. Blood trickled from a gash in her forehead. Alyssa felt for a pulse on the woman's wrist then pressed her fingers to the Carotid artery on her throat.

She poked around for a few seconds desperately searching for a pulse to indicate some life remained in the woman when her eyes fell on a piece of metal beside the Chief's chair. It was a piece of stanchion and very heavy. It must have hit the Chief Engineer in the head when it fell. Alyssa gingerly probed the small wound on her head and felt the soft spongy mass of the woman's brains through the matted hair.

She activated her mic and spoke softly. "Assistant Engineer's log report. I have just discovered the body of Chief Engineer Rononsone. It appears that she was struck by a piece of bulkhead casing. Death was instantaneous. Due to the present emergency I am assuming command of Engineering until relieved by the Captain."

Alyssa grabbed her crew together and they shut down all non-essential power and diverted it to the lifeboats, then they scrambled for their lifeboat stations. Before leaving she activated the automatic dump sequence that copied all the ship's logs into the rescue pods and released an emergency buoy. Out here in an asteroid field, the chances of it surviving were slim, but there was always hope. She ran down the corridor as the lights on the ship changed too red, and the announcement added another phrase.

"Launch in two minutes. Launch in two minutes." They had two minutes to get in and secure everything before the automatic launch sequence ejected the lifeboats. As senior officer in the lifeboat she had the responsibility of ensuring the safety of the passengers and crew under her command. When the last person jumped in, just under the wire, she sealed and dogged the hatch. Then, quickly checking everyone's harness, she strapped herself in tightly.

"Brace yourself," she shouted over the noise. "It'll be quite a jolt. Don't worry if you pass out. The lifeboat is programmed to seek the first habitable planet and land." The alarm changed to a horn sounding steadily. "Here we go!"

Alyssa felt the weight of the world, slam into her chest as the lifeboat exploded from its cradle and automatically steered away from the dying ship. The boat's computerized brain applied full thrust and continued to dodge the asteroids that had destroyed the Carriolion. Being smaller, it could manoeuvre faster and quicker than the big ship; unfortunately it lacked the momentum dampeners of the big ship. The hapless passengers were tossed around like rag dolls.

Alyssa strained to peer through the tiny porthole at the Carriolion. At first she seemed motionless, then Alyssa saw her keel over to the starboard side. A shower of sparks erupted from the ship's side as a giant chunk of rock slammed into her about midway. The life-pod settled into a smooth run as it found a clear space in the asteroid field. Alyssa watched with sadness as another rock slammed into the Carriolion. She floundered and another explosion sent a flame shooting from her side. The Carriolion seemed to be drifting to the left, but Alyssa couldn't see the cause of the drift.

Just before a large asteroid—nearly the size of the Carriolion—hit the ship, the life-pod bucked and weaved as it tried to avoid another swarm. The restraining straps dug into her flesh as she lunged violently back and forth and side to side. Bruised and battered, Alyssa felt consciousness slip away and tried to fight the encroaching darkness. She struggled to catch a glimpse of her companions in the lifeboat, but another violent swing flung her head back against the headrest and she slipped into quite darkness.

Chapter 5

Alyssa, panting and gasping for breath, struggled to swim in the murky, heavy water. Her slow, cumbersome movements only seemed to make it more difficult. She could see the light from the surface a scant few feet away, but just out of reach. Desperately she fought for the safety of the surface. Briefly she stopped her fight for freedom and wondered why she could breathe underwater, but the thought faded and disappeared as she found herself fighting a raging current. Like a wild animal she swam, fighting with all her strength against the current that seemed determined to push her back down. Inch by inch she made her way closer to the surface, glinting invitingly above. The closer she approached the surface, the more exhausted she became. When at last, nearing her limits of exhaustion, she heard a voice, calling and encouraging her to continue.

"Miss Krychech? Wake up, please. Please, Miss Krychech. I'm scared. Please wake up!"

Alyssa strove valiantly for the surface. She wasn't asleep. Couldn't they see she was drowning? Fools! She must reach the surface. She needed to reach the surface. With one last desperate kick, she shot above the waves that had held her back, and found herself floating in the air above the raging stream. She heard the voice calling again, and became distracted. Dizziness overcame her and she lost her balance. The air no longer supported her in her confused state and she plummeted back to the seething waters below. Just before impact the water vanished and she found herself falling onto a body, seated in a chair.

Alyssa moaned softly—her hand coming up to her aching head. Her eyes blinked open and she found the face of a young boy peering down anxiously. She blinked again to clear her vision, the dream fading into forgetfulness. Glancing around with the eyes of a trapped animal, she tried to focus the strange visions into reality

"Where are we? What happened?" She looked at the back of her hand covered in blood.

"We've landed, Miss," said the boy. "You hit your head and now it's bleeding. Please, Miss Krychech, I don't know what to do. The others are still asleep. You slept for a very long time. I got scared when nobody would wake up."

The boy's face registered fear. A fear so strong Alyssa could smell it in the room. But somehow, a hidden inner resolve kept him from bawling his eyes out. Alyssa unbuckled her seat belt and looked around slowly. The first thing she noticed was the upper stanchion. It had broken loose and hung directly in front of her. That's where she had hit her head. Again she tentatively probed the wound. It hurt like hell, but she thought no permanent damage had been done.

"You're Ethan Alaso, aren't you," she said, looking at the boy, recalling the passenger manifest for the lifeboat. *Damn*, she thought, *he can't be more than 13 years old, but he acts like a 6-year-old. Why?*

"Yes, ma'am," he said respectfully.

"Well, you're a very brave young man," said Alyssa, holding the boy's hand as he helped her to stand. "Your parents must be very proud of you."

"I have no parents, Miss Krychech," replied Ethan. "I'm an orphan from the Tantalus colony."

Alyssa shuddered inside. That explained a lot. The Tantalus colony had become the deposit for unwanted and unruly children, more of a penal colony rather than an orphanage, most of its inhabitants failed to get adopted. Those that did proved difficult to handle to the new parents. Complaints of abuse and intolerable language were common. It was common knowledge that children from Tantalus were mentally underdeveloped.

Trying not to show her shock and horror on her face, she looked him squarely in the eyes. "Then I say you're a very remarkable young man. You don't seem to be like the other children from Tantalus?"

The boy smiled, and Alyssa's heart melted. "That's because of Mrs.

Worensky," he said pointing to an elderly woman slumped unconscious in her chair. "Will she be all right, Miss Krychech?"

Alyssa moved nearer the woman and checked her vital signs. After a couple of minutes she turned back to Ethan anxiously waiting—concern written all over his face. "She'll be fine. The strain of everything just made her rest for a while. When she wakes up, she'll be good as new." At the news the boy smiled again and Alyssa felt warm to the boy who had an obvious affection for the old woman.

"Come on," she said, "give me a hand checking on the other people. Can you hand me that first-aid kit on the wall. Yes, that's the one. Now hold this man's arm for me. He broke it and I'd like to set it before he wakes up."

For the next hour, Alyssa and Ethan made the rounds of the rest of the passengers of the lifeboat. Aside from Alyssa's head injury and the man's broken arm, only a few minor scrapes and contusions from the seat webbing needed attention. She had just finished applying a compress to the forehead of a beautiful young woman, when a strong masculine voice sounded behind her.

"Aye, but you do good work, my girl." Alyssa turned to find the man with the broken arm struggling with his straps. She started to move over, but Ethan bounded past her and released the man. "Thank you, son, and who do I have to thank for the assistance?"

"Ethan, sir," said the boy respectfully

"Thank you, Ethan," said the man. "Call me Patty. Everyone does. Now my dear, is there anything I can do to help?"

"I'm sorry," she said, "but I don't recall your name?"

"Ach, just call me Patty. I haven't used my full name in years and I'm not about to start now."

"I don't remember you in my lifeboat drill."

"That's because this isn't my boat," he said. "Things got a little hairy and this was the only one available. I hope I didn't take the place of anyone else."

"I'm sure they got away," said Alyssa unsure about the man. "With over 700 people to evacuate, there were more than enough positions in the lifeboats."

"Aye, but the boats are huge indeed. Although this one seems a tad small!"

Alyssa smiled and explained that this boat and several others were the escape pods reserved for the senior officers. They held only half dozen or so passengers and were designed to land ahead of the bigger pods so that the area could be safely investigated.

"I've got to check the area out so that I can send the all clear signal to main pods," she said. "Look why don't you just sit back and relax."

"Don't judge too quickly young lady. I may be a little banged up, but I can still hold my own. Sixty years in the service of the Star League may have aged me, but it didn't dull me. Here, give me a hand boy. Let's take a look at our situation shall we?"

Patty and Ethan quickly moved around the lifeboat. Patty ran his hands over the various seams in the compartment while Ethan stood nearby in case he needed anything. Alyssa, glad to leave the matter to Patty, returned to her duties concerning the other passengers.

She focused on Mrs. Worensky first. Breaking open a vial of smelling salts she waved it quickly under the woman's nose. Soon the noxious fumes penetrated her sinuses and she woke up coughing and gasping. Ethan looked over and saw her awake and rushed over to her side. The two hugged each other like mother and son and Alyssa turned her attention to the beautiful, unconscious young woman beside Mrs. Worensky.

She didn't respond at first, but then slowly she coughed and tears dripped down her high cheekbones. Satisfied that the girl had finally responded, Alyssa turned back to the old woman. "How are you feeling, Mrs. Worensky?"

"I'm fine dear. Ethan, come here. Have you been a good boy?"

"Yes, ma'am," he said. "I've been helping Miss Krychech and Patty. Haven't I, Miss Krychech?"

"He's been wonderful," said Alyssa and Patty nodded his head behind her.

"Very good," said the woman. "Now help me up. Easy. Easy. I'm not as young as you." She stood up and scooped the boy into her motherly embrace, hugging him tightly. "I'm very proud of you Ethan. And I'm sure your new parents will be."

A slight moan escaped from the full, pouting lips of the young woman. "Get me out of here," she demanded.

"In a minute," said Alyssa. "I want to make sure you're all right first." She moved nearer and started to examine the girl again, when she slapped Alyssa's hand away violently. Alyssa drew back in shock and Mrs. Worensky gasped. Patty just curled his free gnarled fist.

"I said, get me out of here," repeated the girl. "You in the uniform. What's your name?"

"I am Assistant…Chief Engineer Krychech," replied Alyssa coldly, "and before you start making any more demands you better look around and see where you are."

"How dare you," said the girl. "I'll have you brought up on charges. Where's the Captain? I will not be treated this way."

"We don't know where the Captain is," said Patty. "Speaking of which. Chief? With your permission I'd like to scout around and see what I can find. Maybe some of the other pods landed nearby."

Alyssa nodded, cautioning him not to lose sight of the pod, and Patty moved to the airlock. "The readout says the atmosphere is breathable, but it's hot as hell out there. Sorry, ma'am," he said acknowledging Mrs. Worensky.

"My name's Ada, and don't worry. I was swearing long before you were a gleam in your father's eyes." Patty smiled and slowly cracked the seal on the hatch. A small puff of steam entered as the pressure equalized, then a wave of heat bore down on them.

"Oh, close the door," whined the girl. "You're all absolutely mean. I'll make sure you all pay for this. When I contact my father, he'll make sure you'll never work for the League again."

"That will be enough of that, young lady," said Ada sternly. "Chief Krychech and Patty are our best means of survival and I will not tolerate any bitchy, whininess from you. Now sit down and keep quiet."

Alyssa prepared for the onslaught from the young woman obviously from a well-to-do family that had a lot of influence. She was used to getting her own way. Alyssa's anger churned preparing to defend everyone from the verbal assault, but to her surprise the woman sunk sullenly back into her chair. Her eyes seethed and burned but she said nothing.

With a look of satisfaction Ada turned her attention to the hatch where Patty tried desperately to hide a smile. "Well, don't just stand there, Ethan. What did I teach you? Help Mr. Patty through the door."

Patty slipped through and the others waited patiently. After a few minutes a faint voice called to them from the outside. Alyssa moved nearer the hatch and looked outside. Patty stood about 50 feet from the ship on a plain of scorched plants and dark soil. "It's okay," he yelled. "Careful when you come out, the soil is loose around the ship."

Alyssa waved and called out, "Fine, I'll send the all clear signal." She returned to her chair and flipped several switches. The faint readout showed that no pods were in orbit. Obviously someone else had sent the signal.

She turned around and addressed the others, "All right. One by one, we'll leave the ship. I'll caution you that we don't know this planet, so keep your eyes and ears open. When you get out make your way over to Patty. Ethan? You want to be first?"

"Yes, ma'am," said the boy proudly. He scrambled over to the hatch and dove threw like a flash. He slipped a little in the loose dirt that had piled up near the hatch, then regained his footing and dashed over to the waiting Patty.

"Now, you," said Alyssa sternly to the young socialite.

"I'm not going anywhere without my escort," she said haughtily.

"Fine," said Alyssa calmly. "If and when we find them, we'll send them back for you. It shouldn't take more than a couple of days." At that the girl's face blanched and she moved for the door. Ada looked at Alyssa and smiled.

The girl exited the stranded lifeboat and in her tight dress and high heels stumbled and fell in the soft dirt. She pitched forward and tumbled down the small incline, coming to a rolling stop at the bottom. Ethan ran over to give her a hand, with Patty in tow.

While Ethan struggled to help the girl, she started whining and crying like a Banshee. "Ach, what a fuss," said Patty. "You're not hurt, just dirty."

"Don't you touch me," she screamed. "I'll have you all arrested."

"As you wish, my lady," said Patty bowing low. Turning his gaze upward into the hatch he called out, "How about you, Ada? Need any help, or will you have me arrested as well?"

"I would appreciate any help you care to give, kind sir," said Ada and Alyssa helped the old woman through the hatch into the waiting hand of Patty. Gingerly, he helped her descend the loose slippery mound, while trying to control his own descent with one arm in a sling.

Alyssa turned back in and grabbed the E.S.G. Pack off its mount on the bulkhead. Slinging it over her shoulder she scrambled through the hatch. Her last movement closed and dogged it behind her. She slid down the mound carefully and trotted over to stand beside the others.

Purposely ignoring the girl still sitting in the dirt, she addressed the rest. "Now, the odds are high that the other lifeboats landed within a short distance of us. Ethan, please find the locator beacon in E.S.G. Pack for me please," she said handing the boy the pack.

He picked up the lightweight pack and looked it over. On one side the directions stood out clearly in black, bold print. *Emergency Survival Gear—Reg. #335674-C: Contents; 1- Locator Beacon, 1- Emergency Shelter, 1-Pkg. Field Rations (6 persons/3 days), 1-Signal Beacon. 1- Emergency Issue Firearm (Type K2). Note: If any of these items is missing, report the discrepancies to Master stores, Alderran 3.*

"Excuse me, Miss Krychech," said Ethan, "but if anything's missing, how are we supposed to report it out here."

Patty laughed loudly. "The more things change, the more they stay the same. The bureaucratic and military minds work the same way. Our field packs had the same warning, but you never found out what was missing until it was too late."

Ethan ripped open the security seal on the pack and dug through the contents. Shortly he proudly held up a small palm sized device that bore the label "Locator Beacon." He handed it over to Alyssa, then as a second thought emptied the contents of the pack on the ground carefully. "I'm going to check and make sure that everything that's supposed to be here, is here."

Alyssa smiled at the boy's caution and nodded her head. She unwrapped the Locator and activated its tiny display screen. "This will register any other lifeboats in a fifty mile radius. They'll show up as tiny blips," she explained. "We're the big bright blip in the centre of the screen."

The picture took so long to clear, that Alyssa feared that even the long lasting power cell might be drained, or worse. But soon the image came into focus and four other blips registered on the tiny screen. Alyssa studied the readout for a second and made a few mental calculations.

"The nearest one is less than twenty miles in that direction," she said pointing. Then looking up into the sky she said, "it looks like it will be dark soon. Maybe we should wait until the morning." Patty and Ada nodded, the reasoning seemed sound.

"Where do we sleep, Miss Krychech?" Asked Ethan after repackaging the pack. "I didn't see any beds in the lifeboat."

"In the pack," she said, "is a sort of tent. It also contains beds. It's like camping. Do you like camping?"

"I don't know," said the boy softly. "I've never been camping."

"Then we're going to have some fun, lad," said Patty. He placed a protective arm around the boy and started to walk away, his voice fading into the distance. "While we get the tent, let me tell you about this one place where I lived. No buildings. We lived in tents for the whole time. My tent had this…"

"You can't be serious," said the dirty socialite. She had gotten up while the others were talking and moved nearer Alyssa. "I'm not going to sleep in a tent. Having to sleep on your crummy old ship was bad enough, but this is too much. I demand you take me home right now, or at least to a first class hotel."

"Please feel free to summon your vehicle," said Alyssa. Her temper had begun to flare and her red hair waved like angry snakes in the light breeze. The last thing she wanted right now was to listen to a spoiled brat whine.

The girl looked around at the desolation surrounding them and realized the futility of her temper tantrum. Sullen, but not entirely subdued she wisely kept her mouth shut, but she didn't storm away.

"Ada, would you like to give me a hand setting up camp," said Alyssa turning her back on the young woman.

"Happy to," said Ada. "Look, here come the boys. Well you two, if your finished, we'll set up camp. Ethan, would you please assist Patty in assembling the tent while Miss Krychech and I make dinner."

"Yes, ma'am," said Ethan happily. "This is going to be fun." He picked up the package containing the tent and ran off to join Patty who was already searching for level ground.

"We'd better find some water," said Alyssa. "There is some in the pod, but it won't last long. Field rations can be eaten dry, but they leave a horrible taste in your mouth."

"What about her," whispered Ada nodding in the direction of the socialite who was watching the men assemble their shelter?

"I'm sorry," said Alyssa. "I just don't understand that attitude. I came from a similar background, that is my foster parents were well to do, but I don't think I ever behaved that badly. Besides, I can't worry about her now. I have the survival of three other people in my hands. She'll just have to grin and bear it."

Ada nodded slowly then held her finger up, signalling Alyssa to wait just a minute. She walked over to the girl and pulled her roughly by the arm out of earshot of the others. Alyssa could just hear Ada's soft words as they drifted to her on the breeze, "come with me princess, we have to talk…now!" The newly minted engineer watched in fascination as the two women argued. It surprised her to see the young girl suddenly back down and hang her head. She followed Ada meekly back to Alyssa and stood mute beside her.

"Miss Krychech, I have the honour to introduce you to Samantha. She's elected to join us in our search for water." Alyssa nodded without comment to the young woman. She already knew her name of course, from the roster, but the woman's attitude had prevented Alyssa from addressing her directly.

"Over there," said Alyssa pointing. "I see what looks like abundant vegetation. It's as good a place as any to start looking." Samantha took the lead, while Alyssa lay back to assist Ada in case the older woman needed help. When Samantha had pulled ahead, Alyssa whispered to Ada. "What did you say to her?"

"Oh, nothing," said Ada casually. "I just reminded her that her survival depended on all of us and she couldn't rely on 'Daddy' finding her quickly."

"I must admit, Ada," said Alyssa, "you don't seem to be having any problems coping. What did you do that gave you such confidence? Were you in the service like Patty?"

"Heavens no," said Ada. "I'm just an old woman. That's all…Miss Krychech? Can I tell you something in confidence?"

"Only if you'll call me Alyssa."

"Alyssa! What a lovely name. Listen, I'm really scared to death."

"But the way you handle Ethan and Patty, and Samantha…"

"Sweetheart, I raised 7 children by myself when my husband died in an accident at work. He died just before William our seventh child was born. So I had to continue alone. If nothing else it taught me how to handle temper tantrums, and maintain order. A word to the wise dear, when you have children, teach them who's the boss from the start, otherwise they'll run your life."

"What about Ethan, he treats you like his mother or grandmother?"

"The poor boy," said Ada sadly. "No, I never met him until we boarded the ship. He's on his way to meet his new parents. He's an orphan you know." Alyssa nodded. "He reminded me so much of Gregory, my third child. Now there was an undisciplined, troublemaker. He's a surgeon now," she said proudly.

"Well, whatever you're doing to Ethan, I approve," said Alyssa. "From what I've heard about children from Tantalus, they can be a handful."

"Pooh," said Ada. "All Ethan needed was a little love and affection, and some guidance, along with the occasional firm hand."

"Well, he's a wonderful young man," said Alyssa. "You should be proud."

"Of him, or me," said Ada. "Honey, let me tell you something I learned years ago. What we are—good or bad, happy or sad, is inside all of us. Sometimes we need to be shown the other side of our lives. Then we can make a decision…I see in your eyes that you faced that choice yourself. Well, Ethan is facing it now. Continue the way he was or learn to fit in normal society."

Alyssa nodded and gave the old woman a tight affectionate hug. "Where were you when I needed a mentor to guide me?"

"You did all right by yourself," said Ada taking Alyssa's hand in hers. "Chief Engineer on one of the biggest Starships in the fleet is a superb accomplishment. You have a lot to be proud of. You're still young, you may even make Captain."

"No," said Alyssa softly. "I could never be Captain."

"In heavens name why not?"

Alyssa felt the compulsion to confide in the old woman. She felt sure that Ada would never pass judgment, and she was easy to talk to, but Alyssa still couldn't admit her failure. The guilt was still too strong. Fortunately she was spared the dilemma by a cry from Samantha up ahead.

"Water! I've found water," cried Samantha happily. The other two women rushed over to her side and looked in the direction she pointed. Through the underbrush, shone the unmistakable twinkle of a stream as the bright sun overhead bounced and laughed on the tiny windblown waves. Together they beat their way forward until eventually, they stood on the edge of a stream bank.

Samantha looked down at her dirty dress, then at the sparkling clear water, Suddenly she dashed for the water with the obvious intention of diving straight in to wash herself off. Alyssa tried to grab her but missed. She may have missed on the first grab, but Alyssa was no slouch. All those years working out in the shipboard gymnasium to dampen out her bad moods paid off as she appeared to Ada's eyes to leap from her spot and fly through the air. Seconds before Samantha jumped into the water; Alyssa tackled her to the ground in a flying body-block.

"Hey," cried Samantha. "What'd you do that for? I just wanted to wash my clothes. Now I'm even dirtier than before. Can't you do anything right?" She dropped to the bank heavily, crossed her arms, and pouted childishly.

"That's nothing, you idiot," said Alyssa panting from the exertion. "You could be deader than before." Alyssa grabbed the socialite by the shoulders and shook her roughly. Her angry red hair whipsawing in the air. "I haven't tested the water. It could contain any millions of microorganisms, bacteria or other creatures that we don't know about that could kill you. Haven't you got any sense?"

"Alyssa?" Whispered Ada. Alyssa realized her frustration and constant nagging fear that she was in charge had gotten the better of her. She released Samantha and took a deep breath.

"Sorry," she said and helped the young woman stand up.

"Just hurry up," pouted Samantha. "The heat here is unbearable and I'm filthy. I don't like to be sweaty and dirty."

Alyssa grunted then removed the test kit from her belt pouch. Not wanting to get too close to the river's edge, she tied the tiny cup to the end of a branch with some thread and lowered it into the water. Retrieving her sample she poured it into the analyzer and waited for the results. Twenty seconds later the tiny machine pronounced the water safe to bath and wash in. They would have to boil it to drink—untreated it would make them slightly ill—but otherwise it was perfectly safe.

"See," said Samantha with defiance. "There's nothing wrong with it. Now if you don't mind…" She took off her dress and still dressed in lacy undergarments walked into the water. She dove under and surfaced a few seconds later to rejoin the others on the beach. "It's deliciously cool. I feel much better." Her head dropped slowly and a sheepish grin appeared on her face. "I'm sorry I've been such a spoiled brat. Why don't you two come in? Trust me, you'll feel a whole lot better. Oh and bring my dress please. I'd like to rinse it out before I put it on again."

Alyssa looked at the cool water. Samantha dove back in and was obviously enjoying the refreshing swim and Alyssa envied her. Ada stepped forward and started to remove her shoes. "I'm not a swimmer, but I would like to paddle around a bit," she said. "Come on, Alyssa. Relax for a minute. You deserve this as much as anyone."

Alyssa hesitated then saw the peaceful relaxing face of Ada as she slipped her hot tired feet into the stream. With a shrug she removed her tunic and pants. Carefully she moved to the water's edge. Suddenly out of the corner of her eye she saw a movement. Instantly alert she crouched down and gazed into the bush in the direction of the movement.

"Alyssa," called Ada. "Come on girl. It's wonderful."

"Shhh," whispered Alyssa waving her hand for silence. Ada stepped out of the water and crouched behind Alyssa.

"What is it, dear?" She whispered.

"I saw something move, over there," said Alyssa never taking her eyes off the spot.

"Maybe the boys followed us after setting up camp. It could be them."

Alyssa considered this possibility. It seemed a plausible idea. So far they hadn't seen any other form of life on this world. Then she realized she had forgotten to bring the firearm from the E.S.G. Pack and cursed herself for her stupidity. First rule of exploration, be prepared, and like a raw recruit, she had forgotten.

Reaching beside her, she picked up a stout branch lying on the ground. "Patty?" She called out. "Ethan, is that you?"

The brush suddenly parted and they caught a glimpse of fire red eyes staring back at them. With sudden swiftness the creature darted past them and plunged into the water. Its long snake-like body rippling in the water as it moved closer to Samantha.

"SAMANTHA," screamed Alyssa. "Get out of the water." Samantha whirled around at the shout from the shore.

Unable to comprehend what the trouble was she started a slow crawl back to the beach. As she got closer, she could hear Alyssa and Ada shouting and saw them waving and pointing. Treading water she looked around. Scarcely ten feet in front of her, the water rippled and moved. As she watched, a giant head, much like a lion's, rose out of the water. It's long body, resembling a mammoth snake's, but covered with fine soft hairs, whip lashed in the water. Samantha stared at the alien creature and ear-piercing scream escaped from her lips as it moved closer.

Chapter 6

Patty stood up to wipe the now ever present sweat off his brow. Ethan, still crouching on the ground finished tying the last stay on the shelter. "Did you hear that, son?" Asked Patty as he whirled around. Ethan stood up and cocked his head to one side—listening intently.

"No, sir," said Ethan. "I don't hear anything." Patty slowly turned around in a circle. To Ethan he seemed to be sniffing the wind.

"Must be my imagination," said Patty. "Come on. Let's see what this world offers in way of foodstuff. We could be here for a while."

"Then you don't think anyone is looking for us," said Ethan disheartened. Patty looked at the youth.

"Now I didn't say that, did I?"

"Nooo," said Ethan hesitantly.

"They'll find us, lad," said Patty, "but what good will it do us if were dead from starvation, Hmmm?"

"Yes, sir," said Ethan brightly. Suddenly he stopped and cocked his head. "Did you hear that?"

"Yes," said Patty seriously. "I don't know what it is, but we better check it out. Grab the pack." Ethan rushed back to the campsite and retrieved the survival pack. Patty reached inside and withdrew the Mark IV (Type K2) energy pistol from its container. Checking the charge he tucked it into his waistband and broke into a trot with Ethan close behind.

As they approached the bush line, he motioned Ethan behind him and slowed to a crawl. The air split with the shrill piercing cry of a woman. The two men, one old and forgotten, the other young and beginning life, dove into the bush and ran as fast as their legs to carry them.

A few minutes later they stopped to get their bearings and catch their breath. "Which way now, sir," gasped Ethan? The cry came at them again—stronger than ever.

"This way," shouted Patty wheeling to his left and running into the ever-thickening bushes.

They broke free of the bush line at the edge of the river. Glancing up, then downstream, they spotted the women farther down shore. All senses alert and on-guard, Patty motioned Ethan to follow, but not to closely. He wanted room to manoeuvre if he had to. They ran up the grassy beachhead, leaving deep impressions in the soft soil.

As they approached, they could hear Alyssa shouting frantically and pointing into the water. Patty stopped and shielded his eyes from the sun to cut the glare and stared in the direction Alyssa pointed. He saw Samantha's blonde hair bob up and down a few times, then saw her flail her arms in obvious panic.

Then he saw what caused all the commotion. A long undulating shape moving swiftly toward her. Pulling the pistol from his belt he raised it and took aim. A bright blue beam emerged from the end of the pistol then stopped as the power cell discharged. His first shot went wild to the left. "Damn," he swore. Pulling back the cocking lever again, he waited the three seconds for the unit to charge again.

While waiting, they closed the distance between the women. When the unit beeped its readiness, he raised it again and took careful aim. Suddenly the thrashing form of Samantha disappeared beneath the water and the last of the ripples faded, leaving only a smooth shimmering surface.

"Where is she? I don't know where to shoot."

"I can't see her," said Alyssa horrified. They stared at the water in silence. Ada moved closer to Ethan and held him close. Seconds passed like hours as they waited for a sign that the young woman still lived.

"Look," cried Ethan pointing ahead in the water. Small ripples appeared and grew bigger, and bigger. Patty raised his pistol in readiness.

"Wait," yelled Alyssa. "It's Samantha." The blonde hair of the woman broke the surface first, followed closely by her head and shoulders. Her head hung limp, obviously unconscious, but she moved toward the beach smoothly and steadily.

"Please not another one," whispered Alyssa quietly while staring at the unconscious body of Samantha. Only Ada paid any attention to Alyssa's quiet prayer and her eyes narrowed.

As the others watched in horror, the limp body of Samantha rose out of the water. She was draped across the back of the creature. Carefully it swam closer to the shore. Patty took very precise aim at the lion's head of the creature and just before he fired, Samantha stirred on the back of the creature.

"Don't shoot," cried Alyssa happily. "She's still alive. You may hit her." He lowered the pistol, but kept the energy charge active—just in case.

The creature swam to the water's edge then with deliberate care it lifted the semi-conscious form of Samantha off its back with its tail and deposited her gently on the ground. Then heaving its massive bulk out of the water, it moved up beside the young woman. The creature's great lion's head moved up beside the limp form and it opened its mouth.

"It's going to eat her," cried Ethan. Patty raised his pistol again.

"Wait," shouted Ada. "I don't think it's going to eat her. Look…" From inside the ferocious looking mouth came a long slender tongue. Gently, tenderly, it began licking her face then her body. Only then did the party of survivors notice her body covered in tiny blistering welts. Wherever the creature licked, the redness and swelling seemed to subside.

The creature covered her whole body then seemed to give her an inspection. Seconds later it lay down beside her and snuggled up close. Tenderly the prehensile tail came up and wrapped itself protectively around Samantha.

"What's it doing?" Whispered Ethan scared to speak loudly.

"It's protecting her," said Alyssa astonished.

"I'm not sure," said Ada, "but I think this creature just saved her life."

"Or saved her for supper," said Ethan. Ada glared at him and he bowed his head in submission.

Alyssa watched the exchange and once again wondered what power this old woman had over the boy to make him cower so. She turned her attention back to the girl and the creature cuddled together in an embrace.

"It's like watching a dog protect its master," chuckled Patty. "Except this is no dog." Samantha moaned and the head of the creature rose up. It nuzzled her for a few seconds, prodding and pushing her.

Suddenly her eyes opened wide in fear. She stared right into the face of the creature. Then, without hesitation she threw her arms around the great wet shaggy head and kissed it fondly. The creature snaked out its long tongue, and licked Samantha gently.

"Well, I guess I won't be needing this," said Patty turning off the pistol and returning it to his pants. "They seem to know each other quite well."

Alyssa moved closer to Samantha and reached out her hand. Suddenly the creature reared up and emitted a terrifying growl. Samantha reacted unexpectedly by scolding the creature with harsh words. It stopped its growl and lowered its head again. This time it laid its shaggy mane on Samantha's lap. Just like a dog looking for forgiveness.

"I'd thought I'd seen everything," said Patty, "but this has got to be a first."

"It's all right," said Samantha. "He won't hurt you. He's just trying to protect me."

Alyssa moved closer. She watched the creature closely, ready to jump back if it moved. A low growl came from it, but at the soothing touch of Samantha's hand it quieted again.

"Are you all right?" Asked Alyssa stepping closer.

"I'm fine now," she said smiling. "Thanks to my friend here." She playfully ruffled the fur on the creature's head and it pushed up against her hand for more.

Alyssa had now moved up beside the pair. "Let him smell you. Let him see you mean no threat to me." Alyssa held out her hand and the giant lion's head reached forward and sniffed. Then the tongue snaked out and gently licked her palm. Retracting its tongue, the creature pushed its head into her hand. Obviously it wanted some attention, which Alyssa gave by rubbing the back of its hairy head. Satisfied it lowered its head on Samantha's lap again.

"It's gentle as a lamb," said Alyssa addressing the others. "And something else. I get the distinct impression it won't hurt us. Especially Samantha."

"Just let it sniff and lick your hand," said Samantha. Slowly Patty moved in and the greeting process was repeated. When Patty broke into a big grin, Ada introduced herself. Ethan held back, still scared of the giant beast.

"It's all right, Ethan," said Samantha. "He's just like a big dog. You like dogs, don't you?"

"I've never seen a dog," said Ethan. "I've never had a pet of any kind."

Samantha struggled to get up, but the heavy head of the creature still weighed her down. She pushed until it finally moved off her. Finally she stood up, still wobbling. Slowly she moved nearer Ethan and the creature shuffled along behind her. Ethan stepped back, his eyes wide in fear.

"Come on," she said gently. "I promise. He won't hurt you." Hesitantly, Ethan held out a hand. The creature sniffed then licked his hand.

"That tickles," said Ethan snatching back his hand. The creature moved closer and raised its head up. "It's after me," cried Ethan. "It's going to eat me."

"No, it's not," said Samantha. "It just wants you to stroke it."

"H. .How?"

Samantha took Ethan's hand in hers and guided it to the shaggy mane of the creature. Deliberately she pushed his hand into the dense fur and made him rub hard. Ethan tried to pull away—terrified at being so close to the creature, but when it started to rub back, he lost some of his fear. Soon he reached out with both hands and rubbed the fur. A tiny rumbling noise came from within the creature.

"Well, I'll be damned," said Patty. "The beastie's purring. Looks like you've found a friend, my boy." Ethan looked into the brown eyes of the creature, then suddenly threw his arms around the shaggy head and hugged tightly. The creature responded by wrapping its tail gently around the little boy. When Ethan lifted his head, they could see tears in his eyes.

"I'm sorry," he said. "I've read about people and their pets, but I thought I'd never have one of my own." Ada stepped over and put her arm around the boy, and stroked the creature with the other.

"Now you have one," she said gently.

Alyssa turned from this touching scene and faced Samantha. "All right, Samantha," she said. "I want some answers. How is it that on an undiscovered world, you suddenly make friends with an alien creature who seems to adore you?"

"Please…All of you. Call me Sam. My father never let me use nicknames. He said it's not proper for our position."

"Okay," said Alyssa, then gently she said, "Sam, what is going on here?"

Sam moved over to the creature and almost absentmindedly started stroking the fur. "I saw it coming after me," she said, "but it wasn't me it was after. Under the water, I felt something grip my ankles. That's when I screamed. Something started climbing my legs and wrapping itself around me. I couldn't move and this wonderful creature dove down and bit into the things holding me. I got pulled under and could see that it was some kind of plant that had a grip on me. I felt sharp stings and saw blood come out where the vines wrapped around me. My friend here headed right for the plant and started to rip it apart. About then I started to get dizzy from lack of oxygen. Just before I blacked out I saw it's great head come up and gently nudge me onto it's back. When I came too, I was on the beach. The rest you know."

"What about the way you seem to be able to communicate with it?"

"Well," she said slowly. "There's something you should know about me. I have a gift. It's not that unusual, but it has helped on occasion. You see I inherited it from my father, who got it from his mother. Each generation it seems to get weaker. I have only a fraction of my father's ability, and the way he describes Grandma, she must have been something else."

"For Peter's sake," said Patty. "What in the devil are you talking about? What gift?"

"I'm an Empath," she said softly. "It's not as strong as my father's as I said. He can sense the emotions of people. That's why he's so successful in business. I can't seem to do people, but lower life forms, like animals, I can do."

"That explains a whole lot," said Alyssa. "But I know your family. Your father made the fortune. If your grandmother was stronger, what did she do?"

"She was a healer on Meridian Prime." Alyssa nodded her head in understanding.

"So?" Said Ethan still puzzled.

"Meridian Prime," said Patty, "is a world that is settled by people who shun advanced technology. They use only enough to maintain a spaceport; the rest of the world is agrarian based. They use horses and other draft animals to work the land. A doctor without the use of technology would be severely limited. Sam's grandmother being an advanced Empath would be able to use her gifts as well, if not better, than a doctor with a Med-bag full of instruments."

"And you inherited this gift," said Alyssa.

"Only as much as I can sense the emotions of animals," she said. "I told you, it's getting weaker. I'm afraid my children will probably have no ability at all."

"Well, it seemed to work for you quite well in this case. I wonder…An animal this affectionate must have someone else it usually stays with."

"I don't think so," said Sam. "I get the distinct impression that they are a communal group—staying together all the time. This one seems to have been separated from its family. It needs closeness and affection, and I happen to provide it. If I figure right, we have just become its new family."

"It does seem to have grown attached to us," said Patty. "So what do we call it?" Sam looked at the creature that was holding Ethan down on the ground and repeatedly licking the laughing face of the boy.

"I think we should let Ethan name him. I sense a close bond growing between these two." Gently she pulled the beast off Ethan and said, "well? What do you want to call him? Come to think of it, I don't even know if it is a he or she."

"He's a boy," said Ethan confidently, "and he's only a baby. I'm going to call him Scrapper, because he likes to wrestle." The boy smiled and playfully attacked Scrapper to show how they wrestle.

Alyssa started to ask how the boy knew Scrapper was only a baby, when Ada grabbed her arm and shook her head indicating to leave it alone. Alyssa looked at the old woman and saw a brief flash of something in her eyes a sparkle of a hidden secret, of secret knowledge. She stopped, but the look she gave Ada told the story. She wanted the whole story, and would get it from the old woman.

"We'd better get back to camp," said Patty looking into the sky. "I think it'll be dark soon, and I don't want to be too far away from base. What about Scrapper? How fast can he move with that big head and that long snake like body?"

In answer, Ethan darted off. He ran about twenty feet away and turned and called out. "Come here, Scrapper. Come on, boy." Scrapper looked at the boy and with speed remarkable for its sheer bulk chased after the boy.

The others finally got the chance to see Scrapper's entire body. To call it a snake would do it an injustice. More snake like, but with distinctive differences. The soft hairs, previously matted down, now gave the impression of soft orange hued fur. Halfway down the elongated body, a pair of short stubby legs protruded. They seemed to be slightly offset and allowed the creature to run with remarkable agility, using its tail and head as points of balance. Obviously Scrapper could slither or walk as the need be.

"I guess that answers that question," said Patty chuckling. The remainder of the party dogtrotted after the happy boy and his pet.

Arriving at their base camp, Patty built a fire. Even though the heat still made them swim in their own sweat, the sight, and feel of a campfire, made everyone feel safer as night fell over their little home.

"Tomorrow," said Alyssa, "we should begin looking for more

survivors. For now though, I think I'll turn in. I don't know about the rest of you but I'm beat."

"Not before you have something to eat," said Ada. "It's not much, but these rations are all we've got. Now eat this. Got to keep up your strength. Can't let the leader of the group pass out from hunger can we?"

At the last, Alyssa winced but said nothing. While she covered up her fear of leadership quickly, it didn't go unnoticed by Patty. He looked her straight in the eye questioningly. When she refused to respond, he turned his attention to his own food, but the message was clear. He had questions about Alyssa.

Finally after everyone had eaten, they put Ethan to bed in the tent and Scrapper followed and lay on the floor beside the boy. As each of the others entered to go to bed, they rubbed the now dry, soft, furry head goodnight. Scrapper slithered around the tent and nuzzled each one in turn, then planted himself between Ethan and Sam, and within close reach of the door.

"Good night, boy," whispered Patty. "Been a long time since I had a watchdog looking over me." Scrapper laid his big head down and Patty turned out the light. Soon only the soft sounds of light snoring disturbed the still night air.

Several hours later, Scrapper woke the others by growling loudly. His head faced the door and his tail whipped back and forth in agitation. Patty reached under his bunk and withdrew the pistol he had secreted there before going to sleep. He flicked the charger on and waited until the unit quietly beeped its readiness.

"What's going on," muttered a sleepy Ethan. Sam rushed to his side and held him close, whispering to keep quiet. Alyssa rose and crept up beside Patty.

"You take the left, I'll take the right," she whispered. Patty nodded and motioned the others to the back of the tent. Quietly they crept up to the door. Alyssa counted down from three on her fingers. When she reached one, she pulled the lever that would open the door quickly.

It slid into its recess in the tent wall silently, and something shadowed by the moon fell inward. Alyssa dove on the figure and Patty dropped beside her to assist. "Hey. Hold it," said the figure.

"Lex? Lex is that you?" Alyssa reached over and turned on the light. Lying on the floor, covered in dirt with Patty's pistol inches from his head, lay the First officer.

"I can think of much better ways to greet your boyfriend," he said smiling at Alyssa.

Much later, after they cleaned him up and gave him something to eat, they introduced him to Scrapper. Scrapper objected to this night visitor, but with reassurance from Sam and Ethan he accepted the visitor. "Hell of a watch dog…eh, cat, you've got there."

"How in the hell did you find us? And where's the rest of your crew?" Alyssa demanded explanations from Lex. Between her and Patty, they finally got the story from him.

"When it came time to abandon ship, I realized I wouldn't reach my pod in time and jumped into one of the main passenger pods. Alyssa, those things can hold over 100 people comfortably, but this one was jammed packed. Anyway it was too late. The doors shut and we launched. I guess all the extra weight threw the inertial guidance computer off."

He took a drink and collected his thoughts. "We crashed about twenty clicks north of here," he began. "Our pod malfunctioned on landing and coolant gas seeped inside. I blacked out and when I came to, dead bodies surrounded me. I panicked and scrambled for the hatch. That's when I heard a moan. There were still people alive."

Lex's body shivered at the recalled imagery of the dead piling on top of him and hearing the soft moans of the few still alive. "The rest of us stumbled outside and passed out. We woke up hours later. Night had just started to fall. I wanted to go looking for others. The rest wanted to stay. I couldn't abandon them, so I stayed."

He paused as if remembering a bad dream. His big frame shook slightly. Scrapper came over and rubbed his big head in Lex's hand. Without thinking, acting on instinct, he stroked the friendly animal as all pet owners have done when troubled.

"We had no supplies. They were still in the Pod, and that still leaked gas. We managed to get a fire going and sat around talking. About an hour or so later we were attacked by something."

"What?"

"I don't know," said Lex tiredly. "All I can say is it looked like a big piece of multi-coloured gelatine. It seemed to wobble and shake all over. It moved incredibly fast though. Before we knew it, it had enveloped Mr. Hardy. We saw it cover him, then watched as his body disappeared in seconds. Miss Hathaway and I ran for our lives. The creature chased us into the bush.

"I found a big tree. Just before it reached us, I climbed the tree and pulled up Miss Hathaway. There must be something special about that tree, or the thing can't climb, cause it just sat there at the base of the tree."

"Incredible," said Patty. "Sorry, son. Please, go on."

"Well," said Lex, "we remained crouched in the tree for what seemed like hours, but probably was only a few minutes. Eventually I guess it got tired of waiting and slithered off. I waited a few more minutes—just to make sure, then climbed down. I signalled for Miss Hathaway to get down and... She..."

"What happened, Lex?" Alyssa cuddled him protectively. Something had upset him tremendously. His face had taken on a sickly pale green colour.

"She scraped her arm on the bark of the tree getting down. Blood ran freely from her cut and landed on the leaves. I went to help her...but I couldn't...she...the tree..."

Patty sat down beside the younger man. In a fatherly way he laid a hand on the Exec's shoulder. When Lex finished shaking, he finished his story.

"The tree is the devil itself. Somehow, her blood landing on its leaves brought it to life. The branches—thin like a willow's, suddenly started snaking and whipping around. They grabbed her and pulled her up into the foliage. I could hear her scream and tried to reach her, but every time I got close, the branches reached for me. They grabbed me and I just barely broke free. I couldn't do anything. I had to stand away and watch as the branches tore into her flesh. It seemed to be drinking her blood right through the leaves and branches. Eventually she stopped screaming and her head hung limp.

"Minutes later the tree released her and she dropped to the ground. Carefully I moved up near her. Dead, and as near as I could tell, totally drained of blood. The ground beneath me started to shake and I backed away. The roots of the tree came up through the soil, wrapped themselves around her dead body and pulled her under the ground."

"My god," whispered Ada. "What kind of world is this?" Quickly she recounted their adventures including Sam's close call with the underwater plant.

"It would seem," said Alyssa, "that on this world the plants are the killers and hunters."

"What about the blob that attacked us? Plants can't move like that. Can they?"

"Actually, they can," said Patty. "On Sestus Minor, there's a bush that moves about by uprooting itself and rolling in the wind, like a tumbleweed. Then when it finds a likely spot, roots again to feed."

"But they don't attack people and drink their blood, and eat their bodies."

"No, sir," said Ethan who had appeared behind them. "But on Earth there are plants that eat meat. They trap insects and small rodents and eat them. And there is a creature in the ocean called a jellyfish. It's called a fish, but recently they discovered that it contains more plant proteins rather than animal."

"You seem to know a lot about this, Ethan," said Lex.

"It's a hobby," said Ethan. "I've never been to Earth, and I want to go there, so I started studying the plants and animals."

"There you go then," said Patty. "Lots of precedence for this type of plant behaviour already in nature. It's just on this world, it seems to have gone one step further."

"Well, all I know," said Sam who had turned ghostly white, "is that I'll never rest on this world. Plants that attack you! I want to go home. Now!" Scared and frightened she reverted to the only thing she had every known to get results, the spoiled rich brat who cried and whined to get her way.

"Don't start that again," said Alyssa sternly. Sam looked ready to start bawling, but she seemed to draw strength from Alyssa and sniffed back the tears.

"Yes, ma'am," she said quietly. "I'll try."

"Good girl," said Alyssa kindly. "Now listen, all of you. In the morning we'll find the rest of the crew. The Captain will know better when we'll be rescued. For now though, be wary of all plants, until we have had a chance to test them. We spent the day in the bush and had no problems. I think it's only a few selected species, and those we avoid like the plague."

"I think we should get some sleep," said Ada. "Alyssa is right. We must be careful, but if we don't get some rest, we won't be doing anything in the morning."

"What about a guard? I'll stand the first watch," said Patty.

"I don't think we have to worry on that count," said Sam, sounding better. "Scrapper seems to be able to hear and smell things better than we do. I don't think he'll let anyone or anything get at us."

"Well," said Alyssa still unsure of the young woman's empathic claim. "If you're sure…"

"I am," said Sam confidently. Alyssa felt strangely reassured by her strength of conviction and relented.

Lex reached up and pulled Alyssa close as she tucked him into a bed. "Alyssa," he whispered. "My pod…I mean the passenger pod. I tried to control it, but there were just too many people. I tried…All those people dead because I couldn't control the ship."

"Stop it," she commanded. "You're lucky to be alive. You did the best you could." Her words sound hollow in her ears. She had heard them before and they didn't help her then. "Get some sleep," she suggested. "We'll find the Captain tomorrow." He nodded slowly and she kissed him goodnight. Then she ordered everyone else to bed. As an after thought she approached Scrapper and crouched beside the lion head.

"We need your help, boy," she said scratching him behind the ear. "We need you to guard and help us. Will you do that?" Scrapper seemed to understand and licked her hand gently then it moved over near the doorway and settled down in front of it. Its serpentine body stretched out so that anyone or anything passing had to step on it to get in or out. Alyssa smiled, turned out the light, and went back to bed.

Alyssa couldn't sleep. Images and thoughts blurred into one another. She glanced over at the tossing form of Lex and knew what he felt. She wanted to comfort him and tell him everything would be fine, but she couldn't face that challenge herself. Eventually sleep overcame her and she sank into a restless, dream-haunted sleep.

Six hours later, the party woke rested and refreshed the horrors of the past night fading into dreams. "Okay," said Alyssa after a light breakfast of rations. "The locator beacon shows a couple of pods in the area."

"That one there," said Lex pointing, "That's mine. There's no sense going back."

"Fine, that leaves three others in walking distance. We'll split up into groups. If you find any others, lead them back here. We'll search out better facilities later. At least we have fresh water and open space here." The others nodded in agreement. Alyssa looked at the others and smiled. Her gaze fell on Lex and she suddenly frowned.

"I'm sorry, sir," she said. "You are the First Officer, and should be in charge."

"Sweetheart," he said, "the first thing I learned as an Exec is to let your people do the jobs their best at. I'm city born and bred. I've spent most of my career on luxury liners. When it comes to surviving in the wilderness, I'm a babe in arms. You seem to know what you're doing, so until the Captain says otherwise, I'm happy to let you lead this band of rag tag survivors."

Alyssa smiled at the compliment, and enjoyed the faith and trust the others had put in here, then her fears surfaced again and she began to tremble. Patty quickly sidled up beside her and whispered in her ear. "Don't let go. You can do this!"

She smiled at him and hugged the grizzly old veteran. "I'll try," she whispered. Swallowing hard she turned back to the others waiting for her to make the decisions that would save their lives.

"I'm designating each of these blips as Contact 1, Contact 2, and Contact 3," she said pointing to the Locator pad. "Patty, take Ethan and head for Contact 1. Lex you take Sam and head for number 2. Ada you come with me and we'll try for three. Meet back here before sundown. Any questions?"

Ethan stepped forward. "What about Scrapper? Who does he go with?"

"That is up to Scrapper," she said and bent close to the creature. "So who do you want to go with, boy?" Scrapper moved silently between the three groups. He seemed to be studying each one intently, sniffing and licking each person cautiously then it seemed to make up its mind and slithered beside Sam.

"I guess you're still his main priority," said Alyssa.

"Actually, it's quite a logical choice," said Patty. When Alyssa looked at him questioningly, he explained. "Scrapper senses that Ethan will be safe with me, because of my training and expertise. He also senses your abilities to command and lead and does not fear for the safety of you or Ada. But I believe he somehow knows that Lex is unfamiliar in this setting and Sam has no experience at all. Sorry you two, but I call em as I see em."

"No need to apologize," said Lex. "You're right about me at least." Sam nodded her head and cuddled Scrapper. "We need all the help we can get," he chuckled. "Come on, boy. Let's go find that pod." With a cheery wave the trio departed the tent.

"And that would be our cue," said Patty. "Ready for an adventure, Ethan?"

"Yes, sir," said Ethan eagerly.

"Then we will see you all for dinner." The two men, one young, the other old, left the tent.

"That just leaves you and me, Ada," said Alyssa. "I guess we'd better get going as well."

"That was a nice piece of manoeuvring," said Ada.

"Excuse me?"

"Don't try that with me, dear," admonished Ada. "You planned this all along. You want to know about Ethan and me, so you arranged the groups so we would be together. Well, if you behave yourself, I'll tell you."

"You're a very strange woman, Ada Worensky," said Alyssa smiling.

"More than you know," said Ada. "Don't you think we'd better get going?" The two women left the tent and Alyssa sealed the entrance. Hopefully, they would return with others later this evening.

Chapter 7

Patty and Ethan walked in silence, admiring the strange jungle landscape of the alien world. Occasionally, Ethan stopped to smell a flower or stare at an interesting plant while Patty remained ever vigilant for dangers. From the intense scrutiny of the boy, Patty reasoned that Ethan had had very little contact with nature, and wondered about him. Soon Ethan ran up beside Patty. "Can I ask you a question, sir?"

"Don't call me 'Sir.' My name's Patty."

"Patty, you were a soldier," said Ethan. It was more of a statement rather than a question. "What's it like?"

"I don't follow you, son," said Patty looking inquisitively at the boy.

"I mean…You had friends, right? You knew what you were supposed to do, right?"

"If you mean I knew my job and had people I could count on, yeah, I had those. What's wrong, Ethan?"

"I…I don't know. I mean I'm not sure. I don't know who I am, or what I'm supposed to do."

"You're still young," chuckled Patty. "Don't rush it. You'll find out soon enough. I remember when I first joined the Service. I couldn't have been much older than you." He stopped and crouched down beside the boy and looked him straight in the eye. Then in a conspiratorial whisper he said, "If I tell you a secret, do you promise not to tell anyone?"

Ethan nodded eagerly, happy to be let in on a secret from a grownup. "Well," said Patty looking around as if searching for watchers. "I lied on my application. I said I was 16, when I really was only 14. I looked a lot older, and since I had no living relatives they didn't bother to check. Now you promised. This is our little secret."

"Yes, sir," said Ethan firmly. "Do you think I should join the service then?"

Patty rose and said nothing. Instead he started walking and motioned the boy to follow. Ethan trailed after him in silence. "How old are you, Ethan," said Patty finally.

"I don't know for sure," said Ethan hesitantly. "My records say I'm 13 years old, but I know that's not right."

"And how do you know that?"

"Because I know things I've never done."

"Maybe you dreamed them," said Patty kindly.

"How can I dream things that I never knew about? I can remember all sorts of things from years ago. And I've been having even stranger dreams since I got on board the ship." When Patty looked questioningly at him, he continued, relieved to tell someone about his dreams. "I've had this dream about someplace called Maxia. I can see it clearly and the people around me. I know who they are! How can I know about Maxia, and the names and faces of people I never met?"

Patty grasped Ethan roughly by the shirt and lifted him off the ground. His face was stone cold as he glared at Ethan. "How do you know about Maxia," he said harshly and shook the terrified boy. "Who told you? Answer me!"

"No one," bawled Ethan. "I'm sorry, sir. I didn't mean to upset you." Patty regained control of his temper and lowered Ethan to ground.

"My apologies, lad," he said softly. Seeking out a suitable rock he sat down. Suddenly his head hung low and his features fell making him look years older. "It's all right, son. Come here and sit down. Now, tell me what you know about Maxia."

Slowly, fearful of Patty's temper, Ethan moved closer and sat on another boulder near Patty. His face took on a long look as he strained to recall the visions he had seen.

"I remember a group of soldiers, a lot of them were hurt real bad. Some big guy—with the name Magnusson on his shirt—said we had one more fight to go then we could all go home. We all got up, and I remember the guy beside me had a bandage over one eye. He said 'Come on kid. You can do it, but I'll need your help.' Then there was a big flash, and I don't remember any more. But, every once in awhile, just before I fall asleep, I see more of the vision, and I can recall more names."

Patty turned white, the blood draining from his face. Slowly he lowered his head into his cupped hands. Ethan became concerned instantly and moved beside Patty. "Are you all right, Patty? Did I say something wrong? Mrs. Worensky says I really shouldn't tell people my dreams."

"No, I'll be fine," whispered Patty. "Ethan, are you sure no one ever told you this story, or did you may be read about it?"

"No, sir. I mean no one told it to me, and I didn't read it. I didn't even know what Maxia was until I read about it in the ship's library."

"And what did it say," said Patty the colour returning slowly to his face.

"Nothing," said Ethan, his face showing his frustration. "It only said a Peace Keeping Force helped them during a crises. But Patty, I know that's not what happened. How Patty? How do I know, and why am I so sure?"

"Are you scared, Ethan?"

"Yes, sir," said the boy. "I think I may be going nuts sometimes. Do you know what's wrong with me? Mrs. Worensky says they're bad dreams and not to tell anyone."

"Then why did you tell me?"

"Because you shared a secret with me. Isn't that what friends' do? Share secrets? Did I do wrong? I've never had a friend before."

Patty placed a hand gently on Ethan's shoulder. "No, my young friend. You didn't do wrong. Friends do share secrets. Now you must do me a favour. You must not tell anyone else about Maxia until I say its okay."

"Why?"

"I can't explain why just yet, but I will. Ethan I'm asking you to trust me. I believe you, but others might not. So for now, let's keep quiet about it, okay?"

"If you say so," said Ethan a little puzzled but willing to trust his friend. "What about my other dreams?"

"Let's keep walking," said Patty. "We still have a long way to go. You can tell me about your dreams on the way."

*

"You know," said Lex, "you're holding up better than I thought you would."

"What do you mean by that," said Sam, her voice taking on a dangerous tone. Lex held his hands up to ward off the imaginary attack.

"Easy, easy," he said. "I just meant that you're nothing like that spoiled rich kid that came aboard the ship. That's all."

"Can I confess something to you? I am a spoiled rich kid. I've always gotten what I want, when I want it. But I've learned something here. Money and power means very little to someone fighting for survival."

"Indeed," said an amused Lex. "Do tell…"

Missing the sarcasm in Lex's voice or choosing to ignore it, Sam said, "when I thought I was going to die in that stream, I saw the others trying to save me. They weren't doing it for the money. I know that. I really don't know why they tried. I really put on a malicious show when we landed here."

"I can safely say that part of the reason was out of duty, especially to Lyssa."

"You and her… You're pretty close aren't you?"

"I like to think so," said Lex.

"Do you love her?"

"That's rather personal, Sam," said Lex, "but if you must know… Yes, I love her with all my heart."

"And does she return this love?"

"Why do you want to know?"

"Alyssa is one of the few people to stand up to me, and not be intimidated by my position or my father's wealth. I know she still thinks I'm a spoiled brat, but I still like her."

"Well," said Lex, "she says she loves me…"

"But?"

"No buts," said Lex. "I believe her when she says she loves me, I just…"

"You want to marry her, and she says no."

"How did you know?"

"I can see it in your eyes and the way you talk about her." They fell into silence and kept walking, each in their own thoughts. Eventually they pulled up short on a soft grassy knoll to rest.

"God, I'm tired," said Sam, stretching slowly. "I could sleep for a week."

"We can stop for a couple of minutes," said Lex checking the time, "but we can't stay for long."

Sam stretched once more, showing off her ample figure in the process. She could see Lex admiring her form and smiled. Many men had smiled, but few had dared to touch. Sam lay down on the grass and gently placed her head on Lex's lap. Lex adjusted his position so that his back rested on a tree and gently stroked her hair.

She rolled over on her back and put on her best seductive face. "Would you like to make love to me?"

"Excuse me," said Lex a little startled.

"I said, I want to make love to you. Would you like to make love to me?"

"I think you'd better get up," said Lex sternly and tried to rise while gently pushing her off. Instead of moving off, she whirled around and pushed him down. Then straddling his lap she faced him squarely.

"You don't understand," she said coldly. "I want you to make love to me. No one denies me my pleasure, or they answer to my father."

Lex mustered his strength and pushed her off his lap. Standing up smartly he brushed off his uniform and said, "I don't know the type of men you usually hang around with, but I can't be bought, or bullied." Beside them Scrapper emitted a low growl at the angry voices, but hunched down and watched the exchange.

"Can't be bought, eh? Not even for this?" She reached down and before Lex could move, whipped off her shirt revealing her naked form. To her surprise, Lex didn't even blink. Instead he calmly bent over, picked up the discarded garment, and handed it to her.

"I take back what I said before," said Lex. "You are a spoiled brat. Now get dressed. We still have a long way to go, and if you think I won't leave you behind, then you've got a lot to learn about people." He turned and started to walk away. Sam stood there holding her shirt in her hands. As he rounded a bend, she sat on the grassy knoll again.

"I'll wait here," she called after him. When he didn't respond, she started to get nervous. Scrapper whined, looking first at her then in the direction that Lex took. "Well, what are you waiting for," she said the lion creature. "Go get him." Scrapper tilted his head from one side to the other, then settled down on his snake belly and started to whine again.

"Well, I'm not going anywhere," she said. Then realizing she still sat naked, she put her shirt back on, and slumped against the tree. Twenty minutes later and with still no sign of Lex returning, Sam rose and looked around fearfully. Scrapper rose and moved beside her. She reached down to stroke the mane of the beast then made up her mind.

"Find Lex, Scrapper. Go find him." The animal didn't understand what she wanted, but knew it was important. It just stood there whining. Sam moved off in the direction Lex had taken and Scrapper bounded happily after her. When she made no move to return to the grass, it galloped ahead and began sniffing the air.

Sam followed the beast. When she turned at a junction in the tree line, Scrapper put up such a howling noise; she decided that he knew where Lex could be found. She followed the animal deeper into the bush. Ten minutes later they came upon Lex sitting on an old fallen log, eating a ration bar.

"It's about time you showed up. I'm nearly finished lunch, and we still have a long way to go."

"You... You waited for me?"

Lex said nothing and continued munching his bar. Sam noticed the dry meal ration and her mouth watered. "May I have some of that?" Lex reached inside his small pack and withdrew another bar and pitched it at her. Sam dove for the bar and sat on the other end of the fallen log and slowly took a bite.

When she finished eating, she hesitantly approached Lex again. "Why did you wait for me? Duty?"

"Partly," said Lex. "As First Officer of the ship, it is my responsibility to see to the passengers' welfare."

"But that's not the only reason, is it?" She smiled seductively at him.

"You don't give up do you," he said sternly. "It isn't because of your obvious physical charms that I waited. Actually, after your little episode, I'm quite happy to leave you here."

"Then why," she said her face falling in sadness.

"Because of what Lyssa would do to me if I came back alone."

"You're scared of her," said Sam incredulously. "You're nearly twice her size and you outrank her."

"That maybe true," said Lex, "but you've obviously never been around men who are in love. What they think and what they do are two different things. All through history, men built like great oak trees, keel over like saplings in a hurricane at the thought of getting their smaller, weaker women mad at them."

"You really do love her then," said Sam. She stood up and turned away. Lex could hear her mumbling, but couldn't make out the words.

"What was that? I didn't quite hear you," he said in a stage whisper. She whipped around and took a deep breath.

"I said, I'm sorry. For everything! You're right. I don't know people. Nobody has ever turned me down before. I wonder if she really knows how lucky she is to have a man who truly loves her."

Lex shrugged, picked up the garbage, and put it in his pocket. "If you promise to behave yourself, I won't mention this to her. There's no reason to create friction of a misunderstanding. Get me?"

"Absolutely," she said. "Am I forgiven?"

"Let's say that you're on probation. Now, are you ready to continue?"

"Yes," she said, a big smile on her face. The two started off with Scrapper happily bounding in front of them.

*

"Everyone…Quiet, please. Quiet. Thank you." Patty stepped into the middle of the circle of ragtag survivors and looked around. When he and Ethan had arrived at their pod, they discovered that survivors of other pods had joined together. Unfortunately, most of the ship's crew was either injured or dead, and they had no leadership. When Patty showed up, the castaways were perfectly happy to let him make the decisions.

He and Ethan had rounded up some of the calmer passengers, and assisted them in tending to the wounded. Then drawing on his experience in field combat, he fashioned makeshift stretchers to transport the wounded. Eventually he herded them back to the base camp he and Alyssa had set up.

"Listen up," he said loudly. "Our first priority is food and shelter. You and you," he said pointing at two people, "check all the supplies we brought with us and make a list of what we have. You two over there! Start assembling the shelters. Ethan here will give you a hand, he knows how they go together." Ethan nodded and trotted off. The two designated assemblers followed meekly behind the little boy.

"Now for the rest of you. The scouting parties will be returning shortly with more people. We need a sickbay set-up, and I need someone to take names and a headcount."

"I can do that, sir," said a voice from the back.

"Who said that," cried Patty searching the crowd in the twilight.

"Me, sir. Aikens. I'm the ship's quartermaster. If you'll allow me an assistant, I can get all the information you need."

"Thank you, Mr. Aikens," said Patty. "Take whom you need and set up over near the pod. The rest of you, scout around, but don't go too far. We need firewood, and more branches and leaves to make bedding for the sick and wounded." The camp had grown to over 100 people and suddenly broke into a flurry of activity. Most of these people had no idea who Patty was, but he had an air of authority about him. Besides, most of them were so scared; they were willing to be lead and told what to do by anyone who seemed to know what to do.

Shortly, a cry came from the south end of the camp. Patty broke into a run in the direction of the call. Out of the slowly darkening woods came Scrapper. The sentry who spotted him, cowered in fear as the ferocious looking beast approached. Patty smiled and casually walked forward. Scrapper came up and jumped on Patty, licking his face in greeting.

"Scrapper," came a delighted cry from behind the gathering group. A small figure pushed its way through the crowd and raced toward Patty and the animal. Ethan leapt into the air and landed on top of the animal. They both rolled round and round in the dirt. Ethan clasped tightly around the great mane of the lion's head, while the snake like tail whip sawed back and forth in obvious enjoyment. Eventually Scrapper managed to work his tail around Ethan's body and lifted him off. Placing him gently on the ground, he laid his giant head on the boy's chest, effectively pinning him to the ground.

Some of the people began to worry. But they soon lost their fear when they saw the lion licking the boy's face, and listened to the pure joyous laughter from the little boy, reunited with his pet. Patty laughed loudly and dusted himself off. Then walking over to the wrestling duo, he gently pulled Scrapper off his friend.

"All right, you two," he said. "Where's Sam, Scrapper? Where is she, boy?" The great lion's head whipped around and around searching for his mistress. Then picking her scent from the air he bounded off in the direction he came. Patty rounded up a couple of beefy looking guys and chased after the lion-snake.

Five minutes later they came upon Sam and Lex leading a group of 75 people. The beefy boys, who accompanied Patty, relieved the others of their burden of supplies. "Glad to see you," said Patty. "I was getting a little concerned. It's starting to get dark."

"Sorry," said Lex. "Just before we left, a runner from a pod further on came over to ask for help. We went there and found most of them dead. They seemed to have hit a rather large boulder and well, let's just say it wasn't pretty."

"I can see you made out all right," said Sam. "How did Alyssa and Ada do?"

"Don't know," said Patty. "They're not back yet, and it's nearly dark."

"I'm going out," said Lex determinedly.

"Me too," chimed in Sam and Ethan simultaneously.

"No one is going anywhere," said Patty. "Sorry Lex, but in the absence of Alyssa—even though you are the Exec—I must take charge, and I'm not going to allow anyone to go off exploring in the dark. I'll set up sentries to watch all night, and in the morning we'll go out looking for them."

"But they maybe hurt," protested Lex. "They maybe dying, waiting for someone to rescue them."

"Calm down," said Patty. "I have an idea. First, let's give them a little more time. Come on. Let's get these people back to the camp." Amidst grumbles and complaints, Lex and Sam helped their survivors join up with the main camp. Ethan directed them to Mr. Aikens who started asking questions as his assistants assigned them billets and food rations. Patty had to admire the efficiency of the Quartermaster.

"Very good, Mr. Aikens," said Patty approvingly.

"This I know and understand," said the owlish man. "By the way, I've created a list of the various professions and hobbies of the people. I thought there might be some skills we could use to help us survive until we're rescued."

"I am impressed," said Patty. "Well done, sir. Well done indeed."

For the next several hours, Patty kept everyone busy, especially Lex, Sam and Ethan. They complied meekly, but soon gave voice to their concerns about Alyssa and Ada. After the Doctor—who was in the group led by Lex—repaired his broken arm, Patty called them together and asked Ethan to bring Scrapper. When they had all assembled he addressed the crowd.

"Alyssa and Ada are very late now. I still feel it's too dangerous to go off looking for them. We don't know this world and its dangers, but there is one amongst us who does." He looked into the wide eyes of Scrapper the faithful lion-snake. "Sam, he seems to understand you the best. Do you think you could tell him to go find Alyssa?"

"I don't know," said Sam. "I tried to get him to go find someone earlier, but he wouldn't budge."

"That's because he knew there was no problem," said Lex smiling. Sam smiled back at him, and Patty suspected something had happened between the two, but his concern lay with Alyssa and Ada right now.

"Well, he's our only hope right now," said Patty. "Try again, okay?" Sam nodded and knelt in front of the great lion's head. Scrapper's long tongue snaked out and licked her face gently. Some of the survivors, who hadn't really seen the great beast up close, gasped in fear and astonishment.

"Scrapper," she said holding the hairy head in her hands. "Find Alyssa. Understand? Alyssa. Find her." The beast cocked its head and looked at her, then licked her face again.

"Its no use," she said dejectedly. "He just doesn't understand."

"He does understand," said Ethan pushing his way forward. "You just have to talk to him in a way he understands."

"What do you mean, son," said Patty. He had learned to listen to the young boy. Ethan stories had convinced Patty that the boy knew things he shouldn't. If Ethan could communicate with Scrapper it would confirm an idea he had brewing.

"Scrapper doesn't understand words," said Ethan. "He understands feelings and thoughts. You have to think about what you want him to do. I can do it a little, but Sam is far better at it than I am."

"Give it a try," said Patty to Sam. "Don't speak, unless it helps. Think about Alyssa. What she looks like. How she smells. How she moves." Sam shrugged her shoulders and taking the beast's mane in her hands again she concentrated on Alyssa. She thought about how she appeared, the friendship she felt for her after the river ordeal.

Scrapper tilted his head from side to side. He seemed to be listening to something, but only the sounds of night insects echoed in the darkness. Then suddenly he reared up and with a growl dove into a hedge and disappeared. The castaways could hear the sounds of his large snake like body moving through the underbrush. They listened with bated breath until the sounds faded in the distance.

"Do you think it worked? I'm not sure I got through or not," said Sam still on her knees.

"He understood," said Ethan calmly. "If I could hear you, then he could."

"You can hear my thoughts? Ethan come with me," said Sam. "We have to have a little talk." Patty watched the two leave and a huge grin broke on his face. Bingo!

"As for the rest of you," said Patty raising his voice, "I suggest you turn in. Those of you assigned to sentry, don't forget to wake your relief." The crowd broke up and slowly trudged back to the makeshift camp.

Patty reached down and picked up the coffee pot brewing near the campfire. He poured himself a steaming mug full and held it out to Lex. Suddenly the silence broke with an ear-piercing shriek. The two men jumped up and dashed into the night in the direction of the scream.

Just beyond the position of the sentry, they found a woman huddled, scared in the darkness. Someone ran up behind and passed a flaming torch forward. In the flickering light of the primitive torch, the dishevelled form of the Captain appeared.

"It's all right, Captain," said Lex gently. "You're safe now."

"Lex," she stammered, "is that you?"

"Yes, ma'am," he said. "Here let me help you up."

"We've got to get out of here," she said quickly. "There's a huge animal on the loose."

"Wait a minute," interrupted Patty calmly. "Captain, what did this animal look like?"

"Well, I couldn't see it clearly," she said, "but I'd swear it had the head of a lion and the body of a giant snake."

"And you saw it just a few minutes ago?"

"Saw it? It attacked me."

"Calm down," said Patty forcefully. "Now think…Exactly what did it do?"

The Captain took a deep breath and under the military style prodding of Patty, regained her composure. "I was walking towards your camp, when this thing came at me out of the dark. I stumbled backward and fell. Then all I saw was this giant lion's head right in front of mine. It stared at me for a second then it stuck its long tongue out and tasted me. That's when I screamed. It ran off into the woods that way."

Lex chuckled and Patty stroked his chin to hide a smile. The Captain looked at the two men in disbelief. "What is so funny, Mister," she said to Lex, asserting her position.

"I'm sorry, Captain," said Lex, "but you weren't in any danger. You just happened to meet Scrapper, the camp mascot. That's his way of greeting you."

"Really," she said calming down. "I expect this will be an interesting story."

"Captain," said Patty, "did you happen to run across Alyssa while you were out?"

"Why, yes," she said. "She's the one who told me how to reach the camp. In fact I was thinking about her when that beast jumped me."

"That explains it," said Patty. "Ethan was right. Scrapper does read thoughts. It picked up the Captain's thoughts of Alyssa and headed toward her. When he discovered it wasn't Alyssa but found thoughts of her there, it moved on."

"You see, Captain," said Lex. "Since you know Alyssa, and are friends with her, Scrapper welcomed you to the family with a kiss. He's gone off now to find her."

"You mean she's not here yet?"

"No," said Lex. "When did you leave her?"

"Nearly six hours ago. She and, Ada is it? She and Ada found me wandering in the bush. They said they were on their way to another downed pod, and would meet up with me later. I got lost several times. I expected her to be back by now."

"Let's get you back to camp," said Patty quickly noticing Lex's concern in the flickering light. They marched slowly back to the safety of the campsite and the fire. Patty lingered behind a little bit and gazed into the darkness as if trying to see through the gloom and the dense bushes.

Chapter 8

Ada placed one arm under Alyssa's shoulders to support her. Alyssa's limp had become more pronounced over the last few hours, and the tell tale grimace of pain on her face told how the woman struggled to keep going.

"It'll be dark soon," panted the older woman struggling with her injured partner. "We should consider finding shelter."

Alyssa signalled for a stop, and sat down on the grass. Waves of pain and nausea washed over her face. Her features turned ash white as she adjusted her leg. The crude splint made of tree branches and Ada's shawl shifted, and a small controlled grunt escaped from Alyssa's tightened lips.

"Ada," gasped Alyssa through clenched teeth. "I don't think I can go on much further. Listen, the base camp can't be more than a couple of miles away. Just leave me some supplies and you go ahead. With luck, you can bring back help before nightfall."

"I'm not leaving you," said Ada determinedly. She lowered herself gently to the ground beside Alyssa, grasping branches and bushes on the way down. "Besides, I'm not as young as I used to be. I don't mind admitting that I'm beat."

"Beat? Ada Worensky! You have to have the strength and tenacity of Calabrian Bear. I don't think I could have fared half as well as you. No, you go on. I'll be fine here. I'm just slowing you down."

Ada chuckled softly and adjusted her cloak, pulling it tighter against the first cool night air. "A Calabrian Bear, am I? I've been called a lot of things, but never a beast as big and ugly as that." She shook her head. "I'm not leaving you. It's my fault you're in this predicament in the first place, and I don't abandon my friends."

Alyssa's face turned white again as another wave of pain washed over her. Ada shifted around and gingerly rotated Alyssa's leg to get a better look. Carefully she unwrapped the bandage surrounding the woman's knee. When she got closer to the skin, she noticed the bandage had become saturated with blood.

"I'm sorry, my dear," said Ada softly. "This leg needs serious attention. I was wrong not to try and adjust it earlier. The bones have scraped and pushed against each other. Part of your shin is pressing through the skin. I'm going to have to set it."

Alyssa nodded and she reached for their pack. "Inside the med-kit is a blue ampoule. It's a powerful muscle relaxant."

"Why didn't you use that before?"

"Because it's so strong. I didn't think I could control it." Alyssa struggled to sit up and Ada moved to assist. "Tie me off to that tree there," said Alyssa. Unsure as to why, Ada complied with the order.

"Now," panted Alyssa, feeling the bile rise in her throat. "When I say, place the ampoule against my leg, just above the knee. Tap the plunger on top, and it will inject the relaxant. Then, I'm afraid you're going to have to pull my leg, hard. With luck it should snap back into place."

"That's why you had me tie you off," said Ada understanding, "so I could put more effort into it, while you are restrained."

Alyssa nodded weakly. "The relaxant works fast. It'll cause all the muscles in my leg to go limp. As soon as you feel them go soft...Pull with all your strength."

"I've never done this before," said Ada, "but I'm sure it will hurt a lot. Maybe we should wait?"

"Can't," gasped Alyssa. "You were right. It needs setting. I'm bleeding a lot and the pain is getting uncontrollable...you could always go for help?"

"No," said Ada swallowing, "I'll do it." Alyssa nodded then checking her bindings nodded in Ada's direction to begin.

Ada moved to sit at Alyssa's feet. She tucked her skirt under her legs and sought a position to brace herself. One leg, she braced against a boulder, the other she dug a small hole with her heel and inserted her foot. Now she had something to push against. Satisfied with her post, she held up the ampoule in the dimming light. She popped off the safety tab and held it ready in the place Alyssa had shown her.

"Ready?" Alyssa gritted her teeth and nodded. Ada almost hesitantly tapped the plunger. A long needle plunged into the fleshy part of Alyssa's leg and a compressed gas cartridge forced the fluid into her system. Ada withdrew the injector, staring in wonder at the length of the long needle.

Alyssa smiled at her amazement. "The military have used these type of auto-injectors for hundreds of years. For fast delivery they're even better than Hypo-Spray cartridges." Her face fell suddenly and she leaned over and emptied the contents of her stomach all over the grass.

"It's all right," she said seeing the concern on Ada's face. "It's a side effect. My leg should be limp about now." Ada palpated the injured leg carefully. The muscles seemed soft and flabby, no longer tight and knotted.

"Yes," she said. "Are you in any pain?"

"The relaxant loosens the muscles, but unfortunately doesn't diminish the pain. You'd better hurry, before the next side effect."

"What's that?"

"You'll find out. Now brace yourself." Ada adjusted herself and grasped the injured leg. "When I say," said Alyssa, "pull with all your might."

Ada made sure she had a good grip and nodded. With her knees slightly bent and her back straight, she felt sure she could pull hard enough. Alyssa looked at her then grasping her bindings tightly in her hands she nodded.

Ada took a deep breath then pulled back fast. Her legs pushed against her supports and she leaned back. A loud "Crack" echoed in the jungle night as Alyssa's knee popped back into place. The white bone that had started to protrude through the skin slipped back and wedged itself into the section that it had broken away from.

Alyssa screamed with pain and her body thrashed around, trying to get away from the torture. Ada now fully understood why she had requested to be tied up. If left loose, all the thrashing would have caused further damage. Taking great care, Ada started to bandage the leg, then stopped suddenly.

"It's healing," she cried in disbelief. To the naked eye it appeared if the gash in Alyssa's leg had somehow sealed itself and healed over.

Alyssa shook her head and regretted the action as she threw up again. "No. It's another side effect," she said drowsily. "After the muscles have been relaxed, a chemical stimulant is forced into the surrounding tissue. It temporarily increases the tissues' capacity to store water, and causes it to swell to twice normal."

"Sort of like a built in splint, then why not use it before. It could have helped you."

"It takes the water from other areas of the body. If I don't get help soon, I'll die of dehydration as my kidneys shut down."

"Why didn't you tell me? We could have found another way."

Alyssa shook her head dizzily. Just then a loud growl came at them from the darkness. Night had fallen on them so fast they never noticed. "We need shelter for the night," said Ada looking around. "Stay put, I'll be back in a minute."

Alyssa nodded and weakly tried to free herself from her bondage. Ada got up and untied her. After making sure she was all right, Ada disappeared into the jungle night. Seconds later she re-emerged and moved toward Alyssa.

"There's a cave beyond that hedge over there. Do you think you can make it?"

Alyssa nodded, too weak to speak! The older woman reached under Alyssa's shoulders and with a grunt helped her to her feet. Gingerly she checked her handiwork on the bandage and the splint. Together they hobbled into the bush.

Twenty minutes later, Ada gently laid Alyssa on the rough stone floor. Alyssa's head lolled from side to side. For the last ten minutes, she had drifted in and out of consciousness. In the end Ada practically carried her into the cave. After propping the injured woman against the wall, Ada gathered up twigs and branches surrounding the cave and made a small fire.

"It's not much," she admitted, "but it should help keep away the wild animals. You get some sleep, I'll keep watch." Too tired to argue, and racked with pain, Alyssa slipped into merciful sleep. Ada made a quick check on her companion, then settled in the doorway, determined that nothing should interfere with her friend's much needed rest.

*

"Okay now, Ethan," said Sam. "I want you to concentrate. Can you hear my thoughts now?"

"Yes, ma'am," said the boy, blushing furiously. "Mrs. Worensky said I shouldn't repeat things like that. It's not nice."

Sam smiled and hugged the boy. "Sorry, kid," she said. "I had to think of something that you wouldn't be able to guess. Can you read other people's minds?"

"Yes, ma'am. I now know what my strange dreams and visions are. Now that you've told me I'm reading minds. I've been picking up their thoughts, but it's easier with you for some reason. Did I do wrong? Should I stop?"

"No. You didn't do wrong, but you do present a little problem. Listen Ethan; many people wouldn't understand the gift you have. They… Well they don't like other people reading their private thoughts. So you must never tell anyone. Okay?"

"What about Miss Krychech, and Patty? Aren't they my friends?"

"Yes, they are. Let's say, that you only tell people if it's very important."

"All right, but Patty suspects already. I told him some stuff and he got real upset. Then he said not to mention it to anyone."

"Good," said Sam, "for now though, I want to do a few more experiments. Game?"

"Sure," said Ethan eagerly.

*

"Lex, I must admit being a little overwhelmed by your story."

"It's the honest truth Captain," said Lex. "That beast out there is as friendly and as loyal as a watchdog. If anyone can find Lyssa, then Scrapper can."

"I certainly hope so," she said and took another sip of her coffee. "Tell me Ad—Patty, what do you think our chances of being rescued are?" Patty looked at her with wonder on his face.

"Well, we are a little off the beaten path, but with luck, they may locate us in a couple of days. Then again it could be weeks. If they found our ejected log report, they'll search nearer the asteroid belt. But I think it was a rogue belt, wandering around the galaxy. That would explain why it wasn't on the star charts. Then again, the log may have been destroyed in the asteroid belt. I suggest we prepare for the worst." He stopped and stared into the darkness. "It'll be light soon, and then we can begin searching for Alyssa. Lex, why don't you get some sleep? I'll stay up for a while…I promise I'll wake you if anything happens."

"Yeah," said Lex. "I am a little tired. Captain, there's a spare bunk in my tent, if my snoring won't keep you up?"

"I doubt it," laughed the Captain, "and please you two call me Beth, at least in private. I'll be in later. I've still got a small case of the shakes. I'll finish my coffee then turn in. Goodnight, Lex."

"Night…Beth. Night, Patty." He rose from the fire and within seconds disappeared from the warm glow of the fire into the inky darkness.

"Now that junior is out of the way," said Patty leaning closer, "how in the Seven Moons of Glandor, do you know who I am, and good recovery by the way?"

"Patty," said Beth coyly, "I am the Captain of my ship. Very little goes on without my knowing it."

"Well, keep it to yourself," said Patty. "Last thing we need now is posturing. You and your people are in charge. I'll help out here and there when I can. Agreed?"

"As you wish," she said. Taking another sip of coffee, she peered over the rim of the cup at the strange man who wanted to keep his identity a secret. "Not to change the subject, but what do you think the chances are of Ada and Alyssa surviving the night on this hell-hole world?"

Patty stoked the fire then tossed on a few more branches, watching it flare up and light the surrounding area. "She is a very capable officer. If there's anyway to survive, I'm sure she'll find it."

"I see she's made a big impression on you as well."

"Beth, I'll tell you truthfully," said Patty softly. "I've know thousands of people in my life. Every once in a while, I run across someone that just seems to stand out from the crowd. It's not what they say, or do. It's the way they are. These people are destined for greater things. All they need is encouragement to seek it out."

"I agree," said Beth, "but there are demons that war in her. They prevent such things from happening."

"All the more reason she needs friends to support her," said Patty. "Now as my last official order, I order you to bed."

"Yes, sir," said Beth. "But next time there had better be more involved than sleep. Goodnight, Patty…or whoever you are?"

"Off with you, wench, before I call a couple of guards to escort you," chuckled Patty. Beth smiled and turned in the darkness.

Patty stoked the fire again then made his rounds of the sentries. Satisfied that all seemed secured, he retired to his cot and soon fell fast asleep. Anyone watching him could have seen the smile on his face as he dropped off the smile of a man who would have very pleasant dreams.

*

Ada groggily pushed away the annoying tickle under her nose, then her eyes open wide in fear. She had done the one thing she had promised herself not to do. Fall asleep. When her vision cleared from the surprise opening, she found herself face to face with long, sharp pointed teeth.

Suddenly, without warning, the mouth of the creature bearing those formidable weapons opened. A long tongue snaked out towards her and gave her one long lick from the tip of her chin, to the top of her forehead. Her eyes opened wider in amazement.

"Scrapper," she cried happily and hugged the giant beast. The lion-snake rubbed its hairy head in her lap happily and began purring. Their fussing and commotion stirred the sleeping Alyssa. When she moaned softly, Scrapper moved over to her and gently, as if it understood, sniffed her broken leg.

Alyssa opened her eyes and stared into the toothy feral grin of her friend. "Scrapper," she said weakly. "Good to see you, boy." She tried to raise her hand to stroke the animal, but the effort proved too much and she lapsed into unconsciousness again. Scrapper nudged her hand gently then whimpered.

Ada stroked the mane of the great beast that had grown so attached the human survivors. "I don't know how you found us, boy," she said, "but I'm glad to see you. Look, I don't know if you can understand me, but Alyssa needs help. Go find Patty and bring him here, Okay?"

The animal looked at her inquisitively, cocking its head from side to side. "Patty," said Ada trying again. "Get Patty." Scrapper got up on its front paws and gently licked Alyssa's face, then as if reluctant to leave, moved out of the cave.

"That's it," cried Ada happily. "Fetch Patty. Go boy, go!" Scrapper whirled in the darkness in a blur of speed and disappeared into the underbrush.

"Where's Scrapper," said Alyssa waking up.

"Gone to get Patty and the others," said Ada.

"How?"

"I don't know, but I have the feeling Scrapper can understand us." She moved nearer Alyssa and pulled the injured woman's head into the crook of her arm. "Go back to sleep, dear," she said softly. "It's almost dawn, and we've still got a long way to go. Hush now... Sleep. That's it." She kissed the top of Alyssa's matted hair and pulled her shawl around them both to fight off the cold.

Several hours later, Ada heard a commotion in the underbrush. Frantically she scanned around looking for a club to use. Picking up a branch that had to be twice the width of her arm she hefted it in readiness.

"Easy, my good woman," Patty and a rescue team had arrived at last. "If you're going to start braining people, I might just change my mind about rescuing you." Ada dropped the heavy branch in relief and fell into the arms of Patty.

Lex took off his pack and rushed to Alyssa's side. When he saw her leg he motioned for the medical team to come over. The doctor quickly examined the unconscious woman and administered an injection.

"I've given her a broad based antibiotic spectrum. What happened? Why is her leg swollen?" Ada told the doctor about Alyssa using the auto-injector. He rummaged through his medical kit, muttering about amateurs using things they knew nothing about.

Seeing Ada's concerned face at the doctor's ravings, Lex quickly stepped in and explained. "He's not blaming you. The auto-injectors have long been a pet peeve of the doctor. If not attended to quickly, the medicine eventually reaches the heart and shuts it down. The patient literally relaxes themselves to death. They should be used only in extreme emergencies. From the looks of her leg, I think this qualifies."

They turned to stare at the doctor as he injected vial after vial into the limp form of Alyssa. "She'll be all right now," he said standing up. Motioning over two others, he directed them to construct a makeshift stretcher. Then he turned his attention on Ada. "And how are you doing," he asked gently.

"I'm fine," said Ada. "Are you sure Alyssa will be okay? It's my fault she broke her leg."

"She'll be fine," said the doctor. "I've administered the antidote to the injection you gave her. When we get back to base, I'll knit her leg properly. She'll be up and around in a few days. I must say I admire the way you set it a very clean job, considering the extent of the damage. How did you do it?" Ada told how she set Alyssa's leg, while the doctor shook his head in wonder and amazement.

When the stretcher—made out of trees and some type of long strong leaf appeared, they gently loaded the still unconscious Alyssa into it and started back to camp. Patty and Lex hooked an arm around Ada, who now felt every day of her older years. Gratefully she rested on the strength of the two men.

"Ada," said Patty gently, "you said Alyssa broke her leg because of you. Can you tell us what happened?"

"Well," said Ada hesitantly, "it was shortly after we met up with the Captain. She made it safely to you, did she? Oh, there she is! Hi, Captain! Anyway, we finished traveling to the other pod signal. When we got there, there was nothing left but a burnt out hulk. Alyssa said only the emergency beacon still worked, so we started home…"

*

"How are you doing, Ada?" Alyssa had become concerned at the look on the older woman's face. Seeing the bodies of the crew of the pod bent, mangled, and burned, would unnerve anyone.

"I'll be all right, dear," said Ada. "I've just never seen death quite like that before. This must be old hat to you. You didn't even blink and eye. I envy you."

"If you must know," said Alyssa staring straight ahead, "that was my first time too. I've…I've seen death before, but how would it look, if the Chief Engineer on one of the biggest liners collapsed into a blubbering idiot."

"Like she was human," said Ada with a smile. The two women walked in silence. Each buried in her own thoughts about the gruesome sight. So intent on their musings, they failed to notice where they walked. The ground beneath Ada suddenly crumpled away and she fell down. Alyssa, only a step, or two behind her reached out and grabbed the old woman's arm.

The path they had been walking ended suddenly at the stream's edge. Unfortunately at this junction, the stream lay some two hundred feet below them. Ada lay face down in the dirt with more than half her body hanging over the precipice. Alyssa struggled to pull the old woman to safety, but the ground proved too soft to get a foothold. They slid closer to the embankment.

"Ada," cried Alyssa, "don't struggle. The edge is giving way."

Ada carefully reached up and grasped a root protruding through the ground. Just as she grasped it, the soft ground crumbled away, and Ada slipped into the chasm. Alyssa still clutching Ada's arm slid in the dirt, pulled forward by the momentum. Ada summoned strength she didn't know she had and pulled mightily on the tree root, trying to lift herself free.

Alyssa spread herself as flat as she could on the edge of the cliff. Her foot bumped into a large protruding tree root and she jammed her foot under it. "Pull yourself up, girl," she panted. "Use me as a ladder."

Ada started to lift herself up, trying to clamber over her prone comrade. Suddenly the buried root she used for support came free in her hand. For one brief second, Ada fell free into the gorge. Then as if a miracle, Alyssa's arm reached into empty air and grasped Ada's hand before it fell out of reach.

"Ahhh," screamed Alyssa with the sudden jerking pain. Ada tightened her grip on Alyssa's hand and tried to pull herself up. Each movement caused a grunt of pain from Alyssa.

"Let me go, Alyssa," said Ada finally. "I haven't got the strength to pull myself up. Save yourself. Let me go."

"No way," screamed Alyssa. "Never again! I…Will…Not…Give…In!" Alyssa cried out as another wrenching tugged on her already over extended muscles. "Besides," she grunted, "you promised to tell me the story of Ethan, and I'm not letting you off that easily. Now pull yourself up my arm."

"I can't," cried Ada.

"Damn you, woman," said Alyssa angrily. "Pull, or I'll haunt you forever." Amazed at the sound of anger and venom in Alyssa's voice, Ada responded by pulling on Alyssa's hyper-extended arm.

Carefully she swung up her free hand and grasped the sleeve of Alyssa's uniform. Totally swinging free now, her sudden movement caused Alyssa to slip forward and inch or so and let out a scream of pain. Pulling herself hand over hand, her feet dangling and swinging in the open, Ada pulled herself up the prostrate form of Alyssa. Clawing and grasping, digging her fingers into Alyssa's clothing, she climbed up and over. Eventually she reached the ground and grasped tree roots, bushes, and grass. Whatever her reach could touch. Inch by inch she pulled herself up, and on top of Alyssa.

Just when her newfound strength began to give out, she felt a hand reach under her still dangling feet, and push hard. Ada shot forward and tumbled into the dirt. Recovering quickly she moved to assist Alyssa.

"Oh, my God," she said holding her hand to her mouth in horror. Alyssa's leg lay twisted at an obviously unnatural angle. With her foot hooked under the tree, the sudden wrenching from catching Ada had pulled the knee socket out of its joint. Then with all the movement, twisted it most of the way around.

Ada knelt beside Alyssa and lifted the head of the nearly unconscious woman who saved her life. "I've got to do something, and it's going to hurt."

Alyssa could only nod meekly as the pain caused waves of dizziness to wash over her. Ada gently pulled the leg free and twisted gently. The leg returned to its original position, but still looked wrong.

"I think you're knee is out of place," she said. "I don't know if I should try to adjust it or not." Then making up her mind she decided to leave it, hoping it would reset on its own.

*

"…And the rest you know," concluded Ada. "Her leg finally got so bad I had to set it. I hope I didn't do any permanent damage. She saved my life and I owe her more than you know."

"She'll be fine," said Patty shaking his head in wonder at the ordeal the two women had suffered.

"I take it," said Ada trying to change the subject, "that Scrapper came back and told you where to find us?"

"Yeah," said Lex. "He showed up a couple of hours before dawn. After he told us what happened, we gathered a team together and followed him back to you."

"Told you what happened? Do you mean Scrapper can talk?"

Lex scratched the back of his head. "Not exactly. It's hard to explain, but he seems to be telepathically linked to Sam But only if Ethan is around. He seems to act as an amplifier between the two of them. I don't understand it, but it seems to work."

"When Scrapper showed up," continued Patty, "Sam asked him a couple of questions, then called for someone to get Ethan. It was the most amazing sight I'd ever seen. The two of them joined hands and placed their other hands on Scrappers head. They must have been concentrating hard, because they started to sweat."

"They never spoke," said Lex. "Then all of a sudden, they broke up and Ethan fell asleep right there on the ground. Sam told us that Scrapper had found you and said he would lead us back to you then she fell asleep. Right there on the dirt."

"We put them to bed, and posted a med-aide to watch over them," concluded Patty. "Then we set out to find you two."

"Incredible," said Ada. "I don't know who to thank, but I'm sure I do wish to thank Scrapper. By the way, where is he?"

"When we found you, he darted off into the bush," said Lex. "I'm not sure, but I think he returned to camp to check on Sam and Ethan. The three of them make quite a team."

The rest of the trek continued without incident until they met a man running towards them. Fear shone in his eyes Fear and uncontrolled panic. A couple of the rescue party tackled the screaming man to the ground and gently held him down while he screamed incoherently.

Patty rushed up beside the struggling man. "It's Aikens," he said. "He was at base camp making records of the survivors." Taking the man's head in his hands gently, Patty called to him.

"Aikens…Aikens, it's me, Patty. What happened man?"

"G-G-Ghost…Ghost Winds." The man's eyes flew open in terror then he stopped struggling and fell limp. The doctor examined him quickly.

"He's dead," said the doctor. "Whatever happened scared him so much, he had a massive coronary."

Chapter 9

Patty and a small, hastily assembled advance team arrived in a breathless rush at the clearing of the base camp. Tents, tables, wood, and people lay strewn about. Indeed, it was easy to believe a tornado had passed through the camp. Dropping beside the nearest body on the ground, Patty checked her vitals.

"She'll be all right," he said to the others. "Check out the rest. See to anyone who needs help immediately. Thompson, you go back and bring the Doc. I don't like the way some of these people look. Move people, move!"

The woman stirred gently beneath him. Patty lifted her slightly and cradled her head in his lap. The woman moaned and a bright spot of blood appeared at the side of her mouth. Patty wiped away the crimson dot and gently coaxed the woman to full consciousness.

"Easy, Easy," he said softly. "How are you feeling? Can you tell me what happened?" The woman nodded and spoke of whirling winds that swept throughout the campsite. There seemed to be three separate winds, but they moved so fast she couldn't be sure. They attacked twice and she wasn't sure whether the attacks came from different whirlwinds or the same ones returning each time.

From her description Patty could easily visualize the destruction and mayhem caused by these freak winds on this alien planet. Plastic and inflatable furniture tossed through the air like paper kites. Human bodies flung about like rag dolls. The image made him shudder.

"After the first attack," he prodded when the woman had quieted, "what happened then?"

"That's all they just seemed to disappear. The dust settled and we started to clean up. Mr. Aikens and a few others were badly shaken and we made them comfortable. Then suddenly, the winds returned. This time, I know it seems silly, but they seemed to know what they were doing. They moved around throwing furniture and people all over. Mr. Aikens screamed when one of the dust clouds moved toward him. He ran into the woods and one of the whirlwinds followed him until the edge of the forest. Then for some reason it stopped and came back. That's the last thing I remember because it landed on me."

Patty shook his head as the woman slumped forward, asleep. The expression on his face told the story. He couldn't accept all of her story, probably hallucinating, but these mysterious winds did pose a problem. They needed shelter and fast. A cry in the distance signalled the arrival of Thompson and the Doc.

Doc Simmons for all his gruff and grumpy exterior loved his work and the people in his care. He immediately knelt beside Patty and quickly examined the woman. After administering a mild sedative to keep her asleep, he ordered her to be taken away to rest then moved on to the others. Each person received a stimulant, sedative, or antibiotic as needed. A few had sprained wrists or ankles, and a couple had minor breaks or simple contusions.

Later after the camp had been cleaned up and the tents erected again, he approached Patty to give his report. "We came out very lucky," he said wiping his hands on a towel. "Oh, they won't be playing tennis or running the marathon for a while, but they should all recover in a couple of days."

"Thanks, Doc," said Patty. "What about the others?"

"They should be here in another hour or so," he said glancing at his watch. "I didn't want them to rush. Alyssa is in worse shape than I let on. She needs to rest, and I need to prepare for surgery."

"Surgery?"

"The injury to her leg is minor compared to what her ribs are doing. When she wrenched her leg and broke it, she also must have twisted her chest on the ground and she broke a rib. Normally not a problem, but this rib turned and pushed further into her body. It's now causing massive internal bleeding. If I don't stop it soon, she'll die."

"Then why haven't you done anything, man," screamed Patty.

The doctor looked amused at the protective attitude of the old soldier. Then calmly he said, "I couldn't do anything there. I needed her back here where all my equipment is. Don't worry. She'll be fine. Now, I must go and set up."

Patty pulled a chair out of the dirt and sat down heavily. "I'm getting too old for this sort of thing," he muttered to himself.

"Oh, I wouldn't call you old."

"Beth, when did you get back?"

"—A couple of minutes ago. Alyssa was in such a hurry she literally made everyone run. Now what's this about being too old?"

Patty told her the tale told to him by the woman and explained the devastation the winds had caused. Then in a quieter voice he told of Alyssa's injury. Beth moved behind him and gently rubbed his temples.

"Don't," he said. "That feels good and I don't want to feel good right now. There's still a lot of work to do."

"You need to rest," she admonished. "Look, they're taking her to the doctor now. She'll be fine. Come on and lie down for a while. I'll see to the repairs." Patty protested, but Beth put her foot down as Captain and ordered him to bed.

She made him lie down then covered him with a flexible plastic sheet. But Patty couldn't rest. His mind still flew at a million miles an hour and his body twitched with energy. Seeing that he wouldn't stay put and rest, Beth sat beside him and started talking. Soon the twitching stopped and his voice drifted into incoherent mumbling. After a few more minutes, soft gentle snoring sounds were all he emanated. Beth leaned over and kissed his forehead gently, then quietly stole out of the tent to get the cleanup going.

Twelve hours later Patty emerged with a sheepish grin on his face. Beth came over and smiled. She brushed aside his complaints about letting him sleep so long, and took his hand in hers.

"You needed that," she said. "If you didn't, you wouldn't have slept so soundly."

Together they made the rounds of the base camp. Surprisingly, most of the material was undamaged. A few tents had to be repaired and several tables and chairs were complete write-offs. The most distressing thing though was the food supply. The winds had tossed the containers all over the compound and over half of them had broken open. They had managed to salvage what they could, but it left them seriously short on rations.

"The way I see it," said Beth later, "is we have to do several things: One, find a better base camp. Two, find some food, and three, see about rigging up a beacon to send a signal."

"Fine," said Patty taking a sip of coffee. "It's too dark now, but in the morning, I'll take a party and scout around for a better place."

"What about where you found me?"

"Alyssa," he cried and jumped up to greet the woman. Remembering her rib, he hugged her gently. "I thought you'd be laid up for a few more days yet."

"Humph," she said. "Old Doc Simmons is a worry wart. I'm fine, just a little sore. He made me promise not to do anything energetic for a few days, but I can still think and plan."

"How are the bones healing, my dear?" Beth had moved up beside Alyssa and gently planted a kiss on her cheek.

"I have to have the regenerator on for a couple of hours a day, but the Doc says I'll be good as new in a few days." Alyssa looked around at the people seated around the campfire. "Where's Lex?"

"He, Ethan, and Sam took off with Scrapper," said Patty. "Said they had something important to do." He shrugged his shoulders to show that it meant less than Alyssa was thinking.

She sat down in a chair someone had brought up and stared into the fire for a few moments. "Well, as I was saying," she said. "What about the cave where you rescued me?"

"That's a little small," said Patty. "There's no way we all could fit in there."

"No," she said. "Not the one cave. Didn't you see? That whole cliff side is dotted with caves. There must be one big enough for us all. If not, I'm sure there are enough small ones to accommodate everyone."

"Very good, Alyssa," said Beth. "Okay, tomorrow we'll send a team back to the caves to check them out. If they seem safe, we'll move all the supplies and everyone there. Now what about food?"

"Well, according to the list Aikens accumulated," said Patty thoughtfully, "there's a couple of passengers from that farming colony on Setar II. If any one can identify new vegetables and such, I bet they could. The farmers of Setar have an outstanding reputation. As for meat, I'm sure we could scare up a few people who've hunted as a hobby."

"They still do that?" Alyssa seemed shocked. "I thought that hunting for pleasure had been banned on all the worlds in the League."

"Officially it has," agreed Patty. "Unofficially, it's a thriving business. Now don't get all worked up. It's monitored closely. Even the League has a hand in it…unofficially of course. No. We need those hunting skills now."

"Okay," said Beth. "Just make sure that everything is tested by the Doc, before anyone eats it. We know from Sam's experience that the water is relatively safe to drink so that's no problem. What else?"

"That's about it," said Patty mentally running over his checklist. "I'll divide the chores in the morning."

"Will you be in the hunting party," asked Alyssa, "cause if not I'd like to go."

"Be my guest," said Patty. "I'm not much for hunting. Done too much shooting in my life I guess." He fell silent and they others could see him recall events and situations best left unsaid. "Besides," he continued, "I'm more of a fisherman."

"That's the ticket," said Beth happily. "Fishing! I haven't been fishing in years. That settles it. Alyssa, you can go with the hunting party—as long as you take it easy. Patty, you and I will hit the stream and see if we can catch the proverbial big one."

"Sounds good to me," said Patty smiling. "Who's going to lead the expedition to the caves?"

"We will," said a voice from the darkness. The others whirled around to see Lex, Sam, and Ethan approaching the fire. Beside them, Scrapper half skipped, half slithered along.

"Just where have you four been?" Beth was more than a little upset. This little band of refugees was her responsibility, and she didn't like having them take off.

"Sorry, Captain," said Lex all apologetic.

"It's my fault, Captain," said Sam. "When Ethan and I made mental contact with Scrapper, I saw some disturbing images. They were so powerful I just had to explore them. I'm afraid I talked the others into going on an exploration trip."

"Well, don't keep us in suspense," said Alyssa, happy now that Lex had come over and put his arms around her. "What did you find?"

"The remains of what must have been a great civilization. There's not much left now, but you can plainly see that they were incredibly advanced."

"It was amazing," said Ethan eagerly. "We found a big, I guess you could call it a building. Made of glass and shiny metal strips. And we found boxes and all sorts of little things."

Patty appeared thoughtful for a second then said what everyone had on their minds. "Any chance of the owners coming back?"

"I don't think so," said Lex. "I estimate some of those things have been there for thousands of years. The building of glass and metal is broken, and only half of it is still intact. If there is anyone still around, they certainly haven't been there in a long, long time."

"So," said Beth. "Another mystery presents itself. Who were these people and what made them abandon their possessions?"

"Are you all right, Chief?" Asked Sam as she saw Alyssa waver and moved in to help.

"Chief?" Beth looked at Alyssa with amusement

"Sorry, Captain," said Alyssa tiredly. "The Chief Engineer was killed on the ship before we left."

"I'm not criticizing, my dear," said Beth gently reaching out to hold Alyssa's hand. "As far as I'm concerned, you are the Chief."

"No, Captain," protested Alyssa. "I assumed the duties as required, but now there is no need for a Chief Engineer. I return all authority to you."

Patty coughed slightly to get Beth's attention and a knowing wink passed between the two. Beth smiled secretly and sat back in her chair.

"So, you are refusing the promotion," she said gruffly. "Well, let me tell you, Miss I'm-too-important-to-be-bothered. This camp is still under my command, and I say I still need a Chief Engineer."

"But, Captain," protested Alyssa. "There's no motors or engines here. Why bother?"

"If that's the way you feel, Miss Krychech, then I'll have to appoint someone else. Williams perhaps. He's shown a lot of potential."

"Williams," exclaimed Alyssa. "He's a competent enough Technician, but he's no engineer. He doesn't know the first thing about bossing a crew. I mean there's the detailing, the conflicts. A Chief has to know when to…" She stopped her tirade when she realized the others were smiling at her.

"Then I assume you'll take the post," said Beth.

"I don't think I'm qualified, Captain," said Alyssa softly.

"Well, considering what you've done around here, I think you're eminently qualified."

"I didn't do anything," said Alyssa. "Patty did it all. He's the one whom you should be singing praises to."

"I must interject here," said Patty standing. "I didn't do anything that I wasn't authorized to do. To tell the truth, Chief, you've been in command since we left the ship. Think about it. I haven't done one blamed thing without your permission. Have I?"

"But—."

"—No buts," said Beth. "Patty may have done most of the work, but it takes a leader to control and delegate. You've proven your abilities." She stopped and stared at Patty. A subtle nod passed between them.

"Alyssa," said Beth quietly, "by regulations, we are in a crises situation. In an emergency, every officer and crew member, must do there utmost to fulfill their roles and see to the safety of the passengers and crew. As Captain, I need the assurance that someone capable and qualified is in a position I need. That person is you. If you refuse this, by regulations, I must assume that this is a form of mutiny and will so note in my report."

"Mutiny? Captain I would never…Lex you tell her!"

"Sorry, Lys," said Lex. "She's right. By the book, in an emergency situation if an officer rejects the orders given by the Captain, it is an automatic Mutiny."

"Captain," said Alyssa softly. "Beth… You know why I can't…"

"I'm sorry," said Beth harshly, "but we are in trouble and our personal needs are secondary. You may file a complaint with the League when were rescued."

"So I have no choice," she said then with resignation she squared her shoulders and winced. "Very well, Captain. I accept the position of Chief Engineer."

"Very good," said Beth. "I so authorize that Alyssa Krychech is and will be my voice in any and all matters that pertain to her field. I further confer on her all rights and privileges pertinent to her rank and position. If there are no other objections, I so note the advancement."

The rest cheered loudly and began hugging and kissing the still sullen face of Alyssa. She in turn glared at Beth and Patty, but seeing no other way out of the situation, accepted the accolades with discomfort.

"Now, my dear," said Beth gently. "I suggest you get some sleep." Alyssa barely controlled her seething anger and was ready to unleash its full fury when Beth leaned over and kissed her gently on the head. "I know you can do it," she whispered.

Patty came over and repeated the loving gesture. "You have my full support," he whispered. "I'm very proud of you."

Alyssa choked back a tear at these blatant affections of love and support. Her anger subsided and an embarrassed flush crept into her face. She opened her mouth to say something and suddenly felt very dizzy.

Alyssa slumped forward and Lex caught her. Together with Patty's help they took her back to her tent and made her comfortable. "She'll be all right," said the doctor after he had been summoned and quickly examined her. "She just overdid it a little. Let her sleep now."

"Good advice for all," said Beth.

"I'll take the first watch," said Patty. "I just woke up and don't feel tired. Now go. Don't worry; I won't stay up all night. Scoot."

The rest departed for their beds and Beth lingered back. "You know, if you're not tired, I know a perfect solution to make you drowsy."

"Huh," said Patty who wasn't really paying attention. Beth stood silently while Patty replayed the conversation in his mind. "My dear woman," he said feigning horror. "Are you propositioning me?"

"How dare you, sir," she laughed. "I am the Captain of one of the biggest Cruise Liners in the fleet. I do not proposition people."

"Good," said Patty.

"I just offer and if they accept, fine. If they don't I haunt them until the day they die." Her smile said it all and Patty couldn't help smiling as well.

"Then again," he said slowly. "I am still a little tired. Maybe I should get some sleep." Beth moved closer and the two joined in a lovers embrace. "After all," said Patty, "I can't disobey an order from the Captain, can I?"

"Absolutely not," she said and they walked arm-in-arm out of Alyssa's tent and into their own.

Chapter 10

Alyssa woke early the next morning and stretched out her sore, aching muscles. The doctor had done a good job in knitting the bones, but a twinge reminded her how delicate they still were. As she prodded and poked the tender areas, she wondered how they would get along when the battery pack for the knitter ran out.

She threw on her jumpsuit and hurriedly exited to find some breakfast. The knitter could heal broken bones in a few hours, but it left one feeling ravenous as the body's resources were depleted in a hurry. Right now Alyssa felt like she could eat anything that came in sight.

"Morning, sweetheart," said Lex as he kissed her. "Hungry?"

"Starving," she said. "What's for breakfast?"

"Oh, we have a wide assortment," he said waving in the direction of the makeshift camp table. "Steak, Umwa Eggs in Barla Sauce, Toasted Jackfish with Almandine surprise. What will be your pleasure?"

Alyssa looked at the small pile of concentrated ration bars. Wistfully she let out a sigh. "Beast," she said. "Now you've gotten my mouth watering for real food, not this dehydrated, desiccated fodder. "

"Sorry, if you want I can always see if there's anything local I can find. How about one of those big Jelly like things?"

"Make sure it's strawberry flavoured," she said picking up a bar and opening the wrapper. "Hopefully we'll find something today."

"You sure you feel up to stalking wild animals in the woods?"

"Yeah, I'll be fine. I can't just sit here…I'd go nuts!"

"Know what you mean," he chuckled. "That's why I'm off to explore those caves we found you in."

Alyssa nodded while chewing a mouthful of the dry ration bar. "Is Sam going too?"

"Why do you ask?" Lex paled slightly and wondered if Alyssa had found out what happened earlier.

"No reason," said Alyssa eyeing him closely. "There isn't any reason I should be concerned, is there?"

Lex looked sheepish and his head drooped just a little. Alyssa looked into his eyes and said softly, "Who started it? You or her?"

"It was all a misunderstanding," said Lex quickly. "She was frightened and scared…"

"So she offered herself to you and then pouted when you wouldn't give her what she demanded."

"How…How did you know?"

"Sweet lovable man," said Alyssa holding his chin gently in her hand. "You really don't know what effect you have on women do you?"

"Excuse me?"

"Never mind, lover. Let's just say I feel very lucky to have someone like you."

"How do you know I didn't do anything? After all she is a very attractive and desirable woman. And, she was all over me. That's hard for a man to refuse you know!"

"I know," said Alyssa. "Look, Lex, for three years now I've seen just about every female passenger throw herself at you. You never even blinked an eye. I know you! I know you love me. But, even if you did it with her, it wouldn't change a thing. Yes, she's attractive, and yes, she can attract a man with the slightest wiggle, but that's as far as it goes with her. Any man who had desires of making it permanent with Sam would just get his heart broken."

Lex couldn't think of a thing to say and just shuffled his feet uncomfortably. Alyssa let him suffer for a couple of minutes then reached out and grabbed his hand. Pulling, she dragged him across the compound.

"Where are we going?"

"I want to show you something," she said mysteriously and then clamped her mouth shut. Lex followed meekly behind her and started to slow down when they approached Sam.

"Hey, Princess," called Alyssa. "Got a minute?"

Sam came running over and Alyssa glanced at Lex. Tiny beads of sweat had started to form on his brow. "Hi, Alyssa," said Sam, then slower, "hi, Lex…"

"Sam, can you do a favour for me?"

"Sure, Alyssa. What would you like?"

"Kiss Lex!"

"Pardon me?"

"I'm trying to prove a point," explained Alyssa. "Look you two, I'm not blind, but unless this is resolved, I see problems later. Now Sam, please give Lex a kiss, and Lex, you put some effort into it."

"But…"

"Kiss," she commanded.

Hesitantly, unsure what Alyssa had in mind, Lex and Sam moved closer together and gave each other a peck. Alyssa grabbed them both behind their backs and pushed them together.

"I'm not going to get mad," she said. "Listen I know that you offered yourself to Lex, and I know he's attracted to you."

"Yes but, I now know how he feels about you. I promise I won't do it again!"

"Honey, I'm not mad or even upset. Did you offer yourself because you're attracted to him or because you're used to getting your own way and wanted to hurt me?"

Sam looked at the ground in shame and Alyssa moved closer and put an arm around her. "At first," she said slowly, "I thought about doing it to hurt you. I mean you really pissed me off when we landed here. I wasn't used to being treated that way."

"Then—"

"—Then I really wanted him. But please believe me, I wouldn't do anything to hurt you or him. You're… You're the first real friend I've ever had."

"I know, Hon," said Alyssa. "But I also know what effect Lex has on women. You still desire him, don't you? No, don't answer. I can see that you do. And you, my young stud. You feel big and important with the attention this beautiful young woman is giving you. So let's find out how deep this mutual admiration society goes. I don't want you two hungering after each other."

"But I don't want to," protested Lex. "I love you, not her. No offence."

"None taken," said Sam. "Really, Alyssa, this is unnecessary. Lex loves you and you love him. What's the big deal?"

"Humour me, okay," she said smiling. "Now for me, please kiss, and put some effort into it."

Lex looked at Sam and Alyssa could see the glint in his eyes. He wanted her and she wanted him. She knew this would be a gamble, but she preferred it to be out in the open, rather than letting it fester and grow in the shadows. Slowly Lex and Sam moved together.

Hesitantly with both eyes focused on Alyssa, Lex kissed Sam gently. Sam also occupied the same way, responded slowly. As they tried to break apart, Alyssa grabbed their heads and pushed them together. With their mouths mashed together, they had no choice but to continue the kiss.

It took only a couple of moments before they found themselves responding to the feelings and the close contact. Seconds later Lex held Sam in a tight embrace and she returned his attentions with vigour. After a good long solid kiss, Alyssa stepped back and smiled.

The two broke their kiss slowly, and then blushed furiously when they saw Alyssa smiling. Turning away from each other they took several small steps to place them out of reach.

"I have to admit," said Alyssa, "that was impressive. Oh, he can do much better, but under the circumstances I think it will be enough."

"Now," said Sam, her face still flushed and breathing slightly heavy. "Would you mind explaining what all that was in aide of?"

"Okay," said Alyssa. "Sam, what did you feel, kissing Lex?"

"I'm not sure I understand?"

"Did you feel any closeness or attraction, or was it physical. Would you like to be with him, or would you like to bed him? Come on, be honest."

"Well," she said shyly. "I certainly wouldn't have any objections to bedding him, that's for sure. But if you're looking for some sort of commitment from me to him, No."

"What about you, Lex? Any bells or sirens?"

"If you insist on playing this game out Lys, then yes. I would take her to bed in a minute. But that's all that would happen. I'm sorry Sam, but I didn't feel anything other than a physical attraction."

The three friends looked at each other for a moment then suddenly burst out laughing. Alyssa scooped them up in her arms and kissed them both. "Feel better?"

"When did you get so smart?" Lex took her face in his hands and kissed her gently.

"Not smart," said Alyssa, "just maturity. Any person—man or woman—who tries to hold their partner on a leash is fooling themselves. It's human nature to look, and sometimes desire. The problems arise not from this, or from the act or carrying it out. No, problems arise when true feelings are involved."

She grabbed Lex and put him in a headlock. "This doesn't mean you can bed every woman you meet, or that you, Sam, should chase every guy. It just means that it happens, and if it is just a physical attraction, then no harm is done." She let him loose and he stood up and rubbed his neck.

"I'm sorry, my love," she said tenderly. "I had to show you that what you felt was normal. I could see that something had happened between you two, and it was eating you both up from the inside."

"I think I understand," said Sam, "but Alyssa it could have backfired. What if Lex and I found we had real affection for each other?"

"Then I would have kissed you both, and wished you good-luck. Don't look so surprised. I love Lex very much, but I wouldn't want him if he wanted you. It just wouldn't work. In a relationship both parties must be committed. Sam, you must learn that lesson…Before it's too late."

Sam kissed her gently and hugged Lex. This time he responded and they hugged fiercely and kissed gently. They felt comfortable. A new phase of the relationship had begun. They would soon become fast friends, possibly closer than most, but the awkwardness was gone.

"I'd better get going," said Alyssa, glancing at the hunting party now forming at the other end of the compound. "One word of advice. If you two find you can't keep your hands off of each other, at least have the decency to do it somewhere private. After all Sam has a reputation to uphold."

Sam looked dejectedly at the ground. "I already have a reputation," she said softly, "and it's not a good one. I never worried before, because Daddy's money could buy the silence of anyone."

"Well, look around you here," said Alyssa warmly. "These people don't know who you are. We could be stranded here for a long time. They will become your family, friends, and lovers. If you want to bed Lex, go ahead. But if you don't want a bad reputation, be discreet."

"I wouldn't...I couldn't...I mean Lex is yours and he's my friend."

"The fact that you protest so vehemently shows that you're still interested," said Alyssa. "Relax. If it happens, enjoy it. But don't push it to happen, or you'll both be disappointed. Gotta go. Will you two be all right now?"

In answer they flanked and kissed her. Then Lex quickly kissed Sam and took Alyssa's arm to escort her to the waiting hunters. "You're different from when you first came aboard ship," said Lex as they walked. "More sure and confident."

"Thanks to you, and the others," she said. "Lex, I'm serious about this. I know that you love me and wouldn't do anything to hurt me. If you want to sleep with Sam, go ahead, it wouldn't bother me. But, make sure that's all you want to do. If you hurt her, I'll personally make sure you don't have any sort of physical relationship with anyone ever again."

"Don't worry," said Lex laughing. "But why the sudden concern about Sam?"

"You heard her. She's never known a life of love and friendship. She's spent her whole life being waited on hand and foot. She's only now realizing what true companionship and friendship could mean. She's at a turning point in her life and she's confused."

"I think I understand," he said gently. "You like her, don't you?"

"Yes," she said. "Yes, I do. I think she could eventually become the little sister I never had. I don't know why, but I feel drawn to her. She feels like family."

"Then we will become one big loving family," said Lex. "And I promise to look out for her and care for her as if she was my sister."

"Better make it kissing cousin," laughed Alyssa. "She's just too beautiful for you to ignore forever. Look, there's Beth and Patty, come on."

"You still feel up to joining the hunt?" Said Beth, looking concerned at Alyssa.

"I'm fine, Captain," said Alyssa. "You said it yourself when you made me Chief Engineering Officer. I have a duty and obligation to the crew and passengers."

"All right, but take it easy," said Beth. "And if you call me Captain again, I'll take you over my knee and spank you."

"Yes ma'am, I mean Beth," said Alyssa with a smile.

"What about you, Lex? Are you joining the hunting party as well?"

"Nope," said Lex. "That's a little too barbaric for me. I prefer to get my meat already dead. No, I'm joining the group exploring the caves. Besides I feel like a fifth-wheel here. Its time I put my organizational skills into use. If these caves check out, I'll have a full working plan by the time you return."

"Very good," said Patty. "I recommend that we send out several scouting parties, but make sure we leave the base manned. Sorry Beth didn't mean to overstep my bounds."

"When you do," said Beth with a smile. "I'll tell you. For now though, that is a good suggestion. Lex, you might as well put those abilities to work right now. Think you could handle the job?"

"I," said Lex with feigned disdain, "am the Executive Office of the Carriolion, the largest cruiser in the fleet. My job is to organize and delegate. Need you ask such a question?"

"My apologies X.O.," said Beth. "If it meets with your approval on allocating resources, I would like to accompany Patty on his fishing trip."

"Well," said Lex thoughtfully, stroking his chin, "I was about to say we need someone to make the beds…but if your mind's made up, go ahead."

"Lyssa, honey," said Beth in a conspiratorial tone, "you watch him. Sometimes he gets a little rambunctious and needs corralling. Understand?"

Alyssa looked at Lex and with a knowing wink replied, "I do indeed. I promise, he'll be well taken care of."

Patty couldn't contain himself any longer and burst out laughing. He clapped Lex on the back who stood and took the ribbing good-naturedly. "Well, my boy, it seems that we have our duties."

"In more ways than one," replied Lex. Then looking around he asked, "By the way, has anyone seen Ethan or Scrapper this morning?"

"He's off exploring," said Beth. "Earlier he wanted to go and look at the ruins. A couple of the passengers are amateur archaeologists and wanted to go as well. I sent a couple of beefy security guards along to protect them." Lex nodded and after chatting a few more minutes, the group broke up and moved off to the respective jobs.

*

"I've never been hunting before," said Alyssa to one of the hunters. "What's it like?"

"I don't know for sure," he replied. "My wife up ahead is the hunter. We live on a game preserve. She goes out and occasionally has to track and kill and rogue animal. I'm just an accountant. I've practiced in a virtual mock-up, but it's not the same thing."

"My name's Alyssa."

"Tony," he said in acknowledgment. "That's my wife Karen. I promised her a second honeymoon she wouldn't forget. Boy, did I luck out."

Alyssa laughed and they talked as the group plunged through the thick dense bush. Suddenly the leader called a halt and they gathered around a grassy knoll. Unlimbering his pack, the leader called a break then summoned those in his group with actual experience. Of the twenty hunters, only five had any actual hunting ability.

They moved off, away from the rest and formed a huddle. Ten minutes later they returned and the team leader broke the rest into smaller groups. A seasoned hunter became group leader for each. They would hunt together, but also be controlled in smaller groups.

"It's for your own safety," the leader said. "These people have hunted before and know how to behave, the rest of you could just walk into danger without realizing it. Take your cues from them. If they stop and don't move, you freeze. It could save your life."

Alyssa looked around at her companions and saw a sea of nodding, bobbing heads. These people, like herself, never hunted, but for various reasons they joined the hunting party, some of them, because they wanted to experience a hunt, others because they felt that more hunters would be needed and they wanted to learn how.

Alyssa wondered why she had come along. Her reasons of "just checking it out," seemed lame now that they were buried deep in the forest. What was it she was seeking? Surely her skills could be better put to use in other areas. But she knew she needed to be here.

The signal to continue was given and they shouldered their packs. Some carried ropes and slings, others' bags. The hunters in the group carried the tools of the trade. They were issued with a couple of guns from the survival kits, but were under orders to use them only in emergencies, as their charges would soon dissipate. So they had crafted crudely formed bows with arrows, and long pointed spears.

On through the bush they trudged, the blazing sun making it hotter by the minute. Sweat ran freely down the front of Alyssa's jumpsuit making it cling like plastic-wrap to her body. She began to wish she had traded with some of the other women for different clothing.

"Remind me," she said to Tony later, "to send a recommendation into supply to equip the survival packs with some sort of all weather emergency clothing."

"You do look uncomfortable. Wait a minute. I've got an idea." He hurried on ahead and met up with another group. Seconds later he returned with a woman. "Alyssa, this is my wife, Karen."

"How do you do," said Alyssa amiably. She wondered what Tony was up to.

"Tony tells me that that jumpsuit is all the clothing you have. Is that right?"

"Yes, I'm afraid it is," said Alyssa pulling the sticky material away from her skin. "I would have packed better, but we left the ship quite suddenly."

Karen laughed and reached into her pack. From inside she withdrew a short skirt and top made from sort of animal skin. "Here put this on," she said handing Alyssa the outfit.

"Where did you get this," said Alyssa in amazement. She examined and fingered the material and was awed at how soft and flexible it felt.

"As Tony probably told you, we live on a Game preserve. I'm a Ranger and have to be ready to go at a moments notice. I always keep a pack near the door at home that contains a few useful articles. I've gotten so used to doing it I even brought the pack on board the ship. When the alarm sounded it was the first thing I grabbed."

Alyssa nodded understanding. "Where did you buy this? It's so soft!"

"I made it," said Karen. "I'd be happy to show you how later."

"Oh, I'd love that," said Alyssa enthusiastically. "Thanks. I'll put it on at the next rest stop."

"Well then, find a place to change because they've just called another rest." Alyssa glanced ahead and saw the signal for stop from the lead man. Glancing around she spotted a high, wide bush and slipped in behind it. Shucking her jumpsuit she slipped on the skirt and found a pair of panties sown into the lining. Then she donned the top and smoothed the wrinkles out. Karen was slightly more endowed in the bust department than Alyssa, but with a little adjustment, she made it fit perfectly.

When she re-emerged from behind the bush, she was assailed with several whistles of appreciation. At first she blushed, then got into the spirit by modeling and displaying the outfit. Several other women came forward and asked how they could obtain the cooler, comforting clothes. Alyssa introduced them to Karen and not until she promised to hold a class in how to make the clothes did the rest retire.

Several hours later, Karen on the left flank called a halt and summoned the rest. The hunters in the group looked at where she pointed then congratulated her. The rest stood dumbfounded. They couldn't see the reason she had stopped.

Alyssa strained, but just couldn't make out what they were so excited about. Obviously they had found tracks of some kind, but she couldn't see anything and told Tony so.

"You have to look at what's not there," he said. "Look at the setting and see what's not right."

"You're kidding," said Alyssa. "You want me to see something—I don't know what—in a place I've never seen before. How am I to know what to look for?"

"If you can see it, you'll know," said Tony. "Not all things are visible and up-front. Sometimes they're hidden, but still there. We have to focus and concentrate."

Alyssa shrugged and stared into the area Karen had indicated. She tried examining everything in view, but still couldn't see what the others saw and questioned Tony. "I still can't see it. Can you point it out to me?"

"I can if you want," he said. "But to learn, you have to do it yourself. Try it again. Let go of what you think you see and look at it as a whole. Think of it as another way to look at life. Step back and see the whole picture, not just the small portion you are in."

Alyssa closed her eyes then opened them again to view the spot. "View it as a whole," he repeated gently. She changed her focus. Instead of concentrating on looking for a sign, she saw the area as one object. The trees, the grass, the bushes…

"I see it," she cried and Karen came over to her.

"What do you see, Alyssa?"

"Well, Tony was just explaining how to look at this and I can now see it."

"Please describe what you see."

"Well, at first glance everything appeared normal, then I remembered what Tony said, about looking for things out of place, different. Look here. This bush, it has several leaves turned over and this twig is bent at an unnatural angle. Over here, the ground seems fine, except for the way some of these blades of grass are slightly bent."

"What makes you think these are tracks," said Karen. The rest of the hunters had started to silently approach, but kept quiet.

"Because of the way the grass is bent," said Alyssa excitedly. "See? They all bend the same way. Now if a breeze did that, more would be bent, but the spots are spaced evenly apart."

"Very good, Alyssa," said the team leader. "It looks like you're a natural."

"No, really," protested Alyssa gently. "I didn't see anything until Tony told me how."

"Yes, but he didn't show you," rejoined the man. "You had to figure it out yourself. Tell us what else you see!"

"Well," said Alyssa slowly staring at the space. "I can see a broken flower-stem over there and look at that, those leaves have been eaten."

"Excellent," said the man in congratulations. "Anytime you want to join a hunting party, I'll be happy to take you along."

"Thanks," said Alyssa a little embarrassed by all the attention. "So are we going for the small animals, or the big one?"

Karen looked at her in bewilderment. "What do you mean, Alyssa?"

Alyssa hunched down and pointed to the grass. "These tracks indicate several small animals passed through here. See, there's more tracks and the spacing doesn't seem right. They're not even."

"That's right," agreed Karen. "You are very good at this."

"But over here," said Alyssa continuing as if she hadn't heard, "you can see what's left of a break in the bush line. Its quite high and I don't think the animal that made those small tracks could be that big."

Karen and the team leader moved nearer the spot in the bush-line that Alyssa indicated and examined it for a minute. They chatted silently for a few seconds then called the rest of the hunters over. Excitedly the examined the spot then simultaneously nodded their heads and returned to the rest of the group.

"Well, Alyssa," said the team leader. "It would appear you are a natural. None of us saw that break until you pointed it out. You're quite right; a large animal did pass through that hedge. I am very impressed. As for deciding what to search for, why don't we leave it open? We could track for days before actually catching the animal. So we'll continuing searching for a more recent spore. Alyssa, I would like your eyes up front with me."

As they marched, Alyssa did her utmost best to watch for tell tale signs. Soon the strain began to show and she started to develop a headache. She told Andrew the team leader this on the next break.

"You're trying too hard," he said. "Don't concentrate so much, just let it happen. Eventually it will become second nature and you'll do it without thinking."

They found the next spore an hour later, but it was Tony who made the discovery. Not Alyssa or the hunters. He called excitedly and they others merged to examine the site. "Very near," said Andrew. "These tracks are less than twenty minutes old."

Alyssa suddenly stepped back in mild shock. For the last hour she had been so proud of herself. She had a natural ability that didn't depend on training and schooling and had grown over confident. Andrew had just shown her how much she actually had to learn by telling how old the spore was. She felt ashamed at her own ego, but determined to learn everything she could. Fortunately nobody noticed, or cared that she had been feeling supremely proud of herself. Self-chastised she concentrated on the trail and tried determining how Andrew could tell the time.

Andrew started giving orders, sending various groups off in different directions. The hunters in each group nodded their agreements and collected their people and moved off. Alyssa stood beside Andrew and wondered what next.

"I've sent them to encompass the area. They'll check the tracks and hopefully we can enclose these animals in our trap," he explained to her unasked question. "This isn't the best way to hunt, but with so many untrained people it's the best method. Now we'll proceed along the trail. Hopefully, we'll be able to flush some game out and the rest will be able to get it. Ready?"

They moved along slowly on the trail. Alyssa's newly developed senses strained to keep track of the prints, but she lost it several times. Andrew however didn't seem to lose the trail even once. Suddenly he stopped and froze. Alyssa watching carefully did the same thing. Carefully he raised his hand and pointed ahead. Alyssa squinted and peered into the dense bush. Just ahead, she saw several animals that looked liked deer, but had overly large heads.

He glanced first to the left, then to the right. "Okay, the rest are ready," he whispered. Alyssa looked, but could see no sign of the other hunters.

"What do we do now?"

"Timotin and Karen are with their groups to the left. They're our best shots. On my signal we'll drive the herd in that direction." He glanced around once more then with a war like yell, darted into the bush.

The deer, spooked by the sudden appearance of first Andrew and Alyssa, then the rest, darted around frantically looking for a place to escape. With the band of humans closing in on three sides they chose the only open avenue of escape to them. Bounding in great leaps, they ran from the pursuing hunters who were yelling and waving, right into the spears and bows of Karen and Timotin and their people.

Three deer fell in the first few seconds, then two more, shortly after that. The rest weaved and dodged in the underbrush and made for safety in the jungle. Panting from excitement, Alyssa ran up beside the downed animals. The rest of the victorious hunters had slowly gathered around the slain animals. Several of them turned and ran for the bush.

Alyssa breathing heavily moved to the front. On the ground lay the five deer. Three, had arrows protruding from their sides, the others had spears. One had a spear sticking out on both sides. The thrower had so much strength it had gone almost completely through.

Alyssa paled at the sight of the dead deer, but bravely held her ground. That is until one of them moved and made a bleating sound of pain. Then the blood drained from her face. She felt nauseous and ready to faint. A giant lumbering man came forward and made a fist. Timotin—the man from the heavy gravity world—raised his huge monster club like fist into the air and brought it down in a resounding crack on the deer's head. The deer slumped and remained still.

Alyssa turned her head, took two steps, and emptied the contents of her stomach. She dropped to her knees and continued to retch as Karen came over. She placed an arm around Alyssa's waist and held her head as another violent spasm over took her. Eventually the heaving subsided and Alyssa collapsed weakly on the ground.

"How are you feeling?"

"I'm sorry," said Alyssa slowly. "I've just never seen anything killed before. I mean, I've seen dead bodies, but I've never…" She leaned over and heaved violently again. "Wasn't there any other way," she gasped. "He just killed it with one punch."

"Timotin is the kindest gentlest man I know," said Karen. "On board the ship he would play for hours with the children and pets. But he's also a man who knows what to do. Yes, there was another way to kill it, but it would have suffered until it died. We have only bows and arrows. You saw for yourself. One blow from that giant fist put it to rest quickly and painlessly."

"I don't think I could ever be a hunter," said Alyssa after regaining her breath.

"Then be a tracker," said Karen. "My Tony's the same way. He can track pretty good, but he just can't bring himself to kill the animal. He practices though. On the reserve, if you're not careful, its kill, or be killed."

"I'll never eat meat again," said Alyssa sorrowfully.

"Yes, you will," encouraged Karen. "Now we have to cut up the animals for transport. I suggest that you remain here. It can get a little grizzly."

Alyssa thanked the woman and lay down in the grass. Looking over she saw several other people who had become ill also shy away from the gruesome seen. The hunters brought out their knives and carefully hacked up the carcasses into manageable chunks.

Alyssa swallowing the bile got up and approached the butcher shop. Trying to maintain her composure, she watched as Karen meticulously carved a deer up in front of her. She felt her gorge rise, but stubbornly refused to give in and swallowed repeatedly until it subsided.

Karen worked smoothly and efficiently from years of experience. First she removed the skin and rolled it into a ball. She called out for the others to keep the skins then returned to her deer. Alyssa nearly lost it when Karen reached inside and disembowelled the animal. Even though her face turned sheet white, she still watched, becoming fascinated as the woman worked.

In a few short minutes, Karen hard cut the animal into large pieces that could be carried by a person. Then she carefully wrapped them in the sacks they had brought. After that she dug a small hole and buried the entrails of the animal and brushed dirt over the area. Within an hour, Alyssa couldn't tell that an animal had just been butchered in front of her.

"That's better," said Karen washing the blood from her hands and arms. "These deer should provide us with enough food for several days."

"If the doctor says they're safe to eat," reminded Alyssa.

"I'm sure they will be," said Karen. "I've seen enough animals from different worlds to have a feeling of what's good or bad. These will do nicely. The meat should be quite delicious."

Alyssa shuddered again, but bravely picked up a sack of meat and slung it over her shoulder. Andrew called the team together and dividing the spoils, set a course back to camp. Some of the group were still weak from being sick and these lurched behind the rest.

Andrew came up beside Alyssa and spoke softly so no one else could hear. "I saw what happened. I admire the way you came back and stuck it out."

"Thanks," said Alyssa. "I'm just now starting to realize that everyone has their skills and limitations. I think I just found mine."

"Don't be so hard on yourself," said Andrew. "I've been hunting for years, but the same thing happened to me the first time I had to butcher an animal. I've always had servants to do it for me."

"When did it happen to you?" Asked Alyssa thankful that the man shared his confidence with her.

"About an hour ago," he said and walked ahead. He called back over his shoulder. "Have faith, Alyssa. You're stronger than you think." He hurried on to help a couple wrestling with a large hindquarter.

Alyssa stared after the man in wonder. The situation had been ghastly, and gross, and he had the audacity to make light of it. Suddenly the whole thing made sense and she started chuckling. The chuckle quickly developed into laughter and Karen moved beside her.

"Are you all right?"

"Yeah," said Alyssa. "I just go it. I mean I understand now what people have been trying to tell me. Don't take things so seriously. Enjoy life, for even in death you can still do good."

Karen smiled and grabbed Alyssa's arm in friendship. "You're learning, girl. You're learning!"

Chapter 11

Ethan and the two amateur archaeologists—Tomlinson from the Martian research base on the moon Phobos, and A'Serta from Matriarch of Selena—wandered through the ruins found by Sam. Around them the vegetation of the jungle crept ever closer to consuming the few remaining structures and artefacts.

"This is an incredible find," exclaimed Tomlinson excitedly. "Nothing like this has ever been found before."

"I beg to differ," said A'Serta. She came from a female dominated planet and as a matter of course, disagreed with an opinion of any male.

"You know of any other findings similar to this?"

A'Serta found herself pushed into a corner by her arrogance. "I don't know how extensive the research base is on Phobos, but on Selena, we have catalogued and identified every artefact found. I'm sure that there is a match somewhere!"

Tomlinson humphed loudly to show his opinion of her statement! The Matriarch of Selena was still a relatively new world. Founded less than three hundred years ago by a fanatic all female crew, they turned their backs on males and created a society to "Right the wrongs done by men."

Fortunately or unfortunately depending on how you viewed it, something went wrong. Instead of creating a society to foster the peace and love they professed, the women of Selena rapidly reverted to a barbaric state that hunted and attacked any man they found. So ingrained was their hatred that they soon had only a handful of males. Those that arrived on subsequent ships were either hunted or went into hiding.

The founding mothers realized at last that something terrible was happening and appealed to the Star League for help. The League sent a team of female scientists—no man would live long enough to help. By the time the League team had arrived the women of Selena had built themselves into a blood lust and were actively searching every male hiding in the mountains.

The team found—just in time—a microorganism in the water that settled itself into the brain of the host. It attacked upon the rage and logic centres, thereby making the host mentally unstable. These women who had started a venture to raise a world of love and peace without the militaristic, aggressive nature of the male, found themselves behaving as bad as or worse than the men they hunted.

With the resources of the League an inhibitor was found for the bug. It remained immune to any drug they had, but it could be controlled and its actions reduced. Given the choice of abandoning their world or taking the inhibitor for the rest of their lives, the founding mothers decided to stay.

Against their wishes, but realizing the necessity, the Mothers administered the drug to the few surviving males as well. Unfortunately the organism had another side effect by rendering every male impotent. Within a few short years the Matriarch of Selena was in a serious population shortage. Males were needed to inseminate the women.

Gradually a pattern developed. A woman of childbearing age would leave Selena and journey to the Star League. There she would seek out an appropriate mate and become impregnated. The thought of marriage or spending a lifetime with a male was abhorrent. The women of Selena considered themselves all sisters and had no need or use for a man.

If a child was born female, it was given the best education and raised with lavish love and attention. If it was born male, after several years of limited training it would be passed over to the men's houses to be trained in the menial, muscular tasks that men were suited for.

This division eventually caused a separation and two distinctive societies. The women controlled everything and ran the house, the government, and the land. The men became less than second-class citizens and essentially slaves. In the latter half of the century a movement had been underway to educate the males to a higher level. It met with strong resistance, but eventually the males won a reprieve of sorts by being able to school with the women.

"You're not on Selena now, A'Serta," said Tomlinson. "That cocky superiority won't cut with me. If you know of any similar examples, I would be more than willing to hear about them and discuss them with you. But if you don't, we must assume that this is a first find and conduct our research accordingly."

"How dare you presume to tell me what to do," she cried.

"Excuse me," interrupted Ethan. "But don't you think that this can wait. I mean we have to get back to camp soon or the Captain will be angry."

"Well said, son," said Tomlinson. Then turning to A'Serta he said, "I would like to apologize if I offended you. I am used to working with peers and equals. I meant no offence to you or your world."

"I too feel some sorrow at our discussion," said A'Serta somewhat mollified. "This is my first voyage away from my home and I feel the strain of separation."

"I know a little about your world," said Tomlinson. "But Selena is hundreds of light years away. You and I are the only ones to solve the mystery of these ruins. I believe the correct phrase is…'Mistress, May I offer what small knowledge and skills I have to aid you in this project.' I hope I got that right?"

A'Serta smiled. Since she had left Selena nearly three months ago she had run into no one who knew the correct way to address a Mistress. "You have done very well, I will accept your offer."

Tomlinson smiled and clapped Ethan on the back. "Well my son, don't you think we should get started?"

"Yes, sir," said Ethan eagerly. They moved into the ruins then stopped suddenly as Scrapper growled a warning. Tomlinson whirled around in time to see an enraged A'Serta charging him with a tree branch she wielded like a club. Screaming in fury she swung the branch down, intending to split Tomlinson's head wide open.

Ethan watched in horror as the heavy branch came whizzing through the air, then miraculously it stopped and A'Serta found herself flying through the air to land heavily on her backside. Ethan looked up and saw the large form of one of the security guards standing over A'Serta.

"Sorry, miss," he said gently offering his hand for support, "but I can't allow you to do that. I have strict orders from the Captain, not to let any harm come to you two. That means I won't let you brain him either."

"Why are you doing this?" Asked Ethan to A'Serta. "Mr. Tomlinson has done nothing to offend you and has tried to observe your customs. Why do you hate him so?"

A'Serta looked at the young man in wonder. "How old did you say you were?"

"Thirteen, ma'am."

"Well, you certainly don't talk or act like any 13-year-old I've ever met. Still there is wisdom in the youth." She struggled to her feet and with restrained effort approached Tomlinson. The guard stood nearby in case she attacked him again.

"I would like to…apolog…NO! I WILL NOT APOLOGIZE TO A MAN." Then she slumped unconscious on the ground.

Ethan looked around. No one had touched her. Tomlinson bent down and quickly checked her vitals. "She's asleep," he said in wonder. "Give me a hand, let's take her out of here and make her more comfortable."

Together, with the help of the guard, he lifted A'Serta into a fireman's carry and exited the ruins. They moved about fifty feet from the blocks that marked the entrance way and he propped her gently against a wide tree. The guard stood near—just in case—and nodded to his companion who moved closer to Ethan.

Minutes later A'Serta woke and looked around in confusion. "What happened? Why am I on the ground?"

"You fainted, Miss A'Serta," said Ethan softly. Seeing the puzzled look on her face he explained what happened.

"I'm so sorry, Mr. Tomlinson," she said softly. "I don't know what came over me. Honestly I don't remember a thing. I wouldn't hurt you or any man!"

Tomlinson looked at her doubtfully. "I don't mean to call you a liar, but you did try to kill me…And you are from the Matriarch of Selena."

"Yes, I am," she said, "but you should also know that I am the leader of the movement to make males equal in our society. I just don't understand what happened. I've never raised my voice in anger to any man, much less tried to attack him. I am sincerely sorry, please believe me."

Tomlinson smiled and offered his hand, which she hesitantly took. "No harm done," he said. "If you feel up to it, I would like to get one more look at the ruins before nightfall."

"Of course," she said smiling. Flanked by the guards they returned to the site. But once through the stone gates, A'Serta started to become agitated and boisterous. The guards quickly grabbed hold of her as she reached for a rock. Hatred and venom shone in her eyes.

"Take her out," ordered Ethan. So forceful was his command that the guards didn't even hesitate. They dragged her kicking and screaming beyond the stone markers. As soon as they passed the markers, her features relaxed and she sagged in their arms.

"I did it again?"

"Uh-huh," said Tomlinson. "Are you all right now?"

"Yes, I feel fine, thank-you. But what is wrong with me?"

"I think I know," said Ethan. "Whenever we cross the threshold, I sense a presence. I didn't mention it before, because, well, Sam says I shouldn't tell people about my abilities. But I now know that there is a presence there and it affects you, Miss A'Serta."

"Miss," said the guard who had hit her. "I'm sorry I hurt you earlier, but I have a suggestion."

"You were trying to save Mr. Tomlinson," she said sweetly. "I hold no grudge. I must thank you instead. But, you have a theory?"

"Yes, ma'am," he said. "On board the Carriolion I am a security guard. It's an interesting life. I meet all sorts of people and get to travel all over the galaxy. Well on one trip several years ago, I met a woman from Selena. We became close. So close she chose me."

He stopped while the others absorbed this fact. Somewhere on Selena this kindly man had a child that he would never see. It took a special kind of man to accept that fate for his child. That's why the women of Selena searched carefully for a man to impregnate them.

"Anyway," he continued, "she told me all about Selena and the symbiont that is present in everyone. She was a historian so she knew the full details of the first few years on that world. Pardon me for saying so Miss, but what you experienced is very similar to what she described the women from the first landing went through."

"I don't understand it," she said sitting down heavily on a rock "I've had the antidote and there hasn't been a case of the Madness in my lifetime. Why is it affecting me now?"

"I think it's the presence I feel," said Ethan. "It seems to call out as if asking for help, but it seems I'm the only one who can hear it. I think it's this mental call for help that is affecting you."

"Hey that might be it," said the guard excitedly. "I just remembered something that... Well, I can't tell you her name." A'Serta nodded. Part of the ritual insisted that the woman's name never be revealed to outsiders. "Anyway she said that the organism was one reason why no telepaths lived on Selena. It set up some sort of reaction that usually drove the women mad. Any telepaths born usually die shortly after childbirth because of the uncontrollable rage. Maybe this presence that Ethan feels is triggering your organism?"

"Sound reasonable to me, A'Serta," said Tomlinson softly. "If true, it means you could never go into the ruins. It would eventually kill you."

A'Serta didn't want to accept that sentence and tried to counter it with every logical and illogical argument she could muster, but eventually she admitted the truth to herself.

"So what do we do now?"

"Now we return to base," said Tomlinson. "I want the doctor to check you over—just in case."

"But the ruins. Your research! You shouldn't stop because of me."

"Listen," he said firmly. "Those ruins have been there for hundreds, maybe thousands of years. They can wait a while longer until I'm sure you're all right."

"I'm sorry," said Ethan quietly. "This is all my fault. I now know that the reason I really wanted to come here. I must have been picking up the call from the camp. If I hadn't pushed to come here, you wouldn't have been in danger. I'm sorry!"

A'Serta rose from her rocky seat and moved closer to Ethan. Reaching out she drew the boy into an embrace. "I'll be fine," she said. "All I need is a little rest and attention. That's all."

"If we get moving now," said Tomlinson looking into the slowly darkening sky, "I can promise you both."

"Why, Mr. Tomlinson," she said, "that sounds slightly suggestive to me."

"And me," said the guard with a smile.

"But I didn't mean…That is, I meant…" He looked around for help in frustration. He found A'Serta very attractive and was drawn to her even though she tried to kill him earlier.

"Come then," she said. "I still feel a little weak and would prefer to be back before it gets too dark."

The tiny exploration team gathered their tools and started the trek back to camp. At first they had to assist A'Serta, but the further they moved away from the ruins the stronger she got. By the time they returned to camp, Tomlinson and A'Serta had become close and real affection had sprung up between them.

The doctor checked A'Serta, supplied her with a sedative, and ordered bed rest for twenty-four hours. Tomlinson saw that she took her medicine and made her comfortable in her bed. He stayed with her as she fell asleep and refused to leave when the others came to find him for breakfast the next morning.

When A'Serta awoke the first person she saw, was the smiling, unshaven face of Tomlinson. His devotion to her well-being touched her more deeply than anything she had experienced before. Gently she reached out and kissed him lightly.

"Hey, just a minute," he protested gently. "I admit I care for you a great deal. I don't know if they have love at first sight on Selena, but I believe in it. I know why you are here, but I can't be the one. I'm sorry, but I wouldn't be able to live with myself, not knowing whether I had a son or daughter, and never being able to see them."

"I know," said A'Serta softly. "I understand and respect your feelings. I would love to have a child by you. You are a warm, kind, caring man. You have intelligence and a high moral value. But one day I must return home and my child would go with me. It would…I would be very hurt knowing I hurt you by depriving you of your child."

"I'm very flattered that you picked me," said Tomlinson, blushing. "But I can't go to Selena and as far as I know, the Mothers have never let a sister emigrate from Selena…I'd better leave you to rest some more. I just wanted to make sure you were all right."

He rose from the chair he had sat in for the last 24 hours and slowly made his way to the door. Turning around he put on a forced smile. "Maybe you can help me analyze whatever information I get from the ruins. At least that will keep you safe." He quickly ducked out of the tent and returned to his own bed. The last thing he wanted to do now was eat. His heart felt ready to break and there was nothing he could do about it.

Several days later he listened with the others as Alyssa recounted her adventures in the hunting party. When she mentioned the lesson she learned about living life to the fullest he glanced across the fire into the eyes of A'Serta. They hadn't really been avoiding each other, but somehow they had unconsciously managed to be in different places all the time.

"Mr. Tomlinson," he turned and looked into the face of Alyssa. She had finally decided to cut her long red hair into a more pageboy style and it suited her immensely.

"Alyssa," he said. "I'm glad your hunting trip turned out so successful. The doctor tells me the meat is quite safe and we should be able to eat in a couple of days after it's cured."

"Thank you," she said. "But that's not what I came here for. I've been talking to the others. They say you've lost the drive. What's wrong? Anything I can do to help?"

"No, thank you," he said dejectedly. "I'll be fine. It's a personal problem. I just have to work through it."

"It wouldn't have anything to do with A'Serta would it?"

"How did you know," he gasped.

"This is a small community," she said. "We have less than two hundred people, living, eating, and sleeping in close quarters. It doesn't take long for information to spread. Besides, A'Serta sleeps in my tent and she talks in her sleep."

"Really," said Tomlinson nervously. "Does she say anything important?"

"Why don't you ask her yourself, Adam?"

His mouth dropped open. Only one person knew his first name. A'Serta! He had told it to her when she asked before falling asleep.

"She's been calling your name," said Alyssa. "I heard her last night and the others in the tent say she's been calling out to you every night since you got back from the ruins. Look, it's none of my business, and I don't know what went wrong, but I think you two have some real affection for each other. It couldn't hurt to talk."

"She's from Selena," he said softly.

"Oh…Ohhh, I am sorry," said Alyssa. "Uh oh, here she comes now."

"Good evening, Alyssa," said A'Serta. "Good evening Mr. Tomlinson. I reviewed your latest findings on the ruins. I have a few questions if you don't mind?" Her cold approach to the clinical data showed the warring emotions in her.

"Well then, I'll just let you two scientists get to work," said Alyssa. "In a way I envy you both. When we get back, you'll be famous for this discovery. There must be a lifetime's worth of work here. Oh well, see you later." She backed away into the shadows and left the two archaeologists to talk.

A'Serta sat down beside Adam, but not too close. "How are you, Adam?"

He smiled when she called him that. Always a very private man, he rarely let anyone know his first name. "Fine, Miss A'Serta. I hope that you've been receiving everything I found in the ruins. I've tried to make sure you were as up to date as possible."

"Thank you, yes," she said. "Must you keep calling me Miss A'Serta? Alyssa was right. This could be a long-term project and it could get a little awkward. In fact Ethan pointed out that we could be trapped here for quite awhile."

"What would you like me to call you?"

"My name is Kyra," she said quietly so that no one but he could hear. Adam gasped and clasped his hand over his mouth.

"Forgive me if I'm wrong," he sputtered, "but I thought your people never told their first names to outsiders. Only to those they chose to mate with."

"That is correct," she said leaning closer. "We value our names very much. Only our sisters and the man we choose may call us by that."

"Then why tell me? We've already decided that it won't work."

"I have a solution to that," she said and smiled. "First, do you still think you couldn't separate from the child?"

"I'm sorry," he said hanging his head. "I just couldn't…I also couldn't bear the thought of never seeing you again. I hope you won't get in trouble for revealing your name to me?"

"I don't think so," she said. "You see I don't plan to return to Selena. When we get rescued, I'm going to apply to the League to join the expedition that will be sent here to study the ruins."

Adam jerked his head up. "I think by then they will probably put you in charge. Congratulations. This will be a very exciting career for you. Will the Mothers allow you to leave permanently?"

"I don't see how they have a choice," she said. "By the time they find out, I will have broken several of our laws and will be considered an outcast."

"You've broken no laws," he said angrily. "When we get back, I'll petition the Mothers to reinstate you. What grounds could they possibly have to reject you?"

"Well, for one thing," she said, "I want to stay here to do research. Leaving Selena for purposes other than breeding is frowned upon. Secondly I want to have my child here, free from the symbiont…And thirdly…There is no way I'm going to leave my husband and father of my child!"

Adam still seethed with the anger that the Mothers would punish Kyra and didn't listen to her reasons. Then slowly it sank in. "You mean…"

"Yes," she said laying her head on his shoulder. "Adam, I love you very much. I know it goes against everything I've ever been taught, but I can't see myself without you."

"But to give up your home, your family, your world. It's too much for me to ask."

"But you didn't ask," she said firmly. "I am offering. Adam, the first thing you are going to learn about the women from Selena, is that we generally get what we want. And I want you and your children. If that means leaving behind my world to live in yours, then I do so happily."

"But-"

"—No buts," she said sharply. "You cannot live on my world. I can and will live in yours. Now, I've told you my name and while there is no such thing as a marriage between a man and woman in my world, there is in yours. Do you think the Captain would marry us?"

Adam beamed from ear to ear and kissed her passionately. "Why don't we ask her right now. A'Serta…I mean Kyra. Whatever happens to us now, remember that you have made me the happiest man in the galaxy."

He stood and held a hand to her. She clasped tightly then arm in arm they sought out the Captain. They found her sitting in the shadows of the fire talking to Alyssa, Lex, and Patty. When they stepped forward Alyssa applauded before they spoke.

"See," she cried. "I told you they would be here."

"I would be very happy to conduct the ceremony," said Beth before either of them spoke. Adam and Kyra hugged each other tightly.

"Everyone except me new this would happen," said Adam. "Is this the way it will always be?"

"Fraid so," said Lex. "Congratulations, old man. And to you, Miss A'Serta."

"Please just call me A'Serta," she said. "It is the way we are addressed outside Selena. Only my husband may know my other name."

"Then when would you like to be joined? If you can wait a couple of days, we should have more permanent quarters," said Patty. "The team investigating the caves have pronounced them safe and fit."

The two lovers stared at each other and a silent nod passed between them. "We'll wait," said A'Serta. She shivered suddenly as a cool wind blew through the camp. "I think I'll go to bed if you don't mind. I feel a chill coming on."

The others nodded and Beth pulled her cape around her. Patty moved closer and placed a warm comforting arm around the now shivering Beth. Ethan, riding on the back of Scrapper suddenly burst into the circle.

"We've got to take cover now," he cried.

"What's wrong?" Patty searched the night with his keen eyes.

Suddenly Sam appeared and looked at Ethan. "You too?" He nodded and she faced the group. "We have to get to safety. I've got a strange feeling and so does Ethan. Please, call the camp together. We've got to go!"

Beth didn't hesitate and sent runners to collect the rest of the survivors. Some of them still rubbing the sleep from their eyes stumbled toward the fire demanding an explanation. Beth tried calming the irate people when a cry came from the far end of the compound. "They're back. Run! The ghost winds are back! Run for your life!"

Chapter 12

The camp broke into a flurry of uncontrolled panic. The survivors, scattered to the four corners, and the winds followed. Alyssa, running across the compound, made a mental note that only three winds had appeared, just as before. But there was something different this time. The ghost winds acted as if guided by intelligence. They expertly sidestepped the tents and furniture and concentrated on chasing the survivors of the Carriolion.

The whole scene seemed wrong to Alyssa. She stopped and watched. People scrambled for their lives. Jumping over and through obstacles. The winds whipped around the compound at frightening speed. A woman screamed as a ghost wind picked her up and lifted her some 20 feet in the air. With arms flaying and screaming at the top of her lungs, the wind bore her away from the campground.

Alyssa watched with detached interest. A strange feeling passed over her, a feeling of peace and calm amidst all the calamity. She knew there was no way to save the woman, but neither did she feel as if the woman was in any danger. Seconds after lifting the woman aloft the wind slowed its mad rush, fifty feet from the compound and dissipated, lowering the woman gently to the ground.

Alyssa looked around. The winds were only chasing those people still in the compound. Those that had run past the tree line were ignored. She saw a wind approach her and stood her ground.

"Alyssa," cried Lex from the safety of the trees. He moved as if to try and rescue her when he felt a small hand clutch at his shirt. Shaking it off he dove for the open field and was promptly tackled to the ground by Sam.

"Leave her," she panted. "She'll be all right."

"The winds will kill her," he protested, struggling to break free of her hold.

Patty watched this exchange then looked at Ethan. The boy's eyes radiated calm, although they flashed occasionally with the excitement. He started forward and felt Ethan's hand on his back. Turning he saw the boy's head slowly shake a negative.

"Lex," he called. "Come back. You can't do anything now." He gestured to a couple of people beside him. "Go bring him back, but be careful."

Turning his attention to Ethan he questioned the young man. "I'll trust you on this one. If you're wrong so help me…"

Ethan said nothing and pointed into the now deserted compound. Alyssa stood alone as the wind approached. Everyone watched in a mixture of horror and fascination as it picked her up of the ground. Some would say almost gently. She rose gracefully into the air, her toes pointing to the ground, her arms outstretched.

Twirling very slowly she moved across the field and approached the others. The wind seemed to be looking for something as it carried Alyssa along the tree line. When it came to Patty and the rest, it slowed. Ethan stepped out from the bush, his eyes glazed. The wind approached and Patty had to restrain Lex from darting out. Alyssa hovered in the whirling maelstrom and seemed unhurt. When she saw Ethan, she smiled and the wind began to dissipate. Slowly she sank to the ground and when her feet lightly touched the earth, the wind vanished.

Patty came rushing over. "What the hell was that?"

"I'm not sure," said Alyssa calmly, "but Ethan knows." The rest looked at him, almost accusingly.

"They just saved our lives," he said matter-of-factly. "Look!" He pointed to the compound. A dozen or so of the rolling Jelly-like creatures appeared from the one direction the winds wouldn't allow anyone to run. They rolled across the compound in a line that would have trapped anybody still in the field. As they approached the tree line they dropped into a single file and disappeared into the bush.

The refugees cautiously crawled out from the bush. All eyes scanned for the Jelly creatures and the ghost winds. Eventually their fears eased and the people started taking stock of what happened. Everyone had seen what the wind did to Alyssa and they all shouted questions at her at once.

The doctor pushed his way forward and despite her futile attempts to say she felt fine, insisted on performing a full check-up. He grabbed her hand and moved to the tent they had set up as a hospital. Meanwhile Lex and Patty gathered the group together to take a head count.

A startled cry came from the doctor and Patty rushed over. "Just look at this mess," said the doctor. He held up his hand covered in dark greenish goo.

"That looks like one of those Jelly creatures, doctor. Be careful," warned Patty.

"Was would be a more apt term, and just call me Doc—everyone does," said Doc He leaned over and examined a blob of something on one of his machines. "This appears to have no cohesion at all."

Patty examined the putrid smelling gunk while Doc examined Alyssa. The creature had rolled over the small generator that Doc used to power his equipment. Patty checked that the unit was off, but he knew a small charge constantly ran through it to keep the circuitry open in case of emergency. An idea developed in his head, but he needed to test it further.

"Well, she's all right," said Doc emerging from his tent. "Better send over the rest who need help."

"Right," said Patty absentmindedly. He turned still looking at the unit covered in the remains of a jelly creature and slowly started walking back to the assembly.

As he got closer he could hear Beth talking. "As soon as we can, I suggest we move on." Catching Patty's eye she said, "those who need medical attention get it now. The rest of you start breaking camp. Lex will divide you into teams. Any questions?"

"Why didn't those crazy winds attack us this time," said a voice from the back. "I swear it herded me into the bush, but never hurt me." Cries of agreement echoed over the field. Others had experienced similar events.

"Quiet, QUIET," shouted Beth. "I don't know what happened, but I intend to find out. When I know, I will tell you. Now please, see Lex about your assignments." She moved away and approached Patty.

"She's fine," he said in answer to her unspoken question.

"Good," said Beth. "Patty, I may be out of line here, but I could have sworn I saw you stop Lex from approaching Alyssa when she was caught in that whirlwind. How did you know that it wouldn't hurt her?"

"I didn't," said Patty. "Ethan stopped me!"

"I think we should have a talk," she said firmly. "Find Ethan, Alyssa, and I think Sam as well and meet me in my tent."

"Yes, ma'am," he said and threw her a salute. Chuckling she playfully swatted at the man as he made an exaggerated effort of marching away.

Twenty minutes later they were still no closer to the answer than before. Both Ethan and Sam gave the same reason. They just had a feeling they would be safe and Alyssa was equally vague. She claimed that a calming peace came over her and she didn't feel afraid. After several more attempts to gain more information, Beth finally called a halt to the meeting and dismissed them to start packing.

After they had left, Alyssa grabbed Sam and Ethan roughly by the arm. "All right, you two," she whispered harshly. "I want some answers now. Those feelings came from one of you. Now who did it?"

Both protested their innocence freely. Neither could transmit emotions; much less control the thoughts and feelings of another person. Alyssa felt inclined to believe them, but she still had doubts about Ethan's growing powers.

"I didn't do it," he said. "Honest."

"Then how did you know that I was thinking about you," she accused him. The boy turning man suddenly blushed a deeper red than Alyssa's hair and his chin started quivering.

"Leave him alone," flared Sam hugging Ethan. She looked around frantically and then whispered tightly. "If you must know Ethan can read minds. But he can't transmit. I can't transmit. No one can that I know of."

"But you did transmit to Scrapper, didn't you?"

"Scrapper," exclaimed Ethan. Again the change came over him. No longer a frightened child, but calm intelligence that came from years of experience. "That might be the answer. Wait here please." And off he ran in search of his pet.

"Sam," said Alyssa softly, "is it me, or did I just see Ethan change from a teenage boy into a child, then become a man in the space of a few seconds?"

"I saw it too," said Sam. "Alyssa, there's something very strange about our Ethan. I mean at times he seems older than his 13 years. Sometimes older than Patty."

"Look, I'm sorry I got mad at you. I distinctly felt a calming presence and I thought that since you two had mental abilities…Well, I'm sorry."

"No harm done," said Sam hugging the older woman. "Alyssa, I wouldn't do anything to hurt you. Really!"

Alyssa returned the hug and felt the young woman shake in her embrace. Samantha Torens the socialite was gone. Samantha the whinny, bitchy girl was gone. Only Sam the frightened young woman remained.

"We'll get through this," said Alyssa softly. "I promise, but I'm afraid your father may never forgive me for what I've done to you."

"What do you mean?"

"Look at yourself," she said holding the beautiful young woman at arm's length. "When we first crashed here, you couldn't take ten steps without a servant to help you, now you are a confident, self-assured young woman who's maturing before my eyes."

"If I am, it's because of you. I've…I've never had a big sister, and I find myself looking up to you as my sister. In a way I guess I'm trying to be like you."

Alyssa felt a tug in her chest. She too felt a closeness growing with Sam and the two sisters clutched each other in an affection embrace. They stood arm in arm as Ethan came running up followed closely by Scrapper.

"I think I have an answer," he said. "Sam, I want to try something. Please don't listen Alyssa."

Sam bent down and Ethan whispered in her ear. Her face brightened as Ethan's plan took form in her mind, and then she nodded eagerly. Sam took Alyssa's hand and made her stand facing them, then stood beside Ethan and Scrapper.

Alyssa stood wondering what they were doing, when she got the feeling she was being watched. She dismissed it as there were people walking all around them, but the feeling grew. Something dangerous was watching her. Her eyes cast about looking for signs of danger.

Just when she felt she should warn the others, her instinctive warning system—the same one that had been in the human animal since he fell from the trees—kicked in. She whirled around and dropped into a stance ready to fight the thing that was approaching. Then suddenly the fear and the feeling of danger abated.

"I think that proves your point, Ethan," said Sam. "Alyssa, Alyssa honey, I'm sorry, but we did that to you. There is no danger. Look around. Its safe."

"Don't you see," said Ethan eagerly, "it's Scrapper. He picks up our thoughts and broadcasts them."

"Interesting," said Alyssa concentrating on calming her rapidly beating heart. "But why didn't anyone else feel it?"

"Because you have to have some telepathic abilities to pick it up. Obviously the others are psi null."

"But I don't…" Then it hit her. She too had latent mental powers. "Why haven't I noticed it before?"

"My guess is that your so weak it never really showed before," said Sam. "But it's always been there, helping you. Think. How many times have you been in the right place with the right answer?"

Alyssa stopped and it all fell into place. How did she know about Sam and Lex? How did she know about Adam and A'Serta? Her weak psi powers had gently guided her to those who needed help.

"I have a theory," said Sam. "I believe we're all born with these abilities, but the hundreds and thousands of untrained minds that assault us at birth, cause a short circuit. An overload if you will, and we lose it. Only rarely does someone retain any ability, like myself or Ethan. Others don't lose it entirely, but it remains dormant till needed."

"And you think I've always had this ability and Scrapper helped bring it out?"

"I know it sounds silly," said Sam a little shamefaced, "but it is only a theory."

"As good as one I've ever heard," said Alyssa. "Do you think I'll get stronger?"

"I'm not sure," said Sam. "From what research I've done into my own powers, I don't think so."

"Then what use is it?"

"That's up to you," said the mature Ethan. "What we all do with our gifts and abilities determines who we are. You have something very few people have. How you use it, will depend on you."

"I wish I could use it to figure out you," said Alyssa. "Ethan, is there something about yourself you want to tell us."

"There is," he said thoughtfully, "but I don't know what it is…Can Scrapper and I go help everyone pack now." The little boy had returned.

"Sure," said Alyssa. "I'll see you later." Ethan scurried off and Scrapper followed close behind. Sam shook her head the headed for her tent to start packing.

Alyssa thought about packing, but she burned with questions. Questions that only Ada could answer. She hadn't seen much of the old woman lately. Ada had taken to staying with the elderly and those who had suffered physically from the crash.

She strode across the compound purposefully, her face set in an unreadable mask. As she approached Ada's tent she had to dodge around the flurry of people carrying goods back and forth in preparation for the move. Ada could be seen just entering the tent.

"Ada," she said entering the tent, "can I talk to you about Ethan?'

"Of course, my dear," said Ada kindly. "I really don't know how they expect us to pack in so short a time. Here give me a hand with this chest. No, lift with your knees, not your back. By the way, how are you feeling?"

"Fine. I—."

"—I know I'd be scared out my wits if that horrible wind picked me up, And those ghastly Jelly things. Ugh."

"Ada—."

"Oh yes, of course," said Ada still packing. "I'm sorry to keep you. I know you're busy. Listen do me a favour. Ask that handsome boyfriend of yours if he could spare a couple of people to help us. Just to move the stuff you understand. We're not as young as the rest of you."

"I can stay and help you," said Alyssa hopefully.

"Oh no, my dear," she said. "You have far more important duties to perform. Now I won't hear another word. You get on with your job and I'll make sure we'll be ready to move. Oh, and don't forget to ask Lex for some help will you?"

She turned and moved to the back of the tent and helped an elderly couple pack up their meagre belongings in a pack. Alyssa turned and exited the tent and set out in search of Lex. She had taken several hurried steps before she stopped and smiled. The old woman had neatly manoeuvred her into running an errand and once again avoided talking about Ethan.

"One day, Ada Worensky," she said smiling, "you're going to run out of ideas and then I'll have the truth!"

Three hours later the camp had been packed and forced into packs slung on the backs and shoulders of the survivors. Lex took a final role call and reported to the Captain.

"One hundred and sixty-seven people," he said. His smile disappeared at the sight of Beth's face. Of the original 700 crew and passengers they had only 167 people still alive.

"Once were settled Captain," said Lex hopefully, "I'd like to send a search party out. There's still one of the larger pods unaccounted for. There should be over 100 people still out there."

"Yes," she said tiredly. "Yes, of course. We must find them." She straightened her shoulders and took a deep breath. "If we're ready? Lex, would you lead off?"

"Yes, ma'am," he said and caught Alyssa's eye. She read his silent signal easily. "Stay with her. See what you can do."

Lex picked up his pack and signalled for the party to move out. Slowly like a human tidal wave they began to lumber forward. Patty had stationed people he knew at various points in the column of people to assist if anyone needed help. He stepped to one side and watched the sea of humanity trudge past him. Then took his place in the rear of the column.

Alyssa moved up beside Beth and tried to engage her in conversation, but Beth walked in stony silence. Finally she gave up and excused herself. Dropping back she walked beside Patty.

"What's wrong with Beth?"

"The weight of responsibility is heavy," he said cryptically.

"I don't understand."

"Beth is the Captain," he said, "and responsible."

"But she's not to blame for this," protested Alyssa.

"How much Command Training have you had?"

"I've had some," said Alyssa, "but I've missed quite a few courses."

"Hmmm, well I think you'd better bone up on those classes you missed," he said. His face set in a stony grimace. Alyssa could tell that he felt Beth's pain, but for some reason he wouldn't acknowledge it.

"What's wrong," prodded Alyssa.

Patty stopped and Alyssa stopped beside him. "Beth has a lot on her mind right now and she doesn't need some young inexperienced officer butting in where she's not wanted."

"But-."

"Listen," he said more softly. "If you really want to help, complete your training. You're the Chief Engineer now. She's going to need all the support we can give her."

"And just how am I to complete my training trapped on this god-forsaken world?"

"You're the Chief Engineering Officer," he said angrily. "You tell me!" And so saying he started jogging to catch up with the rest, effectively cutting off any further conversation.

Alyssa felt hurt by the brusque manner Patty had talked to her. She wondered what she had done to deserve such treatment and felt angry. Slinging her pack angrily of her shoulder she set a determined march. If that's the way they wanted to be, then fine!

A couple of hours later Lex called a rest break and the party settled down in the soft grass. Alyssa still fuming sat alone behind the convoy. A couple of people approached to chat, but one glimpse of her scowling face they turned and bid a hasty retreat.

Lex came back and sat down beside her. She scowled at him, but he wouldn't budge. He just sat there and stared into the distance. She glared at him, but he just smiled back. This infuriated so much she broke her silence and yelled at him.

"What are you smiling about?"

"That's better," he said. "Now, want to tell me what's wrong?"

"NO."

"Fine," he said lying down in the grass, "but we're not moving till you tell me. And since I'm in charge of this little trip…"

She got up and paced rapidly. Round and round she moved. Soon her rapid pacing slowed as the anger in her diminished. Eventually she sat down beside Lex and told him the conversation she had with Patty.

"And you think he was wrong to talk to you like that," said Lex chewing on a blade of grass.

"Of course," said Alyssa indignantly. "Don't you?"

"No," said Lex firmly. "In fact I think he was very lenient. Lys, I love you, but your ego and stubbornness has finally gotten you in trouble. NO. You listen to me. When you accepted the responsibility for Chief Engineer you accepted all the rules and conditions. It is not my concern that we are no longer near command central for you to receive your training. That is your concern. You have a choice. Find a way to get that information or run away as you always have. Yes, I know about you. Now what are you going to do?"

"Lex, I don't…"

"If you really want to help," he said tenderly, "you have to know what she is going through. I've got to get this crowd moving, but if I were you I'd think about your options." He rose and before she had a chance to say anything had started rousing the group. Minutes later the march started again.

They arrived at the caves just before nightfall and Lex quickly divided them up. Patty posted a watch and they built a large community fire to prepare supper. Exhausted, the ragtag survivors ate in silence. After trudging through the jungle in the heat, most of them were ready for bed. The caves proved to be dirty and smelled a little musty, but they offered something they had never had. The caves were deep into the mountain and the rear promised a cool, comfortable sleep.

When most of the camp had finally retired, Alyssa moved closer to Lex and Patty still stoking the fire. Beth had already retired and as she approached Patty made motions of yawning.

"Wait, please don't go," said Alyssa softly. "I have a favour to ask of both of you. Lex, you were right. I've been so involved with myself for the last few years; it blinded me to helping the people I care about. You both say that the only way I can help Beth is to understand what the problem is. And the only way to do that is to complete my Command Training."

She paused and waited for them to say something, but they just sat there, immobile. Their faces never changed from their stony stare. "I know I can't get the training at the school, but I had a thought. Lex, you've had all the courses and I'm sure you Patty, have had similar classes in the military. Would you two be willing to teach me?"

Lex smiled, but Patty frowned and said, "are you sure you really want to learn? It means you'll be accepting a lot more responsibility than just a title. Think about this. If we teach you all we know. You will have to live with that decision as it will be recorded."

"I figured as much," she said softly. "Lex, Patty, I've been avoiding this for years, but I can't anymore. I can't promise to be the best student you've ever had, but if it will help me understand what is going on, then I'm willing to put all my effort into it."

"Then I must tell you," said Patty. "I am a certified instructor. If at the end of the course, I feel that you are competent, I will so note in the log. This means you can and will be called on to command. If I feel you are not fit I will note that as well, and quite probably you will be dismissed from the service, never to serve on a Starship again. Do you understand?"

Alyssa gulped noisily. All of a sudden all her fears surfaced again. If she took the course and passed, she would be in command. If she failed, well she couldn't bear the thought of never going into space again. Never working on her beloved engines. The third alternative was to not take the course, but she found that that upset her even more than the chance of failure.

"I owe Beth and you a lot more than you could ever realize," she said. "I know I have some problems, but I'm willing to work through them if you'll help. At your earliest convenience I would like to start my training."

"I knew you would," said Patty beaming. He rose and hugged her tightly. She clung to him, relishing again in the feeling of the fatherly affection he had shown. She wanted to make him proud of her and was determined to pass this course, no matter what it did to her psyche.

Chapter 13

"It's been 6 months since we crash landed on this alien world," said Alyssa into her 'corder. They had salvaged several from the pod wrecks and Beth had given one to Alyssa, to record any events of interest. "Things have been a lot better since we moved into the caves. The ghost winds I told you about have reappeared three times. Each time they seem to herd us in a particular direction. Usually they appear just before some sort of danger. We don't know how or why, but they have become our guardian angels."

Alyssa turned off the unit and gazed wistfully into the sky, praying and hoping for rescue. This hostile alien world seemed hell-bent on wiping them out, one at a time. The ghost winds were terrifying, but not nearly as bad as the other hazards.

"Patty thinks he has a plan to stop the Jellyrolls," she said back into the 'corder. "They're those rolling blobs of jelly I told you about. Patty says that an electrical shock will break the membrane that holds it together. The only problem is, he's not sure how much juice it will take, and our generator is suffering from fungus rot again."

The constant heat and humidity proved a breeding ground for fungus. Sure the cool nights slowed it down, but if left unchecked, it would attach itself to anything not moving, and slowly penetrate. Eventually totally consuming the object. During the first few months, they had lost most of their meagre rations to the fungus. Fortunately, the farmers in the group had found many forms of edible plant life and they cultivated a small field just south of the caves.

"Our food supply, while still low is recovering quickly. The farmers are thrilled with the soil and growing conditions. Plants seem to grow at a fantastic rate here. As for meat protein, we found several small animals similar to jackrabbits, which are easy to catch, and cook up well. Personally I think they taste like old shoe leather, but Beth says that it's because my taste buds are used to replicated food. Still, I think I'm actually acquiring a taste for Jack meat. The deer we found on the first hunt appear to be scarce. We've only caught a glimpse of the herd since then."

She paused to wipe the ever-present sweat from her brow. Dressed in the outfit made by Karen, she still couldn't endure the heat. The others had become accustomed to the perpetual 100-degree weather, but Alyssa still longed for the cool, controlled environment of a ship. Karen true to her word, as soon as they moved camp, had started teaching everyone how to make clothes out of the rabbit skins. Now most of the camp now looked like well-dressed savages.

"Oh, for all the botanists who hear this, look out for the Pleasure tree. It looks similar to an Earthly weeping willow, but it's totally carnivorous. The tree remains dormant until a warm blooded creature approaches. Then its branches come alive and whip back and forth until they grasp something. Once caught, the animal has no chance to escape. Doc says it injects a poison into the animals system that causes sensations similar to euphoria. Then it drains the blood and other bodily juices while the victim drifts off into happy land…We lost several good friends until we learned to identify them, and give them a wide berth."

"Hi, sweetheart," said Lex from behind her. He bent over and kissed her softly on the top of the head. Sitting down beside her, he looked at the 'corder in her hands. "Updating the log?"

"Yeah," she said. "Beth said to keep up with the information, and I realized I hadn't made an entry in months. I hope there's enough room on this thing. We could be here a long time."

"No problem," said Lex taking the 'corder and examining it. "This is one of the XJ-23 series 'corder's. They use a high-density crystal that records on a molecular level. You could talk into this thing every day for two years and it would still have room."

"Lex," said Alyssa softly, "do you think we'll ever get out of here? I mean it's been six months already. I would have expected some sort of help by now."

"That's what we were just talking about," he said referring to Beth, Patty, and himself. "Beth remains optimistic. She thinks another couple of months and we'll be out of here. Patty on the other hand, thinks we should start thinking about building a community."

"What about you?"

"I'm in the middle," he said and picked up a long blade of grass and started to chew it. "I'm with Beth. I think we'll be rescued soon, but I also agree with Patty. We can't live in these caves forever. We need more room. We've already had four reported pregnancies. Pretty soon there will be a lot of little babies and children running around."

The news of the pregnancies shocked Alyssa. How could people in such a desperate situation even think about bringing a child into this mess? She thought the men and women involved, foolhardy, and stupid, and she told Lex so.

"Honey," he said gently. "You can't stop human nature. The more dangerous the situation, the more likely we are to have children. It's nature's way of ensuring the species doesn't die out. I know they should be able to stop the urges, but one thing I've learned, When a woman wants a child, no force in the universe is going to stop her."

Alyssa nodded slowly. Thoughts surfaced from many years ago when she and Trenor were together. She wanted to start a family. The more Trenor put it off, the more the desire overcame her. Only the fact that Trenor had left had cooled her fevered desire. Recalling how she felt for that short time, she could easily see how these women would willing have a child, even on this hell-hole of a world.

"Besides," said Lex, "haven't you noticed what's happening? Relationships are being created almost overnight. People who were complete strangers a few months ago are marrying and having children."

"Yeah, I noticed," she said. "I thought they were just clinging, because they're scared. But that instance with A'Serta got me thinking."

"And that little episode with Sam!"

"And that," she agreed. "Lex, don't you think it strange. I mean even the Captain seems affected by this whatever. She and Patty are rarely apart now and Sam seems to be on the prowl."

"Actually, I think she's set her sights on a young hunter, but don't let on you know. She's come a long way since we first landed, but she still can be a handful when upset."

Alyssa nodded. Sam had become the sister she never had. They would stay up late at night giggling and talking about those things that would make Lex or any man blush if he ever found out.

Quickly to avoid being drawn into a speculative conversation she changed the subject back to the problem at hand. "So what do we do now?"

"There's going to be a community meeting after supper," said Lex. "Which reminds me as to why I sought you out. We would like you to reconsider and join the Council. I know, I know. You're an engineer, not a politician. But the people respect you, and follow you. Many of them took it as a sign that we were done for when you refused to join the Council."

"But that's crazy," she said. "Look. You guys are all experienced in these matters. I would just bollix up everything. Don't you see? I only know machines. Everything else I see with a layman's eye."

"And that's exactly why you should join," he said eagerly. Then softly, almost secretively he whispered. "We really need you. The problem with the Council is that everyone is a politician. We spend all of our time arguing. We need a voice of reason and common sense. Someone to remind us why we're here and what has to be done."

"And you think I'm that voice of reason! What makes you think that my voice will be heard amongst all of yours?"

Lex laughed loudly and placed an affection hand on her shoulder. "Sweetheart, if anyone knows how persuasive you can be, it's me. I don't know how or why, but after all this time, with all your refusals to marry me, I still love you. Somehow my paranoid love, you inspire trust and respect in people, and love. Yes, the people love you, but you don't see it." He grabbed her shoulders and turned her to face him. "We need a leader. That leader is you."

"Me," she scoffed. "Beth is the Captain. She should be in charge."

"Beth doesn't want to be Mayor. Yes, I said Mayor. If the people vote to build a community, they will need a Mayor. We on the Council prefer to advise and recommend, but the people will follow you. I know it's a lot, but think about it." He stood up and looked back in direction of camp. "We'll be holding the meeting after supper. If you decide to join us, let me know."

"You can't do this to me, Lex," she cried. "It's unfair to put this on my shoulders. I can't…"

"Why," demanded Lex? "Why can't you? Look I know what you can do, and so does everyone else. You've almost completed your training. We all trust you and have faith in you."

Yes, her command training was going well. Even Patty had nothing but praise for her, but she still felt unsure. She took the training to help Beth, but after finding out what Beth was going through, she realized there was nothing to do but be supportive.

"I'm sorry," she sobbed. "I just can't."

"Then I'm sorry as well," said Lex softly. "Whatever your problem is, get over it." His voice took on a harshness she never heard before. "While I hope to be rescued soon, I must also be realistic and plan on being here a long, long time. We must all work together and use the skills and gifts we have to survive. If you think so little of yourself and us, to deny us the use of your abilities, then you may want to reconsider the way your life is. Honey, I love you, but this is our survival we're talking about. No one person is so important that the rest must be sacrificed. Think about it, Huh?"

Lex strode purposefully away, not even glancing back over his shoulder. The tone and harsh words from Lex upset Alyssa greatly. Hadn't she done all she could? Hadn't she formed the first base camp and kept everyone together? Didn't they realize that she couldn't assume control?

The memories of that fateful time rushed to the surface as if seeking escape: The continual drinking after Trenor had left. The days of abandoning her responsibilities by showing up drunk for work in the morning. The fatal day then lab blew up, killing a close friend, her husband, and scores of others. No, she wouldn't be responsible for anyone else's life again, Command training or no Command training.

She hung her head down in the heat. Sweat ran down her face and mixed with her tears, making a salty wet stain on the front of her top.

Her gentle sobs uncorked a flood of buried tension and emotion and she bawled loudly. Tears and sobs racked her lithe frame, but try as she might to gain control of herself, the tide refused to stem. The tension and stress of the last few months needed to be released. Now it had the opportunity, and it wouldn't be denied.

"Here, here," said a gentle voice behind her. "Whatever the problem is, I'm sure it's not worth flooding us all out for." Alyssa turned and through tear blurred eyes saw the smiling face of Ada.

"I'm sorry," sobbed Alyssa again feeling the compulsion to confide in the woman who had become a surrogate mother not only to Ethan, but Alyssa and many others as well. "Oh Ada. I don't know what to do."

"There, there, my child," said Ada drooping down beside her. "Tell me what's wrong." Alyssa wanted to tell her story, but something stopped her short. Once again that little voice inside her. The one that had tormented her all these years, wouldn't let the story come out.

"It's nothing," said Alyssa sniffing back the tears. "Just a little frazzled that's all!"

"Bull," said Ada. "Don't try to con me dear. I've been around a lot longer than you and I can recognize a problem when I see it. Take my advice. Sooner or later, you're going to have to face those fears. Oh, I don't know what your problem is, but I do know there's something troubling you deeply. If it helps, I promise not to talk about it to anyone?"

Alyssa smiled in-spite of herself. Ada could charm the birds from the trees when she smiled. She treated Alyssa as a daughter and Alyssa welcomed the attention and affection given by the old woman. Slowly, almost reluctantly, the bothersome little voice in her head quieted down, and Alyssa soon found herself spilling the whole story into the patient and understanding ear of her surrogate mother.

When she finished, she looked hesitantly into the wrinkled face of her friend. Not knowing what to expect she feared the worst. That Ada would belittle her for being silly, and chastise her for throwing her life away. But Ada just smiled and opened her arms in invitation—as she had done many times before. Alyssa melted into the older woman's embrace and hugged her close.

"Feel better, my child," said Ada softly.

"Yes, thank you," said Alyssa. "Oh Ada. What am I to do?"

"I can't tell you that," she said softly stroking the hair from Alyssa's forehead. "That's for you to decide. But whatever you decide, remember that I'll always love you. But you didn't confide in me to hear that. You're looking for sound sage advice. Well I'm sorry to say that I have none. This is war. A war with only one player! It will never end until you choose to end it."

"I'm so confused," said Alyssa. "For years I avoided command and control in any fashion. Then later I justified my avoidance to myself in a hundred different ways. Now it seems that once again, I'm being thrust into a position I don't want."

"Are you sure, my dear? It seems to me that while you've consciously avoided command, you nevertheless seek it out. Face it, my dear. You're born to lead and command. The war in you is not about the responsibility of command, nor the lives in your control. No, the war is about your fear of failure."

Alyssa looked at her friend with a puzzled expression, but Ada fell silent, waiting for Alyssa to work it out. Slowly it dawned on her. She had avoided command, yes, but she had also accepted command. But only for those areas she felt confident. Anytime the situation called for abilities or skills she was unsure about, she retreated. Left usually.

Ada hugged Alyssa again, then disengaged, and stood up. Brushing the dirt off her dress she said, "I'd better get back. It's my turn to help prepare dinner."

"Thank you," said Alyssa softly.

"For what? You worked it out yourself. I was only a sympathetic ear."

"Sometimes," said Alyssa, "that's all it takes." Ada smiled and trekked slowly back to camp. The constant dampness had started to affect the elderly woman lately. If this had been any other place, she could have popped into the nearest med-complex and received treatment, but here she had no such resources. Doc, jealously guarded any medication they had, in case of emergency. Alyssa admired the way the woman bore her troubles. She knew that Ada was in tremendous pain, but rarely did she even let out a squeak.

Alyssa sat pondering her situation until the setting sun reminded her to return to camp. It wasn't safe to be outside the protection of the caves after dark. On the way back she detoured by the farms to check on the vegetables. There she found several of the farmers scratching their heads in frustration.

"What's up?" Briefly they explained how the Jellyrolls would sweep by at night and crush the new shoots. Jellyrolls didn't eat the plants; they just crushed them flat when they rolled through.

"The older plants recover all right," said one weather beaten old farmer, "but the seedlings get ground into the dirt. If it weren't for the Jellyrolls we would have twice as much food. Frankly we're stumped."

"We put up a wire fence around the plot," said his wife leaning on her make shift shovel. "But the damn things just seem to ooze right though it."

"Well," said Alyssa thoughtfully. "Patty thinks an electrical shock might cause them to disassociate. Maybe if we energized the fence it might do the job?"

"A good idea," said the first farmer. "But power is at a premium. We can't afford to shoot all that juice into the fence. The generator would burn out in no time."

"Oh, I don't mean charge it enough to kill the Jellyroll," said Alyssa. "If we run a small current through, just enough to give them a shock, then maybe they won't be so eager to slip through."

"It's worth a try," said the third farmer. "That much energy shouldn't seriously deplete our fuel supplies, and it might buy us some time to get a good healthy crop going. Thanks Alyssa. You're a genius."

She brushed off their compliments. "Just trying to help," she said. "Part of my job you know." They thanked her and quickly moved to set up the generator before nightfall.

Alyssa continued walking, waving and shouting to people she passed on the way. Everyone was busily closing down whatever chores they were doing in an effort to get back to camp before nightfall. As she walked, she thought. Then like a flash it hit her. What she had told the farmer was the truth.

"It is part of my job," she said loudly to no one in particular.

"Hi, Alyssa," came a cry from her left. She squinted in the gathering darkness to see who called and found Ethan running happily towards her. His ever present sidekick, Scrapper bounded beside him. "So you're going to become our first Mayor. I'm glad."

Alyssa was about to deny the charge when she suddenly stopped. "What makes you say that, Ethan?"

"I can see it in your mind." Suddenly he stopped and clasped his hands over his mouth in fear. "I'm sorry, Alyssa. I forget I'm not supposed to talk about that."

"It's all right," she said. "I know how easily you forget when playing with Scrapper." She bent down to stroke the furry mane of Scrapper. "How ya doing, boy? Keeping an eye on Ethan? Making sure he doesn't get into trouble?" In response Scrapper snaked his long soft tongue out and licked Alyssa's face.

"You're not going to tell Sam on me are you, Alyssa." He looked so fearful, Alyssa had to chuckle. Sam had turned into his mentor. While he viewed Alyssa more as a mother figure, he bowed to Sam's expertise in these matters. She had proved to be a strict taskmaster, but fair. She constantly reminded Ethan that people objected to anyone reading their thoughts without permission.

"No, I won't tell," assured Alyssa. "It was an accident. I must have been broadcasting all over the place."

"You were pretty loud," said Ethan. "Even Scrapper heard you."

"Well, I won't tell, if he won't." Alyssa smiled and Ethan hugged her while Scrapper did his best to worm his way in-between the two of them. They laughed and rubbed his big head. "Besides," she said. "You helped me make up my mind. Come on you two. It's getting dark, and I'm hungry."

The three friends moved off into the twilight to be joined by farmers and hunters from the forest. When they arrived at the camp, the fire was already blazing, lighting up the compound. Smells of fresh cooked food and appetizing aromas of assorted fruits reached their nostrils.

Alyssa didn't realize how hungry she was until her mouth slavered in anticipation of the feast. She sat on the ground near the fire and waited her turn to get dinner. As she gazed into the flickering flames, Lex came over and sat beside her.

"Alyssa," he said softly. "I'm sorry about the way I spoke earlier. I was out of line and I apologize." In response Alyssa cupped his head in her hands and kissed him passionately.

"Don't apologize," she said. "You helped me more than you know."

"Does that mean you'll be Mayor?"

She nodded and held up a finger of caution. "Only," she said, "if the group votes to build a settlement and only if they all want me to. The Council will rule, with the Captain still retaining command. I'll just organize the community. Is that all right?"

"Wonderful," cried Lex. He kissed her quickly then got up and darted off into the darkness.

Soon it was Alyssa's turn to eat and she gratefully accepted the tree bark plate. As she passed down the log table containing the food, she helped herself to the assortment of food. She heaped her plate with the assorted fruits. They grew in abundance around the camp, so she felt no guilt with them. Then she carefully put some of the hard earned vegetables on her plate. At the end of the table lay the cut up carcasses of several roasted Jacks. Normally she had only a few small pieces; today she allowed herself a full helping.

Mealtime at the camp was always a festive occasion. During the day, the people were too concerned about survival to socialize, but at night, when the sun went down, then everyone would gather and talk about the day's events. Sometimes the stories were short, usually about preparing food or doing the daily chores about camp, but no one seemed to mind. The stories that everyone waited for were those of new discoveries.

A group of hunters announced they had found a pack of deer. They had brought back a small one and held up a large plate of roasted deer meat for a treat. Everyone had a small helping of the soft tender meat. They promised to capture a few more tomorrow. Someone in the dark suggested capturing a few and penning them up. Maybe raise a breeding stock. This brought another discussion of how long they would be marooned on this alien world that wavered back and forth for the next hour.

Soon Beth stood and called for quiet. Eventually only the sound of insects permeated the air. "My friends," she began. "We have been here for six months, and through good fortune and a lot of work, we have survived. We of the Council have a proposal. While we hope to be rescued soon, it is clear that we need more permanent quarters." Not a sound came from the group as they listened respectfully.

"What we propose is to build a community, a settlement, or village if you prefer. All the material for housing is readily available and I can think of no better location than this. It still leaves us the caves in an emergency. Now before you decide I must warn you that there are several considerations."

"If you're worried about food," said a voice from the darkness. "Don't. We're trying an experiment to keep the Jellyrolls out of the vegetable garden and it seems to be working. Thanks to a suggestion from Alyssa."

"As for water," said another voice. "I found an underground stream just above the caves. If we tap it and run pipes, we can have fresh running water in no time."

"Well, it seems we on the Council aren't the only ones thinking about this. Since it's too dark to see a show of hands, I will ask you all to cast a vote whether we build a life here, or continue hoping to be rescued soon. Lex, would you…Thank you. Please pick up a pebble. One only please and cast your vote. Lex will place the buckets near the old tree in the back. The one on the left means we build. The one on the right means we don't. Now one at a time, please vote."

She sat down and Patty placed a protective arm around her. Over the last few months they had grown very close, and he sensed the strain that Beth was under. Time seemed to crawl by as the survivors voted with their conscience. Eventually Lex went to retrieve the buckets. He didn't count them but instead stood in the glow of the fire.

"This is the bucket to build," he announced and upended it. Small rocks and pebbles of different sizes rained down on the ground. "This is the one to continue the way we are. He turned it over and three rocks fell out. "I guess we build."

A thunderous cheer sounded from the group. Then a voice from the back called for attention. "Listen," he said. "If we are going to be a community then I think we should have a leader."

This time Patty stood up and addressed the crowd. "We also agree with that. Not only because it's a good idea to have a central focal point, but also because it helps us to retain a modicum of civilization in this wilderness. I would like everyone to think of someone to nominate for Mayor. I would like to nominate Alyssa Krychech."

"Second," shouted Lex.

"Anyone else interested in being the first Mayor of our community, please give your names to…Sam can you do it?" She nodded and he continued. "Give your names to Sam and we'll have another vote."

Patty sat down and the buzz through the crowd grew louder as they argued who would be the best to lead them in this new venture. Occasionally Beth or Patty's names were mentioned. Patty stood up and announced that all members of the Council would not participate. He explained that they would help and advise the Mayor, but they themselves would not run.

The group returned to their discussions and several people approached Sam. Privately she whispered and talked with these people who disappeared back into the shadows. After an hour, Patty asked if they were ready to nominate their candidates. They all agreed and Patty called for quiet and asked Sam to come forward.

"Now. I want everyone to understand that this is a nomination only," said Patty. "You will get the chance to vote for the person you want later. Okay Sam. Who are the candidates?"

Sam stood up and cleared her throat. "The first candidate is Alyssa Krychech." Then she sat down.

"What about the rest?" Asked Patty, looking puzzled.

"There is nobody else," replied Sam with a smile "Every person who came to speak to me claimed to be speaking for a group of people, and they all wanted Alyssa."

"Then I think we can do without a vote," said Patty. He turned to Beth beside him and said, "My dear, if you will?"

Beth stood up, her posture becoming firm and decisive. Once more showing herself to be the Captain. "The people have spoken. Alyssa my child, come here…As the Captain of the ship and leader of the Council I ask you in front of the Council and the people. Do you accept the position of Mayor and promise to forever safeguard her people?"

Alyssa hesitated. Could she really take full command? Bear the responsibility for the lives and well being of the people, even though true command remained with the Council and Beth. Then her eye caught Ada's smiling face and Ethan's eager expectant smile. "I promise," she said firmly. "To do the best I can. I can do no more."

The crowd erupted in a cheering yelling frenzy. Beth kissed Alyssa lightly. Patty grabbed her, and held her close. In her ear he whispered so no one else could listen. "I'm proud of you." That little phrase made Alyssa warm all over. Suddenly the rest of the group swarmed her. For the next thirty minutes she gave and received kisses in congratulations and support.

Soon cries of "Speech. Speech." Echoed in the firelight. A couple of people grabbed the abandoned buckets and turned them upside down on the ground. A plank was placed across them, and they helped Alyssa to stand on her makeshift podium.

"My friends," she said. "For my first speech as Mayor, I'll make it short cause it's getting late. We have a lot of work to-do. In the morning I would like to see all those people who have had experience designing or building homes. For now though, I suggest we turn in. One thing you may want to think about is a name for our community. Good night my friends and thank you. I'll try to justify your belief in me." She stepped down to thunderous applause and drifted off into the darkness.

As she moved away from the glow of the fire, the stars became more pronounced and lit up the sky with thousands of pinpricks of light. Alyssa looked up and she felt herself drawn closer to the shimmering distant points of light. So absorbed in her sight, she failed to notice when Lex came up beside her. Still she didn't see or hear him until he put his arms around her. Then she suddenly jumped and let out a little shriek.

"Jumpy tonight," he said amused. "Does this mean you're going to burst into giggles in bed tonight?"

She looked at him with a wry smile then poked him in the ribs. The two lovers playful attacked each other for a few minutes until they both collapsed with laughter and exhaustion. They lay down in the cooling grass and stared up at the stars. Alyssa cuddled herself in the crook of Lex's arm and snuggled up close.

Much later, Alyssa confided with Lex. She told him of her fears and how Ada and Ethan had helped her overcome them. She also made special mention of how he brought it all to the front. When he tried to apologize again, she shut him up by kissing him deeply.

"Don't get any ideas," she said at last.

"What about?"

"That you'll get special favours because you're sleeping with the Mayor."

"I'm shocked," he feigned horror. "I would never think that. Just for that comment, Madame Mayor, if you will excuse me, I think there must be some woman around who really wants me." He moved to get up and Alyssa tackled him to the ground.

"You do," she threatened, "and I'll make sure you never walk upright again. Understand me?" To make her point clear she reached down between his legs and squeezed gently.

"Absolutely," he laughed gently prying her fingers away. They cuddled some more, then made their way back to the fire. It had died down considerably and only the night watch remained to tend the burning embers. They waved good night to the tenders and climbed into the small alcove that Alyssa shared with Ada and Sam. In the doorway Lex kissed her good night again.

"Goodnight, Madame Mayor," he said softly. He stole away in the darkness to his cave. Alyssa felt her way gently into the dark recess and found her bed. As she lay down, a small light turned on and she found Ada and Sam smiling at her.

"I don't know," said Sam to Ada in a stage whisper. "She's come so far. And yet she's still unbetrothed. Where did we go wrong?"

"I just don't know," said Ada with an amusing grin. "Children these days are so hard to raise."

"Quite right," said Sam. "In my day if a man pledged his undying love, you nabbed him quick and got married before some other woman took him."

"Oh, I agree," said Ada, "but you know how pig headed and stubborn she is."

"All right, you two," laughed Alyssa. "That's enough. In my day! Pooh. Sam, you're younger than me. As for you, you old fraud…" The other two women laughed and Ada set the tiny light in a niche they had carved out some weeks ago. Then as all good close friends do, they talked into the late hours of the night about life, love, and marriage.

Chapter 14

The next morning found Alyssa up early walking around the small community compound. *I'm the mayor*, she thought, *people are looking to me for leadership and guidance...Can I do it?*

As she walked, she absentmindedly kicked at the loose pebbles and stones making them skip in front of her. No one had shoes anymore. Those few that survived the constant wear and resisted the insipid fungus rot, were carefully sealed in plastic and were kept protected – just in case. Although the first few weeks were a little rough on everybody, they soon developed hardened calluses and could run, jump, skip on the rocky ground as if they wore the most versatile shoe ever created.

But as Alyssa kicked at the inoffensive rocks, one particular stone decided, "oh no you don't either," and her foot smashed into the immovable object causing her to cry out in pain and drop the floor to massage her throbbing toe.

"Some mayor I'll make," she said to the wind and rubbed her sore foot. "Can't even walk without stubbing my toe."

"You weren't elected because of your skills as a ballerina." Alyssa whirled to see the smiling face of Patty coming towards her.

"How long have you been there," she asked?

"Not long," he said with a smile. "Just long enough to see you kick a buried mountain."

"Mountain is right," she said and began to scrape away the loose dirt surrounding the tiny pebble, which refused to move. After a couple of minutes, it was obvious that this was no pebble, but the tip of a rather large boulder.

"C'mon," he waved. "Breakfast will be ready shortly and we all have a lot to do."

The two friends slowly walked to eating area, arm in arm. As they approached, voices called out greetings among them were many "Good morning Madame Mayor." Alyssa flinched each time she heard the cry and automatically clutched Patty's arm tighter.

"Don't worry," he said gently. "Say good morning."

Alyssa waved at people at returned their greetings with as much enthusiasm as she could muster. The mood this morning was one of joy and enthusiasm and Alyssa soon found herself warming to the occasion and soon was laughing and the stories. After breakfast she asked the council members to meet with her.

"Okay, now what do we do," she asked?

"You tell us," replied Beth. "You're the mayor." Obviously the council was serious in giving her the authority she needed to be mayor. For some reason, Alyssa felt strangely comforted by this gesture of faith.

"Well…" she said hesitantly. " I guess we should discuss how to set up a permanent community like we discussed." The others nodded in agreement. When she didn't say anything else, Lex spoke in the awkward silence.

"I've never built a community before," he said loudly. "I don't even know where to begin." He stole a glance at Alyssa who gave a small smile as if to say, "thanks."

" I suggest that we brainstorm what we want, then see what can be done," added Patty. The small council huddled together and with the help of a few electronic pads, and a lot of drawing crude pictures in the dirt, hammered out their ideas for a permanent community.

They broke for lunch, confident that they had found a suitable arrangement and chatted freely during the repast. After lunch, Alyssa stood on her makeshift podium and called for attention.

"My friends, is it still your desire to build a community we can live in?" A chorus of agreement reached her ears. "Then I would like anyone with skills in building, designing and construction to meet with the council in 15 minutes." She stepped of the podium and Lex winked at her.

Twenty minutes later, Alyssa brought the small assemblage together. Each person told of their particular skills and Alyssa divided them into two distinct groups. Those that would create the new community and those that would build it.

She outlined the councils' plan for the fledgling village. The designers found flaws and suggested alternatives, the builders said they couldn't do certain things with the resources at hand and suggested alternate ideas. They worked through diner and far into the night, but when they retired, they had a workable plan.

The next morning, Alyssa met with the several young men and women, who would be the architects and they began the laborious task and laying out the details. Everything from housing to plumbing had to be considered. They rejected individual commodes and opted for central buildings for the time being. Meanwhile the builder group were busy scrounging material for makeshift tools. Pocketknives, pieces of metal from the pods, anything they could get their hands on were hammered and shaped into crude tools.

A week later with all the plans drawn up and approved, construction of the first house began. Trees were sought and marked for felling. Then a team armed with saws made from the casings of the pods moved in, and started to cut down the trees. Another group hauled them out of the forest. While a third, split planks and trimmed them to size.

So smoothly and efficiently did they run, that the first crude shack went up in less than three days! That night a big celebration was held to commemorate the event. The people wanted it to be Alyssa's house, but she said they needed the space for food storage. Her arguments won, and they filled the first shed with food supplies.

Over the next few months, houses and storage sheds appeared in the compound at the rate of one a week. Crude by anyone's standards, they were nevertheless built well and strong. Still though, the villagers were unsure about leaving the safety of the caves. One day a massive rainstorm suddenly developed, sending everyone scampering back into the caves. It was Alyssa with Lex, who stayed in one of the huts. When the storm abated, the rest came out to see them sitting calm, and dry, in the shack. After that, no one hesitated to use the crude shelters.

The first real home was set-up for Adam and A'Serta. They had been the first official marriage on this new world and Alyssa felt it only right they have the very first home.

Occasionally a Jellyroll would wander into camp, but cries of alarm would warn everyone to keep clear. Using Alyssa's idea of a low voltage fence, Patty and a few others, dug a shallow trench around the camp. In this they laid an unsheathed wire and connected it to the generator. When the switch was thrown, a soft hum came from the generator.

Patty walked to the edge of the buried cable and while the current was still on, stepped over it. He didn't seem to suffer any effects and stepped back. Suddenly the cry of "Jellyroll" echoed from the far side of camp. Patty and Alyssa, with many others in tow, dashed to the other side of the village.

A Jellyroll, larger than most, had come out of the underbrush and was charging towards the village. The people scattered, but Patty and Alyssa held their ground. If this was to work, they had to show the people they had no worries. The Jellyroll came on faster and faster as it sought food. Then all of a sudden it slowed and rolled to a stop a scant few feet from where Patty stood.

It backed up, then tried to roll forward again, each time stopping just in front of the buried wire. "It works," cried Alyssa happily.

"Maybe," said Patty thoughtfully. "There's only one way to test it." Before Alyssa could do or say anything, Patty jumped over the buried cable and ran into the brush. The Jellyroll swiftly followed its prey. Patty circled around then sprinted for the compound.

The Jellyroll for all its cumbersome bulk could move with remarkable speed and swiftness. As Patty made a mad dash for safety the Jellyroll extended a pseudopod to try to grasp him by the leg. Patty dove over the line in the dirt where the cable lay buried. The extended appendage of the Jellyroll suddenly stopped short as if it hit a brick wall. The large rolling mass of its body flattened itself out and it pancaked in the dirt. When the dust settled, they saw the Jellyroll formed again into a pulsating blob. It had stopped dead in its tracks on the other side of the cable.

The rest of the onlookers cheered as the Jellyroll moved around the compound trying to find a way into the village. Eventually its primitive hunting mind told it, that it wouldn't find any game here today, and it rolled away in search of other prey.

"I should bust you back to foetus for a stunt like that," said Beth as she helped Patty stand back up.

"I had to know whether it would stop a charging, hungry Jellyroll or not," said Patty smiling. "Obviously it does. But the problem now is…How do we maintain the current? Our fuel supply for the generator is running dangerously low."

"I have an idea about that," chimed in Alyssa. "Where's Shayna? Someone fetch Shayna." When a runner had departed, she turned her attention to the others. "Shayna is the electrical genius keeping the generator going," she explained.

Shayna arrived a few seconds later and Alyssa presented her proposal. "We're getting our water from that underground stream, right? Well what about rigging a water wheel to run a turbine. Could you generate enough electricity to run the fields?"

Shayna thought for a moment, doing the mental calculations needed for the task. "We have most of the materials on hand," she said, "and I can scrounge or adapt the rest from the scrap out of the pods, but I'm sorry, Alyssa, it won't work. The rate of flow out of the mountain is just not enough to provide is with a real steady power. I need something a little more powerful and steady."

So you need a waterfall, thought Alyssa. *Well, it was just an idea. Sorry, folks.*

"It's a good idea," said Patty. "Look. We've almost finished construction. Why don't I take an exploration party out and see if I can't scare us up a waterfall or something?"

"It doesn't necessarily have to be a waterfall," said Shayna. "A fast flowing river or stream would do. Not as well, but I can work with it."

"Very well," said Alyssa. "Tomorrow, Patty, you take several people with you and see what you can find. Remember though that our supply of cable is limited. If it's too far away it might as well be on another planet."

Patty nodded and departed to collect supplies for the next day. Considering the deepness of the underbrush and the jungle, it could take them several days to cover a couple of square miles. So he handpicked the people to accompany him and they collected all their gear.

The next morning Patty with four others, shouldered their packs and amidst cheery waves, set off on their journey. When they passed out of sight, Alyssa directed everyone to fortifying the compound. The electrified cable might keep out Jellyrolls, but there were otherND dangers that wouldn't be so easily dissuaded.

Under her direction, sharpened stakes were jammed into the ground, their spikes facing into the sky. She placed them around the compound at an average height of six feet. Then she ordered a second row to be staggered from the first, behind the others. When Ada wondered why she explained.

"Have you ever seen an animal like a deer run and jump? They can jump pretty high when they want to. This second row is just in case some animal on this world can jump that high. Instead of landing in the compound it will land on the second set of spikes."

When at last all the spikes were pounded into the ground. Alyssa and the Council made an inspection of the grounds. With the spikes and the generator keeping out Jellyrolls, they felt secure and comfortable for the first time since they had landed on this world.

That night after supper, they all prayed for a speedy and safe return of Patty and the others and retired to their huts. Alyssa insisted on keeping the night watch running. Just in case.

The next morning, Alyssa emerged from her hut and stretched lazily in the warm morning sun. Funny, she thought, how the heat didn't seem to bother her as much anymore. She dismissed the thought with a shrug and went to the showers.

The showers were a decadent luxury she had permitted. Until now they bathed under the watchful eyes of armed sentries in the calm river a couple of miles away. Now with unlimited running water from the mountain spring, she had agreed to let the builders construct a series of shower stalls, each with their own spigot to start and stop the flow of water.

It didn't matter that the water was cold. It just mattered that she felt civilized and normal once again. The feeling of the cold pulsing water as it played over her body reminded her, that the decadence of civilization was the vanity of its bathrooms. While anywhere else this would have been considered primitive and uncouth. Here, the cold-water shower, in the rough-hewn wooden stall seemed the depth of depravity to Alyssa. Besides, she felt more than a little proud of the accomplishments of her little band of ragtag survivors.

When she emerged from the shower feeling cleaned and refreshed, she ran across Lex on his way to the showers. "If we lived together," he suggested. "We could conserve water and shower together."

"That is a thinly disguised proposal, Lex," she said and kissed him quickly and continued walking.

That night Lex approached her. He didn't say a word, but instead placed a garland of colourful wild flowers about her neck, then kissed her passionately, in front of the whole village.

"We have no jewellery store here," he said, "but will this do?" He reached into his shirt pocket and removed a shiny gold band bent into a circle. Alyssa looked at the band and felt a tear come to her eyes. Then she examined the gift closely and wept openly.

"Oh, Lex," she cried. "You shouldn't have."

"If not for you," he said gently. "Then for no one. Alyssa, I ask you again, In front of all our friends. Will you marry me?"

She looked deep into his eyes. This wasn't his ordinary proposal, nor one of his never ending gifts. He had given her the most precious thing he owned, His Command Bars. When he was promoted to first officer and given the rank. He cherished the gold bars presented to him. They were the achievement of a lifetime and he cared for them as rare gems.

That he had taken his bars and bent and twisted them into a ring, showed the depth of his love for Alyssa. She tearfully took the crude ring and tenderly turned it over and over in her hand, as if trying to memorize every detail in its construction. She stopped short of actually placing it on her finger.

"Not yet, my love," she said tenderly. Then with a smile she said, "but keep trying. I admit that this unselfish act nearly made me forget…Whatever happens. I do love you!"

"But you still won't marry me!"

"I'm sorry," she said, struggling to find the words that would ease the pain and frustration on Lex's face, but none came.

"How about this then," said Lex with enthusiasm, "In front of witnesses, I say, Let's get engaged. It can be for as long as you need. We'll get married when you're ready. Until then I'll be content to be your fiancée. I love you with all my heart, and I won't give up on us. I know you love me, and I will be there to help you through it. So, what do you say?"

Alyssa stared into those hypnotic eyes, then turned her gaze to the expectant faces of the community, waiting anxiously for her reply. One by one, they smiled and nodded their assent to Lex's plan. They didn't understand her problem, but were willing to help anyway they could. Then Beth pushed her way forward and the muttering died away. Only the sound of insects broke the tension.

"It's time to take the next step," said Beth knowingly. "Let go. Live!"

Without fully realizing it, Alyssa found herself willingly agreeing to the proposition. Suddenly she felt a cold hard knot—she didn't know she had—in the pit of her stomach, loosen a little. It relaxed even more when Lex picked her up and kissed her passionately as the crowd cheered.

Ada and Sam appeared out of the darkness, with a drink for each of them. "We don't have any champagne, but this is distilled from the fruits that grow here," said Ada.

"It's quite good," said Sam and hiccupped to prove her point.

Alyssa and Lex raised their cups in a silent toast to each other and cautiously sipped the liquid. It burned like fire on the way down, but the sensation quickly passed and it left a pleasant fruity aftertaste. The second sip burned less, and the third not at all.

"Easy," cautioned Ada. "This stuff sneaks up on you." She turned and addressed the rest. "We only have a little, but if you all will get you cups, everyone can have some to toast the happy couple." After everyone had received a splash in their cups, they raised them in unison and toasted Alyssa and Lex.

Alyssa and Lex walked slowly around the perimeter, her head resting on his broad shoulders. Everyone had sipped some of the strange brew and partied late into the night. As they drifted off in twos and threes to bed down for the night, Alyssa and Lex started walking in the quiet evening.

"Happy sweetheart?"

"Yes," she said softly, then with more conviction she said firmly, "happier than I have been for years. Only one thing disturbs me…"

"What's that?"

"Can we survive? It's been almost a year and still no sign of rescue. I'm afraid it will never come."

"I've had the same thoughts," he admitted, "so what do we do?"

"We live," she said firmly. Lex stopped and looked into eyes that were bright and sparkling with excitement.

"Don't take this wrong, but why the change of heart?"

"Because of you, you wonderful man!"

"Me? What did I do?"

"This evening you reminded me that we have to live for now, not what may or may not happen in the future."

"So you will marry me?" he asked hopefully.

"Not yet, lover," she said, softly brushing her hand against his cheek. "We all have a lot to do, but I promise, it will always be on my mind. Right now we have a village to build."

"Then Madame Mayor, let us begin our new lives…here."

"We will be a new outpost of humanity," her eyes shone in the moonlight as her vision of a small band of humanity rising up from the depths of primitiveness to survive with pride and dignity.

The next morning, Alyssa told everyone her plan to build and her plan to live. Don't look for rescue, but live and thrive. The villagers talked and mumbled, but finally decided that this was the most logical suggestion. They would survive as humanity as has done for thousands of years.

"What about children," yelled a voice from the back? "I know some of the women are already pregnant, and I want to have children as well. Can we subject them to this?"

Alyssa paused and look at the crowd. 'What about children?' If they were to survive and flourish…

"We now live here," she said firmly. "As human beings we have a basic need to create and procreate. I think any children born to our community will be the luckiest children anywhere because they will know that their parents were exceptional men and women who fought and worked to make a life for them on a new world."

The crowd cheered and Alyssa stepped down to the thunderous applause of the council and her friends. The sound dimmed as her own thoughts filled her head. *We will survive. We are human beings filled with love and determination.* Finally she admitted to herself that she too was happy. A large weight had been lifted from her chest and she felt alive.

"Are you okay, Alyssa?" asked Patty gently.

She hugged the old man tightly. "I'm fine…In fact I feel wonderful," she blurted happily.

Chapter 15

Alyssa Krychech tossed and turned like a whirling dervish on her crude but soft bed of boughs and leaves. Scattered images of her life filled her dream world. The happiest day in her life when she wed Trenor Adwell, Ambassador to the planet Natoth: Her position as Chief Engineer to the planet Natoth, Her friendships with the President Ken and many others, all produced remembered feelings of comfort, warmth and security.

But the nightmares had just begun. The divorce, the incessant drinking, the explosion. Trenor dead having been caught in the blast, as had many of her friends and colleagues. The psychiatric examinations that led to her conviction and banishment from the planet Natoth.

Her fears of command, responsibility, and leadership, low self-esteem. Moving from ship to ship to avoid promotions. Finally ending up on the Carriolion – A large passenger liner. The rouge asteroid belt that hulled the ship and forced them to crash on an unexplored, hostile alien world.

The feelings of love she felt for Lex, the ship's executive officer. The support provided by Beth, the ship's captain and Patty, the old war veteran. Finally coming to terms with her fears and accepting Lex's love and position of mayor in the struggling community.

Alyssa sat up with a jolt. Her body covered in a fine glistening sheen of sweat. Her heart raced and her breath came in shallow gasps. "Did I make the right decision?" she asked the dark.

Suddenly a soft rapping came at her simple door. She reached out and opened the door, allowing the light from the distant campfire to illuminate her hut.

"Ethan," she said in surprise. "What are you doing up at this hour?" Ethan Alaso, an energetic young lad who had taken a real shine to

Alyssa, but who also worried and scared her, because of his strange moods, telepathic powers, and shifts in personality.

"Something's wrong Miss Krychech," he said. Alyssa instantly became alert. Ethan only called her Miss Krychech now when he was seriously troubled.

"Tell me," she prompted.

"You know how close Patty and I are," he said. "Well, we're a lot closer than you think."

"I don't understand," she said. True the boy did look on Patty as a father, but so did she.

"No, he's not my father," said Ethan, picking up her thoughts. "He's…Oh, I don't know how to explain it. Ask Ada. She knows. But the problem is, I always feel Patty up here," he said tapping his head. Alyssa understood. Somehow, Ethan had a link to Patty. She made a mental note to finally have that talk with Ada about Ethan.

"So what's wrong?"

"I don't feel him anymore." He looked ready to burst into tears.

"Maybe he's just out of range," suggested Alyssa, but struggling to calm her own fears.

"No, he's not," said Ethan firmly. "One moment I felt his presence, then all of a sudden it was gone. It feels like a part of me is missing. He's in trouble and we're his only hope of rescue. We've got to go and find him, Alyssa. Now!"

Patty and several others had gone exploring the strange world. Alyssa had approved the trip as mayor, but now was regretting that decision. As she fought down the urge to panic, her old fears resurfaced and made themselves know. Did she make another mistake? Maybe she wasn't fit to command after all, no matter what anybody said.

"Please," pleaded Ethan. "Can we go and find them? I'm worried!"

The boy fought back tears that welled up in his throat. Alyssa knew that the boy did have some sort of mental connect with the old veteran and his fears were almost palpable in the shadowed light of the campfire. Should she trust this exceptional young man?

Chapter 16

Alyssa looked at the young man, thinking how much he had grown in the last few months. Yet she still pondered the strange tale from Ethan. She had no doubts, as did many of the tiny community concerning Ethan's abilities. He had performed some amazing feats of mental legerdemain in the months they had been stranded here. She stared into the deep, thoughtful eyes of the youth and made her decision.

"Go find Lex and Beth," she said, holding his tense shoulders in her hands. "Tell them I want a community meeting right away." Ethan's eyes blinked their gratefulness, but he never spoke. Just nodded and ran off.

Half an hour later, Alyssa mounted the makeshift podium, now made more stable, and presented Ethan's fears to the tiny village. As she expected, many of them still feared the boy's powers. Sam joined her and Ethan on the podium, Fruitlessly she argued with the crowd. They still wanted some reassurance that this just wasn't some child's game. Then Beth made her move toward the podium.

Beth, as leader of the council, held a lot of power. Besides, as the former Captain of the Carriolion, the people held her in highest esteem and regards. The crowd hushed as she moved closer to the dais. She stopped and faced Ethan. Slowly, carefully she stared into the boy's face looking for trickery or deceit.

"I believe him," she announced to the assembly. "We know that Ethan has abilities beyond what we know, and we have seen many of these skills come into play. He is an intelligent, honest member of our band, and I trust him. Therefore, I volunteer to join the search party."

Alyssa stared in surprise. Beth usually never took a stand in matters such as this. She left such things to the wisdom of the council and

Alyssa's judgment as Mayor. Then Alyssa caught sight of Beth's face. Plainly she could see that the thought of Patty and the others missing or hurt distressed her greatly. How much, Alyssa did not find out till later.

"All right," said Alyssa. "Counting myself and Ethan, that's three. This could be a hazardous trip and we'll be gone for a few days. Will anyone else volunteer?"

The sight of Beth facing the crowd, arms folded across her chest, daring anyone to refuse, put a sense of community pride in the people. Sam started yelling at them, reminding them of how it was Ethan and his unique abilities that saved them from the ghost winds and other hazards. Slowly hands started to rise, then seconds later all the hands shot into the air.

One giant, burly man stepped forward. He stood close to six feet and his arms were as thick as tree trunks. Alyssa stared at this giant, desperately trying to recall his name. She knew him of course, but even after six months of close living conditions, there were still a few people unfamiliar to her. Especially those who preferred to live in the wilds, usually the hunters, who provided meat and game for the community. A hunter, that's it!

"Yes, Timotin, isn't it?"

"Yes, ma'am," replied a deep gravely voice that seemed to shake the very air around them. All of a sudden Alyssa recalled the giant. Born and raised on one of the heavy gravity worlds, Timotin could easily break a man in two without straining himself. Colonization of the heavy gravity worlds was still in its infancy. It took many generations for the human body to adjust to gravity, three times or more that of normal, incredibly high death rates, and primitive, to the point of barbaric living. Technology had a hard time adjusting and working in that type of gravity field, so the few inhabitants, lived off the land, and made do with what they could find.

To see a heavy planet dweller off his home world was a rarity, for that dweller to travel in space, on a luxury liner, unheard of. Alyssa made a mental to talk more with the giant. She remembered how he had killed that deer with one blow from his right hand. Yes, she really wanted to get to know this giant of a man better, but right now they had more pressing matters that needed attending.

Timotin stepped forward and faced the crowd. His strong bass voice boomed out over the group, causing more than a few to take a startled step back.

"I lead a group of hunters," he thundered. "We know this land. We hunt this land. We come to camp only to bring meat and collect supplies. We also watch and care for each other. This world has many dangers. As leader of the group, I volunteer my hunters." He turned and with a soft voice that still rumbled in the heavens, spoke to Ethan.

"We know of your power. Where you lead, Timotin and his hunters will follow. It is for the survival. We do not abandon comrades when in danger. Lead on, boy!" Ethan flung his arms around the thick neck of the giant man and hugged with all the strength his little arms could muster. Timotin laughed deep and loud.

"This little fellow has more courage than any of you," he said. He lifted the boy easily over his head with one hand, as if to show, and parade him in front of the others. Then ever so gently placed him down, beside Alyssa.

"Give us thirty minutes to prepare," he said addressing Alyssa. "Then Timotin and his hunters will protect you on this journey." With that, he whirled around and took several steps toward the crowd. They parted as if his very presence created a plough wave that pushed them aside. The wave closed after he passed.

Shamed by the giant's words, some of the group called out, asking if they could help preparing and gathering supplies. Alyssa and Beth huddled together in conversation then Beth left, taking a crowd of people with her. Alyssa could hear her issuing orders and commands to different people to fetch and bring certain items. The rest dispersed, leaving Alyssa, Sam, Ethan, and Lex alone.

"All right, Ethan," said Alyssa bending slightly so she could be eye level with the boy. Soon he would be equal in height to her. "I know the link is broken, but do you think you can guide us to where you last felt Patty?"

"I don't understand," he said quietly.

"She means," said Sam, "can you take us to where you lost the link with Patty. You know? Where he is!"

Ethan suddenly looked fearful. "I thought you knew where he went. I don't know how to guide you there."

"Yes, you do," said Sam gently. "Remember our exercises. Remember how you were able to locate me every time?"

"Yes, but then I was concentrating on keeping a link with you. I no longer have a link with Patty." His eyes started to water, as he realized no one knew how to find his friend.

"Stop it," said Sam sternly. "Now concentrate. Think! The echo of the link is still in your mind. Find it and follow it." Ethan closed his eyes, and his brow knitted in deep concentration. The others could see sweat beading on his brow, as he struggled with his mental powers. Desperately seeking to find the remnant of the link with Patty. His eyes popped open and he stared at them, as if not really seeing them.

"I found the echo, but I can't follow it," he complained. "There's too much going on in my head. I keep losing it."

"Is there any way to amplify the link?" Lex who had been silent till now, grasped at hopeful straw.

Sam shook her head sadly. "No way that I know of. We could be searching for days, or weeks until we find them." The announcement came as a blow to the others. Disheartened they sat down, each immersed in their thoughts. Suddenly Alyssa leapt to her feet. A wild light shone from her eyes.

"I have an idea," she said then started running away. Over her shoulder she shouted, "Wait here. I'll be back in a minute," and was gone out of sight.

By the time she returned, Timotin and the hunters had gathered with their equipment. Beth had also returned with several volunteers carrying knapsacks and bundles heavy with supplies. They gaped in surprise to see Alyssa running at full tilt toward the assembled rescue team followed closely by a bounding, shaking, jumping Scrapper.

"Of course," said Sam, seeing Scrapper. "Why didn't I think of that?"

"What?" Asked Lex, all confused. "How can Scrapper help?"

"We know Scrapper picks up the thought waves of people," gasped Alyssa as she watched the boy and his pet, hug and rub each other.

"We also know that when Sam, Ethan and Scrapper join mentally, they seem to be able to communicate."

"So," said Sam picking up the explanation, "if we three join—and we can make Scrapper understand—he may be able to pick up the link from Ethan and follow it easier than we could."

"Like a blood hound," said Lex understanding. "But do you think he could latch on to a link that's broken and consists only of what you call an echo?"

"There's only one way to find out," said Sam. "Ethan, come here. Now join with me in trying to tell Scrapper what we're looking for." The three went into a huddle and no one dared speak in fear of interrupting something weird, but wonderful as well.

They broke the link and Sam came over as Ethan continued communicating with Scrapper. "We almost had it," she said, "but then the trail became confused and twisted, as if another person was trying to get in the meld."

"Who in the hell could that be?" Lex had almost reached his frustration point and it showed. "You two and that animal, are the only ones I know of who have the power to communicate telepathically."

"I know who it is," said Ethan approaching the group. "And we need that help now." He moved over to Beth and stared at her.

"Me? I have no mental abilities. You must be mistaken."

"No," he said. "I can easily pick up your thoughts, but they're muddled and confused. Sam, help me?" Together the two concentrated, then Sam suddenly burst out laughing.

"I'm sorry," she said. "It's not really funny. It's just the way Ethan's untrained and young mind interpreted the message." She stepped over toward Beth and held out a hand.

"You'll have to join the meld with us."

"Why? What can I do?"

"You too have a link with Patty. It's unfocused, and raw, but it will be the catalyst we need to find him."

"I don't understand! I have no link with Patty. None what so ever."

Alyssa suddenly snapped her fingers as all the pieces fit together. "Beth, I don't want to embarrass you, but remember the speech you gave me on the ship about seeking out a life and grabbing on with both hands. Well, it's time you did that. As much as you may deny it, for whatever reason...You love Patty and he loves you, right?"

Beth looked as if ready to denounce the whole absurd story, but Ethan tugged at her clothes, his pleading eyes boring deep into her soul. Her face softened as she pulled the boy into a motherly embrace.

"Yes," she said softly. "We're in love, but we both felt it our duty to the ship and community to keep quiet about it. I guess you can't keep everything a secret around a telepath."

"We need your connection to him now," said Alyssa understanding. "I know how you feel and what you feel, but for his sake and yours, open up to those feelings. Let them flow."

"What do I have to do?"

"Join hands with Ethan and myself," instructed Sam. "Then let your mind go blank. When it's clear, concentrate on Patty. Think of how he looks to you, how he smells, how he feels! If you've made love, think about your experiences."

"Why would I think about when we made love? How could that possibly help?"

Sam smiled and with a knowing glance at the others she said, "When a couple make love, and they are in love, they form a bond that is stronger than steel. When you make love to the one you love, a connection is made. It's hard to explain, but a connection is made nevertheless. So use it. Patty's life may depend on it!"

Beth nodded and linked hands with the two telepaths. Sam and Ethan placed their free hands on the shaggy head on Scrapper who waited patiently. Seconds later, the three humans went rigid with tension, and Scrappers face assumed a blank, unwavering stare. Alyssa leaned in closer and could hear Ethan softly whisper. "Don't fight it. Let go."

Suddenly the connection broke and all of them sat back, breathing heavily. Scrapper strained his hairy head upward as if sniffing the wind then ran around in circles. Alyssa moved to help the others up to their feet. Timotin picked up Ethan as if cradling a baby and stroked the soft down of his hair ever so gently.

"Easy," he said softly. "Timotin is here to help." Obviously the giant man from the harsh heavy gravity planet had developed affection for the boy in the short time. Ethan's eyes fluttered open and blinked rapidly. He saw the smiling face of the giant and hugged him tightly around the neck. Timotin's face glowed with affection and he held the boy tighter.

"Timotin knows you have made link with Patty," said the giant. "Timotin and his hunters are ready to go, but first you and ladies must rest." Ethan and the others protested, but Timotin would not budge until they had a quick nap and a bite to eat. When satisfied with their efforts, he brought up a length of stout rope woven from the bark of an alien tree.

He hefted the heavy rope and pulled it tight between his arms. His muscles bulged and flexed with the strain of the pull, but the rope didn't part. He coiled the rope then placed a loop in one end. He stepped forward and approached Scrapper, eagerly waiting to go. The lion-snake backed away from the big man as he approached, then stopped, and cocked his head as he stared at Timotin.

"Easy friend," said the hunter to Scrapper. "Timotin means you no harm. This is so we can follow you. See? Timotin will not hurt. Timotin, friend." Alyssa watched the exchange. The man who could easily snap a tree in two, and who hunted and killed animals for a living, seemed so soft and gentle.

Eventually Scrapper made his decision and allowed the hunter to slip the looped end of the rope of his neck. The lion-snake twisted around, weaving his head from side to side, as if checking the security of the harness, then lay down peacefully.

Timotin signalled his team and they picked up their packages and bundles. Reaching down he picked up Ethan easily and placed him on his broad shoulders. The boy squealed with delight as the man mountain lumbered forward.

"Come," he thundered. "We go. Hang on to Timotin, small one. I will protect you." At his command, each of the hunters in Timotin's party teamed themselves with the others.

Alyssa found herself matched with a young man named Allen. She knew him well as he had tried unsuccessfully to attract her attention on the ship. She smiled and he beamed when he realized she recognized him.

"Well, Chief," he said, "it looks like you're my partner for a while." He turned to Lex, and noticed the frown on his face. Obviously Alyssa had told him about his advances. "Don't worry, Lex. She's not interested in me. We are comrades, friends on a rescue mission. I promise she will return to you whole."

"Actually," said Lex feigning disinterest. "I'm more concerned about you. She can be very demanding, and men stronger than you have wilted at her persistence." Alyssa dropped her pack and dove at the startled Lex.

"Demanding am I," she yelled while pinning him to the ground. "You just wait till I get back. I'll make you eat those words." Alyssa had always been fit and strong, but living in this primitive world had honed her muscles to something resembling corded steel bands. She straddled his chest and with her knees, slowly started to squeeze. Lex smiled at first then sweat beaded on his brow. Eventually he cried Pax and Alyssa let him get up.

"See what I mean," said Lex trying to get a last dig in. "Strong as an Ox, and almost as bright. Watch yourself. If she gets out of hand, give her to Timotin to control." He jerked his thumb over in the direction of the man mountain who had Ethan on his shoulders; a pack slung over one arm, and the reins holding Scrapper in the other.

"No," cried Timotin in mock fear. "Alyssa not hurt Timotin. Friends?"

"Always," she laughed hugging the giant. Then she turned back to Lex and kissed him passionately. "As for you, behave or else."

"Yes, ma'am," he said and kissed her again. With packs and bundles all ready, the party set off. Scrapper led the way, gently tugging at the leash held by Timotin. He seemed to know exactly where to go, so Timotin let him follow his senses. He felt no hesitation from his young charge on his shoulders. He knew that the success of this mission hinged on Scrapper and Ethan and he was determined that no harm would come to either of them.

They walked for about an hour, before Ethan still perched on the big man's shoulders said he could no longer see the camp. Wanting to stretch his legs, he asked Timotin to put him down so he could walk.

As they walked side-by-side, Timotin laid a giant hand gently on the shoulders of the boy.

"So tell me about yourself, Allen," said Alyssa striking up a conversation with the young man.

Allen shrugged. "Not much to tell. I was born on Mars and led an uneventful life…Until now that is."

"So how did you end up in the hunting party? As far as I know there are no hunting domes on Mars."

"I didn't fit anywhere else." He shifted his pack to the other side. "I'm a virtual debugger, but there are few systems here for me to play with."

Alyssa nodded understanding. Virtual debuggers were a specially trained group of people. They had cybernetic implants in their skulls that allowed them to interface with most computer systems. Then on a virtual reality trip, they toured the circuit pathways and traveled the endless miles of connections in a computer system. They could find and diagnose problems, easier and faster than any other method.

"That still doesn't explain why you joined the hunting party," she prompted. "I would have thought that, with your skills, maybe a job on the council would be better."

Allen shook his head. From his face Alyssa realized that he found the idea repugnant. "It's because of my skills that I joined the hunters."

"I don't understand?" Allen suddenly reached out and pulled Alyssa back gently just before her foot reached a protruding tree root. "Thanks," she said. "I didn't even see that root."

"You have to be careful here in the jungle," he admonished gently. "It's a wonderful, beautiful place, but it's deadly dangerous as well. Out here, don't assume anything. I've seen…Well, let's just say I've seen things."

"I'll be more careful," said Alyssa realizing that her time spent in the village had dulled her natural reflexes. "So, you were telling me why you joined the hunters?"

Allen remained silent, so Alyssa changed the subject. For a while they talked about the usual amenities, the weather—always hot, being rescued—very soon, etc. When they had exhausted the generalities, they fell into silence. After an hour of listening to the strange insects chirp and squeal, Allen spoke again.

"You haven't asked me why I was on board the Carriolion."

"I didn't think it was any of my business, but since you said you were a virtual debugger, I did begin to wonder. There's no use for someone with you abilities out this far from the League."

"I was on my way to start a new life," he said softly. Alyssa waited. The young man wanted to get something off his chest and it was difficult for him.

"I had to leave. Get away from the computers. You see...I'm an addict." Alyssa gasped, then quickly recovered to hide her shock. Addicts were new. They were a product of the modern civilization.

"I'm sorry," said Alyssa. "If you don't mind me asking, how far along were you?"

"Second stage," he mumbled. "That's why I had to get out." Alyssa praised him on having the strength of will to break it before it got too late.

Neural interfaces with computerized systems were commonplace, but a problem had developed. In a very small percentage of the population thus connected, it created a condition where the production of natural endorphins in the brain was doubled, sometimes tripled. The user felt a rush and a psychological high whenever they connected to a powerful system.

First stage was the high and the feeling of unlimited power. Everyone with the implant experienced the first stage, and most controlled or disregarded the effects. In a very few—and it was still a mystery who was susceptible—the increased endorphin production triggered a psycho/physical craving. They needed to be "Plugged in" to feel, to live.

This was the second stage. While a handful had managed to regain control and lived happy productive lives, the rest would eventually move on to bigger and more powerful systems. The bigger and more powerful the computer, the bigger and stronger the high! By the third stage, the poor souls who were still caught spent the rest of their lives seeking the unattainable. The perfect high! So consuming was this passion, it would blind them to everything else. They would lie, cheat, steal, anything to gain access to a bigger, faster system.

"So you realized you were an addict and decided to break out," she said. "I won't even attempt to say I know how you feel, cause I don't. I applaud your courage, and strength. But it must have been painful for you. The withdrawal symptoms from what I've heard can be excruciating."

"Yes. They are," he mumbled, his eyes glazing over, recalling the weeks of painful thrashing and screaming. Desperately trying to get near a computer that he could plug into.

"When they released me from the hospital, the doctors warned me to avoid any systems higher than a level three nano-processor. Hell, I lived and worked on Mars. Where could I go? Any other job I took, I would still be near those monstrosities. Whenever I went near them, I had to fight to stop from Plugging in."

Alyssa nodded, silently. It must have been a living torture chamber for Allen. The League prided itself on the having the best computers in the Galaxy. It also prided itself on its maintenance engineers and programmers, including the virtual debuggers. She understood now why he was on the ship. In the outer colonies where the Carriolion was bound, he could find peace. No giant super computers existed there yet. Privately she wondered what would happen to people like Allen when even these remote bastions of freedom joined the technology circle.

"When we crashed here," he continued, "I thought that everything would be over for me. There's no medical specialist to help me when I have a relapse. No drugs to control the seizures. I know of people who went mad trying to quit. That's why I chose the colonies. They don't have a super computer, but they do have the medical staff to care for me when I trip."

"Let me guess," said Alyssa. "You 'tripped' while on the planet and Timotin helped you."

"Right," he said smiling. "He's a remarkable man. You can't tell from the way he speaks, but did you know that he's a doctor?"

"You're kidding!"

"No, I'm serious. Timotin found me at the edge of the cliff ready to jump. I couldn't take the pain anymore. The withdrawal was just too much. I wanted to end the suffering…If it had been anyone else, they couldn't have stopped me, but Timotin with his strength, held me until the raging, burning fever passed."

"I still find it hard to believe that he's a doctor," she said, astounded. "I mean, I'm sure he's smart enough, it's just…" Her thoughts returned to the scene of the savage hunt and the barbarian who with one blow killed a full-grown deer.

"It's just that he seems like a big dumb ox who knows nothing other than what he does, right? Well, that's what I thought too. That is until he started to explain what my problem was, as he sees it. Then his speech smoothed out and you couldn't distinguish him from a professor at the Central University Library. He just speaks that way because it's easier."

Alyssa's face showed a glimmer of understanding. All reports of contact with persons from Timotin's planet left the impression that they were big dumb brutes. Now she had second thoughts.

"Life on his planet is rugged and harsh, by anyone's standards. All their energy is put into survival, so they developed a sort of shortened way of speaking. Short talk he calls it. Anyway, he tells me that my body is sick, because my mind is confused. At first I didn't understand, I thought the addiction was all in my head—so to speak. Then he said on his world, survival depended on a sound mind and body. They don't have the advantage of advanced medical techniques, even though their doctors know them—so they had to develop other methods."

"Yes," she said. "I've heard that they apply what could be called revolutionary techniques to cure illness."

"Revolutionary? According to Timotin they're old techniques forgotten and rediscovered. Anyway he says that I must get my mind and body to work together if I want to get better."

"So he treated you?"

"Not really, he showed me how to treat myself. He took me into the jungle—dragged me really—and left me to fend for myself. At first I was petrified, but after a couple of days, when my supplies ran out, I realized that I had to find food and shelter or die. I guess the survival instinct in me was still strong. I learned—the hard way—how to hunt and live in a wilderness all on my own."

"My god," she gasped. "I didn't know anyone was out there. Why wasn't I told?"

Allen laughed. "Blame Timotin. He told the council that he had formed a team of hunters and I was on that team so not to worry. What I didn't know then, but found out after, was that he had placed himself to watch over me. I never saw him or anyone else. I truly thought I was alone, but in truth he was never far away."

"So having to learn to let your body and mind work together to ensure your survival cured you."

Allen nodded. "Not at first. I had another relapse about two weeks into the exercise, but I found I could control the effects better. I started to think clearly, my body became toned and strong. I was fast as lightning and quiet as a mouse. I survived, and felt better than I had in years. Six weeks later Timotin returned, checked me out, and said I was almost cured."

"So you decided to join him in the hunting team."

"Yep," he said proudly. "In fact I'm his second. In the last four months I've only had one relapse and I controlled that with almost no effort. I have him to thank, and the primitive old fashioned ways of his people."

"I am very happy for you," she said sincerely. "What will you do when we're finally rescued?"

"I don't know," he admitted. "I toyed with the idea of staying here, on this world maybe as a guide for the pioneers sure to come. Then Timotin offered me another choice the other day."

"And that is?"

"He was on his way to a medical research station on the colonies. He would be heading the complex. They wanted him to bring an assistant, but you know how his people are. He couldn't find anyone to go. So he offered it to me. I explained I'm not a medical man, but he said needed someone who understood computers and could work with high levels of data."

"Since he has very little exposure to such things, he would be lost," agreed Alyssa. "But what about your illness? Aren't you afraid it would return?"

"Not anymore," he chuckled. "The computers at the complex aren't as sophisticated as the ones back home. Besides, Timotin says he doesn't want to go through that again and says if I start, he'll just break me in two, and mourn the loss later."

Alyssa smiled. Allen and Timotin obviously had a strong friendship. "So are you going with him?"

"I haven't made up my mind yet," said Allen, "but I owe him so much, and what he proposes does interest me. Right now though it's a mute point. We're still here and we must still survive, so I don't think about it much. I'm just enjoying being free for the first time in years!"

Alyssa stared ahead of the line at the gentle giant of a man Doctor, philosopher, hunter, and educator. Time she got to know more about her people, she thought. *Maybe there's hope for me after all.*

Chapter 17

The next morning the heavy, oppressive heat of the sun struck with a vengeance. Inside the makeshift shelters and tents, the temperature rose rapidly. The hot, steamy air made breathing uncomfortable. Alyssa tossed and turned in her bed, sweat dripping from every pore. She had forgotten how hot it got in the depths of the jungle planet. The cliffs near the village afford a small level of protection from the morning sun. She rubbed the sleep from her eyes, wiping away the tiny grains of dust that had built up into a crusty coating. Even with the tremendous heat and humidity, she found herself parched and sought out her water jug at the end of her bed.

Outside, she found the hunters already wide awake and the smell of freshly cooked game and soft tender juicy fruits wafted towards her. Pulling her clothes on quickly, she moved towards the appetizing aromas. Ethan and Scrapper were already playing a game of tag in the tiny clearing around the camp. With embarrassment written on her face, she realized she was the last one to waken.

"Ahhh," said Allen. "Our fearless leader awakens. Sorry, but you'll have to take what's left. Maybe next time you'll wake up in time for breakfast!"

"Sorry," she said. "What time is it?"

"A little after 5."

The time shocked her. With the protection of the cliffs she had been able to sleep until almost seven, before having to rise. Still, she did feel thoroughly rested and once fed, assured the others she could wrestle a Tarkanian Devil Bear. The hunters broke camp with practiced efficiency. In minutes they had the tents, shelters, pots and pans all stowed away, and waited for the leader to signal the journey would continue.

Alyssa finished stowing her gear and went in search of the rest. She found Ethan, Sam, Beth, and Scrapper in a huddle. Not wanting to intrude, she crept up beside them quietly. Sam opened her eyes and signalled her to come nearer. Seconds later they broke contact, and a big smile showed on all their faces.

"Just verifying the link," explained Sam. "I think we must be close, because I detected a hint of active linkage in Beth and Ethan."

"He's alive," said Ethan firmly. He seemed so positive and assertive that Alyssa could only smile.

"Well then," said Alyssa rising and looking at the hunters. "We should get going. Soon it'll be as hot as hell, and I would prefer to have covered a lot more distance than we did yesterday."

Timotin strode over to the group His giant strides shaking the ground beneath them. Alyssa answered his unspoken question and assured him they were ready to move out. From an animal skin pouch, Timotin retrieved the heavy corded rope he used before. Scrapper took one look at the rope and bounded over to the giant man. It raised its head, as if in invitation to place the leash on it.

Timotin smiled and rubbed the shaggy mane of the lion-snake. He gently slipped the leash over the head of Scrapper. Scrapper immediately whipped his head around, sniffing and smelling then started pulling in one direction. Timotin stood and with a yell "HAI," the rescue party picked up their gear and fell into place behind Timotin and Ethan. Slowly, but with efficient movements, the hunters herded their charges into the jungle.

After the noonday meal, when the sun was highest in the sky, Timotin ordered a rest break. Although eager to continue, Alyssa bowed to the wisdom of the big hunter. He and the others knew that to continue without a rest in this heat, meant some of the party would be collapsing from heat stroke and dehydration.

Alyssa found a shady spot under a giant Banyan tree. She slumped down and immediately began to doze. She awoke suddenly to cries of warning and squeals of terror from Sam and Ethan. Coming instantly awake, she blinked rapidly to clear her vision, desperate to see the cause of the commotion. Then she saw it. At least half-a-dozen Jellyrolls had descended on the resting party.

They moved in a classic hunting pattern. They spaced themselves around the camp at one side then rolled quickly into the camp, forcing the humans to flee in the opposite direction. The remainder appeared from the bush, effectively encircling the trapped humans. One of the hunters threw his spear at the nearest Jellyroll. It hit the hideous creature with a soft "smoosh." Then with frustrating slowness it penetrated the alien blob. The humans watched in amazement as the spear passed through the creature. It popped out the other side with the same unhurried speed it had entered and fell to the ground, the creature obviously unharmed.

The humans found themselves being herded and huddled closer together, forming an ever-tightening circle. A Jellyroll near Alyssa extended a pseudopod towards her. In spite of herself she screamed as it snaked towards her. In a split second, almost faster than the eye could follow, Scrapper used his prehensile tail to remove his leash and with a roar launched himself at Alyssa.

His massive body hit her with full force and she flew threw the air like a rag doll. The pseudopod grabbed Scrapper and started to envelop him. At the sight of his beloved pet being slowly absorbed, Ethan let an impressive war yell loose, and dove to rescue his friend. Timotin, for all his bulk, was no slower. He reached Scrapper at the same time as Ethan and together they pulled on the massive head of the giant lion-snake.

While it could be said that Ethan's little arms didn't provide much in the way of strength, his presence seemed to reassure the animal greatly. While Timotin braced himself and pulled mightily on the creature, Ethan wrapped his tiny arms around the neck of the beast and tugged for all his worth. Tears streamed down his face as pulled and tugged, desperately trying to rescue his friend.

Allen and a couple of other hunters, circled warily behind the Jellyroll. They knew from experience that an attack on more than three fronts caused the blob to retract in fear. So while Timotin struggled to free Scrapper on one side, they approached from other quarters and started to stab the creature with their spears.

Inch by inch, the Jellyroll released its grip on Scrapper. Then with a sucking sound, Scrapper popped out of the ooze and shot into the waiting arms of Timotin, who suddenly found himself, holding the squirming lion-snake and a little boy who wouldn't let go.

The Jellyroll, finding itself outnumbered, allowed instinct to take over and it rolled away as fast as it could. The other Jellyrolls continued their advance on the humans, but with the rapid departure of the one, it left an avenue of escape. The humans had one chance to flee through that gap and they took it.

Scrapper now recovered, grabbed Ethan by his prehensile tail and placed him on his back. Then with surprising speed, shot past the trained hunters, who could move quite rapidly if the need arose. Everyone ran as if their very lives depended on it, which it did. Jellyrolls could move fast, but they couldn't maintain the speed for long. Obstacles that they couldn't run over would get in their way. One blob, hot on the heels of Allen, ran smack into a tree, as the hunter dodged and weaved. If it weren't so dangerous, Alyssa would have laughed.

It hit the tree and wrapped itself around the trunk. Slowly the creature oozed around the tree and it rejoined on the other side. As it worked to reform itself, it fell far behind the others. With Timotin in the lead, he ran a zigzag course through the dense foliage. Wherever possible he led the team through the thickest underbrush he could find. It wouldn't stop the Jellyrolls, but it would slow them down a bit. With a final burst of effort, the rescue party came into a clearing. Everyone scanned the area, looking for a safe haven. If they could avoid the Jellyrolls for a while longer, they knew from experience the creatures would give up the chase and leave.

Allen spotted what appeared to be another clearing backing onto to a cliff. If they could reach the cliff face, they could climb to safety. Jellyrolls couldn't climb. The group ran, panting from the heat and the exertion. Reaching the cliff face, they spread out to find a foothold. Timotin shouted that they had to climb at least 10 feet, or the Jellyroll could reach them.

They struggled to find foot and hand holds. Alyssa glanced behind her in time to see the Jellyrolls approach. There were only four left, but those four could kill as easily as twelve. They rolled to the base of the cliff and began extending pseudopods to try to reach the humans. But as they reached and over extended themselves, they fell over and squashed flat on the rocky floor. But that didn't stop them from continuing to try.

Then the thing they feared the most happened. The hunter who had assigned himself to guard Beth, reached up to avoid an extended pod, and the rock came out of its setting. With a scream he fell backward, landing right on top of a Jellyroll. Beth screamed and started to climb down to rescue the poor man, but another hunter reached over and grabbed her firmly, preventing her from descending.

"You can't help him now," yelled the hunter. "He landed right on top of one. It absorbed his body right away. He's as good as dead now!"

The other looked at the horrifying sight. The Jellyroll had completed engulfed the man in seconds. They could see him struggle, but quickly his efforts died, as did he. The Jellyroll pulled back from the cliff face with its prize. Within seconds the humans could see the man's flesh being melted away from his body. Encouraged by the success of one of their own, the other Jellyrolls continued trying to reach their quarry.

"Listen," shouted Timotin. "What's that noise? Sounds like…"

"Ghost Winds," cried Allen. "Great! If the Jellyrolls don't get us the winds will. I picked a hell of a time to get brave."

In spite of the dire circumstances, with death a few moments away the rest of the hunters laughed loudly, including Timotin. Sam thought them crazy and told them so, but it was Ethan who calmed her down.

"Don't you see," he said gently. "It is the way with all people who risk their lives everyday."

"Little one," said Timotin. "We not mock the dead, nor do we have no fear of death. We live each and ever day as if the last. It is good to laugh in face of danger."

"It gives them hope that they will live to laugh another day," completed Ethan.

Timotin smiled proudly at the boy. "Timotin think you grow up and be very wise man someday. Timotin think you may get chance. Look!"

The ghost winds entered the canyon, and instead of heading for the humans, once again they reacted unpredictably and turned directly for the Jellyrolls. Three Jellyrolls suddenly found themselves facing three whirling funnels of dust. The ghost winds singled out a Jellyroll and descended on the creature. It slowly rose into the air, waving its pseudopods wildly as it tried to regain a footing on the ground. The winds carried the helpless Jellyroll aloft, taking it higher and higher. When almost at the top of the cliff, they released the hapless creature, and allowed it to fall to the ground. It hit with a loud splat and spread itself all over the ground. Seconds later the colour changed from a muddy brown to black. The creature was dead.

Then the winds picked up the second Jellyroll and did the same thing. The remaining Jellyroll didn't wait around for its turn. It backed away from the cliff and rolled as fast as it could away from the threatening menace. The human survivors clung to their precarious perches, as they watched in fascination and horror at the slaughter. When the last Jellyroll was either gone or dead, the winds settled down and hovered directly in front of the humans.

"It's been a real pleasure," shouted Allen over the loud whirling winds. "Thank you for all you've done for me, Timotin."

"Do not give up yet," replied the giant. "Timotin has a plan. I will distract the winds while the rest of you make your escape."

"Wait," cried Alyssa. She wanted to explain her theory that the winds no longer represented a threat to the humans.

"Good plan," said Allen not hearing her cry, "but they need you. I'll go!" Before anyone could say anything he launched himself from his perch at the assembled winds. With luck he could startle them and hit the ground running.

Instead of being startled, they moved to intercept the foolhardy man. In mid air, they created a cushion of swirling air, gently, almost tenderly; they supported the falling man, and deposited him softly on the ground. Then they withdrew and dissipated into the air, leaving no trace except for a couple of piles of dust.

Allen quickly checked himself out, just to make sure he wasn't dead or dreaming, then cautiously approached the mouth of the canyon. Seconds later he reappeared and reported the way was clear.

"There's no sign of either a Jellyroll or a ghost wind," he called. "I guess it's safe to come down." The humans carefully climbed down from their rocky perches and stood on the ground.

"What...What just happened here?" Said Alyssa looking around for an explanation. "They've helped us before, but this is too much."

"I do not know," said the giant. "It is if they were operating with a guided intelligence. I would love the opportunity to study and classify these creatures. Perhaps there is some rudimentary intelligence operating at a level we cannot yet comprehend..." He stopped and stared right into the face of an astonished Alyssa.

"You really are a scientist," she exclaimed.

Timotin blushed. "I have some medical training. I'm really a researcher." Then as if in effort to justify himself he explained. "Since you called me that, I assume Allen told you about me. Sorry for the deception, but my skills as a medical man are limited and I didn't want to interfere with the ship's doctor. I normally use the short talk, but when I'm excited about discovering something new, I slip into full language."

"Let's get moving," said Alyssa. "And you can tell me about your research as we walk."

"First," he said, "let me gather up some of this goo from the dead Jellyrolls for study. Maybe I can find some weakness—other than dropping them from a great height—we can use as a weapon." He bent over and carefully scooped some of the black mess into a container then slapped the lid on tightly.

With Scrapper again on his leash, and Ethan at his side, Timotin told Alyssa about his research. She admitted shock when he told her that he was the one who created the serum that saved the people of Alderran from a virulent plague.

"I started my training as a doctor, but found I had skills in other areas," he said. "I had gone about as far as I could with the tools I had on my planet. The league heard about my special gifts—quite rare on my world—and offered me a chance to help with the plague on Alderran. I accepted and moved to the Med Complex on Alderran. After the breakthrough there, I found myself reluctant to return home. I had been given an opportunity to extend myself beyond my wildest dreams."

"So the League offered you your own lab?"

"Yes," he said. "With grateful help from Alderran." Alyssa smiled at how now that the excitement had passed, he reverted to the short talk commonly used on his world.

They continued the trek through the steamy hot jungle until dinnertime then Timotin called a halt. They set up camp and began preparing the evening meal. Ethan and Scrapper, with the energy level of youth had found a stick and were engaged in a joyous game of fetch.

Ethan flung the stick into a thicket, but it didn't hit the bushes. Instead it just disappeared in mid air. Scrapper turned happily to chase the stick and when he reached the thicket, he too disappeared. Ethan screamed and ran after his pet. With cries from the others unheeded, Ethan ploughed right into whatever had caused the stick and Scrapper to vanish.

Before anyone had the chance to react, Ethan disappeared. The others ran to the spot, and only Timotin and his great strength could stop Alyssa from leaping into the same fate. She hadn't realized how much she had grown to love the young boy until she saw him vanish. Now her fears of his loss overwhelmed her.

"Be calm," urged Timotin. "Little one is smart. He will return to us." They waited, and waited, but no sign of Ethan or Scrapper appeared.

Timotin made his decision. He picked up the rope he used for the leash and lashed it around himself. Then, securing the other end around a tree, he instructed his hunters to prepare to haul him back in two minutes if they could.

"I not know what on other side," he said. "Maybe vacuum. Timotin can hold breath for three minutes. Give me one minute safety." With a nod to the others he stepped forward and vanished.

The rope tied to him remained taught. But it looked eerie hanging suspended in mid air. After two minutes, the hunters braced themselves then pulled with all their strength. But instead of meeting a resistance, Timotin came flying at them from the strength of the pull. He landed on the two nearest the invisible wall and knocked the air out of them.

Apologizing profusely, he helped the two stand-up, and brushed off their garments. "There is a room on the other side. The air is clean and cool. I saw the stick and muddy paw prints from Scrapper. They led down a corridor."

"Any sign of Ethan," asked a hopeful Alyssa. Beside her Sam smiled through watery eyes.

"No," said Timotin softly. "Think he may have followed Scrapper. I go back and rescue him now."

"Not without me," said Alyssa firmly and the others piped up their objections as well.

"Someone has to stay," said Timotin. "I could see where the rope entered the wall, but I couldn't pass through. It needs an outside influence to pull you back."

They made plans to leave some behind, while the others went through tied to ropes. The ones who remained would be there to pull them back when they were ready. One by one, the hunters tied ropes securely around Alyssa, Sam, and Beth. Timotin kept his, and ordered two other hunters to accompany him. The remainder would make camp and wait for the signal.

Chapter 18

Inside the grey-walled chamber, thin strips of fluorescent, coloured lights ran along the walls and ceiling. Every few seconds, they would flash in a spectrum of colours ranging from a deep red to a bright yellow. The team tried to examine the lights, but not even the incredibly sharp knives of the hunters could scratch the surface of the material. Nothing broke the smooth surface of the walls. No equipment or furniture of any kind sat in the room.

Alyssa turned around to check that their lifelines still lay on the floor where they had placed them, then addressed the waiting group. "I think we'd better get moving."

They picked up their belongings and started to exit the room. Timotin held a spear out in front as they crossed the threshold of the doorway. Suddenly the spear vanished. An intensely bright green light enveloped the party and held them immobile. Alyssa struggled to break free, but couldn't elicit any response from her muscles. They refused to obey her commands and she stood rock still.

The light held them fast for what seemed an eternity, but in reality lasted only a few seconds, then winked out. Alyssa shook of the slight wave of dizziness and glanced at her companions. Everyone seemed non-the worse for the strange event. Everyone that is except…

"Sam," she cried and ran to the unconscious form on the floor. Timotin dropped down beside her and pulled a small animal skin satchel from his bag. Reaching inside he withdrew a small amount of leaves— green with bright orange specks. He rubbed them between his giant hands and Alyssa soon found herself reeling from a strong pungent aroma.

Timotin passed his hands under Sam's nose and waved them gently. Seconds later—eyes streaming and coughing loudly—Sam woke up.

Timotin leaned back, a huge grin on his face. He showed his hands to Alyssa and Sam. They had turned a bright green from the leaves and the smell of the crushed vegetation still clung to them.

"The smell will dissipate in a couple of minutes," said the heavy planet doctor. "They are Colora leaves, or this planet's equivalent. See the green tinge has faded already and the smell is almost gone."

"I don't know where you learned homeopathic medicine," said Alyssa, "but I'm glad you did."

"Timotin learned back home," he said. "Every school child knows how to identify medicinal plants."

Sam sat up and groggily pushed her hair back from her eyes. "Anything happen while I was out?"

"Yeah," said Alyssa wryly. "The League Council called. They want someone to serve coffee, and are expecting you in ten minutes."

Sam smiled and tried to stand up. She wobbled and Timotin had to catch her before she fell. "Better tell them I may be a little late," she said.

"How you feel," asked Timotin.

"A little woozy, but okay," replied Sam. "Everyone else all right?"

"Yes," said Alyssa holding her hand. "You were the only one to faint."

Sam nodded and took a deep breath. It cleared her head and she disengaged herself from the support of her friends. Taking another couple of breaths, she pronounced herself fit to continue.

"How?" asked Alyssa? "If we try to pass through the doorway again, we'll be stopped as before."

"No," replied Sam firmly. "We've been cleared for entry. It won't stop us again."

"How do you know that?"

"I'm not sure," she replied hesitantly, "but I do know that we are expected."

"Expected," repeated Alyssa, "by whom?"

"Him," she said and pointed at the door. In the bright light from the hallway, a shadowy figure emerged. Alyssa placed a hand to her eyes to try and see better. She squinted into the bright light, trying to focus when Beth suddenly rushed forward and wrapped her arms around the stranger's neck.

"Timotin think Captain Beth has found Patty!"

Alyssa nodded and smiled. "A reasonable supposition."

Beth and Patty were locked in a lover's embrace that spoke volumes of the affection they had for each other. The rest stood by smiling, not wanting to interrupt this touching reunion. Besides, as Timotin pointed out, you couldn't separate them with a crowbar.

Eventually they separated and Patty came in the room. Beth clung to his arm, and he held her equally firm in his hand. "It's about time you lot showed up," he said with a smile. "Ethan's about ready to burst."

"Thank god," said Alyssa. "Is he all right? Are you all right? Where are the others? What is this place? How did we get here? When…" She stopped and looked at the faces as she realized her ramblings.

"He's fine," said Patty warmly. "And as for the rest, well prepare to be amazed and dumbfounded." With Beth still clinging to his arm, he crossed the threshold and passed through without incident.

Seeing no light, Timotin shouldered his pack and followed. When he passed through safely, the rest joined them. Even Sam boldly marched through, but Alyssa could feel the tension in the girl's shoulders. Once through the door, the lighting changed in the hallway. It turned to a soft subdued blue, and cool calming effect overcame the rescue team.

"That's better," said Sam. "Come on. I know where to go from here."

"You too?" Patty looked into Sam's eyes. "That explains a lot."

"Would someone mind explaining it to me," said a confused Alyssa. "You know why Sam seems to know this place, even though we've never been here before?"

Patty nodded and explained as they walked. "That green light you experienced is a sort of watch dog. It checks you out and if you don't fit the profile, it…Well let's just say it's not pleasant."

Alyssa wanted to know how he found out, but the look of horror on his face stopped her cold. Patty was a strong man. Experienced in the ways of war and destruction. If it affected him, she didn't want to know anymore.

"When Ethan came through," he continued, "it knocked him out, just like Sam. We found him with the help of Scrapper—who also appears to be fine—and took him back to the control room. When he awoke he seemed to know everything about this place. In a few seconds he told us more than we've been able to learn in days. It appears the beam also affected Sam the same way."

"But I don't know everything," she protested. "I just, I mean, I only know what is right and wrong."

"That confirms a theory I have," said Patty nodding. "The race that built this place must have been telepathic. It gave Ethan an incredible amount of information, but since Sam is only partially telepathic, it gave her a little. I'm not explaining this too well. You'd better ask Ethan. I'm sure by now that the boy wonder has it all figured out."

He turned down a branch in the corridor and the wall slid aside quietly. The team entered the room and gazed in wonder at the incredible level of technological sophistication. Banks and rows of equipment lined the walls. Some of it seemed vaguely familiar, but the rest was completely alien.

"Alyssa," came the cry from across the room, and a blur of something soft and small jumped into her arms. Alyssa reacted automatically and hugged the form to her. Every sense reeled and she held the struggling body. The scent, the feel, the form!

"Ethan," she cried and hugged tighter. The boy and the woman hugged as mother and son. Tears dropped from her eyes onto the boy's hair and she held him tight and kissed the top of his head.

"I thought I lost you," said Alyssa, voicing her fears for the first time. "Don't you ever do that to me again, or so help me I'll…"

"It would appear," boomed the laughing voice of Timotin, "that mother and son have been successfully reunited. How about a hug for your friend Timotin." Ethan reluctantly left Alyssa's embrace and approached the giant. He threw his arms around the neck of the strong man and hugged for all his worth.

Alyssa seemed slightly embarrassed by her display, and blushed. Beth came over and put a tender arm around the younger woman. "This is one of those other things we talked about. Don't be embarrassed or ashamed. You love him and he loves you. For all purposes, you are his mother. Enjoy it while you can." She kissed the still weeping Alyssa and rejoined her beloved.

Sam looked around the room. "Where's Scrapper?"

"Exploring," said Ethan. "He likes this place. Now that you're here he'll come back."

"What is this place, Patty?" Alyssa had regained her composure and held fast to Ethan's hand.

Patty scratched his greying head. "Near as we can figure, it's the same as that ruin we found when we first crashed here. But everything seems to work."

"It was built by a race called the Providers," said Ethan. "Or at least that's what we would call them. It's a sort of rest stop for them."

"Go on, boy," urged Patty when Ethan fell silent. "What else?"

"It's hard," said Ethan. "I have so much information in head, I can't sort it all out. Let me think for a minute."

They watched in silence as the thirteen-year-old boy with the remarkable mental abilities, turned his concentration inward and focused on the alien information in his mind.

"This is one of seven worlds in this part of the galaxy," he said hesitantly. "They used them as places to refuel and rest on their journey's. I…I'm sorry I need more time. It's hard to think straight."

"That's all right," said Alyssa hugging the boy. "Relax, it'll come to you. Patty, where's the rest of your team?"

"We lost Johnston to a Jellyroll, and Cambridge fell down a cliff—broke his neck. The others are in another room, studying the controls."

"We had our share of troubles with Jellyrolls and Ghost winds," said Allen. "But something weird happened. The winds didn't attack us. In fact they saved my life."

"I know," said Patty. "Please follow me. I have something to show you." They followed him across the room to the far side. A section of the blank wall slid aside quietly and they found themselves in another room. The last two members of Patty's expedition were there and greeted their rescuers with open arms and congratulations.

"Over here," called Patty after the reunion. He reached for the alien controls and touched a lighted pad. In the air an image began to form. It showed the campsite where the remainder of the rescue team waited.

"Incredible," said an amazed Allen.

Patty touched another spot and the dead end canyon where they had been trapped by the Jellyrolls came into view. "Now watch this," he said and touched another pad.

In the image, a ghost wind formed, then another, and finally a third. By waving his hand over a lighted pad, Patty made the winds move about in the canyon. By manipulating the controls, Patty could make the winds climb, bank, pickup objects and drop them whenever and wherever he wanted.

"We saved you from the Jellyrolls," he announced. "We had just figured out what these controls did, when we saw that poor man fall into the Jellyroll. So we used them to create the ghost winds and save you. I don't pretend to understand how it works, I'm just glad they do."

"The winds are the sentries for this place," interjected Ethan. "They are artificial and designed to protect the complex from intruders and animals."

"That's why they seemed to operate with a purpose," said Patty understanding. "Anything else?"

"Nooo, not yet. Just that the first attack on our camp gave the machine time to realize we were intelligent," said Ethan slowly. He turned around and moved hesitantly to a control surface on one wall. Slowly, as if trying to remember, he reached out and gingerly touched a pad. The floating image of the canyon expanded to fill the room. Every rock and bush became life size and the others found they could walk around the room and see all angles and sides.

"It's a holographic projection," said Allen. "We use that in virtual reality. We've succeeded in making small rooms into projection rooms, but it requires sophisticated equipment, and we never could do it in real time, on an outside location."

Ethan reached behind him, as if he'd done it hundreds of times, and touched another pad without looking. The scene vanished and they found themselves in the control room again.

They marvelled at the technology for a while then Beth reminded them they had to go. "I want to get out of here," she said holding Patty tight. "I lost you once and I have no intention of losing you again. Not even to this wonderful alien playground you've discovered."

"The Captain has spoken," laughed Patty. "However, we tried to get out and couldn't. Any suggestions?"

Timotin explained how he was able to leave by being pulled through from the other side. All they had to do was return the same way. Perhaps by doubling up on a line.

"But can we take two people through at the same time?" This from Allen who had been gazing in wonder at the alien technology!

"Nothing to it, but to do it," said Alyssa. "I'll go through first, just to make sure it's still safe, then I'll come back in and take someone through with me."

"Just a minute," argued Timotin. "Timotin should be first." He argued that Alyssa was indispensable while he was totally dispensable. An argument ensued who was more important to their survival. Not until Ethan spoke up did the noise abate.

"There is no reason to test the wall," he said confidently. "I know that two people can pass through easily."

Timotin laughed heartily. "So speaks the voice of reason. Come little friend. You are still Timotin's hero! We journey together, yes?"

Ethan smiled and leapt onto the big man's back. Patty rounded up the rest of his team, and Alyssa did the same. Bundling all their supplies they returned to the room where Alyssa and the others' first arrived.

"What about artefacts?" Asked Sam. "I don't understand all this technology, but some of it should be useful to us?"

Alyssa caught Patty and Beth's eyes as if seeking silent confirmation, then replied. "We can come back later with a properly equipped research team. We know how to get in, and soon how to get out. No huhu."

When they reached the room, Timotin lashed one of the lines protruding from the wall around himself. Picking up Ethan in one hand he tugged on the line with the other. To his surprise nothing happened. He waited then tugged again, harder.

"I know my men are still on guard," said the giant puzzled. "Timotin not understand why they do not pull on moving rope?"

"I think I know," said Allen. "Timotin wait five minutes then tug on the rope again. If nothing happens, join us in the control room. The rest of you come with me please."

They returned to the alien complex control room and Allen activated the image viewer. Carefully he tightened and narrowed the focus until he had the campsite of the others in sight.

"Timotin should be pulling on the rope about now. Watch carefully." They stared into the image. True to their word, one of the rescue team in the camp, held all the ropes in his hand. If they so much as moved a little he would know. They watched and waited…and waited…and waited.

"What are you looking at?" They whirled around to see Timotin stride into the room with heavy thundering steps. "I pulled and tugged," he explained. "Pulled very hard, but Timotin not move at all. So I came here."

"See," said Allen. "It's just as I feared. Whatever that screen, portal, whatever you want to call it, is, it won't allow anything to pass through from this side. Timotin could pull with all his mighty strength and the rope on the other side wouldn't move. I think the portal absorbs energy. Only a force from outside can affect what happens in here."

"Then how do we get out? We have no way of signalling the men outside," said Patty.

"I've been thinking about that as well," replied Allen. "You saved our butts once by manipulating the ghost winds. Do you think you could do it again? This time at the camp."

Patty turned from the image and activated the wind controls. The rest watched the image in breathless anticipation, but after ten minutes Patty resigned in frustration.

"I can't do it," he said. "There seems to be some sort of built in safety control that prevents me from bringing the winds too close to the portal."

Alyssa moved closer to Ethan. "Sweetheart. Have you sorted out all those memories the machine gave you? Can you tell me, how we can get out of here?"

Ethan closed his eyes in concentration. Tiny beads of sweat appeared on his brow. His tiny, but lithe frame shook from the effort he applied to the problem. Presently he opened his eyes, defeat showing on his face.

"I'm sorry," he said choking back his frustration. "I know it's in there, but I can't access it yet."

"It's all right," said Alyssa moving to comfort the boy. Frustration plainly showed at his inability to help them escape.

"We need some way to talk to the system here," said Allen. "Everyone, look around. Try to find an input device—Keyboard, touch pad, voice interface anything."

They split up into teams and scoured the room looking for anything recognisable. For the next half-an-hour, Allen, as the recognised computer expert spent his time running around the room trying the different items found. One by one the teams returned to the centre of the room where the image still showed the outside camp.

As each team reported in, they shook their heads in sadness. Soon everyone had returned from investigating their little section of the huge room. All except Timotin and Ethan. They could still be seen examining a piece of equipment. Curious, the others moved beside them.

"We found something," said Timotin. "Ethan recognises it as a way to communicate with the alien system."

"It's a little unusual, Allen," said Ethan with childlike enthusiasm, "But you should have no trouble."

Allen listened to the boy, but watched Timotin. His features had taken on an increasingly cloudy visage. "What's wrong, Timotin?"

"Allen," he said tenderly. "Timotin is sorry. We found a neural interface."

The others just glanced in puzzlement at each other. They could plainly see that Allen had the port in his head for a neural interface. What was the problem? Alyssa though understood and was horrified.

"Allen," she said taking his hand. "Don't do it. This is a big complex. We'll find another way out."

"My friend," rumbled Timotin, "the danger here to you is great. You have learned much, and healed well, but this is overwhelming."

Allen understood his giant mentor. This alien complex was obviously run by some sort of super computer. He could easily be pushed into third stage if he interfaced with it.

"I don't believe there is another way out. There may be other portal-doors, but I think they may all operate the same way," he said addressing Alyssa. Turning to Timotin he reached up and placed an affection hand on the giant's shoulder.

"Thank you for your concern," he said softly, "but this could be our only way out. Do me one favour though. If I should go to third stage, please let me do no harm!"

Timotin stood mutely then nodded silently. Alyssa gasped and cried "NO." But Allen took her arm and explained there was no other way. The rest clamoured to know what was going on. They didn't understand and wanted to know. Allen, disregarding his privacy explained what he was and what he was about to do.

"That's the bravest thing I've ever known," said Sam and kissed the computer expert shyly.

Allen examined the alien interface and finding it not much different from the ones he knew, made adjustments on his rig to accept the alien insertion probe. Sam stood close by. Clearly she had become enamoured with the young man.

Allen, satisfied that the probe would fit securely turned to Timotin. "Remember your promise." The giant nodded solemnly.

"If you go into this third stage," said Sam, "after Timotin restrains you, we'll get you some help, and when were rescued the best help in League. I promise that."

Allen's hands shook as he held the probe. With pleading eyes he looked at Alyssa. Understanding she took Sam gently by the shoulders and pulled her away.

Sam shrugged out of her gently grip. "What's wrong with you, Alyssa. If Allen gets sick, I want to be there to care for him."

"You really like him, don't you? He's the one you've been talking about. Secretly watching!"

"Yes," she said softly looking back in his direction. "Alyssa, do you believe in love at first sight?"

"For some people, yes," she said. "Do you love him?"

"I'm not sure, but I know I've never felt this way about anyone before."

"Perhaps then you'd better take a tranquil from the med kit."

"Why? Alyssa, I don't understand. I know he stands a chance of becoming seriously ill, but I don't know why you and Timotin are so worked up."

"Allen didn't explain all of it. In the third stage, people get abusive and violent. They'll say anything, do anything to get that ultimate high…Even murder."

"So I figured," said Sam defiantly. "But Timotin should be able to restrain him, then when were rescued I'll make sure that he gets help."

"If he goes third stage, he won't care about you, Timotin, or me. His only goal will be to interface with a high-powered computer. He will literally be mad, and in that condition, he will kill you, or anyone else who tries to stop him from reaching his goal."

Sam stood still puzzled then a dawning realisation hit her. "No," she whispered. "Timotin couldn't. He wouldn't."

"He could and he would," said Alyssa. "Allen knew what he asked of his friend and knew that Timotin would be the only one who could do it. It will hurt Timotin, badly. He cares a lot for Allen, but he also knows what will happen, and has promised."

"But if he cares so much," said Sam tears now running freely down her soft cheeks, " how can he kill his friend?"

"Because to do otherwise is to consign his friend to a lifetime of torturous pain and cruelty. Not to mention that it puts everyone else's life in danger. Look, I don't like it any more than you do, but I understand the reasoning."

"Well I don't," she shouted and broke free, running back to Allen. She reached him just in time to see him insert the probe in its port in his skull. "NOOO," she shouted, but the others grabbed and restrained her.

Chapter 19

"It's too late now," said Patty tenderly. "He's the only one who can break the contact. Don't struggle! If you pulled him free the shock would kill him instantly."

That stopped her struggles and she looked into the face of the aged veteran. He nodded slowly and her shoulders fell. A flare of anger surged in her breast as she saw Timotin remove his field jacket and flex his mighty arms.

Then a serene thought entered her mind and she settled down. *Ethan!* Somehow he had penetrated her hysteria and through mental communication had quieted the raging inferno in her.

"He is not evil or a ghoul," said the boy as he approached her. "Look into his eyes. This hurts him as much as you, but he knows his duty. Death is common on his world, so he doesn't fear it as we do, but it still hurts to take the life of another human being, especially a friend!"

Sam slowed her breathing. She looked at Alyssa and Patty and realised they hadn't heard a word Ethan had said. He communicated only with Sam, telepathically. Suddenly she could read Ethan's thoughts as if wall had been lowered. The boy felt just as strongly about this because Timotin and Allen were his friends, and he grieved for what both men would go through.

But something else caught her attention. Somewhere deeply buried in the psyche of the boy, a seething, bubbling cauldron of courage overflowed. Somehow a hidden reservoir of strength and maturity had surfaced to aid the young man in this difficult situation. She saw that Ethan now appeared older than his young years let on.

"AHHH," came the sudden cry of pain from Allen. Sam tried to rush to him, but Patty's strong grip held fast.

Allen dropped to the floor, his eyes shut tight. Suddenly his body shot out straight and he lay flat his eyes open and glassy. The others waited, hardly daring to breathe and watched as one of their friends began to twitch violently and squirm around on the floor.

Just as a depressed, Timotin moved to assist his friend, the twitching stopped and Allen sat up. His eyes, still glazed and watery focused on his giant friend. He spoke with a soft voice of awe and wonder.

"I'm all right," he said softly. "It was just a problem in communicating with the alien system. I can see its program now, very detailed, very complex. This will take me a little time to work through."

"Are you sure you are fine," asked Timotin concern on his face.

"For now," said Allen. "Alyssa? Alyssa, listen carefully, this is going to take me a while to figure out, but the one thing coming through clearly is there is trouble with the power supply. You must go to the power supply and repair the damage. Quickly we don't have much time."

Alyssa nodded and placed a hand on the man's shoulder. She could feel the energy, as if his body were charged with electricity. "Where is it, Allen?"

Quickly the man connected to the machine explained how to find the source of the power for the complex. She took several people with her and vanished down the hallway. Timotin still stood near his friend. He seemed all right, but Timotin knew that he could snap in an instant.

"Sam," called Allen, "are you still here?"

Patty released his grip on her and she cautiously approached the man still seated on the floor. When she crouched beside him, he turned his head and stared at her through glassy eyes. The sight made her shudder. She got the impression that he was no longer with them.

"Don't worry, my love, I'm fine," he said softly. "Don't let my appearance scare you. This is normal."

"What's it like in there?"

"I can't explain it in terms you would understand, but this has to be the most cleverly designed computer system I've ever seen. The technology is beyond our wildest dreams, and its program is a thing of beauty."

Sam suddenly became concerned. "I'm not bothering you am I? I mean how can you talk to me and still concentrate on searching the computer?"

"You of all people should know that the power of the human mind is barely touched. In here, I can do a lot of things simultaneously. Will you stay with me, my love?"

"That's the second time you've called me 'My Love.' What do you mean?" She tried to make her voice sound like she was carrying on a normal conversation, but inside her heartbeat faster every time he called her.

"I have loved you for many months now," he said, "but until this moment I never thought it could work out, so I kept quiet."

"For God's sake," she cried, "WHY?"

The glassy visage of Allen smiled. "Have you forgotten already who you are and your position? If not, then remember my status. We could never be together."

"Then why tell me you love me now?"

"Because I couldn't face the possibility of dying without telling you. Sam, I'll tell you now. If I get out of this alive and you are interested. I want to marry you and raise a big family."

Sam smiled through tear filled eyes, leaned over, and kissed his lips. They felt cold and lifeless, but she continued kissing him anyway.

"That has to be the worst proposal I've ever had, and I've had a few. But to me it sounded wonderful. I wasn't sure before, but I am now. I love you with all my heart and will willingly marry you, and to hell with what anyone else has to say about it."

Allen's eyes assumed a blank stare even more horrifying than before. "Ethan. You must contact Scrapper. He is about to damage some vital equipment. You must stop him." He told Ethan how to find his pet. With the aide of a member from Patty's group, Ethan set out in search of his mischievous pet.

Sam sat on the floor beside the man who professed his love. Linking arms she snuggled into the crook of his shoulder, but he gave no response that he even knew she was there. Pleadingly she looked to Timotin for help. The giant knelt down and quickly examined him.

As usual when in moments of great stress or concentration he spoke plain English. "From what I have studied about this, I would say everything is going normally. He must be very deep inside the core of the system not to respond. This is where it gets dangerous. Hold on to him my dear. Hold tight. He's going to need all the love and support he can get now to try and keep his own mind."

Sam clung to him as a drowning man clutches a life preserver. No force in the universe would separate her from him. His body twitched and twisted in her grip. Timotin lent his prodigious strength to holding him still. Allen's body began to thrash violently around, making it virtually impossible to hold him still.

Timotin sat on the ground and placed the young man between his powerful legs and wrapped his arms around him. Allen by now had lost control of his body and it fought against the restraints. But these were no ordinary restraints. They were the arms and legs of a man who was born and lived on a heavy gravity world.

Timotin's muscles knotted and bunched with the strain, but he held fast to the squirming figure. "Do not struggle so, my friend," he gasped. "Timotin will not let you leave us yet. Fight! Fight the urge. Remember your lessons in the forest. You control!"

Allen's eyes cleared briefly and he started to speak, but lost the mental control he needed against the super computers influence. Allen descended rapidly into third stage, and there was nothing anyone could do to help him.

Chapter 20

Alyssa led her team down the twisting, winding corridors, according to the directions provided by Allen. Each turn took them deeper into the alien complex. Each bend in corridors changed the subtle hue of the wall coverings. As they moved deeper in the complex, the colouring changed from blue to red, very gradually. Eventually the twists and turns led them to a dead end.

"I don't understand," she said. "According to Allen's directions there should be a passage way leading down, but I don't see any stairs, or lifts. Look around. See what you can find. Check the walls. Maybe it's hidden."

They spread out and started to run their hands over the surfaces of the walls and floors. Alyssa, in the far corner rubbed and pushed the blank walls, looking for a secret entrance. Step by step she ran her hands over the featureless surface, then suddenly her hand disappeared into a portion of the wall. With a startled gasp she called to the others.

They quickly flanked her and found the area was the size of a large double door. No feature or marking was visible, but wherever they touched, their hand would pass through as if nothing was there.

"All right," she said. "Same procedure as when we first entered the complex. I'll go in attached to a rope. Wait thirty seconds then pull me out. Ready? Let's go!" She looped the line around her waist and stepped into the wall. She disappeared as if the wall swallowed her up without a trace.

Her companions didn't have to wait the thirty seconds, before she came back through the wall. "No barriers here. I can come and go as I please. I think I've found the way down. Get your gear and follow me. Oh, somebody better wait here in case of trouble."

One of the men volunteered to remain and the rest walked through the wall as if commonplace. In this ancient alien complex, the strange and unusual were becoming the norm. Humanity always adapts quickly to change. The new, rapidly becomes familiar. So now the presence of invisible doorways, no longer frightened the team.

The other side of the wall left them in a cavern of native rock. The smooth grey-red walls of the complex had vanished to be replaced by rough, jagged rock. A tunnel, very old, had been carved into the rock. Large broad stairs, twice as wide as a normal step, led down a gentle sloping curve.

"Stay together," warned Alyssa.

They started their descent. The farther down they went, the hotter it became. Step after step, minute after minute passed, but still no end in sight of the spiralling staircase. After twenty minutes, the team started to relax their vigil. They found the route safe and comfortable. If only the heat would abate a little.

"It must be close to 120 degrees down here," she said wiping her brow. Her shirt had formed the characteristic sweat pattern on her chest and back.

"I hope this doesn't go much farther," said Walker—one of the team. "The climb back will be hard in this heat."

"Another half-an-hour, then we'll stop for a rest," gasped Alyssa. "Loosen you collars and any constrictive clothing. I have a feeling it will get a lot hotter."

The temperature had risen to well over 130 degrees before they saw the ending of the stairway. With relief they stood on a dirt floor. Strange shadows flickered and jumped in the dim light.

"It seems our alien friends have even provided some form of lighting at this level. But I'll be damned if I can see where it's coming from," gasped Alyssa. "According to Allen's instructions, the power source should be 50 feet directly ahead and round the next bend. I certainly hope so. We can't survive in this heat much longer."

Wearily, gasping for breath in the heat, they plodded on. As they rounded the bend, a wave of intense heat blasted them in the face. Staggering back, they took refuge against the rock surface.

"We need to get in there," gasped Alyssa. "Any suggestions?"

Walker reached into his pack and removed a light animal skin. While the others watched he wrapped it around his head, leaving only his eyes free. Carefully he rounded the bend and disappeared from view. Alyssa and the others waited and watched. A couple of minutes later he reappeared.

Unwrapping his face, they could see the sweat run freely down his face. "Damn, but it's hot in there, but the protection works. The skin will protect you from the heat blast. Try to breathe shallow…You're not going to believe what the power source is!"

The others pulled skins from their packs and wrapped them securely about their heads and faces. Almost as one they took a deep breath and stepped into the furnace. The heat hit them like a physical object, but the skins prevented too much discomfort. Taking little rasping breaths of scalding hot air, they followed Walker deeper into the cavern.

Strange looking pipes—jutting out of the wall, sprayed tiny puffs of steam into the air, raising the temperature even further. The deeper into the cave they went, the more machinery they came across. Soon, the tunnel opened into a giant cavern. Suspended from the ceiling, large glowing orbs throbbed and pulsated. All along the walls, panels filled the cavern with bright hew of orange and green light. But what held the attention of the team wasn't the sight of the alien machinery, but the source of their power.

At the far side of the cavern, a huge waterfall plunged from the ceiling into a pit so deep they could see no end. The closer they got to the waterfall, the hotter it got. Soon, gasping for air, they stood in front of the falls and gazed in wonder at the sight.

Brilliant colours played over the surface of the falls. In spite of the heat, they stared in wonder and awe at the strange beautiful sight. A surge from the falls caused some of it to spray outward. Tiny droplets streaked through the air like tiny meteorites and landed on the ground beside Alyssa.

"That's not water," she cried stepping away from the drops. "It's fire. This is a firefall. The whole thing is made of fire!"

*

Ethan with his friend in tow, concentrated and using the directions provided by Allen, searched for Scrapper. The more he moved through the alien corridors the more he felt he knew the place. Soon he abandoned the instructions and started to run through the well-lit corridors, causing his companion to hurry after him.

He stopped in front of a blank wall, and calmly stepped through. His companion, unsure what to do, stared dumbly for a second then with a shrug stepped through himself. On the other side he found himself in the midst of a jumble of broken and discarded machinery parts.

"Ethan," he called out and was rewarded by the sound of scampering feet. He cocked his head then ran of in the direction of the sound. Careful so as not to trip over the mysterious objects on the floor, he hurried after his young charge. He found Ethan struggling with Scrapper, trying to pull the lion-snake away from a glass enclosure. He moved quickly and between them they managed to rein in the rambunctious pet.

When they finally subdued the animal, Ethan examined the glass enclosure. Inside a swirl of liquid light formed eddies and currents. It shone with a fluorescent blue.

"What the hell is that," asked the man.

"A battery," said Ethan confidently. "They store the energy here. If Scrapper had broken the glass, the energy release would have destroyed this room, and probably the complex."

"How do you…Sorry, I forgot."

Ethan shrugged as if it meant nothing. The knowledge in his mind had been giving him a new outlook on life. He felt confident and assured. With assurance, Ethan moved closer to the enclosure. His keen young eyes quickly found a display panel and slowly at first but with growing confidence, he began activating panels.

"We got here just in time," said Ethan while working. "Scrapper had almost dug through the glass. I've activated the repair systems. It should reseal the glass in a second."

As he spoke the frame of the enclosure glowed and mist ejected from all sides. Soon the fog covered the glass and it disappeared from view. In fascination they watched as the fog condensed on the glass wall and bonded to it. The scratch marks from Scrapper's claws slowly faded from view and the fog dissipated.

"That should hold," said Ethan.

"What happened?"

"The unit just laid a new layer down and patched the holes and scratches. It was the swirling light show that attracted Scrapper in the first place. I've told him to be more careful from now on."

"You mean you can now communicate directly with him? When? How?"

"I'm not sure," said the voice of a little boy, "but I think this new knowledge I've received has also increased my abilities."

"Or possibly freed them?"

"Could be! Could be!"

*

Alyssa and her team returned to the safety of the stairway to escape the oppressive heat. While still well over one hundred degrees, it seemed cool and refreshing compared to the cavern with the firefall. They paused to catch their breath, then made their plans.

"I don't see how we're supposed to fix whatever is wrong with this," said Walker. "We don't even know what to look for."

"I know," said Alyssa leaning back against the cooling rock surface. "Let's go in once more. This time, concentrate on the machinery. Look for something out of place, or whatever doesn't feel right."

"I don't suppose you could give us a hint," asked one of the others jovially.

"If I could, I would," she laughed. "Well, if everyone's ready. Let's do it!"

*

Ethan examined the control panels and a frown came over his face. "What's the matter now? Is the battery okay?"

"Yeah, the battery's fine, but according to these readings, there is a problem with the charger. The complex is drawing more power than the battery can provide, and I'm afraid we're the cause of it."

Ethan explained how the whole complex was using its limited battery reserves to provide light and air so the humans could move about freely. "That's why Allen sent Alyssa to find the source. Something's interfering with the power flow, and the batteries are going dead. Come on, we've got to find her."

"I'm sure she'll find it all right," said his companion with a smile. "She's a very capable officer."

"Yes, but she won't know what to do," said Ethan hurriedly. "I've only just realized the danger myself, and I have the knowledge. We have to find them and help them, before they blow up the planet!"

*

"Well, did anyone find anything?" she asked as they stopped to take a cooling break near the stairway.

"I found two conduits on the southeast wall," said one of the weary explorers. "One is a helix shape, the other straight. The ends closest to those glowing orbs are glowing with the same pulsating light. But the light stops about halfway down the length of the conduits."

"Maybe the pipes are blocked," suggested Walker. "If we free them up, the power should flow."

"But which one is blocked? I couldn't tell from observing them."

"It could be either, or both," said Alyssa. "The again it could be neither. We just don't know…I'm open to suggestions."

They sat in silence for a few minutes, then Walker spoke, "I think it's worth a shot trying to unplug the pipes."

They all agreed and returned to the cavern. Alyssa made everyone hug the wall farthest away from the conduits, just in case. She lifted her spear out of its carrying place in her pack and placed it at the opening of the straight conduit. Slowly she pushed it into the tube then stopped when she met with resistance.

"This one is definitely blocked," she yelled over her shoulder. Slowly she applied more pressure, trying to force the spear through the blockage. When it refused to go any farther, she backed the spear out and prepared to thrust into the pipe.

"STOP," came the cry from behind, but it was too late, she had already started to thrust forward. The cry startled her and she accidentally let go of the spear. It flew from her grasp and plunged into the conduit.

She whirled around to see who called a halt to her attempts and found Scrapper flying at her at full bore. Unable to avoid the flying lion-snake, she took the brunt of the force on her body and Scrapper pinned her to the ground. A half-a-second later the spear came flying out of the conduit in reverse. It flew across the room and plunged into the firefall, burning up instantly.

"If Scrapper were any slower, you would have been skewered by that spear, and thrown into the falls yourself," said Ethan running up beside her.

"Ethan," she said, "what are you doing here?"

"Trying to stop you from blowing up our little world here," he grinned. "Fortunately you didn't try that with the other conduit first, or we wouldn't be here at all."

Alyssa picked herself up and because neither Ethan nor his companion had skins around their faces, quickly ushered them back to the steps. Scrapper seemingly unaffected by the monstrous heat, galloped behind them. Ethan explained that he had only just realized the danger they were in and had Scrapper quickly search out Alyssa.

"So, do you know what the problem is?"

"No," said the boy. "I have to take a look see myself, and hope that these alien memories will tell me what's wrong."

They bundled Ethan up like themselves and returned to the cavern. With agonizing slowness he examined every piece of equipment in the huge cavern. At each stop he strained as if trying to recall what they should look like, then he moved on. Finally he stopped at one of the panels.

"That's the one," he exclaimed. "The intake sensor is malfunctioning."

"Can you fix it?"

"I believe so," said Ethan thoughtfully, "but I can't get to it. It's on the other side of the firefall. The sensor is right inside the wall of fire." He looked helplessly at the others.

"Then we must find a way to breach the fire," said Walker.

The group looked around, but nothing presented itself as a way through the burning wall. No valves to stop the flow, no special heat resistant suits, nothing. Walker moved away from the group and approached the ledge. Crouching down he picked up a piece of rock and was about to throw it into the furnace when he stopped and examined it closely.

"Hey," he cried and the others rushed over. "Take a look at this!"

"It's a rock," said Alyssa, "so?"

"Haven't you wondered why the rock here doesn't burn or melt," said Walker excitedly. "Here's the answer. These rocks are fire proof. See those tiny wispy fibres? I'm willing to bet they're a form of asbestos."

"Very nice," said Alyssa, "but how does this help us?"

"We could weave a suit out of these fibres," said Walker. "Then we could pass through the flames safely." He stopped and realized that while his idea had merit, it would be weeks before they could manufacture suitable clothing from the tenuous fibre.

"Sorry," he said, "wasn't thinking."

"Good idea though," said Alyssa. "Think people. The race that built this had to have some way to service what they built. All we have to do is find it. Any ideas, Ethan?"

The young boy shook his head dejectedly. Suddenly a growl from Scrapper caused them to look in his direction. Scrapper had moved closer to the firefall and somehow now floated in empty space between the falls and the edge of the cliff.

Alyssa knelt at the edge of the gorge and stared into the inky depths. The falls went down quite a way. Even the brilliant light from the flames receded into darkness. If Scrapper, or anyone else fell, there would be no way to rescue them.

"Come here, boy," she coaxed gently. The lion-snake turned at the sound of her voice and with a grin walked on empty air back towards her. When safely on the ground, Ethan hugged his pet then admonished him for wandering off.

Alyssa smiled then focused her attention on finding what had kept Scrapper up. Carefully she felt around in the empty air. Suddenly her hand brushed against something hard and unyielding. With great care she felt out the dimensions of the invisible object. Squinting she tried to see what lay before her, but still saw nothing.

"There seems to be some sort of smooth out jutting here," she said, "but I can't see it."

Ethan snapped his fingers. "That's it," he cried excitedly. "That's what's wrong. Don't you see? The Providers' saw on a different wavelength from us. I've wondered—with all this knowledge—why I've had a hard time reading the panels. It's because they saw at a different end of the spectrum. One we can't see, but Scrapper can."

"Then that thing he stood on," said Walker "is really a bridge to the falls?"

"Right," said Ethan. "If we follow it, it should lead us to the other side."

"Couple of problems with that," said Alyssa. "First, we can't see the bridge. One slight misstep and well, it would be just too bad. And second, burning up in a waterfall of fire is not exactly my favourite way to die."

"We don't have to worry," said Ethan. "Scrapper just told me that he was growling at the doorway. He said that there is a door at the other end of the bridge. That will lead us safely through."

Alyssa sat back on her haunches. The incredible leaps and bounds this young man had gone through never failed to amaze her. That he could easily communicate with Scrapper astonished her, but moreover she knew instinctively to trust him. Then she heard his thoughts in her head.

"I have grown," they said, "and so have you. I can tell that you can read my projections. Don't worry Alyssa. Something tells me we are safe here." She turned to stare at the young man, but he quickly averted his eyes as if embarrassed at his intrusion into her mind.

"So what do we do now?" She stared at the invisible bridge, trying to make it appear by sheer willpower.

"Scrapper can see the bridge," said Ethan. "He can guide us across to the door."

An argument ensued who would make the perilous trip. Alyssa called a halt to the argument and they retreated again to the cooling recesses of the stairway. The debate resumed until Ethan spoke to them loudly and firmly.

"There is no choice," he said. "I have to go. I'm the only one who could recognize the sensors and repair them."

"No way," said Walker. "Look little buddy, you may be mental genius, and have all that alien knowledge floating around inside your head, but I can't justify risking you life. Tell me what to look for and how to repair it. I'll go!"

" I can't," said Ethan shaking his head. "I won't know what I'm looking for until I see it. No, I've got to go, but I will need some help."

"Then it's settled," said Alyssa. "I'll not ask anyone else to risk their lives. NO, I said. It's settled. Ethan and I will follow Scrapper across the bridge. With luck this should be over with quickly…Sorry, didn't mean for it to sound that way."

They returned to the cliff and Ethan told Scrapper what they wanted to do. Scrapper moved directly to the place where the bridge was and without hesitation stepped into open air. With only a second's pause, Ethan followed holding tightly to Alyssa's hand. Alyssa gripped the young man firmly as she stepped into what appeared to her as big nothing. When her foot came down on something solid, she paused to look.

Below her, stretching into never ending darkness, the pit! Yet her foot told her, there definitely was something solid to walk on. Gingerly they fol!owed Scrapper over the yawning chasm. Scrapper moved several feet ahead of them and instantly disappeared.

"Another invisible wall," said Alyssa. "Come on. This heat is unbearable." They inched their way along, following Scrapper. With one hand clutching Alyssa and the other probing the empty air in front of him, Ethan suddenly disappeared from view followed quickly by Alyssa.

On the other side, they found a control room, similar, but much smaller, than the one on the surface. The air temperature had a cool distinctive flavour. After the impossible sweltering heat on the other side, Alyssa found goose bumps forming on her skin—even though it still had to be in the high nineties.

"Okay, Ethan," she said looking around. "Do your stuff!"

Ethan quickly ran from panel to panel and examined them. He stopped in front of one and touched a couple of points. An image similar to the one they experienced before loomed in front of them.

"We're in a room on the other side of the falls," he said. "This view is the backside of the firefall. Look, you can see the rocks it goes over. They're not even singed. If we could take some of these out of here, I think they'd make a wonderful fire pit for the village."

Alyssa smiled at the suggestion. These rocks were far more flame retardant than anything previously discovered. If and when they left this world, scientists and geologists would give their eyeteeth to study these rocks.

"Hurry up, Ethan," she cautioned. "I've got a funny feeling about this." He nodded and continued his search of the panels.

"Here we are," he said with a smile. "This is definitely the broken sensor." Try as she could, Alyssa couldn't see any difference between that panel and the others in the room, but she trusted Ethan.

"Hold out you hands," he instructed her. "No cup them. I'm going to place something in them and I don't want you to drop them." She did as he bid and he fiddled with the panel, then turned and placed something in her cupped hands.

She saw nothing, but felt several small hard objects. Ethan seemed to work like a man possessed. Alyssa watched closely. The young man worked as if he'd been repairing these machines all his life, but now had to do it blindfolded. His small hands, sure and confident, roamed over the surface of the panel, while his eyes remained tightly shut. Every time he turned, she felt another object drop into her palms.

Eventually he moved as if opening a small hatch in the panel. He thrust his hands down and they disappeared from view. She could see his arms moving, but couldn't see what he was doing. Seconds later his hands re-emerged and the panel light flickered briefly.

Without a sound he removed the objects from her hands and began replacing them in the panel, still with his eyes closed tightly. Minutes later he straightened up and opened his eyes.

"There," he said. "That should do it."

"What did you do? I couldn't see a thing!"

"I couldn't either," said Ethan. "That's why I closed my eyes. I knew what to do, but my limited vision kept confusing me. So I did it by touch. The sensors just needed realigning. But that little problem was what was causing all the commotion."

Alyssa hugged the boy. "Have I told you how proud of you I am?" He returned the hug with fervour.

"Scrapper. Scrapper, come on, boy," he said. "Time to leave." The lion-snake headed for a grey wall and disappeared through it, followed closely by Ethan and Alyssa.

Once on the other side, they recounted their adventure to the others. With a satisfied feeling, they made their way back to the stairway for the long climb back. Scrapper bounded on ahead. He didn't seem to mind the exercise, even in the heat.

"Can you still read him," said Alyssa. "Even though he's out of sight?"

"Yes," said Ethan. "He's at the top now." He stopped and his eyes took on a glassy haze. Alyssa grabbed him by the shoulders gently as he missed a step.

"What's wrong, Ethan?"

"We've got to hurry," he said and started running up the wide steps. The others chased after him panting from the heat and exertion.

"Ethan," cried Alyssa. "Ethan, please! Tell me what's wrong."

"I just picked up a feeling from Scrapper," panted Ethan. "He picked up Sam's thoughts. Allen is dying…"

Chapter 21

Timotin rose from his crouched position beside the blank-faced, motionless form of Allen, his doctor persona fully enshrouding his every movement and word. Gently he reached down and laid the still form of Allen onto the smooth floor.

"That's all I can do," he said gently to the others. "Somehow he's avoided third stage, but in exchange he's lost somewhere in the computer's brain."

"I don't understand," said Alyssa. "How can he be lost in the computer?"

"You must understand how a virtual connection is made," explained Timotin. "The technician's mind literally merges with the system processor. He sees and reacts within the computer as if he was the computer. Normally this is not a problem, indeed it is the reason Virtual technician's are so good at their jobs."

"Then what happened to Allen, if this is normal?"

"My diagnosis is secondary," said Timotin. "However, I believe the alien computer was just too powerful. It presented him with what all addicts search and hope for. He just lost himself inside. His mind is now part of the computer and I don't know how to call him back."

Sam returned to her place beside the glassy-eyed Allen on the floor. Since entering the system, she hadn't left his side until Timotin forced her out of the way to examine him. Tenderly she brushed the hair out of his eyes and stroked his cheek.

"He tried to save us," she mumbled. "He knew what could happen, but he wanted to do this. I can't believe that he's lost forever. Going third stage I can accept, but this…"

Ethan burst into the room and sat beside her. He closed his eyes and concentrated. "I'm sorry," he said finally. "I just can't sense his presence at all."

"Ethan," said Sam, "You've got all that alien knowledge in your head. Think please. For me! For him!"

"If there was anything I could do, I would," said the man in the child's body. "To save him we need to enter the system and look for him. Even then, there's no guarantee that he'll come back. He's an addict. This must be his idea of Nirvana."

"Plus," added Alyssa, "no one else has the implant to merge with the computer."

"Sam," said Ethan tenderly, holding her free hand, "I just don't think there is any way to reach him."

"You are wrong, my young friend," said Timotin.

"We're listening," said Alyssa, hopeful that the heavy planet scientist had a plan.

"Recall your link with Patty," he said, "through that link we were able to track and find him through the jungles of this world."

"Yes," said Ethan, "but I have no such link with Allen!"

"No, but Sam does. Did he not profess his love for you, and you returned that affection?"

"Well, yes," said Sam, "but that was only recently. I can't see how we could have developed a link so quickly. Beth and Patty formed their link over time."

"Still, it might be worth it," said Alyssa. "You've been in love with him for sometime, I know! And he admitted that he's been in love with you just as long. It can't hurt to try, Sam, concentrate. Think about Allen...Feel anything?"

Sam focused inward and she desperately searched her mind for a connection, no matter how tenuous to Allen. Slowly she opened her eyes and shook her head sadly. Beth released her grip on Patty and hugged the young woman tightly.

"Is it possible that your powers are not developed enough to read the link?"

Sam considered the possibility. "Then how do we find him?"

"If the link is there," said Ethan slowly. "I can find him!"

"I don't see how," said a sceptical Alyssa. "It took the combined efforts of you two, plus Beth and Scrapper to focus on the link you had with Patty. And we knew that existed."

"That was then," said Ethan calmly. "My abilities have grown tremendously since then. I may look 13 years old, but I have the accumulated knowledge of a race hundreds of millennia old…" He paused to let the impact of that staggering piece of information sink in.

"What I propose," he finally said, "is that I enter Sam's mind and search for the link myself. When I find it, I will ride the link until I meet Allen."

"That means you'll be entering into the system processor with Allen, through his link with Sam," said Timotin. "Do you think you can come out again? Remember, he is a grown man, while although artificially enhanced, you are still young and mentally immature—no offence intended."

"Non taken," said Ethan. "I admit that I'm unsure whether I can do it alone, but I have a solution."

"Let's here it, son," said Patty who had kept his silence until now. He felt a warm affection for the boy turned man and worried for his safety, but he knew that help could only come from Ethan.

"I will need someone to ground me here," said Ethan. "It will be a mental lifeline. If I should get lost, I can follow it back to the real world."

"What do we have to do?"

"I need you…and Alyssa to link with me," said Ethan. "You already know the link I have with you, but Alyssa is only just realizing the link we have."

"You're right," she said. "Now that you mention it, I can feel a connection with you. Ethan, I know we're close, but how can this be?"

"Once we join," he said, "you'll understand why. Do you still want to go through with it?"

"Absolutely," said Alyssa without hesitation.

"Join hands and concentrate on opening your minds to me," he said. "When I've made the connection, Sam, I will link with you and we'll begin the search."

They all nodded and Patty and Alyssa held hands and closed their eyes. Soon Alyssa felt herself growing light headed and she seemed to be floating in a mist. She sensed, rather than saw Patty's presence beside her. He appeared as he always did, but with a difference. In the mist he stood nearly well over 6 feet tall, with broad shoulders. An air of confidence and authority surrounded him.

"So, that's the way you see me," chuckled the image of Patty. "I like it." Alyssa smiled and found she could focus and see herself through his eyes. Patty saw her as a younger version of Beth, strong, powerful, yet very feminine. She approved of what he saw.

"I assume you two are pleased with what you see," the image of Ethan appeared before them. "In here, the mind is not fooled. The picture you paint of each other is the true representation of the way you feel."

Alyssa stared at the image of Ethan. She saw him as young boy, yet with the air of knowledge that surrounds those of tremendous intellect. Yet beneath that, there seemed to be a feeling of helplessness that needed comforting and holding. She wondered how Patty saw him and tried to enter his thoughts, but found herself blocked.

"Don't try to force it, Mother," said Ethan. "He has his reasons and we must respect his privacy."

"Mother?"

"Yes," said the little boy. "Come into my mind."

She felt the tug of his powerful, yet untrained mind invite her in. She looked at herself through his eyes. He didn't see Alyssa the engineer, or Alyssa the Mayor. She looked warmer, affectionate, and loving.

"Ethan," she gasped, "I didn't realize you felt that way about me."

"Oh, but you did," he said with a smile. "You feel the same way towards me. Remember, in here you can't lie."

The image of Patty moved closer to the other two and Alyssa suddenly felt the walls fall and she could clearly see what Patty saw. Ethan wasn't Ethan anymore. He was someone else. Someone she didn't recognize.

"Who is that?" She didn't want to pry, but since Patty dropped his walls, she felt it important to know.

"That is my son, Egan," said Patty. "He died several years ago, but I always remember him this way. He was a crises team leader. On a planet infected with a plague. He contracted the disease and it killed him. Ethan is so much like him that I can't help seeing him that way. I'm sorry, my boy."

"Don't be," said the calm voice of Ethan. "I'm honoured to be included in your thoughts this way. If I remind you of him, then I'm flattered. It means that I meet your expectations and I am pleased."

Alyssa suddenly saw how Ethan saw Patty. Not as a father figure, but as a guide, a mentor, the beloved teacher who inspired one to greatness. Lacking a father, Ethan had latched onto Patty as the one to emulate and make proud. Alyssa felt Patty's warmth and love for the little boy with the incredible mental abilities.

"Here, hold this," said Ethan. "In front of them a rope appeared and hovered in the air. " It doesn't really exist, but it's a representation that you can grasp. This will be my lifeline." The other end looped itself, by its own volition around the waist of the boy.

"Using this I can follow it back to you, when the time is right."

"Ethan?" Alyssa turned to see the image of Sam appearing. Because she was directly linked to Ethan she saw Sam through his eyes. She appeared as a woman, several years older than her real age, but with the beauty that comes from within. Puzzled Alyssa tried to figure out what he saw then it dawned on her. Sam was his older sister.

"We are your family," she said. "But I sense that someone is missing. Who?"

As if in a shadow, the image of Ada appeared Matronly with a kindly face and a lap that appeared big enough for all the children in the galaxy. "Nana," said Ethan. "I don't know what she thinks of me, but this is the way I see her."

The little boy pulled himself together and a young strong man appeared in front of Alyssa. "Time to go. Remember keep a hold on that line. Sam, I'm going into your mind now. Think of Allen, and don't lose the concentration."

*

In the real world, the bodies of their comrades appeared motionless. Timotin carefully checked their vitals and pronounced them safe and healthy. He sat on the floor and waited in silence with the rest, saying a little prayer for the safe return of everyone.

*

Ethan stepped through the wispy doorway that was the representation of Sam's mind. Inside, he ignored the different floating images of people and places that passed by him and sought the link with Allen. He willed himself to travel what appeared to be an endless road, passing other floating lines.

He stopped and grasped each of these lines in turn. The first line, made of a strong stout hawser, connected with an older man with greying hair at the temples. Ethan backed out before he initiated contact. Then moved on to the next line, and the next.

Because Sam had Empathic powers, she had subconsciously created links with anyone who had any meaning to her. Most of these links were very weak and faint. They represented themselves as thin wispy lines no thicker than sewing thread.

Ethan concentrated and removed all images except the links from his view. Sam had dozens of threads, only a few had any substantial mass. Then he saw a link moving and twisting in the fog. He floated near it and saw that it glowed with a pulsating white light. Without hesitation he grasped the line and followed it.

He suddenly found himself immersed in what appeared to be a giant circuit board. All around him, pieces of electronic apparatus seemed huge to their actual size. He knew that he had entered the brain of the alien computer. He also instinctively knew that the imagery was his mind placing details into forms he could recognize.

"Allen," he called out. Ethan drifted through the ever-increasing jumble of hardware.

A swirling port appeared in front of him. A kaleidoscope of colours twisted and swirled, almost mesmerizing in their pattern. The line that

Ethan followed pulsed brighter and disappeared into the whirling maelstrom. Ethan approached the crazy doorway and then willed himself through.

Once through, he found the images confusing and somewhat disorienting. This must be the program of the alien computer. Lacking the knowledge to understand even a simple program, his mind couldn't force the images into a form he could understand. He felt himself grow nauseous and knew he had little time.

"ALLEN," he yelled. The link whipsawed back and forth violently in front of him and he quickly followed it.

Just when he thought that he could go no further without going mad himself, he saw the image of Allen floating in the whirling mists. He lay on his back with his arms and legs dangling freely. He looked lifeless, but Ethan knew that he still lived or the link would be broken.

Desperate now he hurried to the side of the limp form. Reaching out he shook the man. "Allen," he said. "Come on. Wake up. ALLEN!"

Groggily the man responded. "Wha? Ethan? Is that you? How did you get me out?"

"You're not out yet," said Ethan. "We've got to go. I came in to get you."

"No," said Allen. "You go. I'm staying here. You don't know what I've found!"

"Yes, I do," said Ethan. "You've found what you've always wanted. A feeling of power and contentment I do understand. Look at me. Look at what I can do. Hell man I'm only 13 years old and see what I can do."

A wild look came into the boy's eyes and the fog around them vanished to be replaced by a tranquil setting by a peaceful babbling brook. Ethan stood on the grass letting his bare feet revel in the feeling. Allen appeared beside him, looking fit and well.

"I see you've discovered the lure of Virtual," said Allen. "But please, Ethan, get out while you still can. It's too late for me, but you can still leave."

"No way," cried Ethan happily. "This is great!" He started running, weaving in and out of the forest his mind had created.

"Ethan," cried Allen. "Come back. Don't let it take you. Ethan!" Then he saw the lifeline looped around Ethan's waist. "Smart boy," he said and grasped the line.

He took one more look at the tranquil setting and regretted leaving, but he couldn't let Ethan throw his life away. With all the power of his trained technicians mind, he grasped the lifeline and tugged for his worth. Slowly the twisting shapeless line straightened out and pulled taut.

Ethan came flying back through the trees—now dissolving—into his arms. The scene vanished and Ethan came to a stop. He seemed to be resisting the pull of the line. The wildness in his eyes vanished as he stared at Allen.

"Thank you," he said softly. "I felt myself go there, but I just couldn't stop. Is that what happened to you?"

Allen nodded slowly. "But in my case, I don't have the willpower to ignore it."

"But you do," protested Ethan. "You had the strength of will to see I was in danger and tried to rescue me."

"I...I couldn't let it happen to you. You'd better get out of here why you still can."

"Not without you," said Ethan firmly. "I'm not going back and you can't make me. I just can't go back and face Sam. It would kill her."

"Sam?"

"Yes, Sam," said Ethan hopefully. "That's how I found you through her. She has a link with you. She loves you!"

"But we've hardly talked. I mean I've dreamt about being with her, but it never happened."

"Somehow it did," Said Ethan. He slowly floated nearer Allen. "Relax for a moment and feel the link. She loves you and you love her. Is this place what you really need, or is it out there in the arms of the woman who wants and needs you?"

Allen closed his eyes and felt the pull of the link with Sam. Slowly he floated along the tenuous link. It grew thicker and more substantial the further along he moved. Suddenly he opened his eyes and they glowed brightly.

"She does love me," he cried. "You're right. She's what I want. I want to go. I want to be near her. But I've lost my connection with the implant. I can't leave without it."

"Then we'll find it together," said Ethan holding out his hand. "Take my hand. My lifeline will bring us out of this place. We'll search for your connection."

Allen took the boy's hand and Ethan willed his contact with the others. "Pull us back. I've got him!" The line suddenly snapped tight and Ethan was pulled backwards, but not before he grasped Allen tightly in a death grip. He had no intention of losing the young technician now.

Back through the whirling disoriented pattern that was the computer's program they flew. Briefly Allen struggled as the urge to remain grasped him again, but Ethan held fast. They passed through the whirling coloured doorway into the hardware and skimmed over the surface of the electronic equipment.

As they passed through each section, Allen's struggles to break free and return to the computer became weaker and weaker. Soon they were lost in an endless void and settled on the roadway that was Sam's mind. Together they passed over the road until eventually, they saw the open door. A huge image of the neural interface implant floated freely, waiting.

"Thank you," said Allen warmly and hugged the boy. He watched as Allen floated through the door and grasped the image of the implant. His body stiffened and Allen faded from sight.

Ethan broke the connection with Sam's mind and returned to the loving warm embrace of Alyssa and Patty. Slowly the world around them dissolved and the connection broke.

*

Look," cried Timotin pointing to Allen. "He's waking up. They did it. By all the fates, they did it."

"Hey, gang," said Allen sleepily. "What's all the fuss? Who died?"

"How are you feeling?"

"Tired," said Allen. "Very, very tired. Ethan? Where's Ethan?"

"Right here," said Ethan his eyes drooping. "You'll be fine now. I think I'll take a little nap." He turned and with effort crawled over to the waiting Alyssa. She grabbed him and pulled him onto her lap. His head rested against her breast and he fell asleep almost immediately.

"Goodnight, my son," she said tenderly. "I've never been a mother and don't know how good I'll be, but I promise to do my best." She kissed the top of his head as gentle snoring wafted up from him.

"I think you'll make a wonderful mother," said Patty, smiling as he kissed her gently. "And if those two don't cut it out, she'll be a mother before she knows it," he chuckled. All eyes turned in the direction he nodded.

Sam and Allen were locked in a passionate lover's embrace. If anyone had any doubts as to their feelings for each other they quickly vanished. The effort proved too much for Allen though. In his weakened condition he sighed and passed out. Fearful for a relapse, Sam cried in anguish. Timotin quickly examined him then calmed Sam.

"Allen is okay," he said softly. "He's done something no one else has. Gone third stage and passed through it. I don't think you'll have to worry about him anymore. Let him sleep now."

But Sam refused to leave his side. They made them both comfortable on the floor and cradling his head on her chest she held him firmly as they both drifted into peaceful slumber.

Sam woke a couple of hours later and after some persuasion, agreed to get a bite to eat and a drink. A few more hours and Ethan and Allen awoke. Timotin checked them both and pronounced them fit. With Ethan still cuddling in Alyssa's lap and Allen clinging tightly to Sam, they recounted their experiences to the rest.

"That is an incredible story," said Beth, "and don't get me wrong. I'm glad we got you back. But we still don't know how to get out of here."

"Oh, but we do," said Allen rising to his feet. He moved over to one of the strange alien panels and started pushing switches. "I found the answer before I got caught." He flipped a few more switches then turned to the rest.

"The Providers were a telepathic race," he explained. "This whole complex is automatic. It responds to their thoughts. Since we lack the necessary mental abilities, most of the functions won't work. I've just activated the manual override. We can now easily leave."

"But that doesn't explain what happened to Ethan or Sam," said Alyssa. "How come they know so much about this place?"

"I told you it's automatic," said Allen. "When a being enters the complex, they are telepathically given all the information they need. Sam was able to absorb some of it and Ethan because of his advanced mental abilities absorbed more. But they are still incredibly primitive, compared to the Providers."

"Well, in that case," said Patty, "I see no reason to stay any longer. Now we know its safe, we can come back later and explore some more."

The small band returned to the wall where they had first passed through. The lines still floated eerily in mid air, joined only at the featureless wall. Without hesitation, Allen grasped Sam's hand and stepped through the wall, disappearing from view.

With a shrug, Alyssa grabbed Ethan's hand and stepped through as well. Soon the rest followed. Timotin, holding Scrapper on the leash, was the last to appear. The hunters left outside stared wonder as the lost adventurers appeared, seemingly out of thin air. A barrage of questions finally prompted Alyssa to explain what had occurred.

They moved away from the invisible doorway. Ethan and Sam promptly collapsed on the ground. Seconds later they revived and shook their heads groggily. Moments later they discovered that there new found knowledge had disappeared.

"It seems our primitive minds couldn't contain all that alien knowledge once we left the complex," theorized Patty. Ethan struggled to communicate telepathically with Alyssa then Scrapper. Finally he gave up in frustration.

"I can't do it anymore," he said sadly. "I've lost all those powers."

"I know," said Patty gently. "You feel empty and deprived. But think about what you've gained. That should make you feel better."

Ethan looked at him through cloudy eyes then a smile brightened his face. He turned and rushed into the waiting embrace of Alyssa. "Does that mean you still want me?"

"I will always love you," said Alyssa. "I may not be your real mother, but I'd like to be. If you want?"

"You bet!" He hugged her tightly and she returned the affection with equal enthusiasm.

"Time to go," said Timotin. "All this mushy stuff too much for Timotin."

"Faker," laughed Sam and she stood on her toes and kissed the big man gently on the cheek.

"That goes double for me," said Alyssa and repeated Sam's example.

The other hunters laughed at the rising blush of embarrassment on their leaders face. With a smile he playfully swatted at them and ordered them to gather the gear and prepare to move out.

The trek back to the village through the steaming jungle proceeded without incident. Timotin called for rest breaks, but since everyone was full of high spirits, they didn't linger long. They made record time in returning and caught sight of the village just before dusk.

They entered the compound and were quickly greeted by the villagers. They were very happy to see them all safe and alive, but their enthusiasm seemed restrained. Amidst all the back clapping and hugging and kissing, Alyssa searched vainly for signs of Lex. She had learned a lot on this adventure, about herself and her life. More than anything she wanted to be near Lex and share her discoveries with him.

Soon she spotted him walking slowly towards them. She excused herself from the rest and ran into his arms. She wrapped her arms around his neck and kissed him quickly, but passionately. She started to tell him about their adventure when she noticed his face.

"What's wrong?"

He looked at her and she could see that he had had very little sleep. The rest of the part crowded around them. Beth moved in and stared at Lex. "Lex," she said softly. "What's the matter?"

"While you were gone," he said slowly, "we were attacked by Jellyrolls. They caught us by surprise outside the electric barrier. They killed three people, including Tony, you know the husband of that game warden."

"Oh my god," gasped Alyssa. "Poor Karen!"

"Wait a minute," said Patty. "That's not all is it?"

"You'd better come with me," he said softly and turned to march heavily to the shacks.

They stopped outside the shack that Ada lived in. "They attacked us in large numbers. Ada saved a little boy, but was absorbed by the Jellyroll. Fortunately it rolled over a junction in the electric fence and dissociated immediately, but not before it had started to work on Ada."

He choked and sniffled back a tear. "There's nothing Doc can do for her. We got her clear before she started dissolving, but it had infected her with some sort of chemical. It's destroying her from the inside out. Frankly I don't know what's keeping her alive now. I think she waited to here that you were all safe."

"NANA," cried Ethan and tried to rush inside, but Lex grabbed him.

"No," he said softly hugging the crying youth. "She wants to see Alyssa first."

Alyssa blinked back her tears and gently kissed Ethan. "It's all right. She'll see you in a little while. Stay here with Lex!" She opened the door and stepped into the darkened room.

"Ada," she called softly.

"Over here," came a whispered reply. Alyssa moved nearer and saw Ada stretched out on her primitive wooden cot. She looked fine at first glance then Alyssa saw the sunken features and the loss of muscle tone in her form.

"I'm glad you made it out alive," she gasped then coughed fitfully. Alyssa gently cradled the old woman's head and wiped away a trickle of blood that appeared at the corner of her mouth.

"Easy," she said. "Don't strain yourself. We'll get you some help."

"Don't kid a kidder," whispered Ada. "I know I'm as good as dead now, but I had to see you before I died."

"Why?"

"I have to tell you about Ethan," she coughed. "Alyssa I place in your hands a very remarkable boy. I don't have much time. Listen carefully…"

Chapter 22

While Alyssa stayed inside with the ailing Ada, Ethan approached Sam. "I think I know what Nana is going to tell Alyssa. Well, some of it anyway."

"What do you mean?"

"For the longest time I believed, as you, that I was nothing more than a normal child. Now I have strange thoughts entering my head that explain a lot more."

"Sit down here, Ethan," said Sam tenderly, indicating a log bench. "Now tell me what this is all about. Don't be afraid, we're all friends here."

"It's still a jumble. So many conflicting thoughts, but here goes…"

*

"So you're finally ready to tell me the truth about Ethan," said Alyssa firmly, staring at the old woman. "Okay, Ada, I'm listening."

"There's a lot I still can't tell you," coughed Ada. "There would be serious repercussions if word ever leaked out."

"Trouble? From whom?"

"Excuse me?" Alyssa whirled around and found Ethan and Sam standing in the doorway. "Ethan has just told me the whole story At least as much as he remembers. Your decision, Ada, no longer enters into the picture. He now controls his life. Not you. And definitely not the Centre."

"The Centre?" Said Alyssa, "I remember reading about a place called The Centre many years ago. A bio-eugenics lab of some sort wasn't it?"

Ada nodded slowly as Alyssa strained to recall the article so many years ago. "They were supposed to be working on correcting deformities and other problems through manipulating DNA, but they got into some sort of trouble. Wait a minute, isn't that the place that started breeding super humans before they were shut down by the League?"

"That's the one," said Sam nodding. "It really wasn't shut down, just placed under tighter security. The super human project was closed down, officially."

"But unofficially it kept going," concluded Alyssa.

"Yes, and no," agreed Sam. "They did shut it down, but they had several on going projects that couldn't be terminated. After they closed down, they transferred the facilities to a secret bunker under the facility of the children's home on Tantalus."

"That way they could dispose of the failures, without arousing too much suspicion," finished Ada. She looked worn out and defeated. She turned her teary gaze to Alyssa. "I'll tell you the rest. Since Ethan is no longer under my control."

"Allow me, Nana," said Ethan kindly. "You have done a good job. Now rest." Ada smiled gratefully, as if thankful that she no longer had to carry around a dangerous secret. Slowly, painfully, she lied back weekly on her bed.

She reached up a feeble hand and waved the others near. "No," she said. "It's my responsibility and I'll explain." She struggled to prop herself back up then asked Sam to go find Beth.

When they had all assembled in her tiny house she said, "I invited Beth, because I feel she has a right to know. She is still the Captain, and ultimately responsible."

Ada grunted and clutched her side as a spasm of pain racked her frail body. Ethan rushed over and sat on the ground beside her. Gently, lovingly, he took her emaciated hand in his and held it to his cheek. This simple act of affection seemed to provide Ada with the strength she lacked. Clearing her throat she told Beth what the others knew about The Centre, then continued her explanation.

"The project was to create a super human. One endowed with a genius-plus mind, and body capable of extraordinary strength and resiliency. But something went wrong. Of the original twenty-five subjects created, only Ethan remains."

The others gasped in astonishment. The Centre had been closed down nearly forty years ago. How could this young boy be connected to that project?

"Several volunteer women were implanted with genetically enhanced embryos. They had been gene spliced in the laboratory. If you wanted to get technical, the embryos didn't have a mother or father, instead their genes came from a dozen different donors."

"Incredible," gasped Beth. "I knew, of course, about the Centre and their experiment, but I thought it was shut down before it had gotten that far."

"That was the official word released. You see some of these genetically enhanced babies were born before they shut down. They turned out to grow at a phenomenal rate, both mentally and physically. By the time they were three years old, they looked 18 and acted like thirty. Unfortunately they also seemed quite bent on destroying and killing. Something had gone seriously wrong and the scientists realized they had created a race of homicidal maniacs. Now how would it look if we told everyone that twenty-five genetically enhanced Hitler's or Lo-Ping's were about to be unleashed?"

The others could only nod mutely. If word had gotten out about these super humans, then following the pattern of human nature, any child normally gifted would be hunted down and destroyed in fear.

"Fortunately," continued Ada, "their makeup wasn't perfect. None of them survived past 5 years. It seems that their bodies couldn't adjust to the increased power and they literally burnt themselves out. Since they still looked like teenagers, they were able to dispose of the bodies the same way the home above them did."

"But if they all died," inquired Sam, "what about Ethan?"

"Of the original twenty-five, all of them died," she said. "But one of the scientists, a woman of considerable means and intelligence conducted one more experiment. Her name would mean nothing to you, besides she no longer exists. When the first few turned out bad, she studied their gene charts, looking for solutions. Since the embryos were planted at staggered intervals, she hoped to correct the problems in the remaining women before they gave birth."

Alyssa looked at Ada then voiced the question on all their minds. "I don't mean to sound cruel. I admit I've never had children myself and don't know what would happen, but if they had time, why didn't they abort the rest of these monsters before they were born?"

"A good question to which I have no answer. Perhaps they hoped that at least one would turn out all right. I don't know. But back to this other doctor. She found a problem, previously ignored as unimportant in the gene makeup. It seems that when a certain combination was created, the spliced genes interacted and caused a deficiency in chemical makeup. It was this deficiency that made the children go mad."

"So she corrected this problem and tried again," finished Beth. "How did she ever find another volunteer after all that happened, especially since they were legally shut down?"

"You're right, she couldn't. So she implanted herself with the new embryo. Her superiors were furious and threatened to abort the child. But she was a woman of strong resolve. So sure of her facts and figures, she fought them for months, until finally, to abort the foetus would have been detrimental to her life as well. Reluctantly they allowed it to come to term."

"And that became Ethan," said Alyssa. "Obviously her new gene configuration worked."

"Better than she could hope. However, to bring the child away from the madness, she had to sacrifice something, and that was strength. But other abilities, not calculated on, came into being. One of them, you've already experienced, his ability to read minds. Although I must admit, this ability to link minds is new to me."

"You're not telling us everything," said Sam. "Like, when did this happen, and what else can we expect?"

"All this happened, nearly twenty-five years ago," said Ada softly. "You see another side effect was to keep him young. Oh, he ages all right, but at a much slower rate. He ages about one year for every two years."

"Then that little boy…"

"Is over 26 years old!"

"Hey," cried Sam, suddenly blushing, "I've been changing in front of that kid. But he's no kid. He's a man."

Ada laughed until a wheezing cough forced her to catch her breath. "You don't have to worry. Before we left the Centre, a drug, designed by Ethan, was administered to him along with a post hypnotic suggestion."

"That he would obey you," said Alyssa. "And the drug temporarily made him appear as simple as a normal child. So what happened?"

"We were on our way to another facility, also designed by Ethan, on a secluded moon. There, we hoped that he could put his tremendous intellect to use in creating and designing things to help mankind. Ethan never turned into the super human, super soldier they wanted. If we made it, I was to administer the antidote and he would return to normal."

"But we got stranded here, and the effect wore off," said Beth.

"A little at a time," agreed Ada, "but now it appears that he is in full control of his faculties."

"My god," gasped Sam. "What an incredible story. What happened to the woman who gave birth to him?"

Here Ada grew quiet and it took several minutes before she responded. "As far as the Centre knows, she disappeared shortly before I arrived there."

"I don't have Ethan's powers," said Sam suspiciously, "but that's not the whole story is it?" Ada just looked at her face frozen in an unreadable expression.

"If I read you right," said Sam hesitantly, "the woman left the Centre, presumably never to return." She stared at Ada, giving her a chance to refute or deny. "She left, then had her features altered by a plastic surgeon. You must tell me who did it. I've had some done myself, but your scarring is so minimal, I can barely see it."

"You," gasped Alyssa. "You're Ethan's mother?"

"Only his birth mother," said Ada softly. "His genetic makeup contains none of my DNA. I'm sorry, son, I never wanted to hurt you." Ethan leaned up and kissed the old woman gently.

"I couldn't reveal myself in case The Centre found out. So I convinced him that I was assigned to him to guide and protect him.

That's why, as he says, he started calling me Nana. I've always appeared as a kindly old grandmother type. Especially since I continued to age, but he didn't. Soon the pattern became easy and comfortable."

"But he can read minds," protested Beth. "I'm sure he knew who you were."

"Possibly," said Ada, "but he never let on."

"I knew," said Ethan, "but I also knew the reason you hid the truth. As painful as it was for me, I knew it caused you even more grief not to tell me."

Ada nodded and slowly rubbed his head. "I loved you too much. Better to live the lie that you're an experiment, given up by his mother, rather than admit that as a scientist, his mother was too much of a woman to let her child go without a fight. I know it sounds harsh to the rest of you, but Ethan respects and understands science. It's only recently that he's been exposed to the more inaccurate science of emotions and feelings…Besides, I didn't think I could face him, and tell him, I created him for an experiment, not for love."

"But you do love him," said Alyssa tenderly.

"Yes," she said softly. "With all my heart. I couldn't love him more if he where my child. Do you know what its like to have a child for 25 years. Brilliant, yes gifted and talented, yes, but because of his experiences, still emotionally a child, and physically one as well. I'm afraid my maternal instincts are in overdrive."

The other women consoled her now as soft sobs racked her body. Each in her own way, could imagine what they would experience in such a situation, and agreed that Ada did the best thing possible. When Ada's tears subsided, Alyssa stood up and poured them all cup of hot herbal tea. Doc had said that this native tea had a calm soothing effect, and it had rapidly become a camp favourite as the supply of coffee dwindled. Alyssa now took advantage of this soothing effect by doubling the strength in Ada's cup.

Soon she seemed back to her old self, and appeared more relaxed, as if the telling of the story had released a hidden tension she'd been carrying around for years. She lay back down and closed her eyes. Soon soft snoring sounds, punctuated by moans of pain emanated from her lips. The rest sat still and quiet, each buried in her own thoughts.

"That explains a lot," said Alyssa quietly. "Why sometimes you seemed like a child, and other times very much older."

Ethan nodded and looked tenderly at Ada. "I must tell you something though. Please don't tell Nana, my mother. Her dream to create the perfect human is over. I'm dying."

"What," cried Alyssa. "You can't. I mean why?"

Ethan shrugged his shoulders. "Another one of those unforeseen problems. I ran the tests myself a little while ago, before I knew what I was looking for. My system is speeding up. Soon I'll be as old as I actually am, that is, if the internal pressures don't kill me first."

"How...How long?" Alyssa swallowed rapidly. All this seemed like a dream.

"I can't say for sure," said Ethan calmly sipping his tea. "But my best estimate is 8 to 12 months."

"How can you sit there calmly drinking tea and tell us you'll be dead in less than a year," sputtered Sam. Tears ran freely down her face as she flung her accusations at Ethan.

"Don't forget," he said, "I'm over 25 years old and a scientist. I've been trained to think and act logically."

"But you can't die," cried Alyssa. "Ethan, I love you. You've given me life and hope and I can't let you go know. We'll find a way to save you. I'll get us of this world somehow."

"There's nothing to be done," said Ethan.

"There is," gasped Ada from her bunk. The others returned to her side quickly.

"What do you mean, Nana?"

"I knew this would happen," she coughed. "I only hoped that I would be long dead before it happened. It's a recessive gene trait. I discovered it after you were born."

"Then why continue the experiment? Logic dictates that if the experiment is flawed then terminate the procedure."

Ada smiled and looked at Alyssa who nodded. "She couldn't, Ethan," said Alyssa tenderly. "She couldn't for the same reason I won't give up."

Alyssa bent closer to Ada. The old woman was fading quickly and Alyssa had to struggle to hear her words. "You said he didn't have to die. Please tell me how? As one mother to another tell me how we can save our son."

Ada lifted her hand and weekly pointed to the tiny wooden keepsake box on the table. Sam picked it up and gave it to Ada who fumbled with the latch. Her strength almost gone she couldn't undo the simple clasp and it fell from her hands. Alyssa caught the box before it fell on the floor and carefully opened the box.

Inside, was the usual assortment of trinkets. The broach she had worn when the landed, a dried bright blue flower Ethan had picked for her and other odd assortments. Ada took the box then clawed at the base. Her fingers barely even marked the surface as she tried to catch a nail under one edge. Lying back weekly she gave the box to Alyssa who took it carefully.

Alyssa examined the box and her now trained tracker's eyes, spotted a small indentation. She had seen the box hundreds of times before, but never saw this mark before. Since her nails were cut short, Alyssa picked up her knife from around her belt and carefully poked the blade into the depression.

She heard a tiny click and the bottom of the box fell open. A tiny crystal fell out and dropped to the ground. "It's a crystal from a 'corder," she said. "Do you want me to play this? Is that it?"

Ada nodded weakly then closed her eyes. Seconds later Scrapper outside the door set up a mournful howling. Ethan touched her cheek gently then climbed on the bed and lay down beside his mother. Alyssa fighting back the tears quickly checked her pulse and searched for other signs of life.

"She's gone," she said softly. "Ethan, I'm sorry."

"Please leave us alone for a minute," he whispered. Alyssa nodded and taking the now openly crying Sam in her arms, left the shack. Beth stood quiet. Emotion racked her but she held herself in check.

"We'll be right outside when you're ready," said Beth gently. She turned to leave, then a thought occurred to her. "Ethan, don't do anything foolish. There's still hope. Many people still care for you. Including one who really considers herself your mother."

"I know," he said choking back the tears. "Don't worry, Captain. I'll be fine." He laid his head on the breast of the woman who had given him life and cared for him and let the tears run free. Beth tiptoed out of the shack.

Outside her resolve failed and she too burst into tears. Patty came over and put his arm around her. Lex was comforting Alyssa and Allen held tightly to Sam. In-between sobs they told the men what had happened. The three couples held each other for support. Then Ethan emerged from the shack.

He looked at the group carefully. "I suppose you all know by now." They nodded their assent slowly. "So Patty, what are you going to do? Maxia?"

Beth removed Patty's arm and stood to face him. "You wouldn't! You couldn't!"

"Excuse me," said Lex, "but what is Maxia?"

"It was a peace keeping force sent to help war torn Maxia," explained Alyssa, "but I fail to see how this applies."

"Patty knows what I'm talking about and so does Beth," said Ethan. "They'll have to know eventually, and what you're going to do."

"If you so much as touch-," yelled Beth.

"Don't worry," said Patty wearily. "Those days are gone. My friends you'd better sit down." When they had all seated he took Beth's hands in his. "I have to tell them. I don't know how you knew, but I can't carry this any longer."

Beth nodded and smiled then turned to the rest. "What you are about to hear is classified so top secret it doesn't have a name. If you breathe a word of this to anyone, well let's just say that the penal colony on Miridian IV is not a pleasant place to spend the rest of your life."

She gave them the opportunity to leave if they didn't want to risk it, but they sat still and urged Patty to speak. He motioned Ethan over beside him and laid a hand gently on the boy's shoulders.

"Many years ago," he began, "I was part of an exercise. A special unit created to help out on the planet Maxia. I thought I had put that horrible business away until Ethan mentioned it to me when we first landed here." He paused trying to collect his thoughts. The others could see that it was painful for him.

"Do you want me to tell them?" Ethan looked at his mentor and friend.

"No, son," said Patty. "They're my sins. I'll do it...Everyone was told that we were a peacekeeping force to help Maxia. In a way that was true, but the best lie is one of omission. We were sent to find and kill the leader of a viscous fanatical movement. These fanatics believed that the true way to world domination was to brutally murder and torture those who stood in their way."

"My god," said Alyssa, "no wonder they hushed everything up."

"That's not the worst part," continued Patty. "To reach this murderous leader, we had to do unspeakable things. He was well protected and knew how to stop us. He would place civilians in our path. Civilians who were tortured and booby-trapped. Whenever we went near them, they would explode or their bodies pumped full of toxic gas would burst as we approached. Many good men and women were killed."

He stopped the placed his head in his hands. "Finally we received word that this fanatic had planted a bomb of such power, that it could crack the very core of the planet. So mad were these people that if they couldn't rule then everyone would die. Our final orders insisted that we let nothing stop us. NOTHING!"

Patty the soldier, Patty the veteran, started to cry gently. Beth took over the explanation. "Patty and the rest had to stop this madman. With the best firepower the League could provide, and the most dangerous weapons, they destroyed and annihilated everything in their path in one last effort to stop this crazed leader."

"He...He placed civilians, women, and children in our path. In his stronghold he held over a thousand people captive and when we stormed the place he threw them at us as human shields. We couldn't stop. We had to stop him."

"So, you killed all those innocent people," said Alyssa in horror.

Patty nodded. "We just mowed them down as if they were so much garbage in our way. We broke into the stronghold and before he had the time to react we killed him dead."

"Patty," said Lex, "I can't possibly know what you went though, but I can see it affected you deeply. I don't know if I could do that. Kill all those people. But do you mean to say that you would kill Ethan because he's different?"

"He's no threat to you," said Alyssa.

"I'll finish, Patty," said Ethan. "Nana didn't tell you the whole truth. Not all those mad supermen died at such a young age. One of them lived until he was fifteen and escaped."

"Then he was-," exclaimed Alyssa.

"—The one who led the fanatics on Maxia, yes," finished Ethan. "After that incident, the League issued standing orders to all military leaders. All genetically enhanced humans were to be killed."

"Patty," said Alyssa coldly. "I care for you very much, and I respect you and feel for what you've had to endure. But, if you ever go near Ethan or threaten him in any way, I'll kill you myself."

"My orders are clear," said Patty, "however, we're a long way from the League. I have no wish to kill the boy and I won't, but when we're rescued, someone will find out and finish the job I couldn't."

He stood and straightened his clothes. "Ethan, you are so much like my own son. I've seen too much killing in my lifetime. I don't think you're mad and I will do everything in my power to help you."

"Thank you," said Ethan, "but it's probably a moot point. If they haven't told you I'll be dead in less than a year anyway."

"Not necessarily," said Beth. "Alyssa honey, do you still have that crystal?"

"Yes," she said opening her hand. She had been clenching it so tight in anger that it had made several tiny cuts in the palm of her hand.

"Lex," directed Beth, "go find a 'corder. Ada seemed sure that the information on this crystal could help Ethan. Let's find out!"

Several minutes later Alyssa inserted the crystal into the corder and turned the unit on. Ada's voice came through. Clearly she had made this recording many months ago.

"Ethan, if you are hearing this recording it means that I am dead and we are still trapped on this planet. I don't know what to say except that I'm sorry, my son. Yes, I said son. You are my child, at least in part. Very soon—if it hasn't started already—the effects of the drug you took and the hypnotic suggestion will begin to wear off. I had hoped to get you to safety before that happened.

"I can leave you nothing except my love. But there is something I might be able to do. The same thing that killed all the others from the

Centre will soon affect you. I thought I had cleared that problem, but it proved recessive. So, for the last few years I've worked to try and correct this problem. I have worked out a formula that may help. I haven't used it, because it may kill you rather than cure.

"It's a virus, a very potent and potentially lethal virus. It penetrates the cell walls and attacks the DNA. I hoped that I could find time to refine it further, but crash landing here put the stops to that. I can guarantee it will prevent you from burning out, but beyond that I don't know. If you start to accelerate before we are rescued . . Well, I'll leave the decision up to you. I didn't mean to hurt you. I just wanted a child of my own and being with the Centre, I was forbidden. I'm sorry I didn't tell you who I was, but you've given me many happy wonderful years.

"One final note then I'll recite the formula. Because of the situation you've never had a real mother to care for you and look after you. If you can find it in your heart to forgive me, then you might want to consider sharing that love with someone else. Find Alyssa and tell her. I know she cares for you deeply and even though she has her own demons to face, I think you and her can become very close. I love you, my son, and I'm sorry I'm not there for you. Take care of yourself and always remember I'm very proud of you. Now pay close attention to this formula. I hope it works…" She concluded by giving a long list of chemical symbols.

"I don't know what to say, son," said Patty. "She obviously loved you very much."

"What about the formula?" Asked Lex. "Will it work?"

"I recognize some of it," said Ethan, "I'm sure Doc could provide me with the necessary chemicals, but it's the others I worry about."

"Then we need to find them," said Alyssa determinedly. She grasped Ethan tightly by the arms. "I have no intention of losing you and I don't care what I have to do."

"Then I suggest we ask for help," said Sam.

"From whom?"

"Anybody," said Sam. "Listen we may get in trouble for assisting a genetically altered human, but I'm willing to risk it."

"Then I'm going to call a town meeting," said Beth. "Surely there must be a chemist in that lot."

An hour later Beth mounted the podium with Patty at her side. To her left, Allen and Sam sat quietly. To her right, Lex and Alyssa held tightly to Ethan. Quickly she informed them of Ada's death. Many of the villagers wept openly. She had many friends in the tiny community.

"Now to the problem at hand," said Beth. "Ethan here has a problem. Ada was also a scientist and was working on his problem. Before she died, she placed in our hands a chemical formula she hoped would help him. I now ask for your help. Anyone who understands chemistry, or medicine, please, come and see us. We have very little time before Ethan succumbs to this illness and we must work fast. Thank you."

As she stepped down Alyssa whispered in her ear. "Very nice. You kept the whole thing about genetics out of the conversation."

"Better to be safe than sorry," she replied. They waited only a few minutes before several people came forward. Doc was the first one to arrive and Beth explained the whole problem. She had worked with him for many years and trusted him implicitly.

"Don't worry, son," he said. "If there's a way to make this formula your mother left, we'll find it." He then spent the next few moments quizzing those that came forward to see the extent of their knowledge. Soon he had divided the teams into two groups those that would work on the medicine and those that would search for the ingredients.

"I'm glad to see you here, my friend," said Doc. "I don't know anybody who knows more about plants and homeopathic medicine than you!"

"Timotin not abandon little friend now," said the huge hunter. He studied the formula for a few moments then narrowly eyed Ethan. "So, my young companion. You're one of them. I should have realized. Your abilities far out shadow any I have heard of. Don't worry Ethan. We will find a cure for you. I know these chemical symbols. The trick will be to find them in the local plant life."

Alyssa hid the smile she always had when the giant man spoke in whole sentences and stopped using short talk. He saw her smirk and winked playfully at her. "Timotin big dumb brute. We search jungle now. Alyssa you come. Tracker's eyes welcome."

With a hug and kiss for the boy, Alyssa left with the giant and a biologist from the passengers. Doc and a pharmacist, who had volunteered, moved to the hospital and began collecting the other ingredients at hand.

Timotin explained the types of plants he was looking for. "They may be slightly different here, but from what I've seen, they should be very similar." They searched the surrounding jungle foliage for hours. Alyssa strained her natural tracking abilities to the limit. Finally Timotin called a halt for the night. Alyssa protested, but relented when he assured her that they would continue at first light.

They returned to the camp and presented Doc with the plants they had secured. Then he and Timotin went into a deep technical discussion of how to extract the necessary elements. By the time the evening meal was finished several tables were set up to crush, boil, spin and otherwise do all the different things needed to turn the plants into medicine.

"Damn place looks like Frankenstein's lab over there," complained Lex who had volunteered to wash out test tubes and containers.

"I don't care what it looks like as long as it works," said Alyssa.

"Honey," he said gently, "It may not work."

"Yes, it will," she said firmly. "I know it will. I'm so sure, that I'm going to adopt Ethan now. If he'll have me."

"Alyssa, be reasonable. If it doesn't work, he could die. At the very least he'll be dead in a year. Do you really want to put yourself through that?"

"Yes, I do. Oh Lex, I just can't let him die, but if he does, and I mean IF…If he does, he will at least have a mother who loves him."

"And a father," said Lex.

"What?"

"I mean that you're not going to adopt Ethan. We are!"

"But."

"Forget it," he said. "Lys, you've been avoiding making a commitment for years, now you want to make what hopefully could be a lifetime commitment. I care for him almost as much as I care for you. So if you are going to be his mother, then naturally I will be his father."

"Lex, I have been so cruel to you," she said. "I couldn't face a relationship again, but you stayed in the fight. Maybe it is time that I let the past go."

"Then you will marry me? YAHOO! Come on, before you change your mind!" He grabbed her and pulled and stumbling across the compound yelling for Ethan.

The boy came running up and Lex grabbed him. "Listen, Alyssa has finally decided to marry me."

"Congratulations," said the man in the boy.

"But that's not all," said Lex. "We, that is Alyssa and myself, well, we would like to adopt you, as our son."

"Adopt me," exclaimed Ethan. "I'm over 25 years old. You don't adopt adults."

"Maybe so," said Lex, "but to us you're still a 13-year-old boy. And we want to adopt you…Maybe you don't want us as a mother and father?"

"Oh no," said Ethan. "Alyssa already knows how I feel about her and I would be very proud to call you Father. But are you sure you want to do this. I mean not knowing and all that."

"You may be 25 years old," said Lex firmly, "but the first thing you'll have to learn is I am your father and if I say so, then that's it!"

Ethan smiled. "Yes, sir," he said. "That is yes, Father." The three hugged tightly and went in search of Patty and Beth. Both were delighted with the news and Beth promised to perform the ceremony the next day.

"I think Nana would be pleased," said Ethan as he went to bed.

The next day, Timotin and the biologist set off. They still had several plants to find. Alyssa complained and protested loudly when he wouldn't allow her to join them. "You have to get ready for your wedding," said the giant. "We will return in time to kiss the bride."

The whole village buzzed with excitement at the impending nuptials. They sacrificed some of their hard earned timber to create a better setting for the wedding. After lunch the women took charge of Alyssa and the men took Lex away.

What the men did with Lex, Alyssa had no idea, but according to the other women, he was being initiated in the age-old rite of a bachelor party. Alyssa tried to remember if Trenor ever had a bachelor party then decided it didn't matter anymore. The man she loved was having one and that suited her fine.

Just before dinner Timotin returned with the good news that he only had to find two more plants. He deposited the days' collection with Doc then went to clean up. He returned quickly in his cleanest hunting outfit, making a considerable impression on the women in the village.

Alyssa asked him if he would give the bride away. He beamed with pride as he escorted her down the walkway, festooned with garlands and wildflowers. One of the women had kept her dress from the landing and had carefully preserved it. She offered it to Alyssa as a wedding gift and with a little alteration, had transformed her from a sexy barbaric savage, to a lady of beauty and refinement.

Lex waited near the makeshift altar with Ethan as his best man. He had scrounged uniform parts from the remaining crewmembers and now stood tall and proud. Beth had taken Ada's shawl and placed it around her shoulders, giving her a dignified look. She beamed with joy as Alyssa on the arm of Timotin came down the aisle.

When they stood side-by-side Patty stepped forward. "Wait a minute." He said. "Lex, you can't get married like that. You're out of uniform man."

Lex looked at himself. Pants, shirt, jacket, rank bars (made from joining two junior officer bars together, since his were Alyssa's ring), what was missing? Patty reached behind the altar and withdrew a package. "This was mine. I was on my way to secure it in my room when the alarm sounded. I just jammed it in the pod. It got a little beat up, but I managed to retrieve it."

Lex opened the package and found Patty's peak cap. The gold braid or "Scrambled egg," as it was called showed that Patty was more than just an old soldier. Lex thanked him and placed the hat on his head. It was a little tight, but he forced it on.

"Much better, sir," said Patty and saluted him, then took his place beside Ethan.

"We have no Minister or Parent," she said, "But by the laws of the League, the Captain may perform a marriage ceremony. This ceremony is also serving double duty. Lex and Alyssa have expressed a desire to adopt Ethan as well. If there are any here who object to this union of three souls, speak now…Since these two people come from different worlds and have elected to have a non-denominational marriage, I will dispense with the formalities and just ask this.

"Alyssa, do you love Lex with all your heart and promise to be by his side?"

"I will," she whispered.

"And you, Lex, do you love Alyssa with all your heart and promise to be by her side?"

"I will," he said looking at her.

"Now you, Ethan. Lex and Alyssa wish to become your parents, both in love and in the eyes of the law. Will you accept these two people as your parents and heed them in their effort to guide you in love and kindness?"

"I don't know the correct words to say, but I accept Lex as my father and Alyssa as my mother."

"That will be fine," said Beth. "As Captain of the Carriolion, I now pronounce you man, wife and family. May you live together in love and peace!"

The village cheered as Lex kissed his wife, then brought Ethan into a family hug. The meal that night was a festive occasion. More of the homemade wine was brought out and they partied until well into the morning. They moved into the quarters originally occupied by Tony and Karen. After Tony's death Karen had bunked with the single women.

"Well, Mom and Dad," he said with a smile, "I think for your honeymoon night, I'd better sleep in my own quarters." He kissed them both then made a strategic withdrawal.

The next morning Lex and Alyssa didn't arise until the sun was high in the sky. The rest of the village had already had breakfast, but they saved a plate for each of them. While they ate, Timotin came rushing over.

"We've found the last of the plants," he said. "Now all we have to do is make the vaccine."

Everyone waited outside the hospital, as Doc, Timotin, and the others worked to make the life saving drug that would cure Ethan. As the hours passed, the people came to express their hopes and well wishes to the nervous couple. The doctors refused to come out, even during supper. Beth made sure that plates of food were sent in to them.

As the evening sky drew dark, the door swung open and they emerged. "Well, this is it," said Doc. "It's very crude. Ethan? Are you sure you want to try this? We did our best, but this isn't a medical complex…" He left the rest of the thought unfinished. They all new the risks that they had created the serum in these primitive conditions in the first place, showed the skill of the men.

Ethan stepped forward and took the vial. He held it up to see it in the firelight. A greenish-brown liquid sloshed thickly in the flickering light. "I'm already staring to feel the effects. No matter what happens, I want you to know how grateful I am. To all of you."

He moved nearer Alyssa and Lex. Alyssa let the tears flow freely when he threw his arms around her neck. Lex stood stoic, but he too broke down when Ethan hugged him. "Thank you," whispered Ethan. "Thank you for letting me feel what it was like to have real parents. Even if it was for a short time."

"You don't have to do this yet, son," said Lex. "Maybe Doc and Timotin can refine it a little better?"

"You forget. I'm a scientist as well," he whispered. "I know what they've done and they can do no more. No, I must take it. The effects are progressing faster than I had anticipated. Already I feel the pain." He stood up and returned to the Doctor.

"How do I take this?"

"I will administer a series of injections over the next four hours. You will experience a lot of pain. This is a fairly lethal mixture. I hesitate to administer anything untested, but I know it's your only hope."

Ethan nodded and they made their way to Alyssa's hut. They made him comfortable on his bed and Doc administered the first shot. Within seconds his temperature shot up. Timotin stood by with a basin of cool water and several broad flat leaves.

"These will help cool him," he said soaking the leaves and placing them on the boy's body.

An hour later Doc administered another injection and Ethan tossed and turned as pain began to wrack his small frame. A few hours later, the final injection Ethan screamed a blood curdling cry and Alyssa held him tightly to her chest.

"It's all right," she sobbed. "I'm here...Mommy's here."

Lex sat beside her and held them both in his arms. Ethan twitched violently then suddenly heaved and threw up all over Alyssa. She didn't seem to notice and continued to hold him as he shook.

"AHHHHH," cried Ethan and his body went limp. Alyssa tried to rouse him, but he refused to move. With pleading eyes she looked at Timotin and Doc and they moved to quickly examine him.

They worked on him quickly. Then Timotin threw the chair he had been sitting on across the room and crouched down beside Ethan and began applying artificial respiration. He continued doing this for twenty minutes while Doc applied external compression to the boy's ribcage in effort to keep the heart beating.

Finally they stopped and with great sadness in his eyes Timotin said softly, "I'm sorry, Alyssa. It was too much for his heart. He's dead."

Alyssa sat for a few seconds then screamed "NO," she jumped on the bed and started applying CPR to Ethan. "Breathe," she shouted. "Breathe, damn you. Don't leave me now!"

"Alyssa," said Lex softly as he tried to pull her away. "It's no good."

"He's young," she shouted and started pounding his chest. "He wants to live." The others stood back, gently sobbing as the woman who became a mother for one day shouted through her tears at the lifeless body of her son.

"Breathe," she shouted in the boy's ear. She pounded his chest harder and harder as her grief overcame her. "Breathe...Breathe..."

Chapter 23

Alyssa picked up the limp frame of Ethan and shouted loudly in his ear, as if the sound of her voice would bring him back, but he made no movement or sign. Slowly she lowered him gently back onto the bed. Lex came up—tears running freely down his face and squatted behind her. He took her shoulder softly in his hands and laid his head on her back as she laid her head on Ethan's chest.

"A good brave lad," whispered Patty. "For one so young, yet so old, he touched us all deeply. We'll miss you, son. I hope you find peace."

Timotin, the giant man, who could kill with a single blow, stood ramrod stiff! Death wasn't unusual to him considering the harsh life he lived on his home world, but even he had a great affection for the boy and it showed, as his gaze never wavered from its intensity.

"I'm so sorry, Ethan," sobbed Alyssa. She hugged his form to her and buried her head in his chest. Suddenly she sat up straight, her eyes wide.

"I heard a heartbeat," she whispered. "Doctor, I heard a heartbeat!"

"Alyssa," said Doc tenderly. "There was no heartbeat. I checked him myself with the scanner."

"You're just imagining it, Lys," said Lex softly. "Come on. Let the Doctor finish up here."

She leaned down and kissed the brow of her son, then laid her head on his chest for one last hug. Her head shot up fast. "I heard it again!"

"Alyssa," said the Doctor. She reached across Ethan and grabbed Doc by the shirt and dragged him over. When angry her face took on the same hue as her hair and now you couldn't tell where her face ended and her hair began.

"I. Heard…A…Heartbeat," she said angrily. She jammed the Doctor's head onto Ethan's chest roughly. "Now listen, damn you!"

"Alyssa," cried Lex.

"No, it's all right," said Doc and reached for his med-scanner.

"Not with that," shouted Alyssa as she knocked the offensive instrument from his grasp. "With your ear."

Doc looked at her then lowered his head to Ethan's chest. "I don't hear anything," he said gently.

"Wait," commanded Alyssa. He kept his head down and waited. If it would appease Alyssa then he would wait all day if he had to.

Suddenly he opened his eyes wide. "What is it," Timotin had come nearer, in case Alyssa needed restraining.

"I'm...I'm not sure," said Doc. "There...There it is again!" He raised his head and stared at Timotin. "Please listen and verify for me. I don't trust my judgment right now."

Puzzled but willing to accede to a request from a colleague, Timotin placed an ear on Ethan's chest and listened. The only movement he made was to adjust his position and he continued listening.

"There is a heartbeat," he finally declared.

"Thank the great Parent," cried Alyssa.

"But why didn't the scanner pick it up?" Lex had retrieved the device and was checking it for a malfunction.

"Because," said Timotin matter-of-factly, "Ethan's heartbeat is so slow he should not be alive. The machine waited the required time and when no beat registered it proclaimed him dead."

"Please," said Doc, "All of you. Let Timotin and myself do some tests, you too, Alyssa, Lex, get her out of here...Timotin, let's start with a basic series then I want to do some blood-work..." His voiced faded to a mumble as he and Timotin started talking in the language of medical men.

Outside, the group waited. Alyssa sat on a log with Lex while Patty paced back and forth. Beth and Sam, unable to sit idly by, had left to find something to do. Allen had whipped out his notebook and was furiously scribbling notes.

After an hour of waiting, Doc came out and rushed passed them without saying a word. Alyssa tried to peek inside, but a gruff command from Timotin forced her back. In a few minutes Doc returned with a box of supplies and entered the shack.

After another hour, Patty threw up his hands in frustration. "This is ridiculous," he said with feigned annoyance. "They could be in there for hours yet. There's work to be done." He looked around as if trying to find something to do when suddenly he snapped his fingers.

"We still need power," he said, "And I still think that that alien complex is our best chance. If we looked hard enough, I bet we could find something to help us."

"Then I may be able to help," said Allen standing up. "I've been copying down everything I could remember from being in the computer. I'm sorry there's no more, but I got a little distracted in there." He bowed his head slightly, chagrined at his folly.

"Anything you have would be helpful," said Patty taking the notes and looking at them. "What is this? I don't understand a word of it!"

"Sorry," chuckled Allen taking the pad back. "Debugger's shorthand. What I have here is what I can remember about the complex. It's the directions to the different rooms and their names."

"I would prefer a map," said Patty, stroking his chin thoughtfully.

"Oh, I can draw you a map," said Allen. "It will be quite extensive as this complex has 7 levels and over a hundred rooms. And that's only the ones I remember."

"Well, all I need are those that pertain to power supplies and such."

"There's about 7 or 8 rooms that fit that description," said Allen.

"Then let's get busy," said Patty. "Alyssa, we'll be over at the council hut. Please let me know when there's word about the boy."

Alyssa nodded absentmindedly, but Lex assured him they would. Just as Patty and Allen turned to leave the door swung open and Timotin poked his head out. "You can come in now," he rumbled.

Alyssa burst past him and ran to the still lifeless form of Ethan. Doc moved out of the way as she held Ethan in her arms.

Lex moved nearer the Doctor and softly whispered, "Doc?"

"You must understand," he began softly, "that this is totally unknown to either of us. We can only speculate on what happened and guess on what will happen."

"Will he live?" Alyssa rocked back and forth with Ethan.

"We just don't know," he said.

"Something strange is happening to Ethan," said Timotin. "Our tests show that he is breathing, but his respiration is shallow and he only takes a breath every ten minutes. His heart beats only once every two minutes. By all rights he should be dead, the human body is not designed to survive at those levels."

"But that's the keyword," said Doc. "Designed. Ethan was created and his genes manipulated. We don't know what they did to him, but it seems to be keeping him alive somehow."

"It would appear that the serum we administered is rewriting his DNA," said Timotin. "We don't have the equipment to see or chart the changes, but we do know that changes are being made on a cellular level."

"I don't understand," said Patty. "I thought that genes couldn't be changed."

"Yes, and no," said Doc. "When a being is formed, its genes determine whether it will be a boy or girl, animal, or plant. Genes control how we look, and what our abilities will be. But, there are diseases, viruses that can penetrate the cell walls and they infect the nucleus of a cell."

"These viruses then rewrite that cell," said Timotin. "An unsuccessful virus dies out before it can do any damage. A successful one changes the DNA and RNA so that the cell replicates and copies the virus. Which then spreads to other cells, and so on."

"But even the most virulent form," said Doc, "still takes time to move through the host body. This thing that's happening to Ethan is taking place almost simultaneously throughout his whole body."

"We've taken samples from all over and the same thing is happening everywhere. Every cell in his body is undergoing major changes. I don't know how, but it is!"

"What will happen to the boy?" Asked Patty as he stroked the hair out of Ethan's eyes.

"I can't tell you," said Doc. "If I had my equipment from the ship I could chart his genes and make an educated guess, but here and now, I have no idea."

"We'll know in about 24 hours," said Timotin. "If the rate of change remains constant. There's nothing more we can do. Ethan is in a coma so deep we don't know how to treat him. We'll just have to wait and hope."

"I'm not leaving him," said Alyssa. "Didn't I hear that coma patients could hear?"

"The studies are inconclusive," said Doc. "But I believe that the presence and voices of loved ones do penetrate and help the healing process."

"Then I will stay with him," said Alyssa firmly. She took the boy's head and gazed into the sleeping face. "And I'll read to him, and talk to him, and tell him how much I love him."

"So will I," said Lex.

"And me," chimed in Patty and Allen.

"No," said Doc firmly. "I don't want too many people around. Just in case. Let his parents stay. They will be the best medicine I can prescribe."

Disappointed, but understanding, the others left Alyssa and Lex with their son. Outside Patty took a deep breath then said, "We might as well make that map of yours. Let's go," and he and Allen left. Doc and Timotin gathered up their equipment.

"I sure could do with a drink right now," said Doc.

"Then come with Timotin. I have some wine left. We will raise a toast and pray for Ethan." Doc smiled and nodded and the two healers walked away. On the way to Timotin's shack he flagged down one of his hunters and explained they needed to post a watch over the boy. The hunter readily agreed and gathered a few more people. They would sit outside the shack until something happened.

*

"This is a hell of a maze," said Patty exasperated. He had returned to the alien building with several others, including Adam the archaeologist. Allen had been none too happy when Patty vetoed his accompanying them into the building.

"I don't want to take any chances," said Patty. "Once inside you may succumb again."

"I can handle it," exclaimed Allen.

"Maybe, but I'm in charge and I say you stay out here. Besides, A'Serta can't come in and she'll need help analyzing anything we find. You're our best bet for that sort of stuff." Mollified, Allen agreed and turned to help A'Serta set up a worktable near the invisible entrance.

Patty took the map and folded it into a pouch. Without hesitation he stepped through the invisible door followed closely by Adam and Shayna the woman who kept the generator alive.

"All right," said Patty once inside. "These are the best bets for finding what we need." He handed each of them a smaller map that would guide them through the labyrinth of the complex.

"Each of you has two locations to check out," he said. "Pay close attention to where you are going. We don't want anyone getting lost. We'll meet back here in two hours. Any questions? Fine. Good hunting."

The three explorers moved down the corridor and split up through more of the invisible doorways on the way. They didn't know what they were searching for, other than something to provide power to the camp. What made it all the more difficult was that most of the alien machinery was so unfamiliar, they could walk past the very thing they need without seeing it.

After nearly two hours of fruitless searching, the trio reformed, bringing with them those objects that looked promising. They exited the structure and turned the objects over to A'Serta and Allen. Some of them Allen was able to veto straight away.

"I recognize them from my connection," he said.

After a brief rest the three returned inside. "Let's stick together this time," said Patty. We'll examine every room one by one carefully." The others agreed and they approached the first room on the map.

For the next four hours they examined every room that they had pinpointed as hopeful. Finally they came to the last room and Patty stepped through the doorway. Adam quickly followed, but Shayna stayed behind.

"What's the matter?" Asked Patty as he returned to check on her.

"You're in the wrong room," she said.

"This was one of the rooms I investigated," he said slightly defensive.

"Maybe," said Shayna, "but look at this." She unfolded the map and traced their route.

"Well, I'll be damned. Sorry about that. The room we want is the next one." He jumped back through the door and retrieved Adam searching through the equipment.

"My mistake," he said apologetically. "It's the next room over." Adam shrugged and they made their way to the next doorway. Then entered into the room.

"Blast," said Shayna. "There's no light in here. I guess even the Providers had bulbs that burned out occasionally. Now what do we do?"

A small beam of light suddenly stabbed the darkness making everything jump about in the shadows. "I always carry a small flashlight," said Patty. He waved the yellow beam of light around the room quickly.

"The power cell is weak," he said noting the colour of the light. "We won't have much time before it gives out. Let's make a quick search."

The three cautiously searched the room. The light from the tiny flashlight dwindled slowly then flickered and died. "Great," said Patty. "Can anyone see the doorway?"

"Are you kidding," said Adam. "I couldn't see it in the light and you want me to find it in the dark?"

"Search with your hands," commanded Patty. "Be careful. There's stuff strewn all over the place." No sooner had he warned the others when he stubbed his toe on a large heavy object on the floor.

"Owww," he cried. "Stupid place to leave whatever this is." The others laughed and continued the search.

"Hey," came the cry from Adam.

"Adam," called Patty into the darkness. "You all right?"

"I tripped over something," said Adam. They could hear the strain in his voice. "I've twisted my ankle. I can't walk."

"Stay there," said Patty. "Keep talking. We'll home in on you."

While Adam counted out loudly, Patty and Shayna carefully moved through the room trying to home in his voice. "Hey, watch where you're stepping," complained Adam.

"Quit whining," said Shayna. "I found you didn't I. Patty? Over here!"

Patty followed the woman's voice and found them resting on the floor. "I can't see anything," he said. "I wish these aliens believed in windows. I'm going to try and wrap that ankle of yours. I'll have to do it by touch."

Patty searched his clothes for something to use as a bandage when he realized he still held the useless flashlight in his hand. He dropped it beside him; it had no use to him now. He heard it hit the floor and it rolled away. Suddenly light from the tiny flashlight bust into the room almost blinding them.

"I thought the cell was dead," said Shayna.

"It was," said Patty as she reached over and picked up the tiny light. Immediately it went out again.

"Put it back down," said Shayna. "In the same place you picked it up." Patty placed the flashlight back down and it came on again.

"Something near here is powering the light," she said. "If we can find it, we may be able to use it." By placing the flashlight near the different objects they soon discovered which piece of machinery was responsible.

"There's no wiring or any other form of connection I can see," she said and picked up the alien generator. Small and compact, it was no bigger than a textbook and weighed only a few pounds. Taking the generator and the flashlight she walked around the room.

"Portable power," she said. "Let's get Adam fixed up. I want to try something." They wrapped Adam's ankle then with the flashlight found the doorway and exited.

"I knew it," exclaimed Shayna excitedly. "See the light still works."

"But will it work outside the complex?" Asked Patty.

"Only one way to find out," she replied and they hurried as fast as Adam could hobble to the exit. Once outside, Shayna held the light near the generator again and it shone with brilliant light.

Allen came over and quickly examined the object. He turned it over and over, searching for something. "There's no access ports or any other port. If it is a generator I don't see how they connected it to the appliance."

"Perhaps they just laid it beside the whatever they need to power," suggested A'Serta. "Bring it here. Let's see how much juice it can carry." They returned to the makeshift desk and A'Serta opened the back of her 'corder and removed the power cell.

"This uses far more power than the flashlight," she explained and placed the 'corder on the table. Then she took the alien generator and placed it beside the 'corder. Nothing happened and they expressed their disappointment.

"Stupid," exclaimed A'Serta. "I forgot to turn it on." Sheepishly she reached out and turned on the corder. Instantly the activation sequence began and it beeped its readiness.

"There you go," she said. "Instant power."

"Let's get this back to camp," said Patty. "If it works there, I'll return with some portable lights and search for more." They quickly packed up and started the trek back to the village.

When they got back, Shayna took the device to test it with the village equipment. Adam and A'Serta took the other objects they found and returned to their quarters to examine them. Patty went straight over to the hut with Ethan, Alyssa, and Lex. He nodded a greeting to the waiting hunter and entered the dimly lit room.

"How's he doing?"

Lex got up and came over. "No change," he said sadly. "Alyssa's been talking to him for almost 20 hours now." A soft scraping sound reached their ears and in amazement they saw Ethan's hand twitched slowly. Lex stuck his head through the door. "Get Doc and Timotin," he shouted, "Quickly!" The hunter took off as if his feet had grown wings.

Seconds later Doc and Timotin burst into the room followed quickly by Beth, Sam, and Allen. Doc bent down and felt for a pulse. "A strong pulse," he exclaimed.

"Respiration's up too," said Timotin. Ethan opened his eyes so fast it made the others jump.

"Oh, Ethan," cried Alyssa happily hugging the boy.

"A…O…E," said Ethan.

"Don't try to talk yet," said Doc. "Alyssa, please let us work." Lex escorted the happy mother from the shack and amidst cheers and well wishes from the others broke down and sobbed happily.

Thirty minutes later Doc poked his head out and motioned for them to enter. Ethan was sitting up in bed looking every bit as good as he was before. He smiled when Alyssa entered the room.

"Mama," he said in a childlike voice. He threw back the cover and tried to stand up. He immediately collapsed to the floor in a heap.

Alyssa tried to rush to his side but the Doctor restrained her. "Leave him Alyssa," he said gently. "Let him work it out for himself."

"I don't understand," she said puzzled. "What's wrong with him?"

"The virus has wiped any trace of advanced abilities from Ethan. Including most of his memory. He knows, he remembers, but the signals from his mind no longer make sense to his body. It must relearn everything all over, how to talk, how to walk. Everything!"

"We believe his cognitive abilities are untouched," said Timotin, "but he is physically no more coordinated than, say, a two-year-old. From the few tests we have run, he will recover quickly, but he must find out how for himself. Give time for the new neural pathways to become set in his mind."

Alyssa watched in frustration as Ethan squirmed and rolled about on the floor. Time and time again he tried to raise himself up, but failed. Soon though, his arms responded to his commands and supported him. Slowly he learned how to crawl all over again.

Alyssa at the end of the room crouched down and held her arms out. "Come on, Ethan," she said. "You can do it. Come to me. That's it. Come on." The boy half dragged, half crawled to her. The strain on his face told how he struggled to control a body that didn't know how to do anything. When at last he reached Alyssa and collapsed in her arms.

"Alyssa," he whispered. "Mother!" Then closed his eyes and fell asleep.

"He'll be all right," said Doc, "but you have a big task ahead. He has to relearn everything. He's learning incredibly fast, but his body is basically new. It doesn't know how to react."

"It will be just as if you are teaching a baby," said Timotin.

"I don't care," said Alyssa happily cradling her son.

"What about his mind?" Asked Lex. "Was there any damage to that?"

"We believe there was some brain damage," said Doc hesitantly. "Exactly how much we won't be able to tell until he can react and speak normally again."

Alyssa cradled her son tenderly. The man in the boy's body had now become the baby in the child's body. But one thing the others knew for certain. If the boy were to survive he would need help and a lot of it. Looking at Alyssa they knew he had such support.

Chapter 24

"Hey...Hey, Alyssa!" Alyssa turned in the direction of the voice calling her name and saw Adam sprinting across the field. He hugged her tightly when he reached her and she returned the embrace with enthusiasm.

"Adam," she said happily. "How's A'Serta? How's the research coming?"

"Fine," said Adam. "Wonderful, in fact. We've learned some fascinating things about the Providers. That's why I've returned. I need the council and your help."

"What for?"

"I'll explain later," he said, smiling, "but first, tell me. How's Ethan doing? It must be nearly six months since I last saw him."

"Wonderful," said Alyssa proudly. "His recovery is nothing short of miraculous. Doc says that he's almost back to normal."

Adam indicated a soft mound of grass to sit on and plopped himself wearily down. "We didn't really want to leave you, but A'Serta couldn't bear the thought of staying and watching."

"I know," said Alyssa, understanding. Many of the villagers had left in the first few weeks following Ethan's recovery from death. It unnerved them to see a once vibrant intelligent boy, be reduced to crawling and having to be fed, bathed, and changed by hand. But they returned from their explorations after a few months and took an active interest in educating the boy.

"Ethan has almost full control again," said Alyssa. "But, he'll never be the genius he was. His artificially inflated intelligence is gone. So have most of his psychic abilities. Sam says he still retains some, a natural gift, but nothing close to what he had."

"How's he handling it? I imagine that this must be a shock to him!"

"Surprisingly well," said Alyssa. "The transformation left him with an IQ of a well educated 18-year-old. There are some parts of his mind that no longer register on the med-scanner. Doc believes that they are areas no longer functioning. But it doesn't seem to cause Ethan any problems."

"How are you holding up? I know he looks like a 13-year-old, and now acts and behaves like a teenager, but he's still closer to your age."

"I'm doing fine." She smiled. "I worried about that as well, but Ethan says he had no childhood that he remembers. This is his youth. We've grown very close. Ethan and Lex and Patty have formed a bond that can't be broken. 'Male bonding' Lex calls it."

"That's great," said Adam. "I'm very glad everything worked out."

Alyssa nodded. "So tell me? What brings you back to the village in such a hurry? The last report we received from the hunters who visited you, said you and A'Serta would be staying at the Provider complex another couple of months."

"As you know," he explained, "We've been analyzing artefacts from the complex. A'Serta can't go in because of the obvious problem, but she has become quite adept at figuring out the objects I bring out. Oh, and one other thing you might want to know…A'Serta's pregnant!"

"Pregnant," cried Alyssa hugging the man. "How wonderful. I must come out and see her!"

"You can," he said, "anytime. That's part of the reason I'm here. Alyssa, can you call a council meeting this afternoon?"

"Sure," said Alyssa, "but what will I give them as a reason?"

"I don't want to spoil the surprise," he said mysteriously. "Just have the council ready to receive me in, say three hours?"

"If you want," said Alyssa a little doubtful. "How about a hint?"

"Nope," he said smiling. "You'll have to wait just like everyone else. Look, I have to go to talk to Doc about A'Serta. See you in three hours?"

Alyssa nodded and hugged the man tightly again. He left skipping across the field as if he didn't have a care in the world. Alyssa watched him leave and paused to reflect on her life.

In the years they had been stranded on this world, she had gained some of her confidence back, a husband, and a son. She felt good about herself and the world around her. The news about A'Serta's impending arrival only seemed to heighten her feeling of well-being. With a smile she strode back into the village.

The Village as it was now officially called had been transformed into something a little more human. With the aide of the portable generators from the alien complex and a few other devices that Adam and A'Serta had figured out, they now had a few luxuries. The shower that Alyssa used to take with cold water now provided unlimited hot water. The electrical field they used to keep out the Jellyrolls was now completely buried and they had no fear it would suddenly die.

Other amenities included, lighting for each of the huts. The huts were also laid down in a pattern, no longer haphazardly spread out. They had made streets and named them. Alyssa passed several huts while walking along the dirt street and came to the village square. A large sign in the middle proclaimed it "Ada Worensky Square."

The largest hut at the far end of the square was the council chamber. It being midday, she knew that several members of the council would be available and walked inside. A young man greeted her at the door and said that most of the members were on an expedition, scouting a new water supply. But Patty was still around somewhere. She thanked the man and left.

Alyssa found Patty just outside the Village. He was standing in front of a shale blackboard and was giving a class to the young people of the Village. Once things had settled down. Patty had started a school.

"Can't have the young minds going to waste," he said.

As she drew near, his voice drifted over to her. "...And that's why the League has prospered. Okay, who can sum up today's lecture?" He looked at his charges and they quickly scanned through their notes. Slowly hesitantly hands began to rise.

He pointed to one young girl and she stood up. "The Star League represents the ideal of mankind to live in peace and prosperity," she said.

"Yes," said Patty. "That's correct. But if we live in peace and prosperity, why do we have a military?"

A young man, almost an adult raised his hand and Patty acknowledged him. "We have a military," said the teenager, "because we must defend against those that would destroy us."

"That's the official answer," said Patty. "Think about it. I've told you the history of the League and explained how and why. That will be your homework assignment. I want you to think why we have a strong military presence. We have no real enemies. We all live in PEACE. Any questions? Class dismissed!"

The class picked up their pads and ran scrambling into the woods. Personal and ship's clothing had long deteriorated and they were all dressed in animal skins that had been cured and cut to size. Living in the jungle environment had toned their bodies and shaped them into lean athletic young men and women. Alyssa admired the way the seemed to move and flow like animals. She could hardly hear them as they scurried away into the underbrush.

"How are you, my dear?" Asked Patty giving her a hug and kiss.

"Just fine," she replied. "I didn't see Ethan in class today. Is he all right?"

"Oh, he's fine," said Patty. "All this is old stuff to him and he gets bored easily. I've had to create a special class for him. He and Lex should be almost finished for today."

"Why wasn't I told about this class? I'm his mother! Shouldn't I be kept informed?"

"Calm down, calm down," said Patty gently. "Ethan requested that we keep you out of it for awhile. Now don't worry. Lex and I have been his instructors."

"Well," she said a little ashamed of her outburst. "What is this class?"

"I should let Ethan tell you himself. He wants to make it a surprise. Don't ruin it for him. I've never seen anyone take such an active interest before. It's as if this is the one thing that keeps him going."

"Is that healthy?"

"Maybe, maybe not," said Patty. "Ethan is a unique case. He's forgotten a lot of stuff, but retained some memories. I think that without the genetic manipulation, this might have been what he would have done."

"All right," she said smiling. "I'll keep it to myself, until he wants to tell me." They stared walking back to the Village arm in arm.

"Patty," she said. "When will the rest of the council return?"

"Another 2-3 hours I would think," said Patty. "Why?" She explained Adam's request and Patty promised that as soon as they returned, he would conduct a special seating.

"By the way," said Alyssa, "when are you and Beth finally going to tie the knot?"

"Probably never," said Patty. "We both agree that neither of us wants to get married. Don't get me wrong. We do love each other, but we're comfortable this way."

"You hypocrite," she accused. "You nearly forced me into marrying Lex, but refuse to do it yourself."

"Because, my dear heart," he said softly, "you needed it. Whereas, Beth and I don't."

A cool breeze blew across the small open field between the classroom and the Village. Alyssa shuddered and pulled herself closer to Patty. Dressed in what she referred to as "Designer Savage," she felt naked as the breeze blew. It only lowered the temperature a couple of degrees, but after living in sweltering heat and humidity for over a year, it seemed like a cold blast from an icy furnace.

"Is it me," she said through clenched teeth, "or is there a distinctive nip in the air."

"It is getting cooler," agreed Patty. "Our observations show that we are approaching the farthest point of this world's orbit."

"You mean winter's coming!"

Patty smiled. "More or less. I really don't know what form it will take. The orbit of this planet is almost twice as long as Earth Standard. Our figures show we landed here just as summer started."

"Well, I'm cold," she shivered. "If the temperature drops anymore we'll need arctic survival gear."

"Quite true," said Patty. "It must be almost 90 degrees by now. A real arctic chill."

"Very funny," she said sarcastically. "Why do I feel cold then?"

"Your body has adjusted to the climate. I served for two years on a desert world. Beautiful place. Rolling dunes. Swaying trees Average daily temperature of over 110 degrees. When my tour was over I returned to Earth to vacation. I visited Middle Europe in the height of summer. It was the worst three weeks I spent."

"Why? Middle Europe is quite hot in the summer I hear."

"Yes, but to my conditioned body it felt cold and damp. I suffered greatly and was never so glad to get back into space and my climate controlled cabin."

"I see," she said thoughtfully. "I've grown used to the heat, so a little drop in temperature—even though it's still very hot—feels cold."

"Exactly. But don't worry. You'll adjust. The human body is quite resilient, if given half a chance."

"If you say so," she said doubtfully. Right now she wanted to curl up in a warm toasty blanket. Something she hadn't thought about since they arrived on the jungle world.

As they continued walking, Patty became more pensive and quiet. Alyssa looked at her mentor and friend and knew that something troubled him.

"What's wrong?"

"Eh? Oh nothing. I was just thinking about Beth."

"You love her a lot, don't you? I wonder if Lex thinks about me all the time as well?"

"I'm sure he does," he said warmly. "But that's not what concerns me. Alyssa have you noticed anything different about Beth lately?"

"What do you mean?"

"I can't put my finger on it, but she's acting strangely. She's always in a hurry. Rushing about doing a hundred and one different things at the same time. I know she's always been an energetic woman, but lately it seems to be even more so."

"No, I haven't noticed anything unusual," said Alyssa thoughtfully. "But then again I haven't seen much of her. She's always out of camp. Joining some expedition or other."

"That's what I mean," said Patty. "Do you realize that in the last two months, she's accompanied every single expedition team? I mean every one. As soon as she returns from one trip, she embarks on another."

"I'm sure she's all right," assured Alyssa, "but maybe you should have Doc take a look at her!"

"Good luck," said Patty a little angrily. "Every time I mention it she explodes. Tells me to mind my own business."

"That doesn't sound like Beth," agreed Alyssa. "Any ideas?"

"At first," said Patty slowly, "I thought maybe the strain had begun to affect her. You know the command protocols and all that."

Alyssa nodded slowly. Yes, she knew about the command protocols. A few months ago when Beth had been troubled she had pressured Lex and Patty to explain the problems to her. She had been shocked to find out that the Captain of a vessel was solely and totally responsible for the safety of the ship and crew. The League automatically assigned blamed for any incident on the Captain pending further investigation.

"So you think she's worried about the inquiry board when we get back? Somehow that doesn't fit. Her earlier problem I could see, but it's been months and we've survived and prospered. She should be proud of her accomplishments!"

"My thought exactly," agreed Patty. "And she's too strong a Captain, too good a leader to not accept those duties. No, it's something else, but what?"

"Would you like me to talk to her?"

Patty grabbed her shoulders gently. "Would you? I mean be discreet, but I don't mind telling you, I'm a little worried. I've never seen her like this."

Alyssa hugged the man then said softly. "Why don't you take her fishing after the meeting. I remember you both saying that all you wanted to find was the perfect fishing hole."

"Splendid idea," said Patty enthusiastically. "We haven't been fishing in months. I fear though, we may never find that perfect fishing spot here. Far too many dangerous plants under the water."

"There's more to this than you're telling me! What is it?"

He continued walking and kept quiet. Alyssa walked closely beside him. She knew he would speak when he was ready. But as they entered the camp he still hadn't said a word. They strolled across "Ada Worensky Square" and entered the council hut. Still in silence, Patty read the latest reports from the hunting and scouting parties.

"They're back," he said tonelessly. "I'd better round up the council before they disappear again." He moved toward the door then stopped. Silhouetted by the sun in the doorway he turned and with a sad face said, "I've been searching for that fishing hole all my life. I'm too old to continue the search. Much too old," and exited the building leaving Alyssa staring open-mouthed after him.

*

"Captain, Ladies and Gentlemen of the council," began Adam in his address. "As you know we have been studying the complex, supposedly abandoned by a race we know as the Providers. Before I continue, I should tell you what we've found about them.

"The Providers, is the name we have applied to this highly evolved race. It's the best name that fits, but in discovering their complex, and investigating their equipment we have learned that they were so much more."

Alyssa leaned forward and listened intently as Adam explained that the Providers were a race that passed through this portion of the galaxy over one hundred thousand years ago. The complex was the last remaining outpost on this world, but not the last in this quadrant. Seven other such outposts in this area exist and over 1000 others had been found to still be in operation on other worlds.

"How do you know all this?" This from one of the council members: A hunter, who had been seriously injured and was no longer able to journey into the jungle!

"We have adapted several of our scanners to see in the visual range of the Providers, then change the colour spectrum and display it in the wavelengths seen by humans. While studying one of their machines—accidentally of course—I activated the machine and a star map was displayed. By playing with the controls I could force it to focus on any given area."

Alyssa raised her hand to interrupt. "If there are over 1000 of the complexes still around, why haven't we found one by now?"

Adam smiled. "How many suns are there in this quadrant? How many planets circle those stars? Billions! How many worlds has man explored or settled a scant few hundred. If we had found one before, I would have been even more surprised. It is just pure blind luck that we landed on a world where one existed."

Patty cleared his throat gently. "I'm sorry, I don't understand. All this is fascinating, but what can we do about it?"

"Please let me finish and I'll tell you," said Adam. Pacing in font of the council chamber, Adam looked and acted every bit the University Professor giving a lecture. "We all ready know that the Providers were a telepathic species through the contact with Sam and Ethan, and my own dear wife. But, even this advanced race must have had some way to communicate across the vast interstellar distances."

"I always thought that telepathy knew no physical bounds," said Alyssa. "I thought that thought waves were faster than the speed of light."

"In a sense you are right," agreed Adam. "I admit my knowledge is incomplete and second hand, but from what I understand, yes that is so. In theory a telepath standing on Earth should be able to contact another telepath on Mars with no time delay. But, for the sake of argument Let's assume a hypothetical case."

He turned and lifted a shale slab and propped it on a chair. The taking a piece of chalk he began drawing and explaining. "If telepath A lived on planet X, and Telepath B lived on planet Y, how long would it take for their signal to reach each other?"

"We can't answer that," said Beth. "We don't know how far apart X and Y are and how fast thought waves travel."

"IF X is in sector 001 of the alpha quadrant and Y is in sector 001 of the Gamma quadrant, can you figure how fast it must travel to attain instantaneous communication?"

"Well, those two quadrants are nearly side-by-side," said Beth thoughtfully. "Still there's a distance of nearly…900 hundred light years. Therefore, the signal must be able to travel at…" She stopped and made some rapid mental calculations.

"It's obvious," said Lex. "It would have to travel at speeds over 900 hundred times the speed of light. But that's impossible. Nothing can travel that fast!"

"Nothing we know about," said Adam. "Now what if the distance was ten times that or a hundred times that distance. There is no math to support that type of instance, but The Providers seem to have been able to accomplish just that."

"Their outposts stretch across the galaxy and they are all linked together. Now how did they do it? Frankly I have no idea and I'm no engineer, but I have found the equipment that permits them to do this."

"Wonderful," said Lex sarcastically. "All we have to do is send a message to an alien outpost and ask them to save us. Is this what you are trying to say?"

"Yes and no," said Adam patiently. "Remember, The Providers are a telepathic species. They have incredibly vast intellects. I say have because I still believe they are around somewhere. But we humans lack that phenomenal brain-power needed to even power the device."

"By the seven moons of Glandor," exploded Patty, "get on with it, man. What are you trying to say?"

"I think we may be able to send a call for help, using their equipment!" The others looked at him is if he had gone mad. He had just finished saying that their feeble minds couldn't do anything, now he wanted to send a distress signal.

"Calm down," said Alyssa forcefully. Then more gently, "Adam, what you say is very hard to believe after what you've told us. Do you have anything to back it up?"

"Only our research and observations," said Adam. "We believe it can be done, but it must be accomplished in a very special way."

"What way?"

"Individually our minds are weak, immature by Provider standards. Even those amongst us like Sam and Ethan are less than children in comparison. But, collectively we might generate enough power to activate the machine."

Patty stood and the room quieted. "What you propose is fantasy of course," he said gently. "But, let's assume you're right. How do we do this?"

"That's the part I need your help for," said Adam. "I need to run some more tests, and for that I will need the assistance of Sam, Ethan and a few dozen others."

"Absolutely not," cried Alyssa. "He's only just recovering and I will not allow Ethan to be subjected to any experimental tests."

"Then you condemn us to live out our lives on this Hell-Hole," replied Adam angrily. "Ethan has a gift—weak as it is—that could save us. I've given you a choice. Now it's up to you the council. Do we try to rescue ourselves or do we stay here until we die."

"Easy, Adam," said Patty. "I'm sure Alyssa wasn't attacking you personally. Before making a decision I would like to here more about this proposal and these tests."

"Surely you can't truly be considering this," cried Alyssa in wonder. "There's a little boy's life at stake here!"

"And the lives of almost two hundred people," said Beth. "I must use every means possible to ensure the safety of the people. Now I will listen to Adam's theories. If you can't control your emotions then you are dismissed!"

"You're throwing me out of the council," said Alyssa in amazement.

"I have no time to molly coddle anyone," said Beth angrily. "Perhaps you weren't ready for that promotion after all. A true leader needs to think clearly—"

"—Beth," admonished Patty. "This session will recess until tomorrow. Adam, I expect you to explain this proposal in detail then. The rest of you are free to leave. Beth, Alyssa, I want you two to stay."

"I am in charge here," cried Beth. "I say what happens or not."

"True," said Patty firmly, "but under League rules of behaviour, I must assume that you have lost your sense of reason and I therefore assume control of the council."

"If that's the way you feel," said Beth, "then go ahead and play your games. I have an expedition to join."

"Sorry," said Patty. His face was stone. Alyssa couldn't read an expression in it at all. "You are ordered to report to Doc for a physical. Beth, sweetheart, don't make me send you under guard. Something's wrong, and I want to know what it is. As for you Alyssa, I would seriously think about your statements. In here, the concern is for the safety of all. Well, what are you all standing around for? There's work to be done."

Slowly the council members vacated the hut some of them staring back at the trio of friends who now acted like mortal enemies. Alyssa felt a little ashamed at her outburst and said so.

"I'm sorry, Patty, Beth. I was thinking with my heart, not my head. Of course it is our responsibility to get rescued. I promise I'll listen with an open mind tomorrow."

"That's my girl," said Patty. "I promise you that no harm will come to Ethan. How about you my love? Anything you want to say?"

"I don't believe you two," spitted Beth angrily. "It's almost as if you're plotting to take over. That's it isn't it?"

"Beth," cried Alyssa. "How can you say such a thing? Please, go see Doc."

"I will not," she said defiantly. "I am the Captain. I don't have to obey your orders."

"Beth," said Patty gently. "You know I love you, but this can't go on. I've relieved you of the council. Don't make me relieve you as Captain. I don't want to. But I can and will transfer it to Lex if I have to."

"You wouldn't dare," glared Beth.

Patty just stared at her His face rock hard. "You know me," he said quietly. "I can and I will. Now, will you go peacefully, or do I have to summon a guard to drag you there."

"I'll go," she said. Then her whole demeanour changed and she gently brushed Patty's cheek with her hand. "Whatever happens," she said softly, "make sure they get home safely!" Before they could say anything, she left the hut and made her way across the square to the hut Doc had set up as the hospital.

Alyssa stared after the woman. "What…What just happened here?"

"I honestly don't know," said Patty, "but now I'm really worried. I only hope that whatever it is that's bothering her, we can solve. Maybe Doc will find something." Alyssa agreed silently and slipped away to quietly meditate about her own outburst.

In her hut later she confessed to Lex. "I guess I embarrassed you and myself in there. I'm sorry. I've worked hard to keep my temper under control, but sometimes it wins."

"Don't worry about it, Lys," he said holding her close. "You reacted like a mother protecting her young. But don't forget, it's better to act than react...You're worried about Beth, aren't you?"

Alyssa admitted she was then shamefacedly admitted the horrifying truth. "What if whatever is happening to Beth happens to us all. Maybe it's some sort of disease?"

"I doubt that," said Lex. "Anyway we'll know soon enough when Doc examines her. But that isn't what you're really thinking is it? You're worried that if she becomes incapable of commanding I will have to take over, which means you will become second-in-command. You still have the fears, don't you?"

Alyssa nodded slowly then buried her face is his chest. Ashamed at her fears and her weakness, Alyssa sobbed gently while Lex stroked her hair. "I'll tell you this," he said gently. "One day you will command. You will have to face the responsibility, but I have faith in you. I know you can do it."

She smiled at him then gently kissed him. With loving care he kissed away her tears and held her tight. Soon the sobs stopped and she began to feel better. He refused to acknowledge her apologies and sternly commanded her to stop feeling sorry for herself and learn from the experience.

Much later a runner came to the hut and reported that Patty had called an emergency meeting in the council hut. Alyssa and Lex hurried over to the hut. When they arrived, Patty greeted them and ushered them into seats around the table. The only other people present were Beth and Doc.

"I've asked you here because this affects you both," said Patty. "Doc, tell them what you just told me."

Doc placed a hand gently on Beth's shoulder. "I've examined Beth carefully. You'll be pleased to know that she isn't suffering from any mental disease or other viral organism. But, she is far from healthy."

"And the mood swings?" Asked Alyssa as she moved nearer Beth to offer comfort.

"Sorry," said Beth softly. "That's all fake. I was putting it on."

"But why?"

"Go ahead, Doc," she said. "Tell them. We won't be able to keep it a secret much longer."

Alyssa looked questioningly at Doc. "About 10 years ago, Beth suffered a heart attack," he said. "This was before I joined the ship. I didn't know it because she had had her records sealed."

"I didn't want anyone to know," said Beth. "It could have affected my career plans." Alyssa and Lex nodded. If the League found out, they would have placed a monitor on her and at the first sign of trouble had her removed from her post. They couldn't afford to take a chance with the lives of the passengers and crew.

"Why all the mystery and the strange behaviour? Surely you don't think we would betray you? Hell, we didn't even know about it," said Alyssa explosively.

"Beth didn't just have a heart attack," said Doc softly. "She had a massive coronary. It destroyed most of the heart muscle."

"I have a mechanical heart," said Beth. "It's a wonder in technology, but it requires periodic adjustments to meet the physiological changes in my body. My next adjustment was due three months ago."

"The mechanical heart has reached its limit," said Doc. "Eventually it must be replaced with a new one. She never mentioned it to anyone. She's been getting the adjustments and replacements done secretly."

"I still don't understand," said Lex.

"When the heart begins to break down," said Beth, "the soft biotic lining starts dissolving. Eventually the mechanical heart stops completely. I've always managed to find one of the hospitals I deal with long before it happens and get a new one."

"But out here, you can't," cried Alyssa. "Oh Beth, I'm so sorry. Is there anything we can do?"

"I'm afraid not," said Doc. "Her immune system is so strong, that's why she was originally given a mechanical heart instead of a real one. Out here, I just don't have a new one to give her."

"Which means-."

"—Which means that I still wanted to experience everything I could," said Beth. "That's why I joined all those expeditions, and that's why I acted the way I did. I didn't want to leave you like we are. I figured that if I pushed hard enough, then Lex would have to take over. It would make the transition a little easier in the eyes of the courts."

Alyssa looked at Patty. His face was hung and his jaw clenched tightly. "I assume you know how long," she said hesitantly.

"Oh, I'll be fine for sometime to come yet," said Beth brightly and Alyssa smiled. "Doc here ran several tests and has it all figured out. Don't you, Doc?"

"Beth, please," said Doc softly.

"No, tell them," said Beth. "It's better that they know. After all, when I'm gone Lex will be in charge and Alyssa his Second-in-Command. Go ahead, tell them."

"According to my figures," he said slowly, "the decay of the biotic lining has already begun. Normally this would last at least 6 months plenty of time to seek medical attention. But for some reason—possibly the more active lifestyle we lead here—the lining is deteriorating faster. If she relaxes and doesn't exert any more energy I predict complete life support failure in less than 5 days."

"Five days, Lex," said Beth, smiling. "Better get boning up on your command protocols." She continued smiling then suddenly her face dropped and she fell into the waiting arms of Patty and started crying deep wracking sobs, echoed by Alyssa.

Chapter 25

Five days! Beth was living a death sentence and there was absolutely no way to help her. If they were anyplace else, she could be rushed to the nearest facility, but here on this Hellhole she had no hope. Beth had already made her peace, but the rest found the frustration overwhelming.

"I can't believe it," said Lex that night in bed. "She's always been a strong vibrant woman. I always said she was too stubborn to die. Now look at her. Perfectly healthy except for a bad heart that can be fixed anywhere but here."

"I know, my love," said Alyssa softly. Then grasping at a hopeful straw, she sat up suddenly as a thought struck her.

"Listen," she said quickly. "Adam is presenting his proposal tomorrow. Maybe his idea will work and we'll be rescued before her heart gives out!"

"Maybe," said Lex, but he didn't sound hopeful. "Did you know that she's already begun transferring everything to me? She's already recorded in her log the transfer of command…She's also recommended you for First Officer."

"I know," said Alyssa lying back down. With the imminent death of Beth so prominent, Lex and Alyssa comforted each other in the way couples have for thousands of years. Soon they fell into a restless, haunted sleep, their minds still in turmoil.

The next morning after breakfast, the council gathered to here Adam's proposal. Before his arrival, Beth made everyone promise not to reveal her condition. "I don't want the people to feel like the Captain is abandoning them. Don't worry, I have an idea to ease the shock and transition."

Adam arrived to a sea of smiling faces. With quick enthusiasm he set up his display and quickly recounted what they already knew about the providers. Then he pulled a small triangular object from his haversack.

"Before I explain my idea fully," he said, "a little demonstration of what can be accomplished." He went to the door and opened it wide to reveal Ethan.

"Ethan has consented to assist me," he said. "Don't worry, Alyssa. It won't harm him in any way. Ready son? Okay, go ahead!"

Ethan took the triangular object and held it in front of his face. He closed his eyes and they could see the concentration on his features. They waited and watched…and watched. Then the pyramid began to glow softly with a weird pink glow. It grew brighter and began to pulsate. Suddenly it stopped and Ethan slumped forward tiredly.

"I'm all right," he said brushing back Alyssa's concern. "Just tired."

Patty took the pyramid in his hands and examined its smooth flawless features. "What exactly happened?"

"Just wait," said Adam. "The other member of our experiment should be here any minute." Just then Sam came running breathlessly into the room.

"What is it?" She panted and heaved, obviously she had been running hard. "What's wrong, Ethan? I heard you in my mind!"

"Ladies and gentlemen," said Adam, "Sam did not know what was going to happen. I didn't know whether it would work or not, but it has. Please, all of you, be seated. Yes, you two as well and thank you."

Puzzled Sam took a seat beside Ethan who had sat beside his mother. Alyssa wrapped her arms around the boy as if making sure that he was unhurt.

"We know the unique case of Ethan," continued Adam when they all had seated. "He had incredible telepathic powers, but they have been reduced to a mere fraction of their former power. But this pyramid, has given him back some of that power.

"The Providers were telepathic," he said, "but have any of you considered how difficult it must have been to communicate with one particular person. On a planet full of telepaths—all with the ability to communicate instantaneously—it must have been a horrendous nightmare to single a person out. This is what the pyramids are for. They're personal communicators. They take the thought waves, amplify and direct them to the appropriate person."

"So, Ethan was able to send a message to Sam," said Beth slowly. She turned and looked at Sam. "What did you hear, Sam?"

"Well, it was very faint," she said slowly, remembering. "I was on the other side of the Village when I heard Ethan. At first I thought I was dreaming. I haven't heard his thoughts since…you know. But then I heard it again. He needed help and told me to come here straight away."

"Sam is empathic," said Adam. "By her own admission her power is weak, but it was sufficient to hear Ethan's call. Do you understand what this means?"

"You want to send a telepathic call for help," said Alyssa. "But there's one flaw in your theory."

"Only one," said Lex sarcastically. "Sorry!"

"It took Ethan all his energy to make Sam hear his call," she said. "Sam was only at the other end of camp. How do propose to send a message across maybe hundred's of light years?"

"That brings me to my suggestion," said Adam, smiling. "The alien complex contains a transmitter of incredible power. This is how the Providers communicated over the vast distances."

"But how do we make it work? Ethan could barely make a small personal unit function. There's no way his mind will activate the larger unit."

"By himself, no," said Adam. "Even with Sam's help they couldn't do it. But during my tests, I noticed that I—a non-telepath—produced a small response in the unit. With others, I tested a theory. Our collective minds made a bigger response."

"I think I understand," said Patty. "You want to gather a group of people and hopefully turn on the unit."

"Exactly," said Adam. "My calculations show that we need at least 150 people present to fully utilize the transmitter."

"But if the transmitter is designed to work only with one person at a time," wondered Alyssa, "how can we send a message. Sam and Ethan are our only telepaths."

"Ah," said Adam. "We don't have to send a message. Only one of them does. The rest of us will provide—how should I put it—provide the brain power."

"So, we send a message and hope that someone understands it," said Lex. "That's a real long shot, Adam."

"It would work better if there was someone we know who could receive the message. Someone who was telepathic themselves."

"I don't know anyone like that," said Ethan. "I may have at one time, but I can't remember now."

"But I do," said Sam excitedly. The others looked at her. "My father!"

"Of course," said Ethan. "If you could reach him, you could guide him here."

"That's a mighty big if, son," said Lex. "Before we get all worked up, Adam, I want to know how you plan on using us to work this miracle of yours."

"Well, sir," said Adam. "Ethan is the strongest telepath, but he has no connection or link outside of us here. Sam does. To her father, but she can barely read any of us. I propose to allow Ethan to open his mind to the thoughts and feelings of the Villagers. He would act as a conduit for their collective power. He then makes a connection with Sam. She then transmits through the alien device and hopefully we should be able to reach her father."

"That's stretching reality a bit far," said Patty doubtfully. "Are you sure it will work?"

"I can't be sure of anything," said Adam, "but I have conducted extensive testing and feel we have a good chance. It may be our only chance." Patty nodded and leaned back in his chair, deep in thought.

Beth stood and looked around at the others. Some of the faces read a sign of hopefulness, others' scepticism. "I suggest we adjourn for now," she said. "Adam has given us a chance, albeit a small one. This is not a decision to take lightly. We could artificially inflate the hopes and desires of the people. We have made a life for ourselves here, and this could jeopardize everything we've worked for. Think about it, then we'll meet back here this afternoon."

The members rose from the seats and began exiting in groups of two or three. They talked animatedly as they left. Alyssa seated beside Beth, could plainly hear the members arguing the pros and cons of the idea.

After the other members had left, Beth indicated to Alyssa that they should all remain. Alyssa sat back down and took Ethan's hand in hers. Adam was the last person out the door and he shut it quietly while looking back into the room.

Beth looked at the remaining people. Patty, Alyssa, Lex, Ethan, and Sam. "Opinions? Comments?"

"I've heard some crazy ideas," said Lex, "but I'm sorry. This has to be the weirdest one yet."

"Go on," said Beth. "I want to hear your reasons why we shouldn't attempt this. I'm not saying I'm for or against it. I'm looking for input. Now, why do you feel it won't work?"

"For one thing," said Lex, "there's never been anything like this attempted before. How do we know that the machine will do as he says? What makes him think that even if it did work we could send a signal across the Galaxy? Plus, this is an alien machine. A machine I remind you we know absolutely nothing about, except for what Adam tells us."

"Valid arguments, Lex," said Beth. "Anybody else?"

"I think we should try it," said Ethan.

"Me too," said Sam.

"What about you, Lyssa?"

"I'm undecided," she said. "I think there maybe a chance, but I feel we're missing one important element. Telepathy is still relatively new to the human race. We don't understand 1/10th of its power. I would feel better if someone else acted on this rather than Ethan."

"There, that settles it," said Lex with a smug grin. "Even the boy's mother is against the idea."

"I didn't say I was against it," she countered. "Just that I would like another option, that's all."

"I think I may have that option," said Patty. "Think back to when we first arrived here. Ethan's abilities were no stronger than they are now. What changed? What enabled Ethan and Sam to fully use their gifts?"

The other sat in stony silence. Suddenly Ethan jumped up wildly. "Scrapper," he cried. "Scrapper is telepathic, and he's been using it all his life."

"Exactly," said Patty. "Ethan may be able to read our thoughts, and communicate them to Sam, but the real telepathic power here lies in the bond between Scrapper, Sam and Ethan. Scrapper has always been an amplifier between you two."

"So we let Ethan be the conduit and Scrapper the booster station," said Beth thoughtfully. "Scrapper then connects with Sam and that should provide the power and stability we need to make this thing work!"

"I'm still against it," protested Lex, "but if the rest of you want to make fools of yourselves, go ahead."

"If this is to work," said Patty, "we must all be for it. Lex, I respect your opinion, and understand your objections, but I can't buy it!"

"Lex," said Alyssa, "this could be our one chance to get out of here. Why are you so dead set against it?"

Lex lowered his head slowly and muttered and answer. "What? Speak up," said Alyssa.

"I said I don't want to endanger Ethan. He's been through so much and he finally has a chance at a normal life. I will not allow him to risk losing that."

"Lex...Father," said Ethan. "That means more to me than you could believe, but I am quite capable of making my own decisions."

"Wait," cried Beth, "Just hold on a minute. It really isn't up to us. I just wanted your input. It will be up to the council and the people. If enough members vote to try it, well take it to the Villagers and ask them. Now as long as Sam and Ethan are willing, who are we to say no?"

"Captain," said Lex, "what about your responsibility to the safety and welfare of the people?"

"In this case," she replied firmly, "my duty is clear. I have consent and a chance to save everyone. I cannot afford to abandon an idea just because I personally don't like it. That's one of the things you'll have to learn when your Captain."

"Then you're against this too?"

"No, I'm not," she said. "I just wanted you to see that personal feelings have to sometimes take a back seat to what is best for the whole."

"Yes, ma'am," he said a little subdued. "If the rest of the council votes to try it…I will add my support as well."

"We must show a united front to the Villagers," said Patty. "There will be a lot of resistance to a wild scheme like this. Many of the people feel the same way Lex does—no offence."

"All right," said Beth standing. "Ethan, why don't you and Sam go find Scrapper? See if you can make contact and try to explain what we want to do. In all this arguing we forgot how he might feel. He may be an animal, but Scrapper has feelings as well."

"Yes, ma'am," said Ethan and quickly kissed his mother good-bye as he and Sam left.

"As for the rest of you," said Beth, "beat it. Lex you stay. No, you go too Patty. I need to talk to Lex alone. Now scoot!"

Alyssa and Patty left the council hut and Beth closed the door. "What does she want with Lex?"

"I think he's about to get some on the job training in being a Captain," said Patty.

"How are you holding up?" Alyssa linked arms with the old veteran.

"Oh, I'll be all right," he said softly. "I've seen many men die before. But this is different. I feel so helpless. She's handling it better than I am."

"Maybe we'll get lucky," said Alyssa gently. "There's always the chance that her heart will hold together a bit longer."

"Maybe…"

A couple of hours later Lex entered his hut and sat down beside Alyssa. His face was pale and his strong sturdy frame shook gently. He ignored Alyssa's attempts to talk and curled up on the bed and rolled to face the wall. Alyssa sat beside him, not daring to even touch him. Something had really upset him, and he wanted to be alone. She rose and stole quietly from the hut.

Later, Lex emerged, still white, but obviously more in control of himself. He found Alyssa and rounded up Ethan and the rest. They made their way to the council chambers and took their seats. Beth called the meeting to order and reiterated the proposal. Unanimously they voted to try it. Alyssa looked at Lex, but even he voted to continue, before the results were complete.

"Then I suggest we present it to the people this evening," said Beth. "Adam, since you're our expert, you will present the proposal. The council will add their voice of support."

"Thank you," said Adam softly.

That evening after everyone had had their fill of dinner, Beth called a town meeting in the square and introduced Adam. Slowly and distinctly he explained what they wanted to do. Beth added her voice and the support of the council.

"Now, I want you to think about it," she said. A cool breeze whipped up and the Villagers pulled their skimpy rags about them.

"It's going to be cold tonight," she said, "so I won't keep you any longer than necessary. In 30 minutes I will ask you to vote. Any questions? Fine. Be back here in 30 minutes. Thank you."

A runner came up to Patty and offered him an electronic tablet. Patty took the device the young girl scurried off. Clicking on the unit, Patty studied the readout carefully then summoned the others.

"We may have to hurry," he said. "This report shows that the temperature has dropped another 10 degrees in the last 24 hours. We still have several weeks before we reach what we calculate will be winter here. By then it will be well below freezing and if we don't find shelter, we'll freeze to death."

The news shocked the others. This hot, steamy jungle world was about to be plunged into a winter wonderland. Looking around at the tropical plants Alyssa found it hard to believe. Still it had been getting colder lately. She shivered unconsciously.

"I suggest we consider moving back to the caves," said Alyssa. "They should provide some measure of protection and they'll be easier to keep warm."

"We should also instruct the hunters to be on the look out for larger animals," said Beth. "We'll need warm clothes."

Lex caught Patty's eye. "How cold will it get?"

"I don't know," he admitted. "On Earth or any of the other planets, we know how the seasons act and have monitoring devices to tell us when a problem will occur. Here, we only have guesswork and a few calculations. The atmosphere, and the abundant plant life should moderate the temperature a bit, but it will still get very cold. Well below freezing I would think."

"Then I suggest we start making plans to evacuate the Village," said Beth. "Lex, that'll be your job. Make sure that the children and the pregnant women have a safe, secure spot. Patty, tomorrow we'd better check those caves. Alyssa how's the supply situation?"

Alyssa thought back to the most recent report. As Mayor, she was responsible for the maintenance and administration of the Village. "Meat should be no problem if we hustle and start drying some, but fresh fruits and vegetables will be a problem. If it does get as cold as Patty predicts, we'll run out long before it starts to get warm again."

"Leaving us susceptible to scurvy and other problems," said Patty.

"I'll give it some thought," said Alyssa. "Right now though we have a vote to handle. Here come the Villagers."

When they had all assembled, Beth divided the square in half. "Those who want to try it, move to the left side. Those opposed, go to the right. Before you move though I feel we should inform you of some new news." She called on Patty and he told them about the shifting weather patterns and their forecast for the cold.

This set up a murmur of discussion then they slowly moved into position. After almost an hour the decision was made. A hasty head count showed the majority of the Villagers willing to try the experiment, with only a dozen or so wanting to wait.

Beth looked at Adam. "Will that be enough?"

"It should be," he said. "I'll have all the details worked out for you in a couple of days." Beth nodded and turning back to people announced they would attempt the communication using the alien device. Since it had grown quite dark and the cool breeze continued blow, Beth dismissed the gathering and everyone beat a hasty retreat to the warmth of their huts.

That night, Alyssa tried again to talk to Lex. He seemed more amiable this time and reluctantly answered her questions. "It's not what she said," he muttered. "It's how and why."

"I don't follow," she said puzzled. Lex reached into his pouch and withdrew a data crystal.

"This is her log," he said holing it up in the flickering light of the lamp. "Effective tomorrow, I assume full authority."

"Then she's given up completely," whispered Alyssa. "I never would have believed it."

"Neither would I," he said sadly, "but as she pointed out there's no sense in putting off the inevitable. I am the Captain now, and I have to do everything in my power to ensure the safety of the people."

The next morning after breakfast, Beth called a town meeting and made her announcement. "My friends," she began. "I have had the honour and privilege to be the Captain of the largest Starship in the liner fleet. But now it's time for me to step down. We are faced with new challenges and tough times. It calls for a strong young leader. To that end I have recorded the promotion of Lex to Captain. I trust that you will give him the trust and support you have always shown me."

The news shocked the people, but Beth wasn't finished yet. "We will need more supplies to last the upcoming winter months. So I will lead a fishing party to find new sources of food. It will be a long hazardous journey and I didn't want to leave you leaderless. I know that Lex will make a wonderful Captain. Lex? Would you like to say a few words?"

Lex stood slowly and cleared his throat gently. Avoiding the stares of Alyssa and Patty he said, "Thank you, Captain, for the promotion. I'll never be able to fill your shoes. You've shown us what a true leader is, but I will try to make you proud of me. When my time comes to step down, I hope that I can pass on the title and responsibility with equal enthusiasm."

Alyssa stood and choked back the tears quickly. "Three cheers for the Captain. Hip, hip."

"Hooray," shouted the crowd.

"Hip, hip."

"Hooray."

"Hip, hip."

"Hooray!"

Lex and Beth hugged each other gently then Beth stepped down from the podium and left Lex alone. He turned and faced the smiling throng. "We have to prepare for the winter. We'll be moving back to the caves. Go home and pack whatever belongings you have. Will the leaders of the hunters and farmers please come see me before you leave? That is all."

The crowd dispersed and Lex moved off to consult with the hunters and farmers about reinforcing their clothing and food supplies. Alyssa sidled over to Beth and took the woman's hand.

"What's this about a fishing expedition? You never told me!"

"I thought it better than telling them I'll be dead in a couple of days from a heart attack."

"So who's going with you?"

"No one," said Beth. "I'll just disappear one night. It's easier this way."

"You're wrong," said Patty as he came up behind Beth and put his arms around her. "You won't be alone. Who knows we may find that fishing hole yet."

"You dear sweet man," said Beth. "I would like you to be there at the end, but I didn't want to suggest it."

"You couldn't keep me from your side," said Patty softly and kissed her passionately. They held each other tightly, then with a cheery wave moved off on their own.

Alyssa swallowed hard several times and wondered if she could ever face her death as calmly and easily as they seemed to. A soft whimper behind her startled her out of her reverie and she turned to face Ethan and Scrapper.

She kissed Ethan and held him close. Then Scrapper began nudging her hand for attention and she rubbed his shaggy mane affectionately. Together they left the square to begin packing.

The next morning Adam returned with his calculations and explained how the procedure would work. To make the contact as strong as possible they would link and hold hands. Quickly the Villagers positioned themselves into a chain. At the alien complex, Ethan held Alyssa's hand who held the hand of the last of the town's people.

The strength of their support and concentration momentarily made him dizzy. "Wow," he exclaimed. "This is incredible. I can feel the power of everyone's mind."

With his free hand he touched the shaggy mane of Scrapper and allowed the thoughts and feelings to flow through him. Sam placed a hand on Scrapper and completed the connection. Her eyes glazed over as the power of over 200 hundred people focused all their concentration on one thing.

Shaking she placed her free hand on the console that Adam had indicated. The board of lights that had previously flickered now came to life in a blaze of colour. For ten long intense minutes, Sam concentrated on reaching her father through the telepathic link.

After she broke contact, Ethan asked, "Did you get through? I heard you quite loudly."

"I'm not sure," said Sam shakily. "I think I did. I mean I felt him, but whether or not the signal was clear I don't know. He seemed so far away."

" It was worth the effort," said Beth.

"I must admit," said Lex, "I too felt something in the link. I really felt the love and support all these people gave you. It makes me think that maybe we stand a chance."

"Come on," said Alyssa. "It'll be dark soon and we still have a lot to do." The Villagers returned to the town and after packing supplies for a few more hours, settled down for the evening meal.

"I think we should move tomorrow," said Lex. "We still have time, but it will take several days to get organized."

"Good idea," said Beth. "Better to be safe than caught."

After supper, Lex ordered everyone to an early bed. The hunters and farmers had already retired as they had a busy few days ahead of them. Lex bid the rest goodnight and then scooping Alyssa and Ethan in his arms, turned for their hut.

The next morning, Lex organized the teams that would transport the supplies and equipment to the caves. He appointed several people to assist ands they began splitting the people up into the different caves in the mountainside.

When the move was well underway, Lex sought out Alyssa. "Have you seen Patty? He was supposed to help me with this."

"No," she said. "I haven't seen him all morning." She turned and her eyes opened wide.

"Lys?"

"I haven't seen Beth either," she choked.

Chapter 26

"Calm down, Lys," said Lex softly.

"But you know where she's going," protested Alyssa. "We've got to find her!"

"No, we don't," said Lex firmly. "Let her be."

"I'm going to find her," said Alyssa determinedly and she began walking away. Lex grabbed her roughly by the arm and spun her around quickly.

"You'll stay right here," he commanded.

"But we have to find her," cried Alyssa.

"Why?"

"Because we have to. She's…She's not right. Anything could happen out there alone."

"She's not alone," said Lex calmly. He slowly released his grip on her, prepared just in case she bolted.

"How can you be so insensitive," cried Alyssa. "You know why she's gone. You're a cold heartless bastard."

"Maybe so," said Lex, "but you still haven't given me a good reason to go after her. This is her decision, and I respect that. Look, I don't like it as much as you, but it is her wish and I will defend her right to die the way she wants. Clear?"

"But she still had several days left," protested Alyssa. "We could have found something to help in the complex. Why did she leave now?"

Lex took her tenderly in his arms and she gently sobbed against his chest. He waited until her shaking subsided then spoke softly. "Now you knew this day would come. And, you know there is nothing you can do so why all the fuss? Who are you really scared for? Her…or yourself?"

"How could you think that," she shrieked. "She's my Captain, and my friend."

"And mine," said Lex. "The best possible thing we can do for her is to leave her alone."

"That maybe fine for you, CAPTAIN, but I still care."

Lex's face dropped into a stony mask. Clearly his anger lay just below the surface. "If that's the way you feel, then I must order you to continue with the evacuation."

Alyssa glared at her husband and stood ramrod stiff. She raised her hand in salute. "Yes, sir," she said growled and stormed away.

Lex shook his head sadly. Slowly he turned to move across the compound in a different direction from his irate wife and came face to face with Sam.

"I'm sorry," she stammered. "I didn't mean to eavesdrop. I just came to deliver the latest reports."

"It's all right," said Lex gently, glancing back in the direction Alyssa had gone. "Beth has left and Alyssa is taking it hard."

"I know," said Sam. "Ethan and I saw her go with Patty a while ago. I figured out what she was doing."

Lex pulled at his skimpy animal fur tunic. The temperature had dropped another couple of degrees and he was getting cold. "We have a lot of work to do," he said quickly reading the reports.

"She'll be all right," said Sam tenderly.

"I know," he replied. "She just needs to blow off some steam. Let's go. We have to pick every vegetable we can find."

Together the two friends walked arm-in-arm to the fields. They rounded up those of the villagers who were not already occupied in packing, and headed out of the compound. Over the last few months the farmers had done a terrific job of growing the fresh vegetables and grains that the village required. Rows and rows of plants stretched and reached for the sky.

"It's too bad," said Sam. "This planet is a farmer's dream. Food grows so fast and quick here. Now we'll lose it all."

"Not necessarily," said Lex. "See those people over there? They're harvesting seeds and drying them. After winter we should be able to plant again."

Sam humphed. "If we survive the winter. Only a ¼ of the crop is ready for harvesting. The rest is too immature."

"We'll survive," said Lex confidently. "We've come this far and I can't believe that it's all for nothing."

"Forever the optimist, aren't you?"

Lex laughed. "Someone has to be." They divided those that accompanied them into groups and the farmers explained what to look for.

"There will be frost tonight," said one of the farmers sniffing the air. "Only pick those that are ready. Those plants that are nearly ready will be transplanted to a small garden we've set up in the caves. It's not much, but it should help extend our food supplies a bit longer."

The task of harvesting the food by hand was a long daunting one. As others completed their tasks, they joined in the harvest. With a woven reed basket slung over his shoulders, Lex picked and clawed his way though the plants. Occasionally he would stop and pick a mature plant, others he would mark for the team behind him that picked the immature plants.

When he filled his basket, Lex lifted his heavy burden high on his shoulders and started the trek to the caves. Several of them were very deep and it was in these that the food would be stored. On the way he passed a group of returning hunters. They looked tired and each of them carried heavily laden sacks.

"Looks like you had good hunting," said Lex casually inspecting their burdens.

"Some," replied one. "We've gotten enough jack meat for several days, but no larger deer or other animals. Sorry, Captain."

Lex brushed off the apology. Clearly the hunters had taken it as a personal insult the fact they couldn't find any large meat animals to provide food and warmth from their fur. "Where's Timotin? I thought he was in your group?"

"He and a couple of others are still out there," replied the hunter.

Lex nodded. "Better get that stuff back to camp. Set a team going to strip and cure the hides. Small as they are, we can sew them together. Get the meat drying. We won't have the benefit of the sun much longer and we'll have to use a fire."

"Yes, sir," said the hunter and signalling the others, wearily continued his plod to the camp.

Lex finished his trek to the caves and left his prize with others who were placing it carefully in the back of the cave. When he emerged he stretched to take the kinks out of his sore aching muscles.

"Lex," said Alyssa coming up softly behind him. "I'm sorry. I didn't mean what I said."

"I know," he replied. "Feel better?"

"Some," she said quietly. "Do you really think I'm more concerned about myself than Beth and Patty?"

"That's not for me to say, my love," he said tenderly taking her hand. "That's for you to decide. Alyssa, you've been through a lot. We all have. But I need you to be strong. You're my exec, and my wife. I need your support."

"Funny," she said, "I thought you were doing fine all by yourself. Ever since you became Captain, there's been a change in you. You're more confident, self assured."

"That's command training," said Lex. "Believe me, when the time arrives, you'll be as strong."

"I don't think so," she said. "I'm not command material."

"No? Take a look at yourself. As the next highest surviving ranking officer, you are in direct line for the Captainship."

"I couldn't…"

"Perhaps you need more training," he said gently. "Alyssa, I don't plan to have anything happen to me, but I must think about the people. If something should happen, I need to know that they will be taken care. I need to know that my successor will make sure they all get home safely."

"That's what Beth said to you earlier isn't it?"

"Something like that," said Lex with a smile. "She just reminded me of my duty."

"Then why don't I feel the same way?"

"Because you haven't had the same training and conditioning I have. Patty and I have tried to teach you, but you're having to learn the hard way, by experience."

He took her in his arms and gazed across the field. The cave was nearly twenty feet above the ground and except for a few tall trees; they had an unobstructed view of the valley. Below them the village of thatched roof huts sat. On the far side, they could make out tiny figures scrambling and scurrying about in the fields.

"Do you think we'll make it?"

"Absolutely," said Lex, "but we won't if we don't get back to work. Feel up to it?"

"Yes, sir," she said with a smile. "Can't let the people down can we."

"That's my girl," he said hugging her. Hands clasped they made their way down and trekked back to the fields. When they arrived several of the weary pickers hailed them. Sam came running over and put her arms around Alyssa.

"I'm glad you're here," she said. Then with great ceremony gave Alyssa one of the baskets. "Come on. I know where there's a lot of stuff not yet picked." Alyssa quickly kissed Lex and followed her friend into the field.

They continued picking until it became too dark to see. "That's all for tonight people," said Lex tiredly. "We'll get started again first thing in the morning."

As night fell so did the temperature. Before long everyone in their tiny animal skins was shivering with cold. Since the caves were still not ready, Lex ordered the people to their huts.

"If it gets too cold," he commanded, "we'll double up in the huts." The villagers broke off and made their way home.

"I'm worried about the crops," said Lex to Alyssa in their hut. "The cold could kill off the rest of them."

Alyssa nodded and stared thoughtfully into the flickering flame of the tiny fire they had in the hut. "But how do we keep them warm? We can barely keep ourselves warm."

"We don't have to keep them warm," said Ethan snuggling beside Scrapper. "We just have to keep the frost off them, right?"

"Go on, son," said Lex intrigued.

"Something I remember faintly," said the boy. "It's an old technique, I remember reading about, but I just can't seem to remember how."

Alyssa looked at her son as he struggled to remember. Occasionally Ethan could recall little bits of information, but the damaged areas of his mind refused to reveal their answers and it upset him greatly.

"It's all right," she said soothingly. "We'll get by."

"No," said Ethan defiantly. "This is important. You said so yourself, Father, that we could lose some of the crops. If only I could remember."

"I wish I could help, son," said Lex, "but I'm a city boy."

Ethan's eyes opened wide. "That's it," he cried eagerly. "Maybe one of the farmers knows what I mean." He got up and throwing another Jack fur around his shoulders disappeared through the door into the chilly night.

Alyssa looked at Lex then reached for her furs. "Well, don't just sit there. He's going to need some help."

"Yes, Captain," said Lex.

"What did you call me," said Alyssa absentmindedly as she threw on her fur. "Never mind. Are you coming?"

"Right behind you, my love." They ran out of the hut and headed to where the farmers' huts lay.

The farmers had placed their huts at the far end of the village. That way they could tend their crops early in the morning before the heat of the day made it impossible to move around. Alyssa and Lex hurried across the compound and caught a glimpse of Ethan ducking into one of the huts.

As they approached the hut, the door flung open and Ethan with a burly farmer exited. "Captain, Alyssa," acknowledged the farmer. "This boy of yours is a genius. Did you know that? I had forgotten all about smudge pots. We have no need of them back home, being climate controlled and all."

Alyssa pulled up beside Ethan and took him warmly in her arms. "Smudge pots? What are they?"

"It's an old technique," said the farmer, "for keeping the frost off crops. I had forgotten all about them. I remember as a boy helping my father place the pots around the fields. This was before we controlled the weather."

"I still don't understand," said Alyssa. "What is a smudge pot?"

"It's a pot with something long burning in it," volunteered Ethan. "The smoke and heat it generates keeps the frost clear of the crops."

"It won't keep out the snow," said the farmer, "but they should protect them long enough for us to finish harvesting tomorrow. All I have to do is get the materials together."

"Then let's get to it," said Lex. "You tell us what we need and we'll get it."

"First off," said the farmer thoughtfully, "we're going to need help. This will be a big job and it's getting cold fast. Ethan? Go round up the rest of my crew. Quickly now."

Ethan ran off and started rousing the other farmers. "Now we'll need several supplies," continued the farmer. "With your permission, Captain," Lex nodded, "We'd better get scrounging." Within minutes the rest of the farmers arrived and they were quickly brought up to speed on the plan. Eagerly they scoured the compound for the required materials and brought them out to the field. There, Lex and Alyssa, with Ethan, began assembling the smudge pots. As fast as they worked, others took them away into the fields.

A couple of hours later, dense dark smoke wafted over the crops. "That's it," said the farmer. "I hope this works." He bid the others goodnight and returned to his hut. The rest broke away and soon left Alyssa, Lex, and Ethan standing alone.

"There's no use staying out here," said Lex. "Thanks to Ethan, we maybe able to salvage more than we thought. Good job, son. Now let's go to bed."

The next morning the village rose early. A thin white frosty layer blanketed the ground and gave everything a shiny sparkle. As the sun rose and heated the air, it twinkled away into watery droplets then evaporated.

A cursory examination showed that some of the plants had succumbed to the killing frost as their pots had died during the night, but many other still survived. Quickly the villagers finished their harvest and made sure the immature shoots were transplanted into the caves.

Six hours later, they called a halt for lunch. The temperature had dropped to an average in the low 40's by now and the group huddled together for warmth. After they had eaten, Lex made the decision to move the final contents into the caves.

"If we hurry we can all be safe and secure in the caves tonight," he explained. "The temperature is dropping fast and I don't know how much longer we can survive out here exposed." The villagers finished their meal and began the task of moving their tiny community into the relative safety of the caves.

"I'm worried about Patty and Beth," confided Alyssa later to Lex. "It got very cold last night, but they never returned. You don't think Patty would do anything stupid do you?"

"If anyone could survive out there unprotected its Patty," chuckled Lex. "Don't worry. I'm sure he'll turn up soon."

A cry from the far side of the village caught their attention and they rushed over. In the distance they could see figures approaching. As they got closer Alyssa could make out the giant form of Timotin. He had a large bulky object strung across his massive shoulders the other men with him, held several large objects between them.

"Timotin and his hunters return with meat and clothing," said the giant. "We trap many deer in canyon. Must retrieve before other animals eat."

Lex issued orders for the captured deer to be brought in. As a dozen volunteers hurried off, he bent down to examine the deer that Timotin had brought in. He moved to the head of the animal and lifted its head.

"Owww," said Lex. "This thing must way a ton. How in the hell did you carry it by yourself?"

"Because there was no one else," said the giant with a shrug. He bent down and picked up the deer with a grunt. Heaving over his shoulders he plodded over to the campfire to turn the animal over to others to prepare.

The others returned several hours later with the rest of the deer. "We got there just in time," said Allen who had joined the group. "A pack of Jellyrolls was only a few yards away and were closing in. We lost two deer before we managed to chase them out."

"Good work," congratulated Lex. "Let's get them into the caves. It'll be dark soon, and I for one, don't want to be out here in the cold."

Once all the supplies were secured and the animals placed for preparation in the morning, Lex made the rounds of the caves and checked on the safety of everyone. Aside from the cold, they seemed to be in good spirits. Several had already started small fires to warm the interior of their caves.

"All tucked in," he reported to Alyssa, "but now I'm beginning to worry about Patty and Beth." He looked outside as light fluffy white object drifted onto the ground. "It's happening faster than I figured. That's snow!"

Alyssa accompanied by Ethan and Scrapper, scrambled to the cave opening, and peered out. A soft gentle snowfall had begun, bathing the Village in a soft white down.

"It's so pretty," whispered Alyssa. "I just wish it wasn't so cold."

"Tomorrow we'll have to block the entrances of the caves," said Lex thoughtfully. "Damn, but I wish Patty were here. He's lived in these types of conditions. I sure could use his help now."

Suddenly Scrapper started to wag his long tail rapidly. Ethan came up beside his pet and placed a hand on the big lion head. "Look," he cried peering into the darkness. The flickering lights from the small fires cast eerie shadows over the ever-whitening field.

Alyssa stared in the direction Ethan pointed and could just make out a lone solitary figure slowly making its way across the compound of the abandoned village. With a cry she saw the figure fall and struggle weakly to rise.

Without hesitation, Alyssa and Lex darted into the darkness and ran to the village. Still barefoot, because they hadn't yet manufactured shoes out of animal skins, they dashed through the snow. Soft wispy puffs of snow blew into the air with every step.

Alyssa knelt breathlessly beside Patty on the cold ground. "He's half frozen," she declared. "Lex, give me a hand. Let's get him back to the cave." Together they struggled with the shivering frame of Patty. Sleepily he opened his eyes and smiled at them, then collapsed into unconsciousness.

Once back in the safety and warmth of the cave, Lex sent Ethan to fetch the doctor. When he arrived, he examined Patty and said he was suffering from exposure. "He'll be fine," said Doc, "but keep him warm and give him hot broth when he wakes. Keep an eye on him. Watch out for signs of shock. If he should go into shock, get him as warm as possible. I'll check on him tomorrow."

While Lex prepared some broth from dried jack meat and a few precious vegetables, Alyssa bundled the limp form of Patty in her still too few animal skins. She held him close and smoothed the hair on the old veteran.

"It's no use," she said, "I just don't have enough furs to keep him warm. His face is turning blue and his hands and feet are ice cold. I'm afraid he will go into shock."

"Then get into bed with him," suggested Lex. "Use your body heat to warm him." Alyssa nodded and slipped under the thin animal skins.

"No," said Lex taking off his clothes. "You have to strip down. The heat from your body won't transfer as easily through clothes. You take one side; I'll take the other. We'll spoon him between us. Hopefully that should keep him warm."

They stripped down and removed Patty's clothes. Then Alyssa climbed in bed and held Patty close to her. Then Lex climbed in, effectively sandwiching Patty between them. Ethan came over and lay down beside his father. Lex pulled him close and pulled the rest of the skins on top of them. Scrapper whined and Ethan called for him to come near. The lion-snake sniffed and crawled around the bundle of people then climbed on top of them and spread his body over the shivering family.

Soon the heat from Scrapper—who didn't seem to mind the cold—penetrated and they all felt warm, safe, and close. One by one they closed their eyes and drifted off into sleep with their arms around each other.

The next morning, they awoke as the sun penetrated their tiny cave. Alyssa peered out from under the skins. The entrance of the cave was covered with about an inch of snow, and a cool breeze blew into the cave. She shivered and snuggled up against Patty.

"As much as I enjoy this," said Patty, "I need to go to the washroom."

"Patty," cried Alyssa happily. "You had us so worried. When you started to go into thermal shock we had to do something to keep you warm."

"And for that, I thank you,' he said. " Now, will someone get this beast off me." He struggled and pushed against the still sleeping lump of Scrapper.

The lion-snake opened one sleepy eye and looked at Patty. Then lazily flicked out its long tongue and licked Patty gently. "Glad to see you too, boy," laughed Patty. "Now get off. You weigh a ton!"

"Obviously," said Lex with a chuckle, "you're feeling better. The washroom is back that way, but I want you back in bed until Doc makes sure there was no permanent damage."

"Yes, sir," said Patty and he threw back the covers. Only then did he realize that he was naked and blushed furiously. Then he noticed the others were equally attired and shrugged. Slipping his loincloth on, he made his way the spot Lex had indicated.

When he returned, Lex poured him a steaming mug of broth. It had been simmering all night and now had a rich heady aroma, that promised delicious flavour. Patty accepted it gratefully and took a careful sip. Slowly he felt the heat from the broth penetrate and he sighed with relief.

Ethan returned shortly with the doctor and after another quick examination pronounced him okay. "Just take it easy for a while," he said. "Your system's had a shock and you may still experience some after effects." Patty thanked the doctor and sipped his second cup of broth.

"Feel like talking?" Asked Alyssa as she sat down beside him.

"Not much to tell," he said softly. "We went for a walk—at least I thought it was a walk—then she tells me she's not going back."

"So you decided to stay with her," said Lex, seating himself opposite the others.

"I could do no less," said Patty.

"Why didn't you try to get her to return?" Alyssa still sat close to Patty and she could feel the tiny tremors in his weakened frame.

"Because that's what she wanted. She regretted never saying goodbye to you Alyssa, but she felt this way would be better."

"Well, I must say your taking her death rather well," said Alyssa indignantly.

"Alyssa," said Lex firmly.

"No, it's all right," said Patty waving Lex back to his seat. "She doesn't understand. Sweetheart, let me explain something to you. I've seen many good friends die in my life. You learn to cope. It's not easy. Always remember this. You live and learn. Or you don't live long! And that doesn't necessarily mean physically."

Lex nodded understandingly, but Alyssa stood up angrily Her hair flying wildly about her. "I don't understand you two. We've just lost a dear friend and you sit there calmly discussing it."

"Sit down, Alyssa," said Lex firmly. "I'll explain it later."

"NO," she shouted.

"Alyssa," said Patty wearily, "Please sit down. I'll try to explain. You lost a Captain and a friend. Your grief is great. But I lost someone who meant much more to me. Much more!"

"Then I truly don't understand?"

"I miss her terribly," said Patty softly, "but all my anger will not bring her back. Before she died she charged me with two duties. One I must keep secret, the other…" He reached into a pouch in his loincloth. Slowly he withdrew a small shiny object and presented them to Lex.

Lex took the object and slowly turned them over in his fingers. His eyes teared up and choking back the sobs held them out for Alyssa to see. "Her Captain's bars." Carefully he carried them into the back of the cave and placed them in a secure spot.

"It's not easy to lose a loved one," said Patty after Lex returned, "but you must keep going. If you let your misery and sorrow grow, it will consume you."

"But you don't even grieve," protested Alyssa through bleary eyes.

"I'm all grieved out," said Patty slowly. "You see she died the first night out. The cold and her shivering caused the mechanical heart to rupture faster. She died in my arms…The last thing she said to me was to keep looking for that perfect fishing spot I've been searching for. Then she died. I sat there for several hours holding her close. Then I buried her."

"I'm sorry," said Alyssa sincerely.

"I didn't want to live anymore," continued Patty as if he hadn't heard her. "I just sat by her grave and let the cold take me. Then, her last words and her charges brought me out of my misery. I had a job to do and I realized the best way to remember her was to carry out her wishes. So I started back for camp. The rest you know."

"What about this other duty?"

"That's something private between Beth and myself," he said with a smile.

Alyssa leaned over and kissed his cheek gently. "Please forgive me," she whispered. "I didn't stop to think how much this hurt you. Lex? You were right I was thinking about myself."

"Then you would have no objection to a small suggestion I have," said Lex. When Alyssa looked at him inquisitively he explained. "I want you to continue taking the command training from Patty and myself."

"I thought I'd finished the training," she said.

"Only the first part," said Patty. "There's still a lot to learn. I too would like to see you finish."

"Okay," she said. "If it will make you happy. But first, you have to answer one question for me. What is this special class Ethan is taking. Why all the secrecy. Thought I'd forgotten that didn't you?"

Patty and Lex looked uncomfortably at each other. They were saved the problem when Ethan came in the cave. "Fine," said Alyssa. "Ethan, come here. Now I want you to answer me truthfully. What is this special class you're taking with Patty and your father?"

Ethan looked at his father's discomfort and shrugged. "It's no big deal," he said casually. "Patty has been training me in athletics and survival skills, and Father's been instructing me in advanced mathematics, sociology, interpersonal relationship skills, and other courses."

Alyssa eyes the two men narrowly. "Now, why would a young boy need all these high level courses?" she asked loudly. "It couldn't have anything to do with his unique abilities or his background, could it?"

Lex squirmed uncomfortably in his seat. "It was my choice," said Ethan. "It's something I've been thinking about for a long time. With my limited telepathic abilities I'm a natural. So, I asked Father and Patty to help. You see when we get off this planet, I plan to enrol in the Academy as a Communications specialist."

Chapter 27

Alyssa looked at her son in wonder. Her mind thought furiously then she blurted, "You're too young. That's it. You're only 14."

"Physically I may appear 14, but we both know I'm much older than that. Sorry, Mother, but my appearance doesn't factor in. Besides, look what you gained from the Academy."

"The Academy is just the place for the boy," interjected Patty. "He's an outsider. A man trapped in a boy's body. It will be years before his physical appearance catches up to him."

"He's lost his artificially enhanced intellect," said Lex. "The research station he was headed for is out of the question now. What do you propose to do? Send him to some local college with students nearly 5-10 years older than him?"

"At the Academy," said Ethan, "I will be on equal footing with the rest. I will be judged for what I do, not what I am."

"If Ethan ever plans to put his gifts to any use," explained Patty, "he must be able to travel freely in space. Aside from being a passenger on a liner, the only way is to be trained at the Academy."

Ethan took his foster mother's hands in his and said gently, "I want this. Please understand. I've lost my life and need to find out who I am. The Academy will give me that opportunity."

Alyssa sniffed a couple of times. "So, how's the training going," she said trying to sound light-hearted. "Why are you taking advanced math and such? I thought you already understood all that."

"That was the old me," said Ethan. "I've lost those abilities. For all purposes, I'm several years behind the other students and have to catch up."

She hugged him tightly to her breast. "If you're sure this is what you want, then I approve. Only promise me one thing."

"Anything."

"When you get leave. Will you come and visit me? I mean you won't forget me, will you?"

"Forget my mother? How could you say such a thing? Listen lady, you adopted ME! That means that you have to uphold your end of the bargain. You're stuck with me for the rest of your life!"

She hugged him so tight that he gasped for air, but wouldn't pull away. Lex came over and placed a fatherly hand on the boy's shoulder, while Patty stood smiling.

"Well, now that that's all done," said Patty, "what's next on the agenda?"

"First off," said Lex, "we need to know more about this planet's orbit. It got cold faster than we calculated. I want to know how cold it will get."

"We're going to have problems if the temperature drops much more," said Alyssa. "The children and the elderly can't adapt as easily."

"Then we need a contingency plan," said Patty. "Ethan, please run over to Tommy's cave. See if he has any more information on the weather."

"Yes, sir," said Ethan and scurried out of the cave.

Patty watched him go then said quickly, "I sent him out because we need to talk. Before she died, Beth and I plotted the orbit of this world. We hoped our figures were wrong, but it seems they were right."

"Let's hear it," said Lex taking a seat.

"The orbit of this world is like many others roughly oval. More like egg shaped. But the pointed end of the orbit comes out quite a distance. It's a long climb to the apex, then a slow drop back closer to the sun."

"So that means we're on the outward swing," said Alyssa. "Did you calculate how much farther we have to go before the return trip begins?"

Patty nodded. "I can show you the math later, but briefly, it means that this world plunges into an ice age every couple of years. I don't mean a cold winter, I mean a frozen wasteland. I estimate the temperature will drop to at least 100 below, or colder."

"We couldn't survive that," said Lex. "At least not without some specialized gear. How long do we have?"

"I don't know," admitted Patty. "Our calculations seem to be off slightly. This cold set in faster than we anticipated. I hope Tommy has more information."

"Then why send Ethan away to tell us this?" Asked Alyssa. "He'll know as soon as he talks to Tommy."

"Because the only thing I can think of that will save our lives, has a direct impact on Ethan. And a few others."

"Let me guess," said Alyssa. "These others wouldn't happen to be Sam and A'Serta to mention a couple would it?" Patty nodded.

"You want to move everyone into the alien complex?" Lex ran his hand through his hair and paced around the small room. "I don't know. We still haven't explored the whole thing. I have the safety of the people to think about."

"Then think about them freezing to death in the cold," said Alyssa firmly. "We have some furs, and the caves will offer protection for a while, but not against those temperatures."

Lex nodded slowly. "Before I make a decision, I want to hear Tommy's forecast."

"Then you're in luck," said Tommy from the doorway. "I have the revised figures you asked for Patty. Now I want you to understand, weather forecasting is a hobby."

"Yes, but you are also a trained navigator," said Lex.

"Third class, sir," said Tommy. "That's why I always got the boring jobs of plotting orbits and such."

"Still," said Alyssa, "you should be able to plot the orbit of this planet."

"Yes, ma'am," he said. "It is as I described earlier to…to the Captain." He blushed while avoiding Lex's eyes.

"It's all right," said Lex kindly. "She was a good woman and a great Captain. I miss her too. Go on."

"Yes, sir. Thank you, sir," he said relieved. "The orbit is eccentric. I've been taking readings everyday. We're on an outward-bound trajectory. If it followed a normal pattern, I would say that we would have winter for approximately three months. But for some reason—I don't know why—we have accelerated. If the current rate continues, we should start experiencing warmer weather in about 6 weeks."

"That's wonderful news," said Alyssa.

Lex frowned. "Tommy, how cold will it get?"

Tommy shifted his fur-clad feet uncomfortably. "Before it starts to warm up, my best estimate is 150 degrees below zero."

"Oh my god," said Alyssa plopping down on her chair. "One hundred and fifty!"

"It will only last a week or so," said Tommy trying to help.

"Thanks, Tommy," said Patty. The young man looked at him and nodded. He turned and left the cave.

"We have no choice," said Patty. "We'll be dead long before it reaches those temperatures.

"I'm afraid I must agree," said Lex. He moved closer to Ethan and set him down. "Ethan, we must move everyone into the alien complex to survive. You know what that means?"

"Yes, sir," said the boy. "I guessed that when Tommy told me how cold it would get."

"Any thoughts?"

"Well, I think Sam and I will be okay," he said thoughtfully. "Last time it just knocked us out. But I'm worried about A'Serta and Allen."

"My god," said Alyssa. "Allen. I had completely forgotten him. If he gets near that super computer gain, we may lose him for good."

"Not to mention the strange effect the alien field has on A'Serta and her symbiont," said Patty.

"I can't risk the lives of everyone else because of a few," said Lex softly. "Is there any way we can make them safe outside the complex?"

"Not with the gear we have," said Patty. "Look, son, I know this is a hard decision. You've only just taken over and shouldn't have to make these choices so soon, but that's the way it is."

Lex moved to the rear of the cave. When Alyssa approached him, he motioned her away. She returned to Patty and Ethan. "He wants to be alone," she said.

"He has a tough choice," said Patty. "If he leaves them outside, they will die. If he orders them inside, they may die as well. It's never easy ordering someone to their deaths. Even when you have to." He gazed into space as if recalling an unpleasant memory.

Alyssa looked closely at her mentor. This man had done many things in his long career and she still wondered exactly what he did. He was always vague about his military career as if unwilling to discuss it, but obviously he had done things that affected him greatly.

They sat down and Alyssa made a fresh batch of the stuff they had been calling coffee. No one spoke for nearly twenty minutes. They just stared outside at the gentle falling snow. Already nearly 6 inches covered the ground. The tropical plants and trees were cold and limp. They were used to this and had prepared themselves for their cold sleep.

"They all look dead," said Ethan breaking the silence. "I assume that the plants hibernate or something during the winter months."

"I wish we could do the same thing," said Patty.

"Unfortunately we can't," said Lex coming up from behind. "Pass the word. We move to the alien complex immediately. Ethan, find Doc and send him to me. Alyssa, I want you and Patty in charge of the move. Most of our gear should still be packed. Let's make this as quick and efficient as possible."

Many of the people protested at having to move again so quickly, but a quick word from Alyssa or Patty about what they could expect hurried them along. Alyssa set a crew going making snowshoes from the dead tree branches. No one knew how to make them, but with a little experimenting, they came up with a crude shoe. At least you didn't sink all the way in the soft powdery snow.

Timotin gathered his hunters and plunged into the snow-covered jungle. Alyssa could hear the sounds of trees breaking and axes chopping. Soon he returned with several crudely fashioned sleds.

"This make transport easier," he said. Alyssa nodded and ordered the supplies to be placed on the sleds.

The villagers paused only once to eat a hot meal of broth and fresh vegetables then resumed their work. By mid-afternoon they were ready to go. With Timotin in the lead, they headed for the alien complex.

Lex held back and stared at the snow-covered village. Alyssa came up behind him and laid her head on his back. "Come on," she said gently.

"I just hate to abandon it," he said softly. "We've worked so hard, and so many people have died."

"We'll be back," she said. "You're doing what you're trained for. Saving lives." He nodded and turned to kiss his wife. Then holding her close followed the long procession of evicted villagers.

Night fell shortly after and so did the temperature. The people pulled their thin skins around them tighter and leaned into the cold driving wind. The snow began whipping around in tiny whirlwinds, fighting the weary travelers. Occasionally someone would stumble and fall. Others would rush to their side and pick them up. Alyssa smiled at the way they had grown together as a community.

When they reached the clearing that held the invisible doorway into the complex, Lex ordered Alyssa to take everyone through. She moved in front of them all, stepped forward and disappeared. Timotin shouldered his burden and stepped through. One by one the others followed.

Lex stood with Doc at his side. When Allen and A'Serta passed he pulled them to his side. "Just a moment," he said. Adam protested, but fell silent from a signal from Lex.

When the last person entered Lex addressed the others. "As you know, you two have been adversely affected in the past. I can't leave you out here to die, but neither can I run the risk of you hurting yourselves or others inside."

"Just what do you propose, Captain," said Adam placing a protective arm around his wife.

"The doctor will administer a sedative until we have you safely inside in a secure place," said Lex.

"A wise decision, Captain," said Allen.

"Wait a minute," said Adam. "A'Serta's pregnant. How will this affect the baby?"

"She should be all right," said Doc. "Her physiology is slightly different because of her symbiont, but I don't believe there should be any problems."

"But you don't know for sure," protested Adam. "Captain, please?"

"What other choice do I have," said Lex sadly. "She'll die for sure out here."

"Let me hold her," said Adam. "If she loses control, I can restrain her."

"I don't think so, my love," said A'Serta. "Remember what happened last time?"

"Captain," said Allen thoughtfully, "I have a suggestion. What if Timotin held her? I don't think she could break his grip."

"What about it? Would you let Timotin secure you?" Lex looked at A'Serta patiently. She looked at her husband and he nodded slightly. She nodded and Lex quickly entered the invisible doorway. He returned seconds later followed by Timotin.

"Timotin not hurt you, little one," he said as he placed his arms around her. One arm he placed across her chest, pinning her upper arms. The other he wrapped around her waist, clasping her wrists tight against her body.

"Ready? Okay Doc, send Allen to sleepy time."

"Remember to wake me on the other side," said Allen with a smile. Doc placed a hypo-spray against the technician's neck and a slight hiss could be heard. Allen straightened his tunic then slumped forward. Lex caught him before he hit the ground.

"That was fast," he said grunting from the strain.

"I didn't want to wait any longer," said Doc taking Allen's feet.

"You ready?" He said addressing A'Serta. She nodded and still in Timotin's tight grip moved toward the doorway.

Lex and Doc carrying the unconscious Allen stepped through first. On the other side they passed him quickly to Patty and a few others who whisked him away to a secure room. Lex turned in time to see Adam come through then A'Serta held tightly to Timotin.

They waited and watched. Doc ran his scanner over A'Serta. "How are you feeling?"

"A little dizzy," she said, "but otherwise fine."

"No anger?"

"None," she said. "Maybe I've lost the symbiont?"

"No, it's still there," said Doc checking his readout.

"Don't take this the wrong way, sweetheart," said Adam, "but why don't you want to rip my head off."

"I don't know," she said. "Timotin, could you ease up a bit. You're crushing the baby."

"Little one! You are pregnant? That I think explains it. I will release you now." He loosened his grip and stepped back, but stood ready, in case she moved. But she stood there and took several deep breaths. When nothing happened she moved closer to Adam and kissed him passionately.

"I don't understand," said Lex. "I thought you reacted violently near the complex."

"She is pregnant," said Timotin. "Hormones change body chemistry."

"So the symbiont is dormant," exclaimed Doc. "Of course. Yes, I can see that now." He ran the scanner over her again. "I don't think you'll have any worries for now, but if you experience any difficulties come and see me. Now I have to see about another patient." He packed up his kit and hurried off down the hall.

"All right people," said Lex. "Let's get set up. Timotin, check around. See if anyone else needs medical help." They broke and headed down the corridor.

Weary footsore people lay slouched against the walls. Lex passed by with the occasional word of encouragement. He entered the control complex and found Patty and Alyssa pouring over the original crude map they had made of the complex.

"Ah, Lex," said Patty seeing him arrive. "We're just trying to arrange quarters for everyone."

"I thought you said this complex was huge," said Lex.

"It is," said Alyssa pointing to the map. "These rooms are the only ones we've investigated. Until we can explore the rest, it's going to be a tight fit with nearly two hundred people."

"Do your best," said Lex. "Tomorrow we send out exploration teams." They nodded and returned to dividing up the rooms. When they finished they called in the people and sent them to their quarters.

Two hours later, Alyssa flopped wearily in a chair. "That's it," she said. "How are A'Serta and Allen?"

"A'Serta came through okay," said Lex. "I haven't heard about Allen yet. Doc's still with him."

Just then Doc and Timotin came in the room. "Allen is still unconscious," said Doc. "I don't want to revive him until we're ready. Sam's with him now."

"The rest of the group is well," said Timotin. "Several cases of minor frostbite, that is all."

"Very good," said Lex stretching and leaning back in his chair. "We'll revive Allen tomorrow. I suggest we all turn in for now. Patty, I want you to take charge of assessing our supplies tomorrow. Let's see how badly we're hurt. Alyssa, you're in charge of the exploration teams. I want some more room." He yawned widely. "For now though, it's me for bed. Good-night everyone."

A chorus of goodnights reached his ears as he moved to the area Alyssa had laid out as their bed in the control room. Ethan had already crashed out and soft snores came from the boy as Lex lay down beside him. Alyssa came over a minute later.

"Anyone know how to turn out these lights?" Asked Lex through silted eyes.

"Nope," said Alyssa. "Just another thing to add to the list. Here, cover your head with this blanket." Lex took the blanket and within seconds fell fast asleep.

Alyssa looked around the room. The others had paced themselves along the walls. Despite the long day and the trip through the cold, Alyssa still couldn't sleep. Everything had happened so fast, her head buzzed with thousands of conflicting thoughts and ideas. Eventually she fell asleep and cuddled with Lex.

*

Two weeks later the whole village had been divided into separate rooms. The exploration teams had explored every hallway and corridor they could find. The alien complex was huge. It housed more than enough rooms to accommodate the displaced inhabitants of the town.

The main console room had been turned into a general office and it was in here that the council sat. Lex read the reports on the outside temperature with a frown. "It looks like that we could be here for a while," he said. "Latest reading indicates it's well below 100 and still dropping."

Alyssa took the report from him and glanced at it quickly. "What about supplies? How much longer can we last?"

Patty took his notebook out and read out the figures. "We lost a good portion of supplies to the cold. Especially the small farm we had hoped would provide us with fresh vegetables. I estimate we have enough food to last maybe three weeks. If we stretch it."

"Hopefully, the weather will break long enough for us to go hunting," said Lex. "Now what about the people? Being cooped up in here for a couple of months with nothing to do doesn't appeal to me."

"I see no reason why some of the activities can't be resumed," said Alyssa. "Feel up to starting classes again, Patty?"

"Funny you should mention that," he chuckled. "My students have been asking me when school starts. These kids are bored with a capital B."

"Then it's settled," said Lex. "We resume our normal lives as much as possible. For everything else, but be creative and innovative. Let's keep them occupied. The time will go by faster."

The next day Alyssa visited the classroom Patty had made. All the children were there. She smiled at their attentiveness. They were really bored to be so eager.

"If you remember," said Patty, "we were discussing the reason the League has a military. Now, I know your minds are still asleep after missing so many classes, but has anyone given it any thought?"

A little blonde girl about 6 years old held up her hand. "To protect us from all enemies," she said.

"We discussed that," said Patty. "You're partly correct. Anyone else?"

The students stared blankly at Patty. "I said the answer wouldn't be found in any text books," he said. "Think about what I taught you. Ethan! Come on boy. What's the answer?"

Ethan closed his notepad and looked thoughtful for a minute. "Human beings have always had some sort of military," he said, checking off the points on his fingers.

"Yes," said Patty, "go on."

"But we've always sought peace. So the role of the military is to find peace. But that doesn't work, because the military is always preparing or fighting a war."

"Very good," said Patty. "You're almost there."

"Even those societies that abolished their military had a strong police presence," continued Ethan. "And the police are just a civilian extension of the military." He stopped and thought. "I'm sorry, sir," he said finally. "The only answer I can come up with is that human beings are basically barbarians and savages."

Patty smiled. "Out of the mouths of babes," he said. "That my friends, is the answer. Mankind is a predatory species. We hunt, we kill, and we destroy. Only a thin veneer of civilization separates us from the animals we hunt and kill."

The little blonde girl spoke again. "I'm not a killer," she protested.

"No? Directly or indirectly we're all savages. What did you have for supper last night? I'll tell you. You feasted on Jack Meat. That Jack meat came from an animal that we killed."

"But I didn't kill it," she cried.

"Besides," said Ethan. "We needed it to survive."

"So does a lion when it eats a deer," said Patty. "What's the difference?"

"I guess there's really no difference," said Ethan. "We are no better than the animals we hunt."

"No, we're far worse," said Patty. "We hunt and kill our own kind. We destroy anything we come in contact with. The cities you live in back home used to be woodlands, or wetlands. Places where other living creatures lived and died."

"I don't understand," said Ethan.

Patty looked at him with fondness. "I don't expect you to understand immediately, but the difference between us and a caveman is so thin at times it's indistinguishable."

The class sat quietly then one head raised up His eyes wide. Then another. And Another. The blonde girl stood up. "So the reason for a military is not to protect us from an enemy, but to protect us from ourselves."

"Go to the head of the class," beamed Patty. "Without law and order, we would revert to our true nature in a short period of time. But people don't like to think they need to be watched and cared for. In our arrogance we still believe we are in complete control. Nothing could be further from the truth."

"So the military is made up of people, by the people to protect the people," said Ethan. "And not only the military, but the police, and the government."

"Exactly," said Patty. "Every form of authority we empower, is there to protect us from ourselves. That's why we have laws and rules. That's why we have governmental bodies and police to enforce those rules. And that's why we have a military. Okay that will be all for now. Break for lunch and be back here in 1 hour. Class dismissed."

Alyssa stepped into the classroom and kissed Patty gently. "Interesting speech," she said. "I know several experts who would argue with you though."

Patty shrugged. "So what else is new," he said. "Each one of those children will at one time or another encounter someone who has a different opinion. Controversy is what makes the world go round. So-called experts really know very little. I don't claim to be an expert, but I do have years of observational experience."

"Just to play devil's advocate for a minute," said Alyssa taking his arm. "What makes you think your interpretation is the right one?"

"How do you know it's not," he smiled. "But that's not the object of this lesson. Eventually one or more of them is going to think about what I've said. Then they will begin to question my answer. They'll start searching for their own answers. That's what I teach, 'How to think for yourself.' I implant ideas and suggestions that go against the accepted theories. Those who challenge me will never take something at face value. It's those kids who will eventually lead us into a new age."

"I wish I had someone like you when I was at school," said Alyssa. "Maybe I wouldn't have been so trusting."

"It's never too late to learn, my dear." He kissed the top of her head gently. "When we return and you complete you command training, you'll understand a lot more."

"I've been meaning to talk to you about that," she said. "Patty, you seem to know so much a lot more than you let on. Just what did you do in the military?"

"Oh, this and that," he said mysteriously.

She smiled at his evasions. "Were you a spy?"

"I could tell you," he said with a chuckle, "but then I would have to kill you." They laughed at the timeless joke, but Alyssa still felt that Patty hid something from her something terrible and yet wonderful.

Fifteen days later Lex called a general meeting. They held it in a large auditorium style room that just barely held everyone. "Could I have everyone's attention please," he said loudly. When the hum of people muttering died, he continued.

"I called you here today for two reasons," he said. "First. You are all invited to the wedding of Allen and Sam this evening here in this hall." The crowd cheered wildly. Allen had been revived and he faced his addiction with the super computer. With his friends and Sam at his side, he struggled and conquered it.

Allen stood and cleared his throat. "I want to thank you all. With your love and support I have beaten my problem. It wasn't easy, but you were there for me and for that I am eternally grateful. The Captain has kindly consented to perform the ceremony. Sam and I thank-you from the bottom of our hearts." He sat down to thunderous applause and Sam kissed him gently on the cheek.

Lex shook his hand and resumed his spot out front. "Now for some more good news, " he said, "our latest readings show that the temperature outside has begun to rise again." This time the chamber echoed with loud cheers and whistles. Lex waited patiently until they calmed down.

"We should be able to return to the Village in about 4 weeks," he said. "Unfortunately we have a serious problem. We are almost out of food. Even with strict rationing we couldn't hold out that long. What I propose is to go on a hunting expedition. We have observed tracks in the snow, so we know that some animals are still out there."

Hands suddenly shot up as people started to volunteer to go on the hunt. Lex waved them back down. "I appreciate you all wanting to go, but the sheer fact is that we can't. We don't have enough furs to properly protect everyone. So what I want is to meet with the hunters after the meeting. We'll outfit a proper hunting party so they can survive in the cold. As for the rest of you, I know you want out as much as I do. So we will pool the rest of the furs and make up several cold weather outfits. These will be stored here and then each of you in turn can go outside for a little while."

The muttering grew louder and louder until Alyssa stood up. "My friends," she said, "I know we all want to go home, but it is still too cold. Let the hunters go and do their job. Our job is to survive. I promise. As soon as it warms up enough we will return to the village. Please be patient." She sat back down and the rumblings continued.

The council went into a huddle while the crowd milled and buzzed. With a lot of gesticulating they finally reached a consensus. Lex stood and faced the crowd. Raising his hands for attention he waited until things quieted.

"In celebration of the approaching warmer weather, we have decided that the wedding of Allen and Sam will be a grand and festive occasion. Everyone is hereby ordered to relax and celebrate with the happy couple. I even understand that some local wine will be available." The announcement mollified the crowd and they cheered again.

That night Lex performed a simple ceremony marrying Allen and Sam. Patty had dug through supplies and produced a banquet fit for a king. "There'll be hell to pay for using up all our supplies like this, but they need to blow off steam," he confided in Alyssa.

"How badly will this party hurt our supplies?"

"If the hunters don't find food in a few days," he said sadly, "then we won't have to worry about being rescued. I've already passed the word for everyone to be placed on reduced rations. Only the sick and the children will receive a full portion."

The next morning they crowded into the auditorium to wish the hunters good-luck. Bundled up in their furs, they looked more like walking bears. Alyssa moved up beside one bear shaped man.

"I still don't understand why you have to go," she said.

"Because, my love," said Lex tying a drawstring, "if I don't get out of here, I'll go crazy. Don't worry. We'll be back in a couple of days. I'm leaving you in charge until then."

"Let me go with you," she pleaded. "I need to get out as well."

"Sorry, Lys," he said taking her arms gently. "One of us has to remain.

After all, rank has its privileges. Besides. You're the mayor of our little community."

"That's a cheap excuse," she protested. "But take care of yourself. I have no intention of raising a child by myself."

"I will," he said and kissed her passionately. "See you in a couple of days. We'll have a big feast to celebrate." He smiled and signalled his readiness to Timotin who would lead the hunt.

One by one they passed through the doorway into the bitter cold outside. When the last hunter had left the complex, Alyssa turned to face the rest of the Villagers. "Okay," she said. "We have three more outfits made up. Those of you, who would like to go outside for some fresh air, give your names to Patty. No one goes out alone and no one stays out longer than 1 hour. Remember, exposed flesh will freeze in minutes out there." She pushed her way through the crowd and returned to her room.

Inside she found Ethan hard at work pouring over an assignment Patty had given him. "I missed you at the send off," she said.

"I wished Father good hunting earlier," he said without looking up. "I still have a lot of catching up to do. Patty says I'm moving along very quickly, but I don't feel it. Everything seems so slow. My head is always fuzzy and thick like mud."

"That's the effect of this place," she said sitting beside him. "You know that you and Sam are susceptible to its influence."

"I know," he said rubbing his eyes.

"What you need is a break," she said firmly. "Why don't we put our names on the list and go outside for a few minutes. Just to clear the cobwebs. I understand it's a balmy minus 120 degrees out."

Ethan smiled and closed his notes. Together they sought out Patty and added their names to the list. Already he had close to 100 names on it. "I can fit you in the day after tomorrow. In the afternoon, " he said. " Be at the doorway by three o'clock." They thanked him and returned to their quarters.

Two days later, Alyssa and Ethan found themselves being pushed and pulled into a bulky suit of stitched together furs. Alyssa had little difficulty, but Ethan being much smaller, looked more like a mummy.

Only his eyes peered through tiny slits and instead of walking, he wobbled back and forth.

Patty laughed at the sight. "You're going to need help, my lad," he said. "I left the other space open, so I think I'll join you." He quickly donned the suit of furs and the three comrades stepped through the door.

The first thing Alyssa noticed was the cold. Even through all the furs she could feel the bitter biting wind and shivered. "It's still cold," she said. "But boy does this fresh air feel good." She took several deep breaths bringing the frigid air deep into her lungs.

Then she took the time to look around. She hadn't seen outside since they moved into the complex. The once lush greens and browns were now replaced with a blanket of white. A startled cry behind her made her whirl around. Just in time she saw Scrapper suddenly appear through the invisible wall and pounce on Ethan. The two rolled about in the snow, while Ethan giggled and laughed.

"I was wondering when he'd show up," said Patty.

"You knew he would come out?"

"Of course," he said. "Who do you think invited him?" They watched as the boy and his pet ran around in the snow and tossed each other into snow banks.

"That's what it's all about," said Patty laughing at the antics. "Seeing these two, I know everything will be fine." Alyssa nodded and laughed as Scrapper picked up Ethan in his prehensile tail and flung him into a deep snowdrift. Ethan emerged covered in the fine white powder brushing himself off. Then suddenly launched himself at his pet. But Scrapper was too fast and dodged out of the way and Ethan landed in another mound of snow.

Half an hour later, Ethan puffing and panting, called it quits. Snow had worked its way inside his clothes and he started to feel cold. Holding him close to warm him, Alyssa guided him back through the portal. Inside they began to disrobe when Scrapper came bounding through. His shaggy head covered with snow. He stopped and shook his head, wildly spattering snow over the laughing people inside.

Alyssa had just removed her top when another person entered

through the portal. It was one of the hunters. He saw Alyssa and rushed over to her.

"Any luck," she asked hopefully.

"Plenty," he said softly. "We trapped a herd of deer on a cliff face."

"Wonderful," said Patty. "Do you need any more help?"

"No, sir," replied the hunter. "That wasn't the reason I came back. I came to bring Alyssa back with me. Lex has been hurt. Timotin says it's only a matter of time."

"A matter of time for what?" she asked. Then her eyes opened wide, "Lex! Patty, watch Ethan." Quickly she donned her coat and ran out of the room into the snow. The hunter followed.

Chapter 28

Alyssa ran headlong into a deep snowdrift that covered a hole. She sank out of sight briefly then clawed her way back on solid ground. The hunter had just caught up with her and reached out a hand to help. She grasped his hand and he pulled her onto her feet.

"Calm down," he said panting. He stooped over and took several deep breaths. "Besides, you were running the wrong way." He stood and straightened his coat. "It's not far, but there are dangers. Stick close to me."

Alyssa banged the snow out of her coat then nodded sullenly. She would be no help to Lex if she ran off and got lost herself. Together they turned and started the slow plod in the deep snow. Neither had snowshoes on. Alyssa had left in a hurry, and the hunter had forgotten his back at the complex. So each step caused them to sink up to their knees in the cold white powder.

The wind howled and the snow blew with such furry that visibility was reduced to inches in some places, but Alyssa paid no attention. All she wanted to do was reach Lex. She urged the tired hunter to a faster pace. Exhausted as he was, he understood and forced himself to move faster.

Just after sunset, Alyssa spotted a tiny glow on the horizon. "That's the camp," said the hunter answering her point.

Alyssa felt the drain of her own energy reserves and for the first time she thought how tired her guide must be. He had slogged his way back to the complex alone and now had to make the return trip with no rest. Alyssa felt ashamed, but her concern for finding Lex blinded her from anything else.

An hour later they stumbled into the hunters' camp. Her poor guide collapsed from exhaustion and his comrades quickly whisked him away to their tents. Alyssa walked into the fire circle and looked for Timotin. When she failed to find him she turned to the other hunters who up to now had just watched quietly.

"I'll take you," volunteered one of the women. "I know what you must be feeling. Don't think too harshly about my comrades. They are professionals and deal with problems in a different way."

The hunter picked up a brand and lit it in the fire pit. Then she guided Alyssa beyond the safety of the camp. Past where the light of the fire illuminated the snow and through a snow covered tree line. When Alyssa tried to move ahead, the hunter grabbed her and prevented her movement.

"Watch," she said and held the firebrand in front of her. Alyssa looked and as her eyes adjusted to the feeble light she saw they were standing on the edge of a deep precipice. "Follow me," she signalled.

Gingerly, Alyssa followed the woman, carefully testing each step before applying her weight. The woman stopped after a couple of minutes and pointed into the dark. "Down there," she said. Alyssa peered into the inky depths and could just make out a small flickering flame.

"Who's down there? Timotin?"

"Yes," she said softly, "and your husband. There's no way to get him up."

"But we can't leave him down there. There must be something we can do?"

"I'd better let Timotin know you're here," she said. Giving Alyssa the firebrand, the woman cupped her hands and yelled into the canyon. A faint reply came back, but Alyssa couldn't make out the words.

"Timotin says for you to come down," she said. "Let me tie this line to you, then use the line already down there as a guide. Lower yourself down. Be careful. The rock face is very sharp and icy in sections."

Alyssa nodded and tugged on the rope the woman had secured, making sure it was tight. Then she picked up the line that ran over the cliff and noticed the other end was secured to a giant tree. Carefully she held both ropes in her gloved hands and began the treacherous climb down the rock face.

She tried climbing down hand over hand, but the fur mittens wouldn't provide the control she needed and resorted to bouncing. Each bounce dropped her about ten feet. To take her mind off her fear she started counting her bounces. On the seventh bounce her right foot broke through an ice shield and wedged in a rock crevice. She struggled and pushed against the rock face with her free foot, finally freeing the other one.

"I haven't done this since my days in the academy," she said to the rock face.

"Then you are doing very well," said a voice loud and clear. "Keep coming. You're only about thirty feet above me."

Alyssa kicked off the ice face and dropped. She swung in and kicked again. Each swing out dropped her another ten feet. On the final swing she came down hard on packed snow. Catching her breath she rubbed her sore ankles and looked up into the smiling face of Timotin.

"Oh, Timotin," she cried. "Where is he? Is he all right?"

"He's on the other side of that large boulder," he said then grabbed her coat. "Wait a minute. Alyssa. Listen to me. He's hurt badly. LET ME FINISH." He held her until she agreed to listen to him.

"We just set-up camp after capturing the deer. Night had already fallen. Lex spotted Jack tracks, and with another man started tracking them. Suddenly tracks ended. It was just bad luck that Lex was in front. He took one step and fell over the cliff. The other man held him by his safety rope, but a sharp piece of ice cut it."

Alyssa gasped. Then in disbelief she looked up at the cliff she had just descended. Jagged rocks and smooth ice runs jutted out from the 100-foot drop. Her stomach churned when she thought about Lex tumbling helplessly down the sheer drop.

"We couldn't find any other way down to him, so I lowered myself on this rope," continued Timotin. "He was unconscious when I got here. At first I thought he was already dead, then his eyes opened. All he said was to fetch you."

"Can I see him now?"

"Wait," said Timotin. "Lyssa, there's nothing I can do. He landed on a rock and broke his back. He has massive internal injuries and is bleeding into his lungs. By all rights he should be dead now, but for some reason he refuses to die until he sees you. Do you understand? You're the only thing that's kept him alive. So I don't want you doing anything stupid. Be brave."

"I'll be all right," she sniffled. "Can I see him now?"

Timotin nodded. "I'll be here if you need me. Remember, don't move him!" Alyssa nodded and rounded the big boulder in front of her.

On the other side a small fire flickered weakly. In the dancing shadows she saw a form draped over a large mound. It looked unnatural and somehow distorted. As she drew closer, she saw that besides the broken back, Lex had also dislocated a shoulder and his right leg was bent forward. Unconsciously she reached out to her own leg.

Taking a deep breath she moved over to him. His face was paste white and she could hear gasping, ragged breaths. Carefully she sat beside him. "Lex," she called softly. "Lex. It's me, Alyssa. Lex?"

Lex coughed slightly and bright red blood shot out of his mouth and stained the white snow around him. "Lys," he said raggedly. "I knew you'd come."

"Don't worry," she said, swallowing the tears. "We'll get you out of here."

"I don't think so," he gasped.

"Don't talk like that," she said gently. "We'll rig up a board or something. We'll get you up somehow and back to the complex. We'll…"

"You'll shut up and listen," he rasped and coughed up another blob of bright red blood.

"Yes, sir," said Alyssa softly. She reached into her coat and withdrew a rag and wiped the bloody spittle from around his lips. "You are the Captain."

"Not anymore," he gasped. "Effective immediately, you are the Captain."

Alyssa couldn't believe her ears. "You are the Captain! No, I love you. No, say good-bye to Ethan. Just 'you are the Captain.'"

"I do love you," he gasped. "I never stopped loving you. There's nothing you can do for me. But your responsibility now lies with the villagers. You must make sure they get home, safely."

"I can't believe that this is all you want to talk about," she cried. Then her anger began to flare. "I don't believe you. You're about to die and all you care about is making me the stupid Captain. Well, let me tell you mister. I want nothing to do with it so there. You'll have to come back and assume command, because I won't."

But Lex didn't acknowledge her tirade. While she was yelling at him, he died quietly. Alyssa looked at her husband then carefully touched his hand. It felt ice cold and elicited no response from him. Hesitantly she placed two fingers along his neck. She waited, and waited. Without realizing it, she started pressing her fingers deeper into his neck in a desperate search for a pulse.

"Lex," she said. "Lex, you can't leave me. Not now. Lex! LEX GODDAMN YOU! ANSWER ME!"

Timotin suddenly rounded the rock in response to her yelling, but stopped before he approached to close. He could already see that Lex was dead. Alyssa had built up a full head of steam. Her grief had turned to anger and it needed to be released. Timotin stood in the shadows and watched her tirade.

"God-damn you, Lex," she shot at him. "Don't you leave me! I won't be abandoned again. DO YOU HERE ME! BASTARD! COME ON FIGHT! FIGHT!" She stopped and the tears ran freely down her face.

Timotin stepped forward and placed a hand gently on her shoulder. She whirled around and faced him accusingly. "It's all your fault," she yelled. "You could have saved him, but you didn't." Timotin let the accusations wash over him.

"There was nothing I or anyone else could do," he said gently. "It was only his love for you that kept him alive this long."

"Love," she spat, "do you know why that bastard wanted to see me. Not because he loved me. Oh, no! But to make me Captain isn't that a joke. Me? Captain? Did you know I'm banned from the planet Natoth for blowing up a laboratory and killing everyone inside."

"Alyssa," said Timotin tenderly.

"Course, I'm not surprised," she growled. "He probably didn't love me anyway. But marooned on this god-forsaken world he just couldn't leave. So he went out and got himself killed."

"Alyssa, you know that's not true," said Timotin grabbing her roughly by the shoulders. "Lex loved you more than his own life. I know that, and you know that."

Alyssa squirmed in his grip and tried to break away. Her anger was at full boil and she didn't hear a word he said. "You're hysterical," yelled Timotin. He shook her and she screamed like a banshee. "Forgive me, Alyssa," he said softly. Then with one blow of his big right hand knocked Alyssa unconscious. She slumped in his arms and he tenderly picked her up and carried her back to the face cliff.

He fashioned a harness out of the rope and called for someone to pull her up. The woman at the top ran for help and returned with a couple of others. Carefully they lifted the unconscious limp form of Alyssa to safety. Timotin watched her go sadly. Then he turned back to Lex. He still had one duty left to perform. Getting on his knees, Timotin began digging a grave for his friend with his bare hands.

Much later he climbed up and out of the crevice. Without a word to his comrades he coiled the rope and returned to camp. The hunters had stoked the fire against the cold night air. No one felt like sleeping. The fire roared and cast large flickering shadows. Timotin walked into camp and sat down in front of the blazing fire.

Gently, subconsciously, he rocked back and forth. The woman who had helped Alyssa came forward and took Timotin's hands in hers. She gasped when she saw the scrapes and blood on them. Signs of severe frostbite had already set in his fingers. The skin laid peeled back and exposed raw flesh underneath.

Calling for a med-kit she bandaged his hands without a word. Timotin just sat gazing into the fire. When she finished she looked at her leader. "Alyssa is resting in the tent. What happened? Did she fall? There's a whopping big bruise forming on her scalp."

Timotin looked at her with big round eyes and sadly shook his head. He lowered his head and stared at his bandaged hands. The woman understood and placed an arm around the gentle giant. "You must have had a good reason," she said gently.

"She said I killed him," muttered Timotin. "Maybe she was right. I'm a healer, and I did nothing."

"There was nothing to do," said the woman firmly. "You are not at fault. You are a kind, gentle man with extraordinary abilities, but even you can't revive the dead. Alyssa was hysterical. She didn't know what she was saying. You know that." Timotin nodded meekly and moved off into his tent.

The next morning the hunters rose early and strapped the rest of the deer onto their makeshift sleds. Timotin seemed more like his old self, if somewhat subdued. Alyssa had risen with a thundering headache. She stumbled around until her head cleared then helped the hunters secure the deer.

Every time Timotin came near, she moved off in another direction. The other hunters watched this, but this was not their fight. It was something Alyssa and Timotin would have to work out themselves. So wisely they concentrated on their chores.

By mid morning they had started the haul back to the complex. Alyssa still quiet listened with half an ear as the hunters relived the hunt. The female hunter from the previous night lifted her burden high on her shoulders and ran up beside Alyssa.

"How are you feeling this morning?"

"Fine, except for this headache," said Alyssa sullenly. She reached up and touched the spot where Timotin had hit her and winced.

They continued walking in silence then the woman spoke again. "I'm sorry about Lex," she said. "He was a good man and we all cared for him a lot." Alyssa shrugged.

"Maybe it's not my place," said the woman, "but what you're doing is wrong. Timotin is a good man. If there was any way to help your husband, don't you think he would have done it?"

"I'm not so sure," said Alyssa quietly.

"Well, I know," said the woman firmly. "If it would bring Lex back, Timotin would move heaven and earth. You hurt him. He's your friend. I thought you were his."

"We were friends once," said Alyssa.

"I give up," said the woman in exasperation. "Go ahead. Blame everyone for your own shortcomings. I know Timotin tried to save

Lex. And I know what it cost him inside. You want to be alone. Fine! I hope you and you will be very happy together." The woman moved off, stamping hard in the snow.

Alyssa kept her face immobile and looked ahead. Against her wishes, her mind replayed the scene from last night over and over. Slowly the clump of ice that was her heart began to melt. She stopped, oblivious to anything else, and dropped to her knees in the snow. Slowly the tears came, then the flood. She threw herself in the snow and began crying in soul wrenching sobs.

She curled into a foetal position and the tears flowed freely down her face and froze on the animal fur. After an indeterminable time—her chest heaving and hurting—she slowed her sobs and sniffled. Only then did reality make its presence known. Someone was holding her tightly. Rocking slowly back and forth while gently wiping away her tears.

She looked up and blinked rapidly to clear the blurriness right into the smiling face of Timotin. "I'm so sorry," she bawled and buried her face in his coat and started crying again. "I didn't mean what I said," she cried.

"I know, little one," he said tenderly. "Shhh. I understand. Tears are good for the soul. Timotin will help. Timotin will always be friend. Shhh." Alyssa lifted her head and sniffed back the last few tears, then tenderly reached up and kissed the gruff giant gently on the cheek.

A little later, after Alyssa had composed herself, they resumed the journey back to the complex. Alyssa walked beside the giant, leaning on him for support, both physical and emotional. As they walked in silence she noticed that he winced whenever he adjusted the straps on his pack. Then she realized that he didn't wear gloves. His hands were bandaged.

She looked closer and saw flecks of dried blood on the bandages. Calling a halt she asked for the med-kit. Silently, stoically, Timotin let her unwrap his hands. She gasped when she saw the torn ripped flesh and the unmistakable whitening of frostbite.

"When did you do this?" she asked while applying clean dressings. Timotin shrugged and continued staring ahead.

"He did it last night," said the woman from behind. "This big ape dug a grave and buried Lex with his bare hands. All by himself."

Alyssa took the sore hands gently in hers. "Thank you," she whispered and kissed each of them softly.

Their arrival back at the complex was met with loud cheering. Many helpful hands unpacked the sleds as they were brought inside and the meat disappeared as quickly as they could untie it. Patty stood with one hand on Ethan's shoulders. Alyssa came in and looked at her friend, then her son.

"Lex is dead," she said quietly then moved down the corridor. Ethan broke away from Patty and chased after his mother. Patty sidled up to Timotin and quickly saw the bandaged hands.

"What happened?" Timotin quickly explained and a vise closed around Patty's heart.

"Timotin fears for Alyssa," said the giant. "She's hiding. Not good. Help her. Tell her friends nearby." Patty nodded and squeezed the shoulder of the friendly giant.

He stood outside Alyssa's quarters and knocked for entry. No answer came and he knocked again. This time Ethan appeared through the doorway and stepped into the hall. It was obvious he had been crying, but he seemed in control of himself now.

"I'm sorry, son," said Patty holding the boy close.

"He wasn't my father for very long," said Ethan, "but I loved him."

"How's your mother?"

"Alone," said Ethan and Patty nodded. Ethan hugged the veteran and stepped back inside the room to be with Alyssa.

Chapter 29

Over the next three weeks, very little was seen of Alyssa. She rarely came out of her room and when she did, she looked gaunt and wasted. Spoke little, and returned to her private exile. Outside the temperature rose steadily as the planet swung on its tight orbit back to the sun.

Finally all the snow had melted and once again flowers bloomed and insects chirped. Patty stood outside and breathed the clean fresh air. Ethan stood beside him and they watched as Scrapper bounded around in apparent joy the long winter was over.

"I think it's time to move back to the village," said Patty.

"Uh-huh," said Ethan. "Patty, what about mother? It's been almost a month now and she still sits all by herself in our quarters."

"Leave that to me," said Patty with a smile. "Come on. Let's get back in."

Once inside Patty made his way over to Alyssa's room. After several minutes of knocking she appeared in the doorway. "Yes?" She looked thin and pale.

"Snow's all melted and it's warming up fast," said Patty cheerfully. "Time we thought about moving back to the village."

Alyssa shrugged. "So, go!"

"Just waiting for the word, Captain."

Alyssa stared at him angrily. "I am not the Captain," she said harshly. "Lex was the Captain. That post died when he did."

"Maybe you don't think you're the Captain," said Patty calmly, "but you are still the most senior officer alive and as such have a responsibility. I expect you to fulfill that duty."

"You are the council," she said. "Let them make the decisions."

"The council exists only because of the Captain's authority," said

Patty. "Without that we're nothing. Now we want to go home. Are you going to give the order or do we stay here?"

"Why me? I don't want the responsibility. How many times must I tell you? How about I make you Captain?"

Patty shook his head. "Doesn't work that way. Look, you can do what you want. But you have an obligation to these people. Now, they want to go home and you're the one they're waiting for to make the decision. So what's it going to be?"

"Call a meeting," she said sullenly. "I'll talk to them."

"That's my girl," he said with a smile. "We'll be ready this afternoon." Alyssa nodded slowly and returned to the safe confines of her room.

"Oh boy," said Patty softly shaking his head and left to arrange the gathering.

That afternoon after everyone had assembled, Alyssa came into the auditorium. Patty noted with pleasure that she had at least attempted to clean herself up a bit. She looked stronger and walked without the characteristic stoop she had had for the last month.

"My friends," she began as she took her spot on the podium. "I would like to apologize to you all for my attitude over the last few weeks. Things have not gone well for me and I took it out on you. I'm sorry. I know now that Lex gave me great gift. You may not understand, but by making me mad, he saved me the pain of dealing with his death when I was vulnerable." The crowd muttered their dismissal of her apology. They understood and supported her 100%.

"Patty tells me it is now safe to return to the village," she continued. "I think that this is a decision to be made by the council. Which brings me to my next point. When Beth died, we lost a good Captain and friend. We all miss her terribly. Lex stepped in and through his training and natural ability was able to fill the role of Captain admirably. But I don't propose to do the same. I have neither the training nor the natural aptitude. So I will remain mayor of our community and sit on the council. But I will not be Captain and in charge. It's not fair to you…or me. We will now put the vote to the council whether we return or not."

Silence echoed through the room as she took her seat on the dais.

Patty stared at her then cleared his throat and stood up. "Ahem," he said softly. "The, uh, council has already decided to return to the village. If we can have a show of hands I remind you that it is still a bit chilly, but it should continue warming rapidly. Now all in favour of proceeding now, please raise your hands."

He looked around as hands shot up quickly. "Any opposed?" No hands rose and he pulled at his tunic. "Very well. Return to your quarters and begin packing. I want to be able to leave here in two days. It's been a rough hard winter, but thanks to perseverance, we have survived. Now we go home." He sat down and the crowd exited muttering quietly. Alyssa's announcement still left them stunned.

Two days later, they left the complex and started the long trek back to the village. Everyone, man, woman and child were loaded down with heavy packages and packs, but no one seemed to mind. They were out in the sun and going home. It gave their hearts a lift and they walked easily and happily through the growing jungle.

The village had weathered the winter fairly well. Only a few huts needed major repairs and Patty set a team going. The farmers, eager to get the farms growing, ran off to survey the damage.

"Not bad," said Patty that night. "If everyone chips in, we can have the fields ploughed in two days and begin planting. As this is our first night back, I would like a moment's silence to remember those loved ones who passed on. We have been here almost two years and in that time we have lost some very dear friends. Now in the birth of spring, with all the flowers and trees in bloom, I think it fitting that we give respect to those who helped shape the village and save our lives. In particular, I want to mention Beth Bomar, Our Captain and friend, and Lex, a man taken before his time."

He lowered his head and the assembled villagers did the same. Somewhere in the crowd a gentle sob reached their ears as someone fought back the rising tide of emotion. Patty raised his head slowly. "That will be all for tonight," he said softly.

He turned and looked at Alyssa on the dais. She smiled as tears ran freely down her face. "Thank you, Patty," she said. She reached out and pulled Ethan on the stage. "Maybe it's time I stopped feeling sorry for myself. We are alive and Beth and Lex would want us to keep going."

"Then you accept the post of Captain?" Alyssa winced and shook her head.

"I'm not worthy," she said. "We will continue together as a council." Patty nodded slowly and eyed her critically.

As the days passed, the heat rose until it was again a steamy hot jungle world. Everyone had a new spring outfit, as Jack's were plentiful. The old furs had begun to smell and they had burned them. Alyssa slowly came out of her slump and made an effort to smile occasionally.

Weeks passed and she started to feel more like her old self again. She still winced whenever anyone called her captain, but no longer got angry. She recognized that they needed a single authority figure and as much as she disliked it, bore the burden of that duty. Slowly, she reasserted herself and regained her confidence.

Unknown to her, Patty and the other members of the council had been slowly fostering all the decisions on her. While she didn't know it, she had been running the whole village by herself for weeks. Anything of importance came before the council, but they made sure it was Alyssa who made the final decision.

The first tender shoots had risen in the field and Alyssa and Patty were munching on a local plant that resembled squash, but had a slight garlic flavour. Alyssa cocked an ear and stopped eating.

"Do you hear that?"

"What?" Said Patty talking another loud crunch of the bulb.

"Shhh," she said. "Listen!" They sat still and Patty rotated his head slightly to focus in on the sound.

"Must be hearing things," he said. "That sounds like a rocket motor."

"You're not hearing things," said Alyssa excitedly. "That is a rocket motor." Her keen eyes scanned the skies. "There," she cried and pointed in the distance.

Patty squinted. His eyes weren't as good as Alyssa's and it took him a few seconds to find what she pointed at. A small thin vapour trail grew in the distance. Slowly it started to grow and get bigger.

"They've found us," said Alyssa holding back the happy sobs. "Oh, Patty. They've finally found us. Come on. Let's get back to camp."

They ran, skipping and laughing all the way. By the time they reached the village, the white smoke trail could be plainly seen in the sky. The villagers had stared assembling in the town square and were pointing excitedly into the sky.

"Mother? Mother," cried Ethan, running into her arms. "I knew the signal would get through. I told you it would."

"Yes, you did," she said, kissing his head and holding him close.

Soon a small dark spot appeared in front of the smoke. It grew larger and larger until they could make out the fine details of a small scout ship. By now all the villagers had assembled and they were cheering and waving their arms madly in the air. Many were openly crying with joy.

"Must be from a mother ship," said Patty. "It's far too small to be a rescue ship." Alyssa nodded her eyes wide with excitement.

The scout ship approached the village then began to settle just outside the compound. The villagers swarmed and rushed up to the ship, but stopped suddenly when a voice called out on a loudspeaker from the ship.

"Stand back, please," said the voice. "Our ship is very hot. Please stay back until it cools."

The villagers formed a cordon around the ship and waited in breathless anticipation. Soon the steam evaporated and the searing heat dissipated. A small hatch opened in the side and they could see a light shine through. Then a larger door opened and dropped to the ground.

Several men disembarked and placed themselves in a protective ring round the ramp. No one spoke as two men walked sedately down the ramp. One was a middle-aged man with white hair and wearing a dark military style uniform. The other had white curly hair and was dressed in what appeared to be an expensive tailored suit.

Ethan peered closely. "Hey," he said. "I've seen that guy somewhere before. Now where was it?" Before anyone could say anything a figure pushed its way through the crowd and started running across the space between the ship and the people.

"Daddy," cried Sam happily.

Chapter 30

Sam ran across the compound, her hair flying wildly in the wind. She leapt into the arms of the grey-haired man and clutched him tightly. The man taken by surprise struggled to disengage himself from the attractive woman attached to him.

"Princess?" He held her out at arms' length and looked over her lithe athletic body. "Princess, is that you?"

"It's all me, Daddy," said Sam, turning for him to see.

"Humph," he said, looking at her. "Go put some clothes on right now, young lady. I am very happy to see you again, but remember who you are."

"Daddy?"

"We do not run around clad only in smelly old animal skins. You are my daughter and the heir to my empire. I expect you to behave as such."

Sam stood her ground and looked her father directly in the eyes. "If my husband prefers me this way, then I don't see what you have to complain about!"

"You watch your mouth…Did you say husband?"

"Yes," she said excitedly. Turning she ran back to the assembled villagers and grabbed a young man holding a spear. "Daddy, this is Allen. My husband."

Allen nervously stepped forward and proffered his hand. "A pleasure to meet you, sir." The hand remained empty in the space between them.

"My name is William Torens," said the man ignoring Allen's outstretched hand. "Who is in charge of this group?"

Alyssa stepped forward. "No one is in charge. We are ruled by a democratic government Duly elected by the people."

"You," he said accusingly. "Who are you? Well, speak up."

"My name is Alyssa Krychech," she said firmly. The man reached behind him and an officer of the ship handed him and electronic tablet. He thumbed the switch and read the answer.

"Hmmm, Krychech. Engineer—assistant? No, you won't do. Where's the Captain?"

"The Captain is dead," said Alyssa. She had decided she didn't like this overbearing man and her attitude showed.

"Then send me the First Officer or someone with an ounce of intelligence," he pointed to Patty and Adam. "You two take this, this woman away. I want to see whoever is in charge."

"Daddy!"

"Hush, Princess," he said. "You've been through a traumatic experience. No wonder you're delusional about a husband."

"But he is my husband," she protested. "The Captain married us 3 months ago."

"Then I'll have it annulled," he said firmly. "You just relax now, Princess. Daddy's here! I'll fix everything."

Sam moved to stand in front of her father. Her eyes narrowed and through clenched teeth whispered harshly. "I had forgotten what it was like to be your daughter. Now I remember. If being rescued means I have to come back to you, then I'm staying."

"Be reasonable, Princess…"

"I'm not your princess," said Sam coldly. "I am an independent woman. I don't need you or your money."

Alyssa stepped up beside Sam and placed a protective arm around her shoulder. "I am gratified that you received our signal," she said calmly, "but if you expect us to bow and grovel, forget it."

He turned his head and signalled for an officer from the ship. "Arrest this woman. She is to be charged with kidnapping and dereliction of duty."

Two men stepped forward, but were blocked by Adam, Allen, and Patty. Patty stepped forward and confronted the officers. "I wouldn't do that, if I were you," he said in a commanding voice. "Alyssa is under our protection and what is more important—she is under my protection."

"Go away, old man," said Sam's father. "We don't have time for this. It's unbearably hot here and I want to return to my ship. If you won't produce the Captain, then I must assume command here."

"Before you do that," said Alyssa calmly. "I would like to ask one question."

"Oh, very well," he said.

"I assume that you arrived here in one of your vessels. How do you expect to rescue all of us in that tiny ship?"

"Oh, there's a ship coming from the League. Since my ship is smaller and faster we came on ahead to assess the situation."

"Then these officers are not League?"

"No," he said smugly. "They are my own private force. Now, if you will excuse me, I will take my daughter and leave. The other ship should be here in about a week." He moved to take Sam's hand, but she retreated to the safety of the Villagers. They closed in front of her and formed a protective cordon.

"Princess," he said with a puzzled expression.

"My name is Sam," she shouted from behind her friends.

"Your name is Samantha and you are my daughter. Now come out here immediately!"

"No, sir," said Allen stepping in front. "Sam will remain with us until the rescue ship arrives."

"Don't be a fool, man. As soon as the League arrives I'll have you arrested and locked up forever. Is a mild infatuation with my daughter worth that?"

"No, sir, it's not," said Allen calmly. "But since I love her, and she is my wife, it's worth a lot more."

"Daddy," said Sam, softly pushing her way forward. "These people are my friends and family. You've always said that you love me and want what's best for me."

"I do, Prince—Sam. But staying here with these, these barbarians…"

"These barbarians as you call them, happen to be the best most wonderful people in the galaxy. They've saved my life more times than I can count. They taught me there is more to life than money. There's respect, loyalty, courage…and love." She took her husband's hand and stared narrowly at her father.

"I would suggest that you return to your ship," said Alyssa. "With our thanks. But we will wait for the League ship to arrive."

He eyed the beautiful woman coldly. "No," he said firmly. "I've been searching for my daughter for nearly two years. I will not abandon her again."

"That is the smartest thing you've said since you landed here," said Alyssa. "Patty, prepare a hut for our guest. Mr. Torens will your crew be staying as well?"

He looked first at Sam, then at Alyssa. "No," he said and turned to face his crew. "Captain, take the ship out of orbit and rendezvous with the League rescue ship. Apprise them of the situation and bring them directly here. First though, leave me a sub-space communicator. I will stay here."

The Captain saluted and a junior officer trotted up with a small compact transceiver. Patty took the communicator and turned it over to Alyssa. The crew of Torens' ship left; glad to be out of the heat and humidity.

"Well," said Torens, "now what do we do?"

"First order of business," said Sam with a smile, "is to get you out of that suit and into something more comfortable."

"I don't think so," he said haughtily. "I can stand the heat."

"You're the boss," said Sam with a smile. She turned and looping arms with Allen headed back to the village.

Patty came up beside him and motioned with his hand. "This way if you please."

Later after they had found an empty hut for him, they sat down in conference. Sweat ran freely down his head and into his tight shirt. Alyssa and the others sat cool and comfortable.

"Now, I want some answers," he said wiping his brow.

Patty started to explain, but Alyssa cut him off. "Mr. Torens. Around here we treat each other with respect. The watchword is survival. We have learned to trust each other...and ourselves. If you want to learn, you will treat us with the respect that is due to all human beings."

"How dare you," he flustered. "Samantha, I can't believe you tolerate this from the help. It's outrageous!"

Sam stood and addressed the council. "He is my father," she said. "That means he is my responsibility, but I will not put up with this charade." She leaned over her father. Her face inches away from his. "You have never shown anything but your love for money. Money means nothing here. Until you learn that, I place you in Coventry. I will not speak to you, until you learn some manners. Goodbye, Father!"

Sam left the hut in long smooth strides. His mouth hung open in shock as he watched her leave. Patty rose and stood beside the man.

"If you love your daughter as much as you say you do, then I would suggest you open your mind," said Patty. "Sam is a wonderful woman and we love her dearly. We will do anything to protect her as she would for us."

"She has placed you in personal Coventry," said Alyssa. "My responsibility extends to even bastards like you. So I'll give you one warning. Do not step out of the boundaries of the village. There are dangerous creatures here. If you ignore my order, then I will not be responsible." Alyssa gave a signal and the council emptied the hut leaving the man all alone.

Word spread fast because when he emerged, the villagers ignored him completely. He squared his shoulders and began wandering around the village. Slowly a grudging admiration for the people emerged. They had a thriving, self-contained community going on a hostile world. William Torens may have been a businessman and hard to get along with, but he recognized when he was out gunned.

While walking through the town square he saw the refurbished plaque declaring it Ada Worensky Square. He stopped to admire the craftsman ship in the crude sign. Out of the corner of his eye, he saw a figure dart quickly between the huts.

"Wait," he called and hurried after the vanishing figure. "Please. I only want to talk. Stop." He rounded a corner and came face to face with Ethan.

"Yes, sir," said Ethan.

"What's your name, son?"

"Ethan."

"Ethan, I'm sure you understand. I only care for my daughter as does your mother and father."

"My father is dead," said Ethan.

"I'm sorry. I'm sure he was a good man."

"He was," said Ethan coolly. "Now if you'll excuse me, I have errands to finish."

"Just a minute. Please, will you tell me how I can find Sam?"

Ethan looked at the man. "She will not speak to you," he said. "Sam is my friend. You hurt her. She was so happy to see you and all you cared about was your power and control. I have nothing but contempt for you."

Ethan ran off leaving William even more puzzled than ever. He looked up. The sun had risen higher in the sky. He loosened his shirt and took off his jacket. He felt dizzy in the heat and sat down on a convenient rock.

"It will be noon soon," said a voice behind him. He turned and saw Patty standing there. "The temperature will really shoot up then."

"Is there any way to keep cool on this accursed world?"

"No," said Patty. He started walking away when William called him.

"Sir," he said softly, "I would appreciate a cool drink of water."

Patty pointed to the square. "Over there," he said and continued walking.

"Please, sir. You seem to have some influence here. Can't you make my daughter, and the others understand?"

"My name is Patty and no, I can't. You brought this on yourself, coming here blustering about arresting people. Ignoring your daughter's happiness. Dismissing her husband as if he didn't exist."

"Perhaps I was a bit hasty. Patty, please. I just want what's best for my little girl."

"In case you haven't noticed," said Patty, "you're little girl is all grown up."

"I noticed," he said and hung his head. He stared into space. "She really is a beautiful young woman isn't she? Looks a lot like her mother."

Patty sat down beside the man. "Then her mother must have been a very beautiful woman."

"That she was," he said leaning forward. "That and more. She had the beauty inside as well, but what a temper. Funny, that's what attracted me to her in the first place. I was a rising young executive and bowed to no one. She wasn't concerned who I was and had no problem telling me so."

"In that case," said Patty, "I can assure you that her daughter is the same way. You sound like you were very happy."

"Oh, we were. When Samantha was born, she was such a beautiful child, I felt my life was complete."

"So what happened?"

"My wife died in a shuttle accident," he said sadly. "I lost touch with the world that day. I turned my anger and grief into the business."

"And alienated your daughter along the way."

"Yeah. Oh, I made sure she lacked for nothing. She had the finest clothes, and when I became rich and powerful, I hired the best private tutors. But I couldn't give her the one thing she needed. A father. I couldn't bear to be with her. As she grew up, she started looking more like her mother."

"So you distanced yourself, because you couldn't bear the pain."

William nodded slowly. "Now look at us. She won't even speak to me."

"Mr. Torens-."

"Please, call me William."

"William, it's still not too late."

William shook his head sadly. "I don't even know how to be a parent, much less her father. She's all grown up and doesn't need me anymore."

"Children always need their parents and it's never too late to start." Patty placed an affection hand on the man's sweaty shoulder. "Will you take some advice? From one father to another?"

William nodded. "I'm willing to try anything."

"We have here in our community a young man who's had a similar problem. He never knew what a family was, until he came here. He was adopted and now is happy. Talk to him. Talk to his mother. I'm sure they could help you."

"It can't be the same thing," said William. "He's still young. He can adapt easily. My daughter is a full grown woman."

Patty smiled. "Ethan is a, unique case."

"Ethan? Yes, I believe I met a young man by that name. He wasn't very pleased with me. Not that I blame him."

"I wouldn't worry about Ethan," said Patty. "It's his mother you have to win over. You see, she's still new at this, and is learning how, as you are. But the difference is, she's trying. Now, what will it be? The ship will be here in a few days. Are you going to try and reconcile with Sam, or go on without her?"

"I would like to try," he said earnestly. "Please tell me about her. What's she like? How about this young man she married?"

"Ask her yourself," said Patty. "Just remember she's not the same spoiled kid you sent on a trip anymore." He looked at William critically. "Ready to reconsider our offer for other attire. I promise you will be a lot cooler."

"Thank you," he said gratefully. The two men rose and began walking to Patty's hut. "Can you tell me about your community I admit, I'm impressed. It takes strong leadership to make things work in this type of environment."

"You don't know the half of it," chuckled Patty.

"Your Captain must have been a remarkable person," he said.

"She was," said Patty softly. "But she didn't do it alone. There were others, and some who kept us alive when all else failed."

"Who took over when the Captain died? The First Officer?"

"Yes," said Patty. "Lex was a good man. He died in a hunting accident. His wife is now the Captain, as next senior officer."

"Then why didn't she come forward when I asked?"

Patty scratched his head. "Our Captain is different. She's had a rough life and had to learn many hard lessons in a short period of time. When her husband died, she retreated into herself. She's only just now acknowledging her responsibilities and duties."

"Then she shouldn't be Captain," said William. "There's one thing I know. It takes a strong leader with a strong will to keep a company alive. Otherwise that leader is just a threat to the continuation of the business."

"Better not let the villagers hear you talk like that. Let me just say that this woman means more to us than ourselves. She is the most responsible, qualified person I've ever met. All she needs is time and our support. And we all give her that. Understand?"

"She must really be some type of woman to inspire such devotion."

"She is," said Patty firmly. He opened the door to his hut. "Over there you should find a suitable change of clothing. " I'll go get Ethan and his mother. Make yourself comfortable."

"Patty," said William as Patty started to leave. "Thank you for everything. I haven't talked about my wife in years. It felt good." Patty smiled and slipped out the door.

William scrounged around the pile of animal skins until he found a breechcloth and a light tunic that fitted him. A brief examination showed him how to wear the unusual clothes and he gratefully shucked his own suit. He stood admiring himself. The best physical trainers, money could buy, had kept him fit and trim. He had to admit that the skimpy animal skins were much cooler and better adapted to the searing climate.

A knock came to the door. "Come in," he said. The door open and in stepped Ethan.

"Patty said you wanted to talk to me and my mother," said the boy, eyeing him suspiciously.

"Yes, that's right," said William. "First, let me apologize to you and your mother about my behaviour. It was disgraceful and I'm sorry. But where is your mother? Didn't she come with you?"

"Yes, sir," said Ethan, "but she preferred to wait outside."

"I understand," said William. "Please tell her that I am here to learn. Patty says you two can help me with Sam."

"If your serious about trying to reconcile with Sam, then we'll help you," said Alyssa from the doorway. William's face registered shock when he saw her.

"Madam," he said respectfully. "I do apologize for my behaviour earlier. Please, I beg you. Help me!"

Alyssa nodded and indicated him to a seat. "There are some things you must understand first," she said sitting opposite him. "I will not tolerate any heavy handiness or power playing authority. Start those games and I'll leave you out to hang. Do I make myself clear, Mr. Torens."

"Yes, ma'am, you do. Please call me William."

"My name is Alyssa and this is Ethan, my son," she said. "I think I'd better start at the beginning. Our ship was severely damaged and we escaped in the life pods, only to land on this world…"

For the next several hours, Alyssa and Ethan gave William an abbreviated version of the last two years on this Hellhole. William struggled with the idea that hundreds of people had died. He shuddered when Alyssa described the living conditions and various creatures that inhabited this jungle planet.

A knock came to the door. "Yes," said Alyssa. The door swung open and Adam stood framed in the twilight of the setting sun. "Yes, Adam. What is it?"

"Excuse me, Captain, but dinner is ready. Do you want me to bring something here or will you be coming out?"

"We'll be out shortly, Adam, thanks," said Alyssa. Adam nodded and quietly closed the door.

"He called you Captain," said William.

"That's right," said Alyssa. "Although I personally don't like the title."

"Oh my god," said William holding a hand to his mouth. "I think I owe you another apology, Captain."

"You will if you keep calling me Captain," said Alyssa with a smile. "Here, we are run by Council. I'm Captain in name only."

"Not according to Patty," said William then shut his mouth quickly as he recalled what Patty said about their Captain.

"Patty is a wonderful dear man," said Alyssa, "but he lets his imagination run away with him sometimes. Now, if you are hungry? It's not exactly gourmet food, but we like it."

"If you don't think it will be a problem," said William, "I would be happy to share a meal with you. Tell me. Will…Will Sam be there as well?"

"I don't see why not," said Alyssa. "We eat all our meals together." William nodded and rose. Ethan rushed to the door and held it open as the adults exited.

William took a place in the food line between Ethan and Alyssa.

When he reached the head of the buffet table, someone handed him a polished wooden plate and a pair of smoothed sticks.

"Chopsticks," volunteered Ethan as he saw William stare at the implements. "They're a lot easier to make than knives and forks."

"It's been years since I used chopsticks," admitted William.

"Don't worry," said Alyssa from behind him. "You'll get the hang of it."

They moved down the line and Alyssa pointed out the various foods on the table. Carefully he placed small portions on his plate, while Ethan heaped his high. "What a feast," exclaimed Ethan.

"The cooks have out done themselves tonight," agreed Alyssa and helped herself to more fresh vegetables.

William looked at the strange food on his plate. He knew that they didn't have a synthesizer, but the idea of eating fresh meat and vegetables turned his stomach. He sniffed cautiously and his stomach rumbled with hunger. Gingerly he picked a small piece of Jack meat and took a small bite.

It was tough and chewy, but it had a sharp musty flavour he found pleasant. "Not bad," he admitted. "What did you say this was again?"

"We call it Jack meat," said Alyssa. "It's really an animal that looks like a giant Jackrabbit." William choked as he realized that this meat had once been alive. He coughed and choked while Alyssa chuckled.

"Don't worry," she said. "We all reacted that way the first time too. Have some fruits and vegetables."

"No, it's all right," gasped William. "I've eaten some strange things in business deals. I can handle this."

They moved to a spot near the campfire and sat down on the warm ground. William watched as Ethan and Alyssa dug into their meal with fervour. Then slowly he took another bite of Jack meat and forced himself to chew and swallow it. When it didn't come back up, he took another. Before long his plate was empty and he still felt hungry.

"There's more," said Alyssa. "Help yourself." He looked at his empty plate and felt his stomach rumble again. Nodding he got up and moved over to the buffet table.

Torches had been lit because of the growing darkness and he had a hard time distinguishing one food from another. "Wish I could see what I'm eating," he said softly.

"That's a local version of Cabbage," said a quiet voice behind him. William jumped at the sound and whirled around. "And that's a fruit that tastes like an apple," said Sam.

"Samantha," he whispered. "It's good to see you again."

"That bowl over there contains roasted Jack meat," she said ignoring him.

"Sam, please," said William placing his plate down. "Please talk to me. I've been absolutely horrible. I'm very sorry. Can we start over?"

"That depends," said Sam, "on how sincere you are!"

"Anything," he said. "Please, honey, Talk to me." He stopped floundering for words, but nothing came.

"I hear that you've been talking with Alyssa," said Sam reaching for Jack meat.

"Yes, she's a remarkable woman," said William. "You all are. Sam, I know how you feel about me, but hear me out. I lost your mother when you were a little girl. She was my life. When she died, a piece of me died as well. I lost your mother but I don't want to lose you. Tell me it's not too late. Tell me you can forgive a selfish bitter old man."

Sam looked at her father and her eyes softened. "We'll see. Why don't you pick up your plate and come and sit with us. Allen would like to meet you properly."

William smiled. "And I would like to meet him." Sam took her father's plate from his hand gently and together they walked back to the campfire. William glanced over his shoulder and saw Alyssa smiling at him in the flickering firelight.

Over the next few days, the villagers showed William their proud accomplishments. Before long he became an accepted member of the tiny community. They were pleased when he announced to the whole village, that he was going to devote the rest of his life to helping more, rather than being around less.

"You've made me a very happy man again," he said to Alyssa one night. "You've given me back my daughter and a purpose to my life."

"I've done nothing," said Alyssa. "You did it. What will you do now? I just heard from the ship. They'll be here tomorrow."

"I still have a business to run," he said, "but things will be different. As a matter of fact Allen, I have a proposition for you."

"Yes, sir," said Allen.

"I've been talking to Timotin," said William. "It seems that the research station he was headed for is owned by me and leased to the League. When he didn't show, the League cancelled its lease. That station is still out there. I've offered it to Timotin to continue his research. He wants to know if you still want to be his assistant?"

"That's very generous, sir," said Allen, "but it's no place to take a wife and raise a family."

"I've been thinking about that too," said William. "I propose to expand the facilities to include suitable accommodation for the married members of the team. You won't be alone. Several others from your Village will be going there as well. Including Adam and A'Serta. I have offered them a full lab, to study the artefacts from the Providers. So what do you say…son?"

Allen took his wife's hand in his and she nodded slowly. "We accept," said Allen. "Only if you come and visit occasionally."

"I would be honoured," said William. "Thank you. What about you, Alyssa? What will you do?"

Alyssa glanced at Patty. "I don't have much choice," she said. "As soon as the League ship grounds I will be placed under arrest."

"That's outrageous," said William. "Let me handle this. I'll get you the best lawyer around."

"No. Thank you," said Alyssa softly. "Just promise me one thing. You'll make sure that Ethan is well taken care of."

"I'm entering the Academy," said Ethan. "I'll be fine. And we will get you some help."

Alyssa brushed off their offers of help. She knew it was her responsibility. "In a way, I'm glad it's over," she said softly. Patty looked at her affectionately.

A scraping came at the door and a soft whine. "Please let Scrapper in, Ethan," said Alyssa. Ethan bounded up and ran to open the door. As soon as he did the giant lion-snake slipped in and tackled Ethan to the ground. William jumped up and started forward to rescue the boy, but Patty held him back.

"It's all right," he said chuckling. "I forgot you haven't met Scrapper yet. Scrapper? Scrapper. Come here, boy. That's it." He rubbed the shaggy head while its long tongue snaked out and liked his face.

"Scrapper, this is William," he said introducing the animal to the stranger. Scrapper slithered over to William and sniffed him cautiously. "Hold out you hand, William. Let him get your scent."

William held his hand out and Scrapper sniffed again. Then as if deciding he passed, rubbed his shaggy mane against the outstretched hand. Slowly then with joy, William rubbed the head of the Lion-snake.

"I guess that makes it unanimous," said Alyssa and the others laughed heartily.

The next morning the League's ship appeared above the horizon and slowly grew in size as it approached. With a blast of smoke the giant ship settled about a mile from the Village. The Captain of the ship had chosen his landing site well. Only a few trees were knocked down as the giant ship descended.

"I am Captain Veron of the League Starship Adventure," said the man as he descended a boarding ramp. "I'm very glad to see you all. Ah, Mr. Torens. You're here as well good."

"Captain," said William, "allow me to introduce my daughter Sam, and her husband, Allen."

"So this is the special young lady who can send a telepathic message across the galaxy. Glad to meet you, my dear. And you, sir."

"It wasn't just me," said Sam. "We all did it."

"I'll be interested in hearing the whole story," said Captain Veron. "If you wish, we can leave as soon as everyone is aboard."

"Captain," said Patty approaching, "we have been here a long time. Frankly this is our home and we're reluctant to leave it to be destroyed."

"No worry about that, sir," said the Captain. "When we received your message, the League put together a fully equipped team of planetary explorers. They will be very happy to watch over things for you."

Patty looked at Alyssa and she nodded to his unspoken question. "Fine Captain. If I could speak to them, there are some things about this world they should be aware of."

"Of course, of course, please feel free. The deck officer will show you to their ready room."

"Thank you, sir," said Patty and he boarded the giant ship.

"If the rest of you will gather your belongings," said Captain Veron, "we'll get you comfortably on board. Before that though, I must ask to see the Captain of Carriolion."

"The Captain is dead," volunteered William.

"Then the First Officer or the highest ranking officer still alive," he said.

"That would be me," said Alyssa stepping forward.

"Alyssa," hissed William.

"No," she said. "I'm tired. Let it be finished. One request first though, Captain."

"Of course, ma'am," he said kindly. "Please believe me, I do not relish this duty. But rules are rules. Now, what is it you want?"

"We have a pet of sorts. Would it be all right if he came with us?"

The Captain thought for a moment then saw the look on Ethan's face. "Is it your pet, son?" he asked kindly.

"Yes, sir," said Ethan. "He's really good. He won't get into any trouble. I promise."

"Well, it is against regulations to transport unknown animals," said the Captain thoughtfully, "but I think I can make an exception. Go ahead, son, fetch your pet."

Ethan vanished into the woods calling for Scrapper. "Thank you, Captain," said Alyssa.

"My pleasure, ma'am," he said. "I'm sorry to do this, but under regulations I must place you under arrest. If you promise not to do anything foolish, I think we can dispense with confining you to quarters."

"I won't make any trouble," said Alyssa. "Here comes Ethan and Scrapper now."

Captain Veron was taken aback by the lion-snake, but when he saw how friendly it appeared, he loosened up and approached the creature. "Good boy," he said and rubbed Scrapper's head. "Quite an animal you've got there, son. Will he be all right on board the ship?"

"Oh yes, sir," said Ethan hugging his pet. "He'll stay with me. Come on, Scrapper. Let's go." Ethan started to move up the gangway, but scrapper backed down. "Come on, Scrapper," Ethan called again. But the lion-snake refused to move.

Ethan ran back down the ramp and knelt beside his friend. "What's the matter, Scrapper? Don't be afraid. It won't hurt you." The animal raised its head up and leaned on Ethan.

"I need Sam," said Ethan. "Scrapper wants to talk." Alyssa sent for Sam and she came running up.

Captain Veron and William watched in amazement as Ethan, Sam, and Scrapper locked in silent mental communication. Alyssa explained the unique relationship between the three friends and they waited.

Soon Ethan's eyes watered and he started to cry. They broke the link and Ethan ran crying into the ship. Sam approached the others, tears streaming down her face as well. Allen rushed to hold her as her body shook with deep sobs.

"Scrapper won't come with us," she cried. "He says that his place is here. He would die if he left. He will stay with the explorers."

"You mean that the animal is intelligent?" William looked in disbelief.

"More than that," sobbed Sam. "Scrapper is a descendant of one of the original animals left here by the Providers. They were guardians and friends. He can't leave. His system is geared to live here."

"How do you know all this?" Asked Captain Veron sounding sceptical.

"If my daughter says its true," said William, "then it is. She has an unusual gift, and obviously, so does Ethan. I'm so sorry, honey."

Scrapper slithered back into the crowd of Villagers. One by one they rubbed or kissed his head good bye and he licked each one in turn. Patty came down the gangway, a puzzled look on his face.

"What's wrong with Ethan," he said. "He blew by me crying his eyes out."

Alyssa explained the situation and a dark cloud passed over the old man's face. "Oh, I see." He approached Scrapper and crouched down. The lion-snake moved over to him and nuzzled his hand gently. Patty stroked the soft fur on Scrapper's head for a minute then stood up. When he turned they could see tears in his eyes. Without a word, Patty boarded the ship.

Scrapper crouched and watched as his friends entered the giant ship. When everyone had boarded, Patty emerged followed by the team of explorers. He introduced Alyssa, then Scrapper. Scrapper weaved in and out of the strangers. Then gave his signal of approval by nuzzling the hand of the leader.

The explorers picked up their gear and headed in the direction of the village. Scrapper started to follow them then stopped. It whirled around and charged for Alyssa. It hit her flying through the air, knocking her to the ground. Captain Veron reached for his sidearm, but Patty stopped him.

Scrapper pinned Alyssa to the ground and began to lick her face feverishly. Alyssa wrapped her arms around the giant lion's head and hugged with all her strength. Her tears matted the hair down and Scrapper whimpered mournfully.

Slowly the beast disengaged himself and with one last look, followed after the exploration team. Patty rushed over to help Alyssa stand again. "I have a feeling he'll be all right. This is his home. Come on. Let's get aboard."

Patty helped Alyssa ascend the ramp leaving Captain Veron alone. He continued watching in the direction the exploration team had gone. "Incredible," he muttered. "Absolutely incredible!" He shook his head and boarded his ship. Minutes later the jungle shook with a roar as the great ship slowly lifted into space.

Below them in the village, the exploration team looked up and waved good-bye. The leaving was made all the more painful as Scrapper sat howling and whimpering until the ship was out of sight.

Chapter 31

"Miss Krychech, as the highest ranking survivor of the Cruiser Carriolion, the responsibility and burden fall on your shoulders. Are you prepared to accept the judgment of this tribunal?"

Alyssa stared coldly at the hooded and cloaked judge. According to the law, the Captain of a ship is responsible for the safety of the ship, crew, and passengers. If the Captain is dead, then the next in command assumes the mantle of responsibility. With everyone else dead, the burden fell on her tired and defeated shoulders.

Alyssa straightened her back. A grim determination possessed her. The safety of everyone had been placed in her hands when Lex died. Even though she hated the idea of being in command, she bore it stoically, and over the last few months had proven herself a capable and sometimes brilliant leader. Now, she must answer for her actions.

"I accept the judgment of the tribunal," she said formally.

"Very well," said the judge. "Alyssa Krychech, former Chief Engineer of the Cruise Liner Carriolion. As acting Captain, you are charged with the safety of the ship and crew. The charges against you are numerous. Will the Proctor read the specified charges?"

Alyssa stood very still, staring straight ahead as the Proctor rose and read from the Tablet. "Charge one. On 35678.34 did Alyssa Krychech wilfully-."

"I think we can dispense with the usually formalities," said the judge softly. "Miss Krychech has to answer to them. She doesn't have to have them thrown in her face."

"Yes, my lord," said the Proctor. Alyssa threw the judge a look of gratitude, but she kept her rigid stance.

"Briefly," said the Proctor. "The charges are loss of League property; Namely the Cruiser Carriolion. Destruction of League property;

Namely, the afore mentioned cruiser. Failure to maintain and sustain the well being of the afore mentioned cruiser. Failure to maintain and sustain the passengers of the Carriolion: Death of the senior officers of the Carriolion, including the Captain and the First Officer. The deaths of several hundred crew and passengers, then under protection of the Company…There are more specific details. Do you wish me to read them, my lord?"

"Thank you, no. That will be all," said the judge. He leaned forward and faced Alyssa. "Miss Krychech, you have heard the charges. Before I ask you for your plea, I am at liberty to remind you that while you yourself did not cause these problems, as the one still in charge, you are responsible. Should you enter a plea of not guilty then the record will show so. You will be free to go. However, the chances of employment in the space service will be terminated. I must caution you that you are responsible under space law, and at the discretion of the court, could be held in contempt for treason."

"Then I'm stuck either way," returned Alyssa. "If I plead guilty, then I'm to be subjugated and held on trial. If I plead not guilty, then I'm to be ostracized, possibly punished. Not exactly a fair choice is it?" Behind her Patty tapped her shoulder.

"Remember what I taught you," he whispered. "You are in command. Not your emotions. Do what you must. I can't advise you, but don't let emotions rule you. Use them to your advantage, not your defeat."

Alyssa smiled at the old soldier. Turning her attention back to the bench she addressed the tribunal. "My Lords. When the safety of the passengers and crew where placed in my hands by the First Officer on his deathbed, I vowed to see them safely home. I also accepted the terms and conditions of Command, of which I was fully aware. I have done my job, and I'm not backing down now…To the specified charges as acting Captain I plead…Guilty as charged. I await your decision."

"Very well," said the hooded judge. He looked at the silent others on the bench and said, "This court will resume in two weeks to hear a final statement. You have until then to prepare your testimony, Miss Krychech. During that time period, this Tribunal will interview the remainder of the passengers and crew. At the end of the case, a judgment will be passed with recommendations. The first ruling will be to decide whether a court martial concerning Miss Krychech is in order. This Tribunal is at rest."

The Proctor rose quickly and said loudly. "All rise and pay homage…My Lords have left the bench. You may depart." He scooped up his notes and quickly followed the judges through the anteroom door.

Alyssa turned to talk to Patty and found herself face to face with a security guard. "Where is everyone? Where's Patty?"

"Sorry, Miss," said the guard, "but as soon as you pleaded guilty, the courtroom was cleared of all persons concerning the case."

Alyssa stared into the cherub face of the security guard. The woman looked small and frail, but Alyssa knew the training these people endured. This pretty little security guard with the disarming smile could take on a half-a-dozen men twice her size and not even work up a sweat.

"So, what happens now?"

The guard smiled. "Now, we get you back to your quarters for some rest." Alyssa followed the other woman meekly out of the courtroom. Patty had never mentioned any of this before and it worried her.

"Miss Krychech? For what it's worth, I admire you very much," said the guard.

"Thank you," said Alyssa numbly. "When can I see my friends?"

"Not until the final judgment has been rendered. According to the law, you are forbidden contact with anyone concerning this case. The Tribunal wants to question them without your influence."

"What about me?"

"You will be provided with transcripts of the interviews after each has occurred, to give you a chance to prepare a defence."

"Wonderful," said Alyssa sarcastically then remembering her training reined in her temper.

"Here is your room, Miss Krychech," said the guard indicating the door they had stopped beside. "If you need anything I'll be right outside."

"Why? Am I under arrest?"

"Not at all," replied the woman. "You are free to come and go as you please, but I have been assigned to protect you and answer your needs and questions."

"Protect me! From who?"

"That is not for me to say," said the guard.

"Well, if we're going to be close, you might as well come in. And please call me Alyssa. Miss Krychech is a little too formal for me."

"I can't do that yet, Miss," said the woman hesitantly. "Perhaps later."

Alyssa shrugged her shoulders. "Suit yourself, but you might as well come in anyway. We can have a cup of coffee while you explain what's happening."

The woman's face brightened. "Thanks. I'd like that. By the way my name is Beth."

"That was my Captain's name," said Alyssa softly.

"I know," said the guard. She stepped inside and headed straight for the tiny kitchen and started to make a pot of coffee.

Alyssa followed her, wonder and puzzlement on her face. "You seem to know a lot about what happened. How?"

"I don't think I should say just yet, Miss Krychech. Maybe later. Now come sit. The coffee's ready and we have a lot to do."

Over the next two weeks the two women were inseparable. Along with her duties as a guard, Beth also proved to be a worthy defence counsel. Since the banning of lawyers over three hundred years ago, the courts had decided that people could defend themselves better without all the usual nonsense. If a defendant lost the case he or she had no one to blame but themselves. The facts and the people spoke for themselves.

Each day the transcripts of the interviews arrived by messenger to Alyssa's door. She and Beth poured over the contents, looking for damaging evidence. "Alyssa," said Beth. She had finally relented after a week and began calling her by name. "These people all seem to adore you. The only negative comments are from people you ignored after your husband's death, but even they support you."

"Then I shouldn't have any worries," smiled Alyssa.

"Not quite," said Beth. She hesitated for a moment and motioned for Alyssa to sit beside her. In two weeks they had grown a fast friendship. "Look, I'm not going to lie to you. The charges against ship's Captain's rarely go unpunished. Someone has to take the fall."

"I anticipated that," said Alyssa smiling, "but somehow it doesn't really matter anymore. Beth, can I tell you something?"

"Sure."

"I never wanted command. When it was thrust on me, I just did the best I could. To my surprise, I found I was good at it, and I even enjoyed it." She picked up a sheaf of interviews and waved them in the air. "These are my justification. We went through life, and death together. Sometimes my decisions weren't popular. But against all odds of surviving, and sometimes against the wishes of my friends, I made my decisions. I never thought of myself as really being in charge, but after reading this, I am ready to fully accept the title of Captain and everything it implies."

"Even if it does mean your dismissal from the service."

"Yes," said Alyssa firmly. "I am the Captain of the Carriolion and I must accept the responsibility for her. And before you ask, no, I have no regrets. There are some things I wish didn't happen. But given the same situation and the same circumstances, I would do the same things again."

"I'm glad to hear that," said Beth hugging her tightly. "That's one of the things the Tribunal will be observing. Whether you are competent and capable or not."

"Since the court resumes tomorrow," said Alyssa finally, "don't you think we should go over the final draft of my statement?"

Beth smiled and saluted. "Aye-aye, Captain." A small thing, but it had the obvious effect of making Alyssa smile.

The next morning found them side-by-side in the same room that Alyssa had stood many days before. Alyssa looked around the room and it seemed more crowded than last time. As she gazed over the spectators, it gradually dawned on her that everyone from the expedition who was able had attended.

Beth leaned in close and whispered. "You still can't talk to them, but I know they're all here to support you, as am I."

"Thank you, my friend," said Alyssa and gently hugged the other woman. The room suddenly went quiet as the Proctor entered the hall.

"All rise and pay homage," he said. "My Lords enter the chamber." The hooded judges moved sedately into the room and seated themselves on the raised bench. The head judge gave a small signal to the Proctor.

"Be seated," he said, and took his place.

"Alyssa Krychech," said the judge. Alyssa stood up and squared her shoulders. "Have you received copies of the interview transcripts and are you prepared to make a statement."

"Yes, my Lord," she said firmly. The judge motioned for her to continue and sat back in his seat to listen.

"My Lords," she began. "The story of the Carriolion is one of sadness and loss. It is also a story of bravery and adventure. This august body is familiar with the details the names and dates. But that is not the whole story. It is a story of independence, of the struggle of people to survive against all odds. It is also the story of growth. The names and dates of the dead mean nothing but statistics to you, but to me they mean a lot more. These people were friends and lovers. I knew each of them. When I hear their names I don't add a tote board, I see their faces, hear their laugh, share their sorrows, and relish their joys.

"With the help of friends, I grew, both as a person and as a leader. If I could, I would gladly sacrifice myself to bring back the dead, but it won't happen. I can only honour their memories. My responsibility is to the passengers and crew, and I stand by my decisions. I will offer no defence, as I did not commit any crime, but I will accept the responsibility for whatever actions were taken, because My Lords, I am the Captain of the Carriolion." She sat down gracefully to the sound of thunderous applause from the spectators.

"Order," shouted the Proctor. "Order please, or I will have you removed." Slowly the noise dwindled to a hush.

"Miss Krychech," said the judge. "The title of Captain bestowed upon you is honorary. You have not officially been instated as such and I caution you to refrain from calling yourself such. Personally, I commend your attitude and actions, but it is not for me to decide. I sit as moderator only. The Tribunal will now consult."

The judges rose and left the bench, but the Proctor didn't call everyone to attention. Seconds later they reappeared and resumed their seats. A gasp rose from the audience. Such a quick decision usually meant that guilty verdict was imminent.

"Before we render our decisions and recommendations," said the judge, "I feel it's only right to inform you that aside from the charges officially laid against you, there is a civilian charge also pending. The plaintiff has agreed to hold charges until the outcome of the Tribunal has been reached. Do you understand?"

"Yes, My Lord."

The judge took a deep breath and to Alyssa he seemed to take an extremely long time to exhale. Finally he spoke. "Miss Krychech?" Alyssa rose and stood at attention.

"In regard to the charges and specifications regarding the loss and destruction of the Carriolion, this Tribunal finds you…guilty! In regards the charges and specifications concerning the deaths of the crewmembers and the passengers, this Tribunal finds you…guilty! And finally concerning the death of the true Captain of the Carriolion, this Tribunal finds you…guilty as charged!"

The crowd erupted into a mob, yelling and shouting. Cries of foul and unfair rained down on the ears of the Tribunal. A small tear came to Alyssa's eye as her friends shouted their disapproval of the judgment. The judge sat back and let the crowd vent its anger for a few moments then called for silence. Slowly, grumbling they quieted to a low murmur.

"Thank you," he said. "Now, if I may continue? Due to mitigating circumstances, no charges of treason or mutiny will be considered. It is the judgment of this Tribunal that you, Miss Krychech, acted with the best intentions, and while a little unorthodox, did maintain the proper discipline and conduct of a Commander. Therefore, under the recommendations from the sealed records of the late Captain Bomar and Admiral Jherok, you are to be placed in the Academy at the rank of Commander and given the appropriate training. Upon completion of the training you will be commissioned with the rank of Captain, and given your own ship."

The crowd cheered and stamped their feet in approval. Whistles and clapping drowned out the Proctor as he tried to maintain order.

They tried to rush forward to congratulate Alyssa, but the guards held them back. Finally order was restored and the judge spoke again.

"There is one condition though," he said. "If the civilian lawsuit of wrongful death finds you guilty, you must forfeit this commendation and accept a discharge. Now we will find out. Proctor?"

"Miss Krychech, a lawsuit of wrongful death has been filed against you concerning the death of the Captain of the Carriolion by Captain Bomar's niece. Will the Plaintiff please state whether she will continue this course of action."

"My Lords, I will not pursue this case, and I offer my support in your decisions as well." Alyssa turned to see who the niece of the Captain was and found herself staring into the smiling face of Beth.

"I'm sorry, honey," she said. "Tradition dictated that I file the charge. At the time I had no problem with that, but after meeting you and getting to know you, I knew I couldn't do it, regardless of the outcome of the Tribunal."

Alyssa gripped her new friend's shoulder in appreciation the turned and faced the Tribunal. "My Lords, may I speak?"

"Of course, Commander," said the judge.

"I must clarify a few things first. I do not wish to return to the Liner service. If it is possible I wish to join the Military service. I feel the skills I have learned would be put to better use in exploration. Furthermore, I do not know anybody named Admiral Jherok, and question his authority over me."

"May I answer her questions, My Lord?"

"Of course, Admiral," said the judge smiling. Alyssa turned to the voice behind her and found Patty smirking.

"Admiral Jherok? I thought…I mean…Oh hell."

"Surprise," said Patty. "Admiral P.T. Jherok at your service. Sorry for the deception, but I had to keep my identity secret. Beth knew, but I swore her to secrecy."

"You're the one," cried Beth the guard. "You're the one she wrote about. She loved you a lot."

"And I loved her. A part of me died when she did, but she made me promise to care for Alyssa. You see, my dear, she loved you as her own daughter. She knew what you were capable of and charged me with helping you find it in yourself."

Alyssa felt the tears well up and rushed to hug the old man, the suddenly remembering his rank she stopped suddenly. A war fought inside her. She desperately wanted to hug the stuffing out of her friend, but the discipline held her fast.

"I'm still Patty to you, my dear," he said softly. "Now come give me a hug, or do I have to make it an order." The two friends hugged tightly for a few moments then Patty broke away. "Now in answer to your other question. Your commission of Captain will be military. I recently found out that a new branch—totally devoted to exploration has been formed. The first ship, completely outfitted will be ready by the time you graduate. All she needs is an experienced Captain, and that is you. Interested?"

In response she hugged him again. "I thought you'd say that," he chuckled. When they broke apart, Patty addressed the Tribunal. "My Lords, I thank you for this opportunity."

"My pleasure, Admiral," said the judge. "Now I have a little surprise of my own. I took the liberty of bringing down the officers soon to be under your command Miss Krychech. They all have followed this case intently and have unanimously offered their support. They now wish to meet with you. Proctor?"

The Proctor moved to the anteroom door and the first command crew of the new exploration branch of the military marched in crisp bright green uniforms. Alyssa went down the line and met each of them. At the end she felt a swell of pride a good crew, capable and willing to follow her lead.

"Admiral, I mean Patty," she said. "There are positions missing. I know our job will be exploring, but I'm going to need a full crew."

"We already thought of that. We currently don't have the people to fill those positions, but will have by the time you take command. They are currently training at the Academy. Including someone very special to you. Unfortunately, he's in the Academy and can't attend today."

"Ahem," said the judge. "I took care of that little problem. Alyssa, if I may call you that, may I present your new communication expert, Ensign..."

"Hi, Mom," said a soft voice from the doorway.

"Ethan," she cried happily and scooped the young boy up in her arms kissing his wet cheeks. Realizing that it was undignified for a Captain to kiss her crew, she reluctantly put the boy down.

"How? When?"

"As you know, because of the boy's extraordinary talents, I received permission to allow him to enrol. I had taught him most of things he needed to know while marooned on the planet. When he graduates he will be a full Ensign and ship's communication specialist."

The crowd cheered loudly and this time the guards moved away to allow them to reach Alyssa. Tears ran unashamedly down her face as each of her friends and fellow survivors hugged, kissed, and congratulated her.

Patty moved closer and whispered in her ear. "You've come a long way, and beat your own demons. I know you'll do me and Beth proud. I'm equally sure Lex would be proud of you."

"Thank you," she whispered, "for everything."

"No charge," he said. He backed up and slipped away in the throng Confident that the young woman whom he held in fear and joy, would do wonderful things in the years to come. He looked forward to seeing her off on her first voyage. He glanced back for one last look, but failed to find her in the midst of the happy group.

Stepping into a travel tube he called the destination of the parking garage. It slid away silently then slowed to pick up another passenger. To his surprise Alyssa stepped in.

"What are you doing here?"

"Well, I just thought of something. When we started this journey, you told me, that you weren't wanted anymore, and were being put out to pasture, right?"

"Yeah, so?"

"Well, over the last few years, I've come to realize that you are far from ready for retirement. And since you don't really have any plans, I was wondering if you would like to come with us."

"On the ship? Are you nuts? I'm as old as the hills. You don't need a retired Admiral around to foul things up for you."

"Oh, you wouldn't be, Admiral Jherok," she said, smiling. "No, the position I had in mind was as advisor. As Captain, I can choose those people I think would be most beneficial to safety and survival of my crew, and I choose you. So, what do you say, Patty. Care to explore the Galaxy with us?"

Patty saluted her and said, "Happy to be aboard, Captain. Maybe now we'll find that perfect fishing hole."

Printed in the United States
63595LVS00003B/13-75